Disreputable Allies

Disreputable Allies

WREN WESTON

Topsy-Turvy Publishing

Topsy-Turvy Publishing
512 West MLK Jr. Blvd, Suite 264
Austin, Texas 78701

Copyright © 2016 by Topsy-Turvy Publishing
Cover Design by Deranged Doctor Design

ISBN 978-1-68381-021-6 (print)
ISBN 978-1-68381-022-3 (epub)

Visit Topsy-Turvy Publishing on the World Wide Web at www.topsyturvypublishing.com.

Visit Wren Weston at www.wrenweston.com.

1

Lila had everything under control.

She padded silently into Senator Edward Serrano's office, pulling the door closed without a sound. She had not chosen the man or his office randomly. The puffed-up politician favored oversized leather furniture and velvet drapes. Both would provide Lila with plenty of cover if a patrolling guard peeked inside. She wasn't worried about being found, though. Her partner had carefully timed the men's paths. According to Tristan, she would have at least twenty minutes to steal the files and withdraw from the Bullstow compound.

Flush with time, Lila raided the senator's mini-fridge and opened a bottle of Saveur, taking several deep gulps of the expensive beer. It tasted lightly of vanilla and smoke and money. A lot of money. She slid the bottle cap into her trouser pocket and let her fingers skate over the slick wooden box on his desk. She didn't need to open it to know what was inside, for the mild scent of tobacco drifted throughout the office.

After pocketing a few cigars, she tossed her black peacoat upon the senator's desk. The heating would not be turned on again for another hour or two, but she was glad to be rid of the coat despite the chill. It was a cover of poverty she was unaccustomed to, a strange weight that barely flowed past her hips.

Shivering, she tossed her frayed newsboy cap and the thermal hood on the desk. In a perfect world, her cheap gray shirt and trousers would come next, followed by her stiff work boots, which had already worn blisters into her heels. She could have done the entire job in her thermal suit. The skintight material kept her from being seen on thermal cameras, but she would be marked as a high-end thief if anyone saw it.

Lila took another swig of Saveur and plucked the senator's laptop from his desk. Stretching out languidly on the couch, she began her second break-in of the evening.

Tapping quietly on the keys, Lila tried the most common passwords at the login prompt. Breaking into the senator's laptop was the only part of her plan that she had not accounted for. Perhaps she was getting sloppy, but these jobs had begun to feel too routine, too monotonous, and too easy. Perhaps they didn't come often enough to counter the drudgery of her day job. Perhaps she'd partnered with Tristan for too long, and his irresponsibility had rubbed off on her.

Yes, she thought, narrowing her brown eyes. It was probably Tristan's fault in some way.

Lila typed yet another permutation of the word *Odin*—the most commonly used password by men in politics—into the login screen. She hoped for the sake of her government that Serrano's password would not be so simple, but those hopes were dashed on her fourth attempt, as was the chance to test her new password-cracking program.

She was in.

Brushing her dark curls from her eyes, Lila scanned the senator's desktop. She spied a folder entitled *Toys,* but on this occasion she chose not to trespass against Senator Serrano's privacy. He had nearly two dozen children, after all, and at this time of the year, it might be nothing more scandalous than a gift list for the Winter Solstice. If it wasn't so innocent, she knew she didn't want to see what the folder might contain.

Instead, Lila logged into the senate's network under Prolix, the username of one of her fake accounts, and transferred a few programs to Serrano's computer. She depended on such programs to hide her activities and to keep an eye out for snoops, and she updated them often. While they ran, she set the entire BIRD to back up on her star drive, a slice of memory the size of her knuckle. She then leaned back into the cushions of the couch and checked her watch. The guards would not patrol the second floor for another twenty minutes. She still had plenty of time.

A light on her snoop program flashed red.

Lila sat up instantly and put down her beer. She squinted at the snoop's user ID. Her programs did not recognize it, which meant that the account was fake. If someone had laid a trap, she might have just armed it. She couldn't be caught in the Bullstow compound, copying files from senate's network. A conviction for pilfering files from the BIRD would place a hacker's neck in the hangman's noose.

Lila stood up and paced back and forth while the database copied. When the screen flashed green, she dove back to it at once and brought up her programs.

Save data on snoop: Zephyr?

The cursor blinked on and off.

"Of course," she muttered, hitting enter, watching lines of numbers and letters blur across the screen. "What kind of name is Zephyr?"

Data copied.

Delete all logs and programs?

The cursor blinked again, waiting for approval.

Lila slammed the enter key once more and ripped the star drive from the laptop. The computer's fan whirled as she twisted the memory stick into a pendant and hung it on the little gold chain around her neck. She frowned as the laptop worked. She had never been caught by a snoop before, and though she was confident in her programs' ability to keep her hidden, she didn't want to remain in the office one second longer than she had to.

She crouched over the laptop once again, holding her finger over the shutdown menu.

A loud screech pierced the air.

Lila startled, nearly shutting down the computer before it had finished. Every fire alarm in the building shrieked with the volume and shrillness of a thousand distressed toddlers.

Covering her ears, Lila madly sniffed the air.

She smelled nothing but the muted, stale scent of cigars.

Had Tristan hit the alarm as a warning? Were guards surging upstairs ready to capture her? Was it another mistake? If he had bungled things again, she would kill him. What would be the excuse this time? How hard was it to relax in the shadows, waiting to intervene only if the militia pinched her?

Sometimes it seemed like Tristan wanted her to get caught.

"Hurry up!" Lila hissed at the senator's laptop.

As if it understood her, the computer finally shut down. Lila slammed the lid closed and returned it to Serrano's desk, exactly as she found it.

Slipping on her coat, Lila broke for the window and yanked back the velvet drapes. She pulled her thermal hood over her curls and thrust her newsboy cap into her pocket, thumbing the coin-sized pendant inside. The jammer would scramble any cameras nearby.

Tugging her thermal gloves higher on her wrist, she snatched up the bottle of Saveur, opened the senator's window with a dull creak, and crawled onto the second-story ledge. She took care to replace the drapes behind her so that they hung straight once more and then closed the window. It sealed electronically behind her with a little beep.

Luckily, Bullstow did not keep logs of such things. Not yet.

Lila dangled her legs over the granite ledge and pressed her back into the glass. The stone leeched heat from her body, causing another shiver to flow up her spine. Her breath smoked in the cold autumn darkness. The floodlights on the roof flashed across the compound, highlighting the garden and marble statuary below.

Lila squinted through the patchy fog. The boys' school buildings and university, the private cafés and restaurants, the government buildings full of administrators, social workers, and the militia, all hid from her sight. Even Falcon Home and the stone wall surrounding the compound played coy, hidden by swirls of gray.

Lila drained the rest of her beer and scanned the area for a means of escape. The searchlights should have been on a program. Tristan had captured their movements on camera days ago. The program was supposed to make it impossible to avoid detection, but Lila had found a way. Unfortunately, the fire alarm had kicked the beams off their program. Guards now aimed them manually, swinging the beams so erratically that she could hardly find a pattern at all. What should have been easy had turned into a tripwire attached to a thousand kilograms of dynamite.

Lila stowed the empty bottle of Saveur in her coat pocket and lowered herself off the ledge. Swinging her body away from the first-floor window, she dropped to the cement below, stamping loudly as her boots hit. The impact jarred the knife she kept inside.

Crouching behind a shrub, Lila tensed to sprint away.

She heard voices around the corner of the building.

Lila circled behind the nearest marble statue and peeked around its pedestal, narrowly avoiding the domain of a floodlight that butted up against the back of the building.

Two men appeared, clad in the gray and black uniforms of Bullstow security. Their leather blackcoats had been hemmed only a dozen centimeters above the ground. The golden piping on their uniforms matched the rose stitched on their breast. The cut and style would have been at home in the Allied Lands three hundred years before: the style of Britain, Spain, Portugal, and France before the alliance. A Weberly revolver hung on their right hips. On their left, the hilt of a short sword peeked out. A German Shepherd trotted beside them, unfazed by the floodlights, the fire alarm, and the shouts of its masters.

"I'm telling you, this is a test," the shorter guard hollered over the alarm, his voice imbued with a nasal tone. He scanned the statuary as if they might suddenly hop off their marble bases and run away. "Sergeant Bates told me all about them. Someone's out here, Nic. Someone sneaking around."

Lila ducked down, making herself as small as possible.

"Sergeant Bates is an idiot. 'Bout time you learned that. The fire department never shows up at tests. Chief Shaw always warns them."

"If it's really a fire, why hasn't anyone seen or smelled any smoke, huh? Sergeant Bates says if we catch the snoop, we get the bonus."

"I'm going to bonus your face in a minute, rookie. We just had a test this summer. Mark my words, it's the wiring."

"No one caught the snoop. We're having another test."

Lila rolled her eyes. It would be two men who shouted privileged information to anyone who might be near.

Sloppy. Very sloppy.

When the voices finally disappeared around the corner, Lila didn't pause to check the searchlights. She merely sprinted toward the tree line as soon as the beams turned away, and hoped for the best.

One of the beams swung around instantly.

Lila sprinted faster, adrenaline taking over where her natural speed left off. Her worn boots scraped at her blistered heels until the sting shot throughout her body.

The beam edged closer, gaining, as if it spurred her toward the park.

It caught up before Lila reached the tree line. As it nudged against her heels, she launched herself the last few meters into the trees and dove behind a marble bench.

Lila froze where she landed, hissing as the beam lit up her boot. She didn't move, not to scratch her wrist, not to settle into a more comfortable position, not even to hide herself more completely. Movement would only attract the attention of whomever aimed the light and squinted at where it was pointed. There was still a chance they had not yet noticed the outline of her boot.

The night was foggy, after all.

Lila panted, waiting. The lights would have blinded her if her head and torso hadn't been hidden behind the bench. But she didn't hear any voices. She didn't hear any boots squelching in the mud, either. She didn't even hear the expected croaks and chirps within the trees. The entire park listened, frightened at the light.

Still the beam did not move. The guards on the roof might have stopped to pick their noses, to sip chocolate, to talk, to take a piss off the side of the building. They might have radioed for a patrol to investigate the bench. On the other hand, their superior might have ordered them to check thermal imaging.

Lila breathed heavily in the darkness, hoping for the latter. She would be invisible over thermal, and the searchlight would move on.

After several moments, the light whipped back to the grounds, crossing with another beam over the statuary.

Thanking her luck, Lila crawled across the soggy ground and progressed deeper into the trees. When she thought she had gone far enough, she hopped to her feet and slipped from trunk to trunk, coming closer to the stone wall that enclosed Bullstow.

A boot squelched in the mud behind her.

A flashlight beam lit up the area.

Lila spun behind a tree.

"Told you it was a snoop," came a triumphant, nasal shout. The shorter guard sprinted toward her, cocked his gun, and aimed a flashlight at the tree. Nic huffed along behind him, clutching his side.

Lila's hand flew to her hip with a practiced movement. She drew her gun and crouched low to the ground, wincing at the metal in her grip and the thoughts in her mind. Firing her gun would complicate matters significantly, but she had no other choice.

She was no fighter.

Swinging from behind the tree, she aimed her Colt at the rookie's neck.

His flashlight swung up at the same time, blinding her.

The tranq dart hit the rookie's forehead instead.

"Son of a…" The blackcoat lurched stiffly. His flashlight slipped from his grasp and struck a rock as he tumbled to the ground, struggling to brush away the dart.

The bulb shattered.

The rookie landed beside it with a fart-like splat.

"Rookie?" Nic called out, wheezing beside his partner.

The guard peered into the trees. Lila didn't have time for her eyes to adjust to the dark, but neither did he. Groping wildly, she sprinted deeper into the park, shoulders smacking into limbs, face smarting from the occasional whack of a branch. She could only hope that her eyes would recover first.

She heard a *whoosh* of air.

Something grazed her sleeve.

Lila whipped behind a tree and brushed her arm where the phantom touch had landed. Her cheap woolen peacoat had caught Nic's dart, and she flicked it away with gloved fingers.

Then she gripped her Colt and fell onto the soggy grass with a thud.

The blackcoat advanced slowly, his outline coming into clearer focus with every step. Towering over her, he nudged her with his boot. When she did not move, he turned his head toward a radio perched on his shoulder. "Nichols to base. I'm in quadrant two. Send a med team. I caught the snoop, and my rookie is down, over."

Static erupted from the radio.

Nic winced and turned his head away, rubbing his ear.

With the blackcoat distracted, Lila drew her Colt and fired in one quiet, crisp movement.

This time the dart hit its mark perfectly.

The tranq overwhelmed Nic more quickly than his partner. He fell atop her, pinning her shoulder and her Colt to the ground. The man's heavy chest crushed her fingers inside the trigger guard, and she barely kept herself from crying out.

Digging her arm into the man's side, she worked herself free and gingerly stretched her fingers. Nothing seemed broken.

"Idiot."

A loud snore erupted, calling out their location like an over-powered homing beacon.

"I pity your lover." Lila turned the man onto his stomach to stop the bulk of the noise. She ran her fingers along Nic's neck and retrieved her dart, then ran quickly to the rookie to do the same.

The job had gotten far too hot. With nothing stolen and no other crimes evident, the first thing Bullstow would consider was the security of its computer network. Even if Lila didn't get caught, she might never work again after such a mess.

Neither would Tristan, if she had anything to do with it.

Lila stowed the darts in her pocket and sprinted toward the stone wall at the edge of the compound. She ran up the side and stretched toward the top, lifting her head over the cold stone, mentally cataloging all the ways she could torture her partner with an expensive beer bottle and a few used sleep darts.

Luckily, the searchlights on the street still had a rhythm to them, not thrown off by the blaring alarms or the fire truck hurtling closer to Bullstow's front gate. Since she could predict the beams again, she could avoid both the light and the blackcoats who patrolled the front gate.

After the fire truck wailed past her position, she scrambled over the wall and dropped onto the street, littered with wads of trash and grime. She skirted the domain of the floodlights and peered at the guard post a block away. A herd of blackcoats shouted back and forth to the driver of the fire truck, surrounding it in a press of skittish eyes and cocked revolvers.

Lila removed her thermal hood and cast about the streets, settling her newsboy cap over her curls once more. She thrust the hood into her pocket, waited for the correct pattern in the search lights, then crossed the street toward a lowborn perfumery. The clash of a hundred floral scents invaded her nose, fighting for control of her stomach.

Holding her breath, Lila walked steadily toward the alleyway next to the shop. From now on, she was nothing more than a citizen of New Bristol out for an early morning stroll.

"Halt!" someone shouted down the street. The group of black-coats sprinted away from the fire truck in a swirl of confusion. Their boots clomped against the asphalt, disturbing bits of paper and shopping bags that dotted the street.

Lila kept walking despite their presence. A cackling radio struggled against her jammer and called out the location of the perfumery. She slipped her hands inside her pockets and thumbed off the device.

Instantly, the static disappeared.

"Halt, under order of Governor Lecomte!" one of the guards called out again, Weberly revolver drawn and pointed at her chest.

Lila turned slowly, a practiced look of innocence pressed into her features. She did not look directly at the men. Instead, she scanned the streets for Tristan and his people. At any moment, they would appear and provide a distraction so that she could run away.

The guards formed a ring around her, guns swaying in the air. Guards, she couldn't help but notice, who were unmolested by a roaring swarm of criminals.

"Hands up," another guard ordered, punching the space between them with the butt of his gun.

Lila was too shocked to comply immediately. Her eyes danced across the rooftops, peered into alleys, and even squinted hard at the guard post. But the man behind the glass was far too young and far too plump to be confused with Tristan.

"The man asked you to put your hands up. I think you should comply, madam." The leader of the guards marched closer, a swagger heavy in his gait, a gun held tightly at his thigh. He was smaller and leaner than the others. He'd pressed his uniform just a bit sharper, and polished his boots to a brighter shine. The stars pinned to his collar revealed his rank as sergeant, and if Lila had to put money on it, he'd been a sergeant just long enough to become antsy for his next promotion. A deep scar ran across his cheek, marring an otherwise average face. Any doctor could have tended such a wound. Any half-decent plastic surgeon could have corrected the scar it had left behind, and Bullstow contracted with the best plastic surgeons in the world.

"What did I tell you, boys?" the sergeant called out to his brethren as Lila finally raised her hands. He dug into her pockets, ignoring the cigars and beer bottle in favor of the thermal hood and tranq gun. He held them up as trophies, neglecting to pat down her boots.

Sloppy.

"If you turn on the thermal camera on nights like these, you never know what you might find. A bodiless head floating down the street, for instance." He snickered. "My man behind the thermal camera nearly soiled himself thinking we had some sort of ghost on our hands. Congratulations for that."

Lila cursed under her breath as he studied her hood. "Using thermal imaging on the streets of New Bristol is against regulations, even for the mighty Bullstow." She dropped her hands and pitched her voice deeper, the change straining her throat. "Do what you want within your compound but not outside. The city doesn't take kindly to perverts peeking into their homes and businesses."

"My unit does not suffer perverts. I would not allow it." The sergeant's focus drifted from her hood. "Keep your hands up, madam."

"There's always a pervert or two. Perhaps in this unit you're the pervert, since you wanted to use the thermal cameras so badly."

"Madam, I'm a sergeant in the government militia. I—"

"Yes. I can see that from all those pretty little stars on your collar."

Several of the men chuckled.

The sergeant clenched his jaw and shoved Lila's possessions into the chest of a subordinate. "Hands," he growled, stepping closer toward her, withdrawing a pair of handcuffs from his belt. "Under the authority of Governor—"

"Yes, I'll be sure to note your adherence to proper procedure. Of course, I will have to inform Chief Shaw that you only caught me because you used thermal imaging. Illegally, I might add. The bonus will go unclaimed this season. Again."

The guards around her fidgeted, and the barrels of their guns dipped slightly. Here and there, the men took their eyes off her, too engrossed in silent conversations with one another to watch her carefully.

The sergeant frowned at Lila. "This isn't a test, madam. We already had one—"

"Yes, this summer. You've done little better since my last visit, boy."

One of the men whistled at the jab.

The sergeant's lip curled. He clasped her wrists and shoved her back across the street, slamming her into the stone wall around the compound. "I take my reprimands from Chief Shaw, not a hireling thief he may or may not have hired to poke at our defenses."

Lila wiggled in the sergeant's grasp.

The man cursed as his handcuffs clattered at his feet. He shoved his body against hers, pressing her into the wall.

The beer bottle in her pocket pressed into her ribs. She worried it might shatter.

"Be still, you filthy workborn, else you might get hurt."

"I'm—"

"A very good liar," he finished for her, shoving her into the wall even harder.

The men circled around them, mouths open wide. Lila had riled their sergeant too much for him to keep his anger in check. Only the lowest workborn displayed such violence. It reflected poorly on his men and all of Bullstow that his temper broke now.

"So you're a pervert, after all? Do you have mommy issues? Is that why you took offense when I called you boy?"

The sergeant trapped her wrists with his right hand. With his left, he removed a pen from his lapel. He dug the tip into her neck, and she felt a needle pierce her skin.

Lila yipped at the bite. With that one little prick, she knew that everything was over. In less than ten minutes, the pen would transmit her DNA profile across the Bullstow network, directly into Chief Shaw's office. Within the hour, the sample would be run against the public database, matched, and saved to her government file. She might have altered the shape of her nose and chin with a bit of rubber prosthetics, she might have changed the color of her eyes with contacts and modified the sound of her voice, but she couldn't change the truth in her blood.

Given the sergeant's disposition, he might not even wait until she was arrested before he dosed her with truth serum and began an interrogation. She would confess everything and break the encryption on her star drive, and she would do it with a drunken smile on her face.

The media vans would line up outside Bullstow, the journalists frothing at the faintest whisper of a treason charge, long before Chief Shaw even stumbled into work. She'd be on the news and plastered all over the net before the citizens of New Bristol sat down to breakfast.

Why hadn't Tristan come to her aid?

Had he set her up?

"My cuffs." The sergeant snapped his fingers.

The guard holding her possessions retrieved the handcuffs from the sidewalk and handed them over, sliding back before the sergeant's temper could pass to him.

Lila stopped struggling against the officer's body. There was really no point anymore. She leaned her forehead against the cool stone of the wall. Things were about to get complicated enough without her panicking or wasting her energy.

That was the last thought Lila had before the ground shook under her feet. The sergeant slammed into her once more, pinning her against the stone, crushing her ribs into the bottle of Saveur. But it wasn't just her chest this time that threatened to break. Her fingers and toes and forehead all pressed into the wall as well.

A terrible boom erupted behind her, slapping against her eardrums as though the sergeant had driven a DNA pen into both her ears.

The world muted. She no longer heard the blackcoats' radios, the fire truck's wailing siren, the still-screaming alarm. Even the crickets and frogs on the other side of the wall went silent.

The night erupted into yellow and orange flames behind her. The air smelled of gasoline and smoke. The worst of it retreated so quickly that nothing caught fire, like a welder who turned his blowtorch on and off for a lark. Lila slid her fingers to her side as chunks of stone and wood and plaster hurtled through space, battering the wall around her in one last, rumbling barrage.

Dust and soot covered the wall, her clothes, and even her tongue.

Through the grit, Lila tasted blood.

2

The sergeant's body shielded her from the worst of it, from the shock wave, from the blazing chunks of rock that peppered the street and skittered along the asphalt with sharp little hisses. Lila squeezed her eyes closed and turned her face away from the heat. The floodlights on the street had shattered, and shards of glass rained from the sky.

The sergeant moaned behind her and collapsed, finally relieving the pressure on her chest. She stumbled slightly and lurched against the wall for support.

The handcuffs clattered impotently on the pavement once more.

"Shit," she grumbled, too late in realizing that she had bitten her tongue.

Lila turned and stared at the mushrooming black spire behind her. It climbed higher and higher toward the stars, as if it might swallow them up like it swallowed up the building beside the perfumery. Tendrils of fire lashed out at the businesses next door, threatening the structures, the flames providing the only light for several square blocks.

Even Bullstow had gone dark.

Lila struggled to remember what the business had been only seconds before. A restaurant? A coffee shop? Some sort of office?

Whatever it was, someone had cut it out of New Bristol, right under the nose of Bullstow. She recalled the last attack against the city, the charred and twisted train cars stopped only by a flattened row of houses. The faces of the dead. The faces of the living.

Blood. Bones. The smell.

Lila squeezed her eyes shut. If the Almstakers had become active in America, then she would likely be executed just for standing near the explosion, regardless of whether she had anything to do with it.

It was better to be safe than to be just.

The wind changed, deepening the smell of gasoline, igniting the perfumery's peppermint-dressed awning. At least all the businesses on the block belonged to highborn families. No one slept above the shops in this neighborhood. The only thing lost would be profits.

A muffled siren caught Lila's attention as though oil covered the sound. The fire truck inside Bullstow had changed directions. She rubbed at her ears, still aching from the explosion, and tried to judge how long she had left until it reached the gate. All she could see over the wall was a blur of red and white flashing lights near the High Senate Office Building.

The chubby guard stepped out from the guard post, glancing through the gate into Bullstow.

"Orders, sergeant?" he shouted helplessly at his superior. "Can you hear me, sarge? Do I wait here until the truck rolls through? Do you need me? Is everyone all right?"

Lila squinted at the men sprawled on the sidewalk. Several had not stirred since the blast, though she could see their chests rising in the dim light of the fire. The few who could move were sluggish, as though they might have been infants surfacing from a heavy, sweat-filled fever. The blast had disoriented them, and none were in any condition to stand up, much less give chase, should she decide to bolt.

"They're all still breathing," Lila shouted back, her voice sounding dim and faraway to her own ears. "Call for medical, then see to the gate. The truck needs to get through."

"You shut up!" The blackcoat glanced at the approaching fire truck and back again. He pulled his tranq gun from his belt, took aim carefully, and fired.

The heavy dart fell to the ground halfway between them.

"You better stay put." The man gestured with his gun. "It'll go worse on you if you run. I swear to the oracle, I'll track you down myself!"

"Of course you will," Lila muttered.

She ignored the shouting blackcoat and stepped over the sergeant, kneeling at his side. "At least your temper was good for something, Sergeant Perv." She rifled through his coat pockets as the man batted weakly at her prying fingers. A dart in the neck would have stopped it, but perhaps his condition was worse than it looked. "I doubt I'd be able to walk away so easily if I didn't have such a fine officer of Bullstow shielding me from the blast. Imagine how happy Chief Shaw will be when you tell him. He might even give you another one of those pretty little stars you're so proud of."

Lila snatched up the DNA pen, which she then dropped and crushed underneath the heel of her boot, stopping it before it could finish its work. The little red light blinked out, and she yanked the brains of the device from the pen. She could only hope that nothing had been transmitted across the network before the blast knocked out the power.

Her thermal hood, tranq gun, and spent darts were strewn on the ground, covered with a thin layer of ash. Lila quickly retrieved them, hoping her gun would work if she needed it.

She stuffed the remains of the DNA pen and the rest of her possessions into her coat pockets, then sprinted into the alley near the charred perfumery. The smoke and fog covered her escape while a strange blizzard of flyers fell around her, offering even more cover. She snatched one of the drifting papers from the air as she ran. *American Abolitionist Society* had been printed in large black letters, along with a column of red print she hardly had the time, the energy, or the interest to read.

At least it hadn't been the Almstakers this time. As a citizen of the commonwealth, Lila bore no love for the Holy Roman Empire, but she almost felt sorry that they had to deal with the extremist nutjobs.

She tossed the flyer away as soon as she reached the alley and shielded her eyes, finally following the paper trail up into the sky. Several figures in plainclothes watched the scene from the roof of a three-story apartment building nearby, craning their necks toward the fire. They held radios to their ears and counted down the seconds until militia reinforcements would arrive, their voices far too loud for the thick silence that hovered in the air, a silence free from the hum of electricity and the buzzing of lights. A few children leaned over the side, dwarfed by oversized coats and gloves, tossing fistfuls of the AAS papers from worn satchels slung around their chests. A ginger-headed boy laughed and laughed in their midst, flinging the papers from his grasp like Frisbees.

One man stood apart from the group, perched on the corner of the building. Shaved head. Long brown coat. Black trousers. Black sweater. Purple scarf swinging in the wind. The toes of his blood-red boots hung over the side, so red they were almost black. Dixon would leap from rooftop to rooftop to follow her if Tristan demanded it.

Lila hoped he had not.

She retreated back into the shadows and skirted the perfumery, emerging on Leclerc Street moments later. She passed law office after law office, each geared for a specific sort of client. Highborn, lowborn, workborn. All would find representation on Leclerc.

Shoving her newsboy cap atop her head, Lila considered her options. Tristan had come through, all right, but this stunt had not been for her. It had not been improvised. It had been planned. It had been why she needed rescuing in the first place. He had used her as a diversion. If Dixon was on the roof, overseeing the operation, it meant that Tristan was elsewhere.

Lila turned east on Leclerc.

Dixon followed.

Gritting her teeth, Lila kept to the shadows, avoiding the occasional soul who stumbled into her path. The bystanders stared, each one entranced by the blast and the smoke and the fire, not content merely to pull back their curtains like the rest of polite society.

Most people who lived near Leclerc Street were lowborn professionals, that class of citizens who owned at least one business. They had either been born into their lowborn status or had beaten the consequences of a poor birthright as slaves or contracted servants, capitalizing on every educational opportunity and business loan they could find. These were the rare success, these few who had burst through the workborn ceiling, and they all strived for more. Some even held positions in Low House, the lesser, lowborn chamber of the senate.

They had been asleep like proper ladies and gentlemen, that much was certain, for their dresses sat askew, their breeches had not been properly tucked into their boots, and the collars of their elegant matching coats were twisted at the neck. Though their attire might have been made of fine wool and tailored elegantly, all of it was wrinkled.

Thankfully, they kept to their stations. None of them stopped to chat with the poor workborn servant. They sidestepped her completely and tried the doors of the nearest apartment building, ready to rush upstairs for a better view.

One enterprising child—she could swear it was the ginger boy from the roof—even held open his building's door and charged admission. Given the twinkle in his eye, Lila was hard-pressed to believe that he lived there at all.

She scanned the roof line. Dixon stared down at her from across the street.

Lila slid into the darkness and walked on.

She avoided everyone she saw, brushing away the ash and grass on her coat whenever someone new came into view. She hid whenever she heard a siren. The highborn militias had either sent a few patrols to assist Bullstow or to spy.

The increased security helped Lila as it hampered Dixon. She finally caught sight of him on a far-off rooftop, peering down at a street she had passed ten minutes before.

His companions had long since scattered into the night.

"Told you I was better." Lila smirked, emerging under the closest functioning streetlight, blocks away from the fire. She turned her back on Dixon and continued on, hoping he would not pop up again later.

The size of the buildings shrank the farther she traveled from Bullstow, and the paint became more chipped and faded. Flattened cigarette butts, chip wrappers, and crumbled scraps of paper dotted the street more frequently until the gutters overflowed.

Shabby pawnshops and liquor stores soon replaced the bookstores and cafés of the more well-to-do workborn. She ignored the blisters on her heels, both bleeding and stinging, and moved her gun into her front pocket. People here would notice the telltale bulge, whether or not the weapon had survived the blast intact.

Plenty had ventured from their homes after the explosion, workborn mostly, all wrapped in ill-fitting coats and cheap scarves. Some huddled on the stoops of apartment buildings or in the yards of crumbling houses, smoking cheap cigarettes and stamping their feet against the chill. Their heads turned infrequently toward the tower of smoke.

Not everyone paid attention to it. These workborn contracted with the poorest lowborn families, falling into bed late and rising early. It was not curiosity that drove most from the warmth of their beds. If they didn't prove to their neighbors that such commotion would wake them, they could expect to be burglarized before the end of the week.

She already saw a few sideways glances at darkened windows.

The front door of an apartment building opened.

"Radio says it was a gas explosion across from Bullstow," an old woman called out to her neighbors. She joined them on a stoop, her shoulders wrapped in a frayed knitted blanket. She held a steaming, chipped mug in place of gloves.

Lila did not ask for details. She kept her eyes to the ground, hoping no one would remember her tomorrow or notice that her peacoat and hair had been dusted with ash. It wasn't much of a stretch to think that they wouldn't. Studying a person too intensely, especially one's face, was not done in this part of the city. Indeed, if Lila's habits slipped and she looked around too closely, it would mark her instantly as a highborn. And that they would not forget.

The wealthy did not travel here. They sent proxies.

Lila turned down an alley, the stench of urine and month-old trash choking her throat. She stepped carefully, eyes tracking behind dumpsters and overturned boxes, with only a dim, flickering street lamp down the block to guide her. No one lay in wait. Only rats and cockroaches skulked in the filth.

She marched to the end of the alley, finally reaching a door that had been graffitied in a rainbow of hoary cartoons and letters. A stenciled red phoenix had been spray-painted above the sliding peephole. The door hung partly ajar, one hinge broken. For some reason the carelessness only made her angrier.

She took the thermal hood from her pocket and pulled it over her face, shoving her newsboy hat atop it and tugging the small brim down low. There was no telling who had already come back from the job or who had stayed behind. No one in the motley group had ever seen her face, except for Tristan, and she would keep it that way. The only thing that his people might recognize was her disguised voice, for plenty had heard her speak. Tonight they would hear her yell. She already had a half-composed tirade perched on the tip of her bitten tongue, waiting.

Lila yanked open the door and stepped inside.

The backroom of the old hotel was empty. Not just empty of people but empty of everything. The only things inside were grimy paint, the ever-present musty smell of an old building, and four piles of trash pushed to each corner of the room.

She bent down, snatched up a piece of crumpled-up cardstock, and unfurled it over her thigh. It was another AAS flyer, exactly like the one she had caught in the air near the explosion.

There had been a table there the day before. A lookout controlling entry into the safe house, more with his body than his mind. A refrigerator had taken up the corner, filled with cheap beer and leftovers from the Plum Luck Dragon. The empty sink lurked in the corner like a stranger. It had always been piled high with dishes, for none of Tristan's people would lower themselves to do slave's work now that they were free.

Not unless it was a punishment from Tristan.

Lila balled up the flyer and tossed it back on the ground, then slipped into the hotel lobby. Everything had been removed: the threadbare rugs; the battered black couches and mismatched ottomans; the chairs mended with unstained wooden legs; the table that wobbled unless you jammed a wedge of paper underneath; the worn tapestries over the windows that had held in warmth from overtaxed heaters; the stolen paintings that had lined the walls. Even the new pool table had been removed, as well as the wall of computers that had cluttered the front desk. Everything was gone except for random piles of litter, peeling wallpaper, and dust.

Lila ventured upstairs into Tristan's room, empty now. Bed gone, closet devoid of weapons and ammunition, the little string of bottle caps snatched up from the window. She stepped inside, not prepared for the shock of it all. It was as if her own family had stolen away in the night, vanishing without even providing her with a hint of their return.

She kicked a lone bottle cap in the center of the room and listened as it echoed against the walls.

A door opened somewhere in the hotel, creaking.

Dixon.

Lila slipped out of the room, prowling down the hallway. But no matter which room she looked into, she found nothing but the occasional beer bottle.

She chucked them against the wall as she came to them, one after another, the shattering glass mocking her with every crash, forcing her to throw the next one harder and harder and harder.

She ran out of bottles long before she ran out of anger.

The bottle of Saveur in her pocket was the last instrument of solace, destroyed in Tristan's room. She dropped its cap next to the only one he had left behind.

With nothing else to do, Lila washed her face in his bathroom sink, ridding herself as best she could of her makeup and prosthetic nose and chin. She dried her pale face on her sleeve and peeked out the window. Sunrise was still a couple of hours away.

A door slammed in a far-off room, rattling against its frame.

Lila stepped over the shattered glass and took off her boots, then rushed through the hallway on silent cat paws and peeked over the upstairs balcony. Two lean figures crept across the lobby downstairs.

Neither form belonged to Dixon.

Lila drew her tranq gun, stilled her breath, and waited.

"Did the door shut?" a teenage boy whispered in the darkness.

"I had to slam it closed," a girl replied. "I don't like this. What if the owners come? What if someone's already squatting here?"

"Meeting a junkie is better than being burned alive. Did you see that fire? Do you really want to sleep under the stoop tonight?"

The friend mumbled something that Lila could not hear.

"We'll leave in the morning when it's safe."

Turning away, Lila put on her boots, pocketed her gun, then slipped out through an upstairs window. She had no more time to dawdle. Not for children and certainly not for an asshole like Tristan.

Time had grown sparse, and she was expected at home.

3

Lila hid behind a pecan tree across from the Randolph compound, soaked in the cool humidity of the morning. She had arrived at precisely five o'clock, two and a half hours before sunrise, and had spent much of the last half-hour crouched behind the tree. Safely under the hood of her thermal suit, she studied the compound, its defenses, and the people who patrolled it.

The Randolph family enjoyed tighter security than the politicians of Bullstow, for the Randolphs were one of the wealthiest families, not just in New Bristol but in the entire state of Saxony. Wolf Industries boasted ten square kilometers of architecture, ranging from mirrored skyscrapers filled with offices and condos in the north, to the neo-classical mansions of the fifteen heirs scattered widely around the southern entrance, the oldest segment of the estate. Each building and statue shone in the night, as clean and perfect as those in Bullstow, surrounded by extensive grounds. Slaves and servants had coaxed every shrub into beauty, clipped every blade of grass close, and scraped every sidewalk to reflected glory.

It wasn't only the staff who kept the estate so clean. Due to pollution concerns, the Randolphs had moved their manufacturing plants to the outskirts of the capital city more than fifty years ago, long before High House had placed pollution restrictions on the highborn. The chairwoman had built a rail system to link them, positioning the station one street away from the estate's north gate. The bullet train stretched for an entire block, chauffeuring everyone to the plants and back home again every hour. All but the slaves, of course, for they lived in a series of residences next to the plants.

The Randolph family, or Wolf Industries to be precise, owned much more than just manufacturing plants, though. At least thirty percent of the land under New Bristol belonged to the Randolphs, which made much of the city its tenant. In addition, Wolf Industries partnered with, or invested in, at least a quarter of the lowborn shops in New Bristol. The family also traded extensively throughout Saxony, dominating several key industries in the region, including manufacturing and research, headquartered in New Bristol, and oil refining, which was centered three hundred kilometers away in La Porte and farther east in New Orleans. The family had even managed to procure a small but significant share of the natural gas market around Beaulac, the second largest city in Saxony after New Bristol.

To protect the estate, their matron had erected security towers every two hundred meters around the perimeter of the compound. Like every other highborn family, the Randolphs employed their own militia, women and men who functioned as a security force and defensive regiment for the estate. Lila watched them patrol, searching for one woman among the blackcoats.

The ubiquitous floodlights shifted direction.

Lila dashed from her spot and climbed over the wall.

As she scrambled to gain purchase, her boot caught the edge of one of the signs that ringed the exterior of the compound, glorifying the Randolph family's coat of arms and the accompanying motto, *Mutual Benefit*. The words were far older than the city of New Bristol, even older than America itself. The motto had been brought over from the old countries, long before the Allied Lands formally recognized America as a sovereign territory of the commonwealth. Indeed, the first prime minister had even appropriated it as one of the defining values in society, business, and government.

Unity, above all else, had been declared the first.

Lila landed safely on the other side of the wall and thanked her luck that the sign had been bolted on securely. Dewy grass immediately latched on to her boots as though ratcheted on by static.

"Stop. Who goes there?" called out a woman in a sentry uniform—black with crimson piping—and a long leather blackcoat to match. She pulled on the lead of her German shepherd. The dog barked in excited aggression as both sprinted across the grounds to intercept.

Lila pulled up her thermal hood briefly as the pair reached her.

"Chief Randolph." The woman bowed, wearing her sentry cap and blackcoat with the same grace as an evening gown. As she straightened, her face broke into a wrinkled grin.

The beast next to her breathed out in moist white bursts. It strained on its lead, confused when it couldn't scent Lila through the gasoline and smoke, too surprised by it to keep barking.

Lila wished she could say the same about the dog. The odor of wet mutt filled her nose, and she stepped back from its tinkling chain. "Commander Sutton," she returned with a stiff nod, wondering if the woman would question the state of her clothes or their smell.

Sutton said nothing. Perhaps she didn't notice. Everything smelled of smoke on the estate, for the direction of the wind had changed half an hour before.

The commander turned away and murmured a few words into the radio affixed to her collar, then keyed in a code for the security office on her palm computer. A search light that had been on a path to inspect them swung back around into place, and the commander slipped the palm computer back into her pocket.

"How'd you know it was me, chief?" Commander Sutton asked, her mouth twitching at the corners.

"Patience. It didn't take long for me to recognize your walk among the others."

"I have a walk?"

"You drag your left leg slightly. You're also the only blackcoat on patrol who kept looking out for my arrival. I doubt anyone else noticed your interest."

"You did." The woman rubbed at her thigh, scanning the rooftops. "I suppose it's too chilly for me to ignore the stiffness this morning, or perhaps I'm getting so old I don't even notice it anymore. I suppose you heard the blast earlier?"

"Heard it? You can see the smoke from here. What was it?"

"The news called it a gas explosion, but I'm not buying it. Didn't have the right feel to it. Can you imagine a gas explosion less than a hundred meters from High House and Falcon Home? What if the prime minister had been in residence?"

"He wasn't. Besides, accidents can happen anywhere." Lila stuffed her fists into her coat pockets. "Time never passes for an old soldier, does it?"

"I suppose you're right." The commander motioned for Lila to fall into step beside her. The dog trotted after them obediently. "My head's too full of the past tonight."

"You're not the only one." Lila thought back again to the explosion five years before. She had been a lieutenant directly under Sutton's command back then. When the explosion shook New Bristol, both women had jumped into a militia truck and sped to the scene, witnessing the fear spread after the Almstakers claimed responsibility through a hastily posted video online. The video hadn't held up to the evidence, though. Bullstow ignored the Almstakers' claims in the official report and blamed Bryan Rail. They claimed that a commercial train from the company had jumped the tracks, an accident later attributed to its poor safety record. It wouldn't have been so devastating if one of the cars hadn't been carrying a shipment of fertilizer.

With thirty-four people dead and scores injured, the outside shareholders sold their stakes of the lowborn business in a rage. Wolf Industries had swooped in and bought Bryan Rail at a steep discount.

That was the price of failure in New Bristol.

"The government militia is on the scene," Commander Sutton said as they dodged a floodlight and sidled around the nearest building. "I suppose Bullstow wouldn't lie."

"I suppose they wouldn't."

"I sent a dozen blackcoats to assist, headed by Sergeant Tripp and Sergeant Nolan. Perhaps they'll sniff out something useful for us while they're there." Sutton inclined her head. "You managed to take care of every camera along this path tonight. They're not out. They're just pointed a bit out of line. Thermal, too."

Lila frowned, slightly annoyed that all it took to beat her own security was a thermal suit and a jammer. She knew it was better than that, though. She had taken to breaking into the estate every month or so, all to shore up the compound's defenses and keep her militia on its toes. She did the same to other Randolph properties whenever she visited.

At least Randolph engineers had been the ones to create the thermal suit and the jammer. Their energies had now turned to creating cameras to see through Lila's toys. Chairwoman Randolph was unsure if the family would market either technology, though. Lila understood the chairwoman's reasoning, for she enjoyed having toys the other families did not. Then again, the family would lose out on a great deal of potential revenue by keeping the technology to themselves. Lila could afford her own mansion if she sold either device on the black market, provided that the structure had not been built on Randolph property. Beatrice Randolph never sold any land she didn't have to.

But Lila had no intention of selling her toys.

"It was part of the test," she told her commander.

"I thought you wished to test thermal?"

"I did." She grinned, giving Sutton another half-truth. She had tested the thermal, just not on Randolph property.

"None of our patrols caught you snooping around the compound tonight. I suppose you've beaten the whole damn lot of us again."

"It's not a question of winning and losing. We can't protect against every threat, commander. We'd drive ourselves mad trying."

Sutton nodded. "Well, we're at changeover. No one will notice if you come through. You don't even need to use your jammer, and I'd be grateful if you didn't. You might spook Captain McKinley, and I'll never hear the end of it."

"I'm not going to alert Captain McKinley, commander. Tonight is a blackout. The militia does not need to know about this test of our defenses."

"I said I was old, not senile or infirm."

Lila did not apologize, though she felt bad for reminding the woman how to do her job when it was unnecessary. At twenty-eight years old, Lila might outrank the older woman, but Commander Sutton had been her superior officer for most of her militia career. When Lila had been promoted to chief of security nearly three years before, Sutton had been the first name on her list as her replacement. Sutton had proven time and time again how much she deserved the promotion. It was a pity that no one else had recognized her potential.

As commander, Sutton ran security for the New Bristol estate, having the last word unless Lila overruled her, which Lila rarely did. She needed someone like Sutton, someone she could trust with such responsibility, for Lila's time was split among a dozen other commanders and properties in Saxony. The family compound was merely the crown jewel.

An image of the empty hotel entered Lila's mind, and her regard for Sutton rose. The commander would never do anything like that to Lila, to the family, nor to the estate. Not only was Sutton good at her job, but her adopted mother had been an heir once, one of the fifteen women in each generation who might become the family's chairwoman by birthright. Even though there was no hope of the frail Edith Randolph ever becoming the chairwoman now—short of a particularly fatal epidemic or an ill-advised murder spree—the woman's wealth and position made it very unlikely that Sutton would ever betray their matron.

That and her temperament. If the commander suspected what Lila had really been up to that night, she would have dragged her in handcuffs to Chief Shaw's office herself. Sutton's brain was composed of laws and codes; no gray permeated her heart. It made her predictable. Lila could bend that trait to her advantage, and she frequently did.

"Your people looked good tonight, commander. You've done well with them," Lila said as they kept to the shadows and skirted around the estate's mail facility.

Beyond the structure, Lila spied the Randolph family's great house, a sprawling mansion that housed the chairwoman's family and assorted staff members assigned to their security or care. Elegant and palatial, the neoclassical building boasted a fountain out front, commissioned from the great artist Frederic Batholdi. Four gray wolves sprang out from the center, impatient to conquer from all sides, similar to the family's coat of arms. The fountain and the building, called Villanueva House after its architect, were the first things anyone saw when entering the estate from the south entrance. That and the security office. Both were intended to overwhelm, rather than welcome.

The pair saw little of the famous building. Instead, Commander Sutton passed a keycard through a security panel. The dog's claws clicked against the linoleum floor as they entered the mail facility's back entrance and shuffled down a hallway. The group soon passed through another locked door, descended a staircase, and crossed into the basement level, gaining entry into the extensive tunnel system below the estate.

"You know, I don't think I've ever seen you without an officer's uniform, Commander Sutton. Not in my entire life, except on nights like this." Lila's voice echoed against the concrete, competing with the jingle of the dog's leash. The group stepped through the tunnels, the air smelling of soil and grease, the constant *plink* of dripping water surrounded them as they walked. Lila had always liked the tunnels despite the smell and noise. She found them restful, perhaps because she had spent so much time getting lost in them and finding her way out again as a child.

"Well, I rarely see you in the clothes of a workborn, except on nights like this."

Lila smoothed the breast of her peacoat, the absence of her family's coat of arms tugging at her once again. It was as if someone used to slumbering under thick blankets had been given only a dirty sheet to pass the night. At least the coat of arms had not been on her when the sergeant had begun his arrest. Every single man under his command would have known instantly that she was a Randolph and a highborn on sight.

That wasn't her only worry. Did Zephyr have proof of her actions in the BIRD? Would the snoop figure out Prolix's true identity? Had she destroyed the DNA pen quickly enough, or was Bullstow matching her DNA at that very moment? Were government blackcoats already on the way to intercept her and throw her into a holding cell? Had her client heard about the explosion yet? Were Tristan and his people laughing at how they had used her as a distraction?

It would be a long day finding out the answers.

"How about this weather? Shouldn't be so cold in October," Sutton said suddenly, tugging uncomfortably at her collar.

"This is New Bristol, commander. If you don't like the weather, just wait fifteen minutes. I'm sure we'll be back to sweating by the weekend. Unless it decides to rain."

Sutton nodded.

The pair walked down another stretch of tunnel in silence.

"Is everything okay, chief?"

Lila realized that she had said nothing for most of their journey. Usually, she filled all interactions on the estate with militia chatter, endless questions of protocol and procedure, double-checking arrangements for whatever security nightmare the matron had planned next. Lila typically had a thousand things to do and only ten minutes to do them, and Sutton bore the brunt of such attention. "Everything is fine, commander. I'm just tired."

The commander unlocked the door into the dim basement of the great house, and Lila retrieved her own set of keys from behind a stack of boxes. "Enjoy your day off, chief." Sutton bowed slightly, concern evident in every wrinkle.

Lila pulled off her thermal hood and slipped through the scullery and into the kitchen. A stout, middle-aged woman stood at the counter, wearing a flour-dusted apron. She skipped through her pop music playlist, too busy to notice when Lila skulked through the room behind her. The muffled warbling of some overpaid and autotuned singer, desperate to make a hit, leaked from around Chef's earphones. The smell of bacon hung in the air.

Chef was up early, and Lila didn't know what it meant.

She quickly put it out of her mind once she reached her bedroom on the top floor. If the cameras in the hallway had recorded her movements at all that night, they would only prove that Lila had exited her chamber at one in the morning and returned at half past six.

There were spies everywhere on the estate, especially in the great house.

Not in her bedroom, though. She made sure of it.

Lila snatched her palm computer from her desk. It was little more than a palm-sized touchscreen display only five millimeters thick, made of flimsy waterproof rubber and black plastic. The metal and circuits inside could slide and adjust when bent, making it virtually indestructible. Though it possessed only eighty percent of the power of her desktop computer, it was much more flexible in its capabilities, much like its frame.

Lila set the device to search for the telltale signals of bugs and waved it along the dark gray and white walls. She eyed the screen while she aimed it at the few pieces of furniture in her room: a bed with black blankets and a pop of crimson, a long black couch with one stray red pillow, a coffee table, a chest of drawers with photographs of her family and friends arranged on top, a bedside table, and a massive desk. Artisans had carved each piece from ebony and stained it to the blackest black. Despite the room's large size, Lila had never possessed the time or inclination to fill it with anything more, and its minimalist style made sweeping for bugs so much easier. In fact, the only decoration in her room was a silver Randolph coat of arms, hung above the couch.

Finding nothing in the sweep, Lila dropped her palm on her desk, yawned, and kicked off her boots. She stuffed her peacoat, clothes, thermal suit, and the remains of the DNA pen into a canvas sports bag and hid it inside a secret compartment in the closet. She tossed the cigars in a drawer and slipped the star drive into a hidden panel in her desk for later processing. Then she hopped into the welcoming embrace of a hot shower, stripping off layer after layer of smoke, gasoline, and ash. The last layer she scrubbed away was Canidae, created to erase its wearer's scent from the purview of nosy dogs. Randolph researchers had concocted the recipe, and she had tested it for the first time that very same night. Perhaps it had helped cover the scent of gas and smoke.

Once Lila was in the shower, it was hard for her to step out again. She had spent the last several hours cold and wet, and warmth was now a welcome friend. After a good scrub with apple-scented shampoo, Lila turned the water off and dressed in a thick white robe, stitched with the family coat of arms on the left breast. She felt more like herself with its return, and glanced longingly at her bed.

Unfortunately, there was no time for sleep. The first order of business would be a mug of hot chocolate and a pain pill for her pounding headache, followed closely by a stroll through Bullstow's computer network. She needed to see what the DNA pen had managed to transmit before it had been smashed under her boot.

There was a soft knock at the door.

Lila stepped to the door and peeked through the peephole. "It's barely six o'clock, Alex," she muttered. The slave's crisp white blouse and skirt had not a wrinkle anywhere, and her blonde hair was styled perfectly, even at such an early hour.

As soon as Lila opened the door, Alex lifted her silver tray and bowed deeply, exposing a tiny scar on her neck from her slave incision. Lodged deep inside was an identity chip and homing beacon, placed far too near her arteries and veins for all but the most competent of medical professionals to dig out again. Not that it stopped some from trying, and dying in the attempt.

Keeping her back low, Alex tilted her head up at Lila. "I assumed you were asleep," she whispered, still obediently bent at the waist.

"I assumed you know by now that I am unpredictable."

"Who was he?" Alex said, a twinkle in her eye. "Is he still here?"

"He?"

"She, then? My, my, my, I suppose things really have changed since university."

"Shut up, Alex."

"As you wish, Chief Randolph." The slave bowed deeper, her face the very model of seriousness and propriety, except for a slight sarcastic twist on one side of her mouth.

Lila tugged Alex into her room. It was such a quick movement that the slave nearly tripped over her heels. She barely managed to avoid dropping the silver tray.

"Would you knock it off?" Lila growled once the door had closed.

Alex surveyed the room, even peeking into the closet and the bathroom. Lila drew the line at her old friend checking under the bed. "There's no one here."

"Then you went out? I'm glad to hear it. You've been starved for months. The staff was beginning to worry. I thought I might have to work my old contacts and lure some highborn scoundrel here for you to devour. I still know several who would meet your requirements."

Lila tried not to think about the truth in Alex's pronouncement. She *was* a bit starved. She hadn't been with a man in over a year, which she knew was far too long. If the staff of the great house was already beginning to whisper about it, the family would be sure to follow. Things would get awkward if that happened.

As if she needed one more thing to worry about.

Lila put it on her list of things to do. One, figure out if Bullstow had matched her DNA. Two, find Zephyr. Three, find and kill Tristan. Four, send a report to R&D about the Canidae trial run. Five, invite a man over for dinner and a show.

Six, avoid contacting her client until she had sorted out what had happened at Bullstow.

"I'm not starved, and I didn't go anywhere," she lied, somewhat amused at Alex's rather accurate description of her past lovers. But at least wastrel sons of insignificant highborn families never wanted to get her pregnant. It would please their mothers and matrons too much. "I've been home all night."

"Fibber. I know you were with someone because you have that post-sex glow about you—"

"That's gas."

"Plus you're awake at an ungodly hour of the morning, at least for you—"

"I had insomnia."

"And you just got out of the shower," the slave finished, as though it were the end of some magic trifecta, condemning Lila to some post-coital state.

"I do bathe occasionally, Alex."

"Yes, but all three of those things at once are not a coincidence. Who's responsible for your rosy cheeks and lazy smile?"

"A warm shower will do that for you."

"Oh really?"

Lila snatched up the missive on the silver tray.

"I suppose sometimes you just have to take matters into your own hands. I'll find those numbers for you this weekend."

Lila crushed the letter in her fist. "Damn it, Alex, I don't need—"

"Okay, I'll make that tonight, Chief Fussy."

"You're impossible, Alex," Lila said as she flopped on the couch.

Alex laughed and sat onto the cushion beside her. "Did the blast wake you?"

Lila tapped the envelope against her thigh. "Did anyone sleep through it?"

"Not likely. I bet half the city is awake."

"It wasn't a train this time," Lila said, tearing the envelope open. "Just a gas explosion."

Alex leaned back into the couch. "So what does the chairwoman want? Has she ordered you to run around the compound five times, shouting, 'Glory to the Randolphs'?"

"It's more likely a summons. And you should mind your tongue before someone overhears it waggling." Lila dug into the envelope and read the request for an early breakfast in the morning room. The rest of her plans would have to wait. "Tell Chairwoman Randolph that I shall arrive with great anticipation in fifteen minutes."

"Great anticipation?"

"Yeah, make it sound sincere if you can."

The slave gathered up the tray once more and paused at the door. "What do you think she wants?"

"Security for the Wabash Fundraiser next week, I suppose." Lila's easy tone belied her anxious stomach. The summons so soon after the botched job worried her, especially if the chairwoman was awake at such an early hour. The Randolph family was not known to be early risers. The estate was only six or seven kilometers away from Bullstow, though. It was likely the blast, and nothing more, that had woken the chairwoman.

"Are you going?"

"I'll send a security team for the chairwoman and another if Jewel plans to attend, but I'm staying here. That's the nice part about being the boss. You can delegate unpleasant tasks."

Alex fingered the tray. "Sometimes I hate you for that, you know. You're a highborn. You could still be a part of it all if you wanted. The dances, the season, the balls."

Lila joined her at the door. "You turned your back on it long before you ended up in this situation, Alex. Don't make me a part of your disappointments and regrets. It's not fair."

"I don't have regrets. Not really. What happened was my own fault. I never wanted to be an old woman, stuck at the end of my life, wondering 'what if.' That has to be worse than slavery, don't you think?"

"You've done well for yourself here," Lila said, squeezing her shoulder. "The chairwoman respects you well enough to keep you in the great house, and your new coat of arms is much better than the old."

"The chairwoman only wants me close so that I can be watched."

"Do you think it's any different with me? You might be a fallen heir from another family, but you are a highborn nonetheless. You know our ways, and you can be trusted. I suspect you'll keep moving up if you want such things."

"Well, if I want such things, I should probably get back to work before I'm accused of sloth." Alex waved goodbye with the silver tray and closed the bedroom door.

4

Lila dried her dark hair, arranged it into a loose wave, and then donned her uniform. The black woolen trousers, white cotton blouse, and red officer's jacket hugged her figure, yet stretched well enough for her to run or fight should the occasion arise. Her militia blackcoat, trimmed with red piping, went over it and skimmed her calves. Lila felt like herself again under so much leather, and she hummed under her breath while she finished dressing.

Tucking her trousers into her boots, she considered paging Isabel. The leather could do with a bit of a polishing, but there was no time for it. Instead, she swiped a towel over her boots and called the job done. She then holstered her backup Colt at her hip, slid her officer's short sword into the scabbard on the opposite side, and rammed her knife into a sheath in her boot. Before leaving, she glanced in the mirror one last time and brushed off the four silver stars on her collar.

Tugging on her black gloves, Lila descended the main staircase and passed through the main hall. It had been paneled in mahogany and adorned with crimson silk tapestries. The silver Randolph coat of arms hung on the wall, made by Jewel Randolph, painter, sculptor, and prime heir to the Randolphs. Portraits of the family surrounded it, spanning backward into the eighteenth century. The heirs' crimson ball gowns had hardly changed much at all in that time. Neither had the men's tailored coats and breaches.

Lila stepped deeper into the house and entered the morning room. It should have been called the room of windows, for three of its walls had been built of glass. The rising sun streamed into the room, casting beams of light on a table, heavy with platters of pancakes and syrup, eggs, bacon, toast, yogurt, and blackberries. A bottle of Gregorie and a pitcher of orange juice peeked over the food. A male slave stood in the corner, dressed in crimson breeches, tights, and a matching coat, waiting for instructions.

The chairwoman studied Lila. Her silver hair had been styled into a severe bun at the nape of her neck. Though the matron claimed the hue was natural, Lila knew it had been dyed. Most people likely assumed it, for the woman was only forty-six years old. The color matched her coat, which bore the family coat of arms in crimson thread. The silvercoat was cut more stylishly than Lila's militia jacket, but it still retained a regal and military air, as did her high-fashion boots of the same shade. She wore a flowing sheath dress in crimson underneath, and her body had been liberally dotted with rose-scented perfume.

"Chief," the chairwoman said by way of greeting, gesturing at the chair across from her.

"Mother. Isn't it a bit early to discuss security arrangements for the Wabash Fundraiser?"

"Why would I summon you on your day off for that? Especially so early." She dropped her gaze down to the proffered chair once more, hinting.

Lila sat and removed her gloves for the meal.

The chairwoman picked up a bowl and offered it to Lila. "Would you like some blackberries? Chef reminded me of how much you like them. They're quite fresh."

Lila took a few and piled her plate with more food than she really wanted, pretending an appetite. She tried not to wince around her injured tongue, still sore from where she had bitten it in the explosion.

"Leave us," Chairwoman Randolph said to the slave in the corner.

He bowed immediately and left the room.

"You're up early," Lila said, stabbing at her pancakes, soggy with maple syrup.

"I could say the same for you. The explosion woke me, just as I'm sure it woke everyone in the city. Didn't wake you, though, did it? You were already up."

Lila schooled her face into blankness and sipped her orange juice. "What do you mean, madam?"

"What do you know about the disturbance?"

"Disturbance? That's a strange way of referring to a gas explosion."

Her mother's eyes narrowed. "Tell me something that's not already on the news, Lila."

"Okay. There are about a dozen members of the Randolph militia assisting Bullstow at this very moment. I'll know more when they return. That's not on the news."

"Good. What about your spies?"

"It's still early yet. I'm sure they're still out there. Spying," Lila said, waggling her fingers. "I suppose yours have already reported in?"

"A few have. One told me they saw something rather interesting a few hours ago. What were you doing, sneaking through the tunnels under the estate at half past four this morning?"

"I don't know what you're talking about." It had taken a great deal of money and cajoling to flip one of her mother's best spies, but she had done it. Finally.

The fake alibi couldn't have come at a better time.

"I checked the cameras, Lila. You snuck out. What were you all night?"

Lila picked up her glass and focused on the pulp that stuck that to rim. "What do you think I was doing, Mother? I was testing my people. I'm afraid Commander Sutton is the only one who can confirm it, though, for the rest of my people were in the dark. Supposing your spy is employed by the militia, they might have gotten a promotion for spotting me if they had come to me instead of you. I hope you're paying them well enough to make up for that."

"Testing?" Her mother snorted, knowing of Commander Sutton's impeccable honesty. "You and your tests. You only engage in them because you're bored with your position. You think I don't know that?"

Lila had no desire for a lecture when she had so many other pressing matters to attend to. She stood, breakfast half eaten, and bowed her head curtly. "A pleasure as always, madam."

"Sit," the chairwoman commanded. The word was a leg swinging at Lila's knees.

She toppled back into her chair.

"Yes, you abdicated your role as prime heir. Yes, you will no longer take over the role of chairwoman when I retire. Yes, your younger sister has taken up the whitecoat and become the president of Wolf Industries because you continue to shirk your duty. Yes, you have abandoned your responsibilities to the entire Randolph family—"

"Yes, sometimes I cheat at cards," Lila said, threading her fingers together and propping them on her knee. "Yes, I drink far too much hot chocolate and eat too few vegetables. Yes, I sometimes chug milk straight from the carton. Yes, I—"

"Elizabeth Victoria Lemaire-Randolph, it would be wise not to bait me so early in the morning."

"I'm sorry. I thought you were listing every single fault you have with me. I was only trying to help. Yes, I am sarcastic when—"

"I allowed you to circumvent your birthright in order to engage in this foolishness," the chairwoman said, waving absently at Lila's uniform. "I thought you'd tire of it and eventually accept your duty by my side. A decade has passed while I've waited, a decade spent clawing your way to the top of the mountain, but I see the boredom on your face, child. You're not having much fun at the summit."

"It's a job. It's not meant to be fun—"

"The right job is."

"It's meant to be meaningful. I never wanted to become chairwoman of Wolf Industries, or its president. You know that."

"Yes, and haven't I been a benevolent matron in allowing you to play in your security office?"

Lila frowned, unsure how to answer the question. "*Your* security office, madam. We have a contract. What exactly do you want from me?"

"Want? Need is more like it. I need a lot of things. I need a competent prime, yet you refuse, leaving your little sister to flounder with every decision she makes. I need a granddaughter, an heir for the next generation. Yet Jewel has not been able to produce one, and you continue to insist that you will remain childless." The chairwoman poured herself a glass of wine. "Since I can't have either of those things, I want the best chief of security in all of Saxony. This explosion happened hours ago. You should know more by now."

"My people are on it. Let me remind you, chairwoman. You have the most secure estate in the country. Out of forty-seven attempted intrusions last year, only three even made it over the wall. My people caught each of them in less than sixty seconds. We had one hundred and eighty foiled attempts by hackers on our system, and those are only the serious intrusions. In fact, the last successful large-scale attack on our system was six years ago before I was promoted from sergeant to captain of our tech division. If you remember, that's why I became the captain."

"I remember, Lila."

"Good. I didn't become chief because I'm your daughter. Don't talk at me as if I don't know my job."

"Fine, but one day, you're going to look at your life and wonder why you settled for the security office instead of Wolf Tower."

"That's unlikely. I don't have any regrets."

"Not now, perhaps. But later? I suspect you will, Lila. What am I supposed to do when I don't have enough time to teach you all that you should know?"

"I don't want—"

"You don't want, you don't want, you don't want. It's always about what you don't want. That's what got us both into this mess. Ms. Wilson wanted a lot of things. Now her entire family will fall because Chairwoman Wilson has no prime and the woman is too old to bear another daughter. That's where wanting gets you, Lila. That's where—"

"We're not a dying family like the Wilsons, and I'm not the only heir to Wolf Industries," Lila said, annoyed that she must rehash a very old and frequent argument. "Alex lost her mark because she was the only heir left in a generation, a daughter surrounded by half a dozen boys."

"No, she lost it because her business failed."

"It failed because you helped tank it. Then you scooped up her mark at a discount. Now you're gambling that her mother won't bear another daughter. You're hoping she won't since you control the only living Wilson prime. They were our friends."

"Ms. Wilson was your friend. Her mother is an embarrassment."

"Alex didn't even have a real chance."

"That's business. That's competition. We live on a razor's edge, Lila. Within one generation, the Wilson Empire will fall and come into our hands because we control its only heir. We will assume possession of all their interests because they could not manage them effectively."

"I'm glad you're not reveling in their misfortune," Lila said before swallowing a blackberry.

"You think they wouldn't have reveled in ours? Ms. Wilson's current position is due entirely to her own poor choices and your friendship. How many other matrons would be so fair to a fallen heir? She still wears fine clothes and might even be in charge of the great house staff after Ms. O'Malley retires, so long as she continues her good work and discretion. I'm nothing if not fair. More than."

"It's not Alex's fault."

"Not all of it, no. It's also the fault of her grandmother for trifling with German princes and not having more daughters. Her mother, too."

"She had three."

"Yes, and two are dead. Drunk drivers should all be hanged." Her mother shivered and snatched up her glass once more.

Lila fiddled with the end of her short sword, watching her mother's face. The rumor was that her mother had been behind the accident, just to leave Alex exposed and ripe for the plucking. Neither Lila nor Alex believed it, of course. A smart matron would have bought Alex for a song at auction and then arranged for the accident to take out the other two.

And Beatrice Randolph was very smart.

Sometimes Lila had to wonder what her mother was capable of, though, especially when she became so terribly blunt and pragmatic.

"Ms. Wilson erred when she didn't birth an heir to the Wilson-Kruger line," the chairwoman said. "She should have had one and signed it over to her mother before striking out on her own if that's what she wanted to do. Now any child she bears will be born into slavery. All the while, her mother takes a basketful of medication while chasing senators and meeting with doctors to harvest her eggs. It's unseemly and desperate at her age, and her business is suffering for it. Our business, in another fifteen years or so, if anything is left of it."

"Sooner or later, one of those eggs will take," Lila said, pouring her own glass of Gregorie. She considered Chairwoman Wilson, a woman of nearly sixty, fighting against hot flashes and time in order to bear another daughter. Science had given her extra time and a better chance than most, but it could not work miracles. Even if such a child was born so late in life, Chairwoman Wilson would not have long to teach her any business sense. The only saving grace of such a plan was that the child would have so many well-placed brothers and cousins in the senate to assist her. They had enough political acumen to smooth over a few mistakes of youth, but they could only do so much.

Besides, it wasn't as if the woman had that much sense or decorum to pass on. Lila could never figure out how Alex had come from such a ridiculous line, for her friend's grandmother hadn't been any better. Alex was one of the rare instances of a well-bred father making up for the mother's lack. Perhaps it was fortunate that Senator Craft had died before he witnessed what had become of his daughter.

"None of her eggs will take. I control the woman's doctor. Once the chairwoman dies, we will own her company, her capital, and the land underneath."

"Hooray for us," Lila said halfheartedly. It was a pity that Chairwoman Wilson had never gone to Randolph General. Lila never would have allowed one of the doctors at her hospital to take bribes that impacted patient care.

Unfortunately, the Wilson matron obviously did not trust it.

Lila couldn't blame her.

"Yes, hooray for us. I've tripled the profits of the Randolph family in the last thirty years, but do you honestly think I wanted this responsibility at fourteen when my mother died? Do you honestly believe there weren't other things I wanted to do before taking up the position? I didn't have enough time with my mother to learn what I needed to know. I made mistakes in my youth that I shouldn't have made. I—"

"You're doing just fine. You've tripled our profits, remember?"

"Yes, and I had to figure out too much of it on my own. It's all just a game, Lila. And it's a far better game than the one you're playing now. I can only correct for Jewel's mistakes while I live. Once I'm gone, the full extent of her carelessness will be in full view. You'll be forced to take over then. Your own sense of duty won't allow for anything else. You should drop this nonsense now while there's still time."

"You don't lack for sisters and nieces, Mother. One of them will be more than happy to do the job whether or not you're too stubborn to accept it. Go have this conversation with one of them." Lila stood up from the table, straightened her uniform, and bowed, as befitting the chief of security to her matron.

Lila then stalked out of the room, leaving her mother and the rest of her breakfast behind.

5

Lila changed out of her formal uniform and into cargo pants and a black sweater, which had a coin-sized Randolph coat of arms stitched on the left breast. Rifling through her desk drawers, she found a packet of stale chocolate chip cookies to tide her over until lunch. Popping one into her mouth, she turned on her desktop computer, readying herself for the first part of her to-do list.

The first and most unpleasant task of them all.

Lila snatched up her palm and typed out a message. *What on earth do you think you were doing?*

Frowning, she read her first attempt again, then shook her head and deleted it.

I could have been killed!

Lila deleted each letter of her second try, her scowl deepening. *Where did everyone go? Where are you?*

The words stared back at her, much too simple to reflect the soup in her mind.

Would you have cared if I had died?

Lila barely paused before hurriedly erasing the message, chiding herself for writing it at all. In the end, she replaced the text with a simple, noncommittal question mark. The vague symbol held every single question she wanted to ask.

She was curious to see which one Tristan would answer.

Lila tossed the palm across her desk and rubbed her forehead. At some point, she had forgotten what Tristan truly was. A criminal. They weren't friends. They could never be friends. The man hated the highborn. He hated their money; he hated their lifestyle; he hated everything they stood for. He only worked for her because it suited his agenda, and the money was too good for him to pass up.

"Should have gone with 'What were you thinking, asshole?'" Lila grumbled to herself as she logged into her desktop computer.

BullNet was an easy hack. Though the government kept strict controls over the net, Lila always managed to find a way through Bullstow's network. Even Unity's network had never presented much of a challenge.

It was the not-getting-caught part that made it slightly more difficult and time-consuming. Despite the controls on private networks, no public content was censored on the net, except for what might be inappropriate due to age. Every citizen left entries in logs, though, regardless of class. A citizen's logs could be scrutinized with a warrant as long as the officers in question had a case number and narrowed down their interests to a certain date range. Such a warrant trapped the individual, just as firmly as the iron bars of a cage.

Lila simply stepped around such measures. Her first snoop programs had constantly scrubbed her logs clean and substituted innocent content when necessary. Unfortunately, there were also logs on the other end to worry about, and her programs could not always alter them. The easiest and most low-tech way to get around that was to use someone else's account, but the user might figure out that their logon had been compromised.

The more difficult—and ultimately more secure—option was to create a fake account, separate and hidden from one's own identity. Barely traceable, it remained illegal and dangerous if any part of it led back to the creator, but Lila had enough skill to evade that trap.

Very few others in Saxony did.

Using proxies, Lila slipped into the Bullstow militia network with one of her fake logins. She snuck through the logs, first searching for the data from the sergeant's DNA pen.

Lila breathed easier as soon as she opened the file. It was short. Nothing much had been transmitted. It did not even contain enough of her DNA to mark her as female, much less compare it to her samples within the Saxony DNA database. It surprised her, but perhaps the male sergeant had not kept the pen charged. Perhaps it just didn't have enough time to send anything to Bullstow before the blast knocked out the power.

In any case, no one had opened the file.

Lila erased the data and the accompanying logs, then read over the sergeant's report. Bullstow had pulled in their sketch artist to work with him and his men, none of whom had been seriously injured in the blast. Clearly their memories had focused more on the size of Lila's prosthetics than on her features. No one would confuse her with the sketch, much less the facial-recognition software. Lila didn't bother to alter the report.

She skimmed through the rest of the file that focused on the bombing. Bullstow had managed to keep the true cause of the explosion from the press, not wanting to cause a panic. They had used extra men from the local militias to create a wide perimeter until every flyer had been retrieved by Bullstow. Luckily, the damp had kept the flyers from blowing too far.

Bullstow knew nothing about the American Abolitionist Society other than its name. Lila wondered how long it would take them to find the hotel, or if they'd find it at all. She imagined Sergeant Perv questioning the workborn about the flyer, a flyer that extolled freedom for all slaves. Such an approach wouldn't take him very far. Slaves didn't help the militias in the best of times, and most servants had at least one relative who had been condemned to a slave's term. Both classes of workborn would be more likely to hinder the investigation than help.

She was safe, at least for now.

Lila signed out of BullNet, for she had work to do for her client. She retrieved her star drive from its hiding place, still glinting on its golden chain. The entire BIRD fit into the palm of her hand. For such a small thing, it was certainly worth a great deal of money. Some of the files in the BIRD, the Birth Identity Records

Database, would fetch a high price if offered to the right people, for the parentage of everyone in all four American states had been recorded inside it.

Most of the data was public knowledge, but secrets abounded within. Sometimes mothers, usually highborn or wealthy lowborn, kept the father of their heir or subsequent children private. Bullstow sealed the records but allowed citizens of any class to query the database for their own records by their fourteenth birthday, inputting the name of anyone they had intentions of bedding. Submitting a potential lover's name to the BIRD ensured that the pairing would provide a good genetic match in the case of non-private births, but it also ensured that an individual did not inadvertently bed one's own half-sibling. Of course, Bullstow might visit if too many requests occurred in too short a time, for it was illegal to use the feature as a means of ascertaining a hidden father's identity.

Blackmail was always an option for anyone who could hack the BIRD. Not that Lila needed the money. She wasn't interested in blackmail, and neither was her client.

She put the star drive into her computer's port and, for the next hour, reviewed the data captured by her snoop programs. It did not take her long to untangle the code and figure out how Zephyr had hidden within it. The trap had been woven into the BIRD itself, the strands of code suspended like crude spider webs, waiting for a juicy fly to walk inside.

Lila had activated the program, and likely alerted the snoop, the moment she logged into the BIRD with a fraudulent ID. Zephyr knew exactly what files she had taken, knew when she had been inside the network, and knew when she had gotten back out again. What would the snoop do with that information? What had the snoop already done with it?

When Lila attempted a trace on the snoop's counterfeit ID, she didn't get far. Although she was somewhat mollified by the fact that she found so many telltale signs of fraudulence, the ID was good enough that she couldn't penetrate the identity behind it. Not quickly, anyway.

Lila cocked her head, and was considering another way of tracing the snoop when her computer beeped. A window popped up on her screen flashing from red to green and back again.

Her client.

Lila cursed. She pulled on her VR spectacles, flipped the switch on the earpiece, and clicked *Initiate* on the browser window before hopping up from her chair. The bug-eyed lenses curved around her nose and cheek and forehead, making it difficult to see anything around their edges, not even her body. Her room disappeared slowly, devoured by smoke until nothing remained.

"Lila, girl." A deep voice rumbled into the void.

The fog cleared. Lila found herself standing in the middle of an office, not unlike Senator Serrano's in style, though this office had been carved from cherry rather than mahogany. A man sat at the desk, surface covered with papers, pens, stacks of documents thicker than novels, color-coded folders, hastily scribbled notes, paperclips, and star drives. He dwarfed it all, though not with his size. His mere presence and keen stare were enough, as though he were a prizefighter only a week from his last fight.

His body resembled it as well.

Lila knew he worked hard for it.

Prime Minister Lemaire reclined in his expensive leather chair and scratched his salt-and-pepper stubble, coat and breeches cut in white, eyes red and tired. He motioned for her to sit. The gesture and his voice occurred slightly out of sync. Lag. The bane of VR transmissions. It was not a good start to the conversation.

Lila flopped down, hoping she would not miss her real chair in her bedroom, for the chair in her client's office and her own were not remotely in the same place. The software corrected with a brief sizzle and flicker as soon as she sat down.

"Father, how's your chair?"

"Comfortable."

The question and reply was a constant joke between them. Right after Lila's twelfth birthday, her father had moved to Unity as one of the newest members of the national High House, America's senate. Lila had been distressed about the change, for she had spent a lot of time visiting her father at Bullstow, sneaking around the compound, and seeking out her younger brother Shiloh in places she had no permission to be. In an effort to placate Lila, her father had told her that he would come back if his chair was not as comfortable as the one in Saxony's High House. Before he arrived in Unity, Lila had already bribed a slave to swap out his expensive leather office chair for a wooden stool.

Prime Minister Lemaire did not ask for a replacement. He stubbornly used it, even during meetings, for an entire legislative session. Predictably, Lila realized that she could survive without her father while he tended to the business of the country. She bought him a new chair for the next session, the most expensive and lavish one she could find, but he did not throw out the old stool. Even now, it lived in the corner of his office, chipped and beaten, a splash of blue paint on one of the legs. A little plaque had been bolted to the edge of the seat. *Remember Your Sacrifice* had been etched into the metal.

Lemaire had added it himself.

Lila spied a plate on his desk, captured by the cameras inside his office. "Is that bacon and sausage, Father?"

Frowning, he picked up his breakfast and hid it behind a stack of papers. "Things have been busy in New Bristol. I've already spoken to Governor LeComte and Chief Shaw twice this morning. What do you know?"

Lila settled into her chair. "I know your doctors told you to stop eating bacon and sausage."

"Lila."

"I know that the heart-clogging capabilities of your breakfast do not suddenly disappear just because you've hidden them away. What are you, five?"

He fixed her with a stern gaze and hunkered over his desk. A loud creak cut across the transmission, delayed by half a second. "This gas explosion at Bullstow has your friend written all over it."

"I don't know what you mean," she said, keeping her answers vague and free of names in case the line had been bugged.

"Lila, was he involved?"

"I don't know."

"Yes, you do. Or at least you have your suspicions. I know that face. I've seen it on your mother too much." He sighed tiredly. "Lila, you cannot... We cannot afford to be in league with his sort."

"His sort?"

"You know what I mean."

"Yes, I do, but keep in mind that I could only trust his sort, not unless you'd rather face an endless drain on your bank account every week for the gift of silence."

"I'd rather have that to deal with than a governor who believes the Almstakers have resurfaced under a different name. Cut ties. Immediately. It's too risky."

"No, I've invested too much time and energy. I'll not have my contact burned. Besides, he's the best option for our work in the region."

Lemaire stroked his chin, considering her face. "You have your orders. Report."

"You want a report? Fine. Bullstow is a lovely place to walk in the middle of the night, especially when you have business."

"Last night?"

"Of course."

Lemaire's shoulders fell. "I was afraid of that. Did you finish your walk successfully?"

"Yes, but as you can see, there were complications. I'm not yet aware of the details."

The prime minister leaned back in his chair. "I don't like being kept in the dark. I don't like how you're handling this mess, either. What of the information?"

"I'm reviewing it now."

"What have you found?"

"It's early, but I found our spider and its web. Unfortunately, I don't know who the spider is or where it lives. I need a bit more time with the details."

"I need that information soon, Lila. The situation has become more desperate."

"Another woman?"

The prime minster winced. "Yes."

"Send me what you have, then. I'm going to figure it out, Father. Soon."

"Good," he answered, tapping his leather armrest. "Lila, I'm going to be blunt. If Chief Shaw hasn't had a break in the bombing case by Saturday morning, then I'm turning in your friend's name as a suspect. You're to do the same the moment you believe he's involved."

Lila's eyes widened.

"Don't look at me like that. There's a big difference between ignoring a stolen car here and there and ignoring an act of terrorism. If he's innocent, Chief Shaw will clear him. Quietly."

"Give me until Monday. I'll solve it myself," she said, wanting to buy a few extra days for Tristan to leave Saxony. Maybe she owed it to him. Maybe she didn't.

"Lila, you don't have the time, the resources, or the jurisdiction to work on the case. If Chief Shaw requests your assistance, then I'll certainly approve it, but—"

"You know that he'll ask for my help anyway. It's the natural consequence of training every boy who attends Bullstow as some silly—"

"Senator. Bullstow trains senators. From birth. It's tradition."

"It's a stupid tradition that has resulted in a militia who can't even investigate the most basic online attack, much less—"

"They aren't inept. You're just much better than they are. Besides, you have other work right now with the BIRD investigation."

"If you want to keep me doing that important work, then you'll give me until Monday."

He fixed her with a stern eye. "Chief Shaw will treat him fairly, Elizabeth. We can't cover for someone like him."

"I need him for this case. What I don't need is the threat of our friend's capture being held over my head."

"It's not a threat." His eyes cut to her face and held her gaze. "Fine. You have until Monday morning."

Lila inclined her head.

"On a more pleasant note, I'm meeting with the oracles next week."

Lila stifled a groan. She could scarcely hear the word oracle or see their symbol—an eye with wings attached—without wanting to vomit.

"Don't give me that look. Those women are the spiritual backbone of the alliance."

"Those women are the spiritual claw prying open the treasury."

"Well, as long as the meeting goes smoothly and nothing delays my flight, I should be in New Bristol in time for Father's Week. *Should.*"

"Should?"

"I think there's something the oracles aren't telling me."

"They're oracles, Father. There's always something they aren't telling you."

"More so than usual. The oracles are disappearing, Lila, but the infernal women won't discuss it with me."

"You were just talking to me about jurisdiction? The oracles are sovereign, Father. You have absolutely no recourse if they don't want you involved. They've been taking care of their own for over a thousand years, with the exception of demanding their yearly allowance."

"It's not an allowance."

"My point is that you can't expect them to let outsiders get involved now. Besides, it's not exactly a secret that their numbers are declining."

"No. It's a fear. It's a hypothesis. It's a rumor. We don't know for sure. Only the oracles do, and I can't help them if they refuse to discuss the matter." Lemaire sat back into his chair like a striking cobra. She knew that look. She'd seen it on her father's face, mid-speech before the senate and mid-fight with her mother.

"I'm sorry, Lila. I'm bringing other issues into our time together. We'll have dinner when I come into town, just the pair of us. Perhaps we'll dig up Shiloh after we're done talking business. I'm the prime minister. They should be able to rustle up an evening pass so that a boy can see his father." He winked, knowing Bullstow would lift the entire boys' dormitory if he snapped his fingers and asked for it.

"I'm sure he'd like that."

"I hope you will as well. This unpleasantness should be over by then."

"Unpleasantness? Is that what our friend would call it?"

"I know you're upset, but I won't apologize for trying to keep my family safe. I never should have dragged you into this business, Lila. I'm sorry for that."

"Asking me for help is exactly what you should have done. I'll always do what I can, for you and for Saxony. It's how you raised me."

Lila mused on her father's face, so tired and old this morning, upset that he had brought her into his troubles. While at the same time, her mother demanded that Lila become involved in hers and called it a birthright.

6

Lila rubbed her eyes. They'd begun to lose focus after straining at her monitor for so many hours. Lunch had long since come and gone, consisting of a quickly eaten sandwich at her desk. She hadn't made any further breaks in Zephyr's identity, and dinner loomed. Given how poorly breakfast had gone, Lila had no desire to share a table with her mother.

She twirled her sapphire ring and checked the messages on her palm, scrolling through a few updates from Commander Sutton and Captain McKinley, as well as a reminder from Commander Fitzgibbons about her upcoming visit to the New Orleans compound.

Lila propped her boots upon her desk and sighed. The season would begin in a month, and her mother would begin a new round of arguments. She'd want Lila to join in the season: to attend the balls and dinner parties, to find an eligible senator, to reverse her birth control, to bed a new beau and bear a daughter. A daydream popped into her head, a lovely daydream of her sneaking from one Randolph compound to another, too busy to attend a single event for the entire season.

But Beatrice Randolph would never accept such a ruse.

The chairwoman had been right about one thing. Very few matrons would have allowed a prime to skip her birthright, not unless the prime was deficient in some way. It had only been a moment's lapse on her mother's part that had allowed Lila to duck the responsibility at all.

After Lila had caught a hacker in WolfNet at the age of seventeen, a hacker who had nearly made off with a third of the family's capital, her mother had thrown a party in her honor. It had been one of the most lavish, expensive affairs that Lila had ever witnessed. The entire Randolph ballroom had been packed with every highborn on the compound. As a crystal chandelier sparkled above them, slaves dressed in immaculate tuxes brought tray after tray of wine and champagne; guests feasted on endless platters of delicate sandwiches, sliced fruits, and sweetened pastries; and everyone danced to lively waltzes, played by a group of white-gloved musicians.

Her mother was shrewd in her opulence. The party showed the family what they could expect after Lila took up the heir's whitecoat, for hadn't Lila been given Our Lady of the Light for her fourteenth birthday? Hadn't she renamed the hospital for the glory of the Randolph family? Hadn't she built it up and made it the most successful medical facility in all of Saxony?

It didn't matter that Lila told everyone that the hospital's success lay mainly with those she had hired to advise her. She hadn't come up with any ideas of her own; she'd merely sifted through their ideas and picked the direction she liked the most.

They thought Lila modest for such confessions. It made them fawn over her more.

At the end of the night, the chairwoman gathered the crowd and toasted Lila for her business sense, for her computer skills, for her watchfulness. She had promised to give Lila a reward. Did she want the rarest of antique cars? A large-eyed puppy with a champion's pedigree? A month-long vacation to an island paradise? A closet full of new clothes designed by Madame Thayer? Did she dream of a new heir's mansion built for her and her alone?

Her mother raised her glass, her silvercoat and crimson dress flowing about her, her diamond necklace twinkling in the dim light, waiting. So beautiful. So happy.

So proud.

"No, madam," Lila answered, her voice as bold as she could make it. "I wish to abdicate my position as prime and join the militia."

Half the musicians stopped playing at once due to surprise. The others hadn't heard Lila's words and continued on, falling out of time when they realized something had gone horribly wrong.

Silence soon devoured the ballroom.

No one breathed, least of all Beatrice Randolph. The pair stared at one another, poker hands clutched to their breasts, the chairwoman's eyes burning with rage that Lila would dare ask such a thing before the entire family.

Lila refused to take back her wish. She'd never get such an opportunity again, and she'd be damned if she would waste it.

The chairwoman had been forced to grant her request, signing a contract later that evening after a long battle between two sets of shouting lawyers.

"Such a waste, such a loss," her mother had despaired at every opportunity during her first year, usually at meals and in front of guests. Eventually, it had devolved into prim sighs and frowns.

Arguments followed. So many arguments.

The same argument they'd had that morning.

Lila laid her head upon her desk and tried not slam it into the ebony.

One thing was clear. Her mother was getting antsy about the contract, and if she didn't want the chairwoman to toss it out, then she'd have to pick a few events during the season and attend, appeasing and teasing the woman.

Three really busy, really crowded events.

Perhaps she'd take a lover this season as well, a senator who wanted a season's break from the heir carousel. Though Bullstow was home, school, and work to all firstborn sons of Saxon heirs, they only chose the most beautiful, the most pleasant, and the most charming men amongst themselves to serve as senators. Despite their annoying tendency to talk too often about their children— and the promise of them—she had occasionally paired off with one out of season. Some of them could be quite fun, not to mention attractive in their tailored Bullstow coats and breeches.

It was only sex, after all, and she hadn't gotten enough of it in the last couple of years. Her mother's only recourse would be to prattle on about reversing her birth control, something Lila had no intention of doing.

Ever.

Lila sat up, rubbed her forehead, and scrolled through the rest of the messages on her palm, shaking off thoughts of children and senators and contracts. She had bigger things to worry about, like the fact that Tristan had not bothered to reply to her message.

Annoyed, she pulled up the *New Bristol Times*, checking if a certain column had been posted that morning. The column was famous within the city and beyond, as was its Sunday counterpart. One from Mael Faucheux, the other from Alexandre Bouchard, two columns on opposite sides of every issue, an ever-evolving conversation between two writers.

One was always just a bit more persuasive than the other.

Tristan DeLauncey penned both, not that he could use his real name—not that Tristan DeLauncey even was his real name. It always surprised her that a man as infuriating as Tristan could write so persuasively, so beautifully, and so intelligently.

Unsurprisingly, he'd chosen the Slave Bill as his topic, that piece of rumored legislation that might one day free lowborn and high-born from the consequences of business failure, allowing them to retain their mark if their businesses failed.

He'd managed to turn in his column on time, not bothering to spare two seconds to send her a message. It must have been too much for him, too taxing while he was so busy, subtly changing public opinion to his own views.

Grumbling, Lila typed his ID into one of her programs. She drummed her fingers against her knee while her computer traced his location.

East New Bristol. Shippers Lane.

Lila didn't need the rest of the address to know exactly where Tristan had gone.

She switched off her computer, silencing her radio before leaving. The explosion had managed to drown out talk of the Slave Bill. Today the announcers had filled the air with remembrances of the train derailment years before, calling out the names of the dead and their bios, rehashing conspiracy theories that involved the Almstakers.

At least they hadn't begun to question the gas explosion, though she doubted that Bullstow could keep a lid on it for too much longer. People liked seeing patterns, especially where there weren't any.

She dug into her closet and changed into a pair of Kevlar jeans, throwing her leather riding jacket atop her a gray sweater, neither marked by her family's coat of arms. Stuffing her jammer and some cash into her pocket, she wrapped a plain matching scarf around her neck and sprinted down the hall, hoping that Tristan would not leave his location before she got to him.

"Going for a ride?" Alex asked as Lila trundled down the great house stairs.

"Whenever possible." Lila darted across the parlor and through the front door. She marched across the garden path and entered the family garage, ignoring the sports cars, antiques, and sensible vehicles inside. Instead she picked up her keys from a peg near the door and slipped her helmet onto her head, swinging her leg over her silver Firefly.

She scrolled through her snoop programs on her palm and waved it over her bike, a bike that would have cost a year's pay if she depended only upon her militia salary. Lila would have bought it anyway, even if she didn't have her substantial dividends to fall back on. Motorcycles were her one weakness. Before she had settled on her Firefly, she had owned four of various makes and models. But after her Firefly, Lila had been spoiled for all others. She had sold the rest within the month.

Her palm beeped. She hopped up and dug a little gray chip from the seat cowl. The device beeped again near the front fairing, and Lila picked out a GPS tracker and an audio bug. Instead of crushing them under her boot, she tossed the chips on the Firefly beside hers. Her sister had bought the red bike the same day as Lila bought hers, not out of jealously, but because she found the bike beautiful and had never ridden one before. She wanted the experience.

Of course, Jewel had not gone near it after the first week, but Senator Dubois, the man her sister had spent the last four seasons with, took great delight in it.

As did the Randolph family mechanic and her assistants.

Lila started the engine and sped through the compound, waving at Sergeant Tripp as she passed by the guard post outside the south gate. The blackcoat puffed on his pipe and waved back, leaning in to whisper something into the ear of the rookie beside him.

Lila zoomed down Leclerc Street, a block away from the capitol. The building sat at the epicenter of the city and its twelve highborn estates, with their walled and gated compounds scattered around it, their pockets of skyscrapers, high rises, and glass-domed towers. The estates shot through the mud of the lowborn and the muck of the workborn like rose bushes of varying beauty and size, sporadically planted, struggling through weeds in a large garden.

And these rose bushes towered over Bullstow.

Lila slipped briefly onto the interstate before disembarking two exits later in East New Bristol. The foot traffic moved briskly down the sidewalk on either side of the street, boots clomping on graceless feet, heads undulating like a ribboned wave. They stamped over the grit, soot, and litter on the streets, and their conversations pitched up and down like a rollercoaster depending on the topic. The bells on wire-framed bikes rang out as their riders impatiently threaded in and out of the crowd.

The road became grittier as she traveled down Wickersham, and the smell of damp, sooty air choked her nose. She cruised past the yawning gates of the Wilson-Kruger compound, its name sculpted in twisted steel. Dirty as a workborn slum, the estate stood as a cautionary tale to the rest of the highborn in the city. These days,

Chairwoman Wilson abandoned more structures than she filled, leaving the skyline pockmarked and chipped and covered in grime. Vandals had shattered the windows in many buildings, sprayed the doors with paint, and even cracked the bricks in their boredom.

At one time the noise from the plants had been deafening, but the sound of the machines had decreased year after year, traded for the squeals and shouts of the idle. The last time Lila had been inside the compound, half-drunken groups had milled inside like hordes of zombies, for there wasn't enough money to keep all the plants open and there wasn't enough sense in the chairwoman's head to find them other employment. There would be even more people now, in want and in need of something to do. She did not envy the woman's chief of security for having to deal with the fallout.

There might not be anything left of the estate after Chairwoman Wilson died, except for the land underneath it. Fortunately, Beatrice Randolph was very fond of land and considered the investment worth it. If Lila's mother did not raze the plants and erect skyscrapers in their place, then she would likely rent out the property to lowborn businesses. On the day of the transfer, every highborn inside would become members of the workborn, dividends cut off, bank accounts slashed to pay the Randolphs for their marks. They'd have no prospects until they bound themselves in service to another family through contract, picking up their old roles for pay as doctors, architects, programmers, or perhaps clerks and landscapers if they could not find better. Many would move for new opportunities and anonymity, starting fresh elsewhere.

Lila emerged on Shippers Lane after changing her license plate to a fake one in an alley. The street sat on the border of East New Bristol, the poorest section of the capital. The buildings looked little different than the Wilson estate, except that there were no walls surrounding them to keep anyone in or out.

She parked her bike in front of a worn, yet well cared for, Chinese restaurant. Smells leaked out of the Plum Luck Dragon: fried rice, chicken teriyaki, sweet and sour pork, beef lo mein, barbecue ribs. People stood outside chatting with one another, shaking hands, and laughing. Lila knew the restaurant's name well, even by its Chinese characters. It had been spelled out on every takeout packet in the old hotel.

She glanced at her palm, which had continued to trace Tristan during her ride.

He had not moved from his spot.

Circling around the restaurant, Lila crossed into the alley and wrinkled her nose at the smell of piss and rotting food. Her stomach lurched, and she thought she might be sick.

Behind PLD. Now, she messaged Tristan.

Her nose had just begun to adjust to the stench when a rangy man stepped into the alley, casting his dark, wary eyes over her. His long brown leather coat smelled faintly of smoke and gasoline, a welcome relief from the odors in the alley, and his white scarf was gray from soot. It smeared onto his face as he unwrapped it from his jaw. The ends dropped around his neck like a loosened tie, exposing his slave's incision and a deeper scar where it had been cut out.

Lila thought, not for the first time, that Tristan would have fit in well in High House if his mother had not been born a slave. Even with his low birth, he might have made something of himself. Instead, he had run away from his masters at seventeen and had taken out his slave chip six months too early. It was much too late for him to claim respectability now.

Even still, Lila wondered how he'd look in a burgundy coat and black breeches.

"I'm not a member of your militia to be ordered about, chief," he grumbled. His words hung in the air, wrapped in the remains of an accent from the western state of Bordeaux, infused with the rolling waves of the sea. He thrust his sooty knit cap into his pocket, and his close-cropped dark hair stuck up oddly, so unlike the long locks of the proper senators of Bullstow. He mussed it, furthering its disarray. "How'd you find me?"

"I traced your palm. I shouldn't have had to."

"Reaper said it couldn't be traced."

"Your hacker isn't as good as I am. You neglected to answer my message."

Tristan's mud-caked work boots scratched against the ground as he backed away to the opposite side of the alley, only three paces wide. "I've been busy today." He studied her from head to toe with his dark eyes. "What do you want?"

"What do I— What do you think I want? I want to know what in the world you were thinking last night." She slipped her hand into her breast pocket and turned on her jammer.

Tristan eyed her pocket.

"The AAS?" She rolled her eyes. "Why didn't you just call it the Anti-Slavery Society?"

"A-S-S. ASS? You think we should call ourselves ASS?"

"It fits you better."

"Dixon said you were limping last night. Are you hurt?"

"Do you care?"

"I asked, didn't I? Dixon lost track of you, and the others never saw you cross their checkpoints. I figured you were okay when you finally sent me that message, vague as it was."

"Why'd you ignore it, then? Is typing out a few letters so strenuous?"

"I could say the same thing." He prowled across the alley and rested his hands on either side of her head. His breath smelled of whiskey, and warmed her cheek. "How am I supposed to reply to a damn question mark? Would it have killed you to type out 'I'm okay'? Now you've pulled me from my dinner and ordered me into this putrid alley like I'm some sort of criminal—"

Lila drew her Colt and pressed the barrel under his chin. "You are a criminal, Tristan, and you'll want to step away from me with that temper."

Tristan scowled and shoved himself off the wall. "Of course, chief. Very well, chief. I forgot how much you love to order everyone around, chief. Wouldn't do to get too close to the riffraff, would it?"

Lila holstered her gun. "You could have killed people, Tristan. Do you even care?"

"No one was hurt. You weren't, were you? Shirley said that you'd be fine."

"Oh, so now you're worried about me?"

"I worry about all my people." He sniffed and retreated to his side of the alley.

"I'm not one of your people."

"Clearly."

"That's a good thing, since you don't give two shits about the highborn. Where were you this morning? Your one job was to watch my back. Instead you left Dixon in your place. You nearly got me arrested and blown into tiny pieces while you were doing gods' know what, and now—"

Tristan's dark eyes narrowed. "No one was nearly blown into tiny pieces. We were careful. You were far enough away from the blast when we detonated. I had to get you free from those blackcoats somehow, didn't I? Here you are, instead of a holding cell in Bullstow. I held up my end of the bargain. You should be thanking me."

"The only reason why I got caught was because you triggered the alarm in—"

"What alarm?"

"The fire alarm inside the Bullstow compound," she explained, keeping the details to herself. She only told Tristan what he needed to know, and her purpose in Bullstow was not part of that.

"None of my people triggered an alarm. We weren't even inside Bullstow when the bomb exploded, so don't blame me and mine for your mistakes."

"And before?"

"No."

"I suspect that's the truth. Most of them were probably still moving your things from the hotel, is that it?"

"You went back there," he said, rubbing at his eyes. "That's why we couldn't find you. I can explain—"

"No. I don't want to hear it. You're too sloppy, Tristan. This was our last job together. Do you understand me? You went too far this time." She had hoped he'd apologize, or at least say something, anything to make her understand. But her father was right. She wouldn't turn his name in to Shaw, but they couldn't work together anymore. Not after this.

"What do you mean this is our last job? Who else are you going to use if not me? Hawk? Natalie? Someone—"

"Someone competent? Maybe someone who won't use me as a distraction to cover up his own aims? Someone who won't put my back in danger when he's supposed to be looking out for it? I'm not one of your people, Tristan. Don't act like I am."

"You got pinched. I acted. That was the job, chief."

"No, the job was to make sure I didn't get arrested, not blow up a building. Don't talk like you did this for me. You'd planned it out already."

"Why would—"

She held up her hand quickly, silencing his rebuttal. "You wouldn't have moved out of your safe house unless you knew there'd be a need for it. You wouldn't have had thousands of flyers ready and waiting to rain down on the streets unless you had a reason for them. That wasn't a backup plan. You don't go to that much effort. You used me, and what I can't figure out is who you think you're going to work with after this."

"What do you mean?" Tristan cocked his head to the side. "With you, of course."

"You're serious right now? You just shrugged off potential casualties like we were talking about the weather, and you think I can still work with you? You think I can trust you?"

She hadn't meant to say it out loud, to acknowledge she had trusted him before the bombing no matter what her brain had told her.

But she had, and Tristan didn't even seem to notice. "I had half a dozen people watching you the entire—"

"Do you have any idea the heat this will generate for you and your people? How much heat it already has—"

"How is it different than anything else we've done for the past few years? Breaking into Bullstow? Sneaking into highborn estates? Fine, you didn't like how we handled this job. We'll be more careful next time. We're in this together, both of us against the—"

"Tristan, take it down a notch. You and I aren't locked in some war against the highborn and the government. At least I'm not. You know why I do the things I do."

"You think it's any different for me? We're on the same side, whether you admit to it or not. This is our war."

"It's not a war, Tristan."

"It should be. One day soon, slavery will be abolished in—"

"Slavery isn't going to be abolished, and you know it. Not for your kind, anyway."

Tristan's jaw clenched.

Lila didn't care. "Your kind fall into slavery because they broke the law. The Slave Bill will never apply to you. Pardon me if I don't have much sympathy for murders, thieves, and rapists. Few in the country do."

"Few of my kind, as you so elegantly put it, are any of those things. They're not criminals, not unless you count crossing the street in the wrong place as a crime, or looking at the militia in the wrong way, or sleeping in the park because you don't have anywhere else to go."

Lila leaned against the wall, settling in for another of Tristan's rants. "If you don't have money for your fines, then you have to pay them off somehow."

"Do children have fines to work off?"

"They do chores to pay for their room and board, their medical fees, and their schooling until they age out. What else should we do with them? Take them away from their parents? We're not animals, Tristan. A child only stays with a slave if they don't have another parent available. It's the best of a bad situation."

"They shouldn't stay there at all."

"Well, we disagree on that point," she muttered. "Yes, a few slaves here and there have been unjustly sentenced, but it's no reason to throw out a system that works. It just means you clean up the system. You don't abandon it."

"Of course you'd say that. It takes a lot of slaves to drill all that oil. How convenient that the council rubber-stamps it, a council you sit on."

"Don't be naïve, Tristan. What else are we to do with criminals? Execute them? Stick them in little cages like they do in the Holy Roman Empire, letting people rot and drain the government coffers? Slaves get experience that can help them land a better job when they complete their sentence. It's cheaper and more efficient to let the matrons deal with them."

"Yes, because we can't solve any problem without the damn matrons getting involved."

"I'm not going to argue with you. I spent the morning listening to important people ask me questions that I can't answer, and I spent the afternoon listening to the radio speak of terrorism. Have you listened to it today? People are scared, and Bullstow thinks you're a terrorist. With your attitude right now, I'm not so sure you aren't."

"And you've always been so afraid of important people," Tristan said. "If what we're doing together is just another contract, then act like it. This has been a mutually beneficial arrangement for the last couple of years. We both made out on it. Don't go ruining it now."

"None of this was part of the job."

"Neither was going back to the hotel."

Lila snorted. "Now you're upset with me for not following the plan? That's priceless. What if I had needed medical attention or a new palm or...something? Anything? Damn it, Tristan, were you even going to tell me where I could find you?"

"Eventually. After everything blew over. If you'd been pinched, you could have led Bullstow back to the safe house while under the influence of the serum. I had to protect my people."

"So much for *me* being one of your people," she said. "I'm Chief Shaw's only suspect. What do you think will happen if I'm picked up for this? I can talk my way out of a lot of things, Tristan, but not a terrorism charge." She hugged her helmet to her chest and shook her head. "You want to talk about protecting people? You protect a dozen. I protect thousands. What are they supposed to do if I'm thrown into a holding cell?"

"They'd find another chief."

Lila's mouth gaped.

"I didn't mean it like that."

"No, I think you meant it exactly like that. I want to know why. I deserve to know why. Why that building? Why last night?"

Tristan scratched his chin and considered her for a long moment. "The building was a law office called Slack & Roberts. We've been watching them for the last six months. We have reason to believe that they've been throwing cases for certain highborn families, instead of defending their clients. Occasionally the lawyers pass evidence to the prosecution. Sometimes they even help fabricate it."

Lila said nothing, annoyed with Tristan's conspiracy theories, knowing any response might inspire more of his nonsense. Highborns dealt with criminals found on their families' properties. After an arrest, the family militia handed the accused to Bullstow for trial and filed the necessary paperwork for the judge. The trial was usually a brief affair, given the level of surveillance on most highborn estates. If found guilty, the accused compensated the family by relinquishing their mark for the duration of their sentence. The family could then use the prisoner as a slave until their term concluded. If the family had no use for a slave, the mark could be sold to another family at auction.

Marks could also be purchased directly from the government, for Bullstow held the marks of those caught breaking laws on public property as well as on lowborn and workborn property. Most slaves were bought by mining or agricultural families who used the cheap labor to run their farms, ranches, vineyards, fisheries, and meat-processing plants, spreading the slaves among the servant class who worked the same jobs for pay. Even the Randolphs used prisoners, the bulk of which were sent to their manufacturing plants just outside of New Bristol or their oil platforms and refineries along the Costa Sur.

"Why would a highborn family do such a thing, Tristan?"

"Why does your kind do anything? Money, of course. The Wilson-Kruger family has done it at least a half-dozen times in the last few months, maybe more. They pick a group of innocents off the streets, frame them, then petition the court for longer sentences—"

"I find that hard to believe. They don't even have enough work for their own family. They certainly don't need any extra hands."

"Of course not, but they could certainly use the extra money from selling a few marks. Chairwoman Wilson has even done it to members of her own family. She's desperate for funds."

"Tristan, there's not that much money to be made in selling marks." Slave labor didn't fetch all that high of a price—after all, the slaves became a dependent of the family, forcing the highborns to clothe and feed them, not to mention cover the cost of their healthcare tax. They also required extra militia to ensure they did not harm the other workers. It could be even more expensive if a slave died under highborn care.

Yes, it was cheaper than using contracted workborn, but only just. The only real perk was having a steady stream of workers who either did the job offered or faced the hangman's noose. Tristan had been correct: the country had a need for cheap, captive labor.

"It doesn't matter if there's not much money in it," Tristan said. "Maybe Chairwoman Wilson doesn't need that much money to begin with. I'm guessing some of the cases are to get rid of undesirables or threats to her family. Sending someone to the mines for twenty years is a slow, quiet death sentence."

"The Wilsons don't have mines."

"They auction people off to those who do."

"How do you even know this? I can't see you paying for the information. You don't care if the highborn sell one another for profit."

Tristan grinned. "No, I don't. The highborn can take care of themselves."

"Is that what you thought when you detonated the bomb? 'It's not my fault if one of them dies. The highborn can take care of themselves'? How many highborn would have had to die to make you regret it?"

"There was a fire truck ready and waiting, and Bullstow has a clinic on site." He stuffed his hands in his pockets. "No one got hurt. Not permanently, anyway."

"That wasn't my question."

Tristan only shrugged.

"If I had died, would you have regretted it?"

"You didn't."

Lila shook her head. "I gave you too much credit. Killing people doesn't bother you. Then again, you don't see the highborn as people. You have much more in common with some highborn than you think."

Tristan did not answer her.

"You admit to pulling the alarm? So you'd have a fire truck standing by just in case?"

"No. It just seemed like a good omen. Look, I did you a favor, chief. Bullstow thinks that the woman who broke in last night was part of the AAS. No one has a clue who you really are or what you were doing inside, and no one will ever look at you as a suspect."

"There's a sketch of me. A bad one, but it's out there now."

Tristan tugged at his scarf. "I'll take care of it."

"Wrong. I can't trust you to handle it. I can't trust you with anything. What were you thinking? What do you think the prime minister will do about a bomb exploding so close to Bullstow? What in the world did you think this would solve?"

"It wasn't supposed to solve anything. The problem is too big for that. But at least my kind will have one less place they'll get screwed over in this city. Bullstow will investigate, but it won't be a high priority. No one died. It was just a few singed eyebrows near a lowborn—"

"It's terrorism," she insisted. "I'm to turn you over to Chief Shaw, did you know that?"

"So you'll just do as you're told?"

"It's because I don't do what I'm told that you even know. Unless I can convince my father otherwise, he's going to turn your name into Chief Shaw on Monday as a suspect."

"Of course he will."

"Hey, I bought you what time I could, and I don't like my chances of convincing him to let this go. People are going to want answers if the true cause of the explosion gets out, so you better hope that Chief Shaw can keep it under wraps. It hasn't been so long since the Almstakers, or have you forgotten?"

"No, I haven't forgotten, but Bullstow forgot about the Almstakers when they couldn't prove that the group was responsible. They'll do the same now."

"Bullstow didn't forget. They found the cause of the explosion and the culprit. It wasn't even terrorism. But this one? This was—"

"What we did wasn't terrorism. It was an escape, for you and the slaves in this city. What do you want me to say, Lila?"

She startled at the use of her first name. Even after several years, Tristan had never used it. "I don't want you to say anything. I always knew you didn't respect me, but I thought you at least respected the work."

"I respect you, or I wouldn't team up with you. You're angry right now. Fine. Just drop me a line when the next job comes up. I'll—"

"You don't get it, do you? There won't be another job. As long as I don't hear another word about the AAS, I won't report you to Chief Shaw, and I'll try to convince my father not to, either. Don't push it, though. The AAS is dead, do you understand?"

She crept forward and rifled through Tristan's pockets until she found her stolen jammer.

He held his hands at his side and let her.

"I've bought you what time I can, but you and your people need to leave Saxony before Monday morning. Your life depends on it. Don't contact me again."

Lila turned her back on the man and slipped from the alley, cutting off the jammer as she hopped back on her bike.

She needed to get back home, dive into her work, and find out Zephyr's identity. She couldn't do that by lingering with petty criminals. She shouldn't even have come. Her father would be livid if he found out that she had warned Tristan to skip town.

But she owed him that much. They both did, whether her father admitted to it or not.

Lila shoved her helmet over her head and flipped the kill switch on her bike.

A blackcoat called out across the street, trotting toward her, two pieces of paper lodged in his fists.

Lila pretended not to notice, and hit the start button on her Firefly. The man sprinted toward her as soon as the motor roared to life. He stood in front of her, finger tapping on her helmet, Saxony rose stitched onto his blackcoat.

A scar crossed his face.

Lila cut her bike's engine, pulling off her helmet. There wasn't enough room to go around him, anyway.

"You're in an awful hurry to ride away," Sergeant Perv said, the moment her engine sputtered and died. He stared at her face, not as though she were a person, but a room in which all the furniture had all been moved a few centimeters to the left.

It wasn't that he recognized her as an heir. Though she was of age, she had never formally assumed her position as heir, nor had she ever given an interview. Therefore, newspapers could not legally run her picture. Neither could they post it online without dire consequences. As such, few people in New Bristol recognized her face when they saw it.

Lila enjoyed the loophole and the anonymity it provided.

"I'm late," Lila said, slipping her keys into her pocket.

"Late for what?"

"For a date with your father."

The blackcoat glared. "This is an expensive bike. Where'd you get it?"

"At a dealership."

"Which one?" he asked, circling her, his eyes locked on the bike. "This is a lot of bike for someone who lives in East New Bristol."

"Who says I live in East New Bristol?"

The sergeant stared at her for several long seconds. "Do you recognize this?" He stuck a copy of the American Abolitionist Society flyer in front of her face.

Lila skimmed the text, humoring him, and shrugged. "No, I do not."

"What about this woman? Have you ever seen her before?" He held up the picture that he and his men had cobbled together with the aid of a sketch artist.

Lila whistled at the drawing. "Is she your sweetie? Have you lost her? With your charming personality, I can't say I'm surprised."

"You can't help yourself, any more than you could help your-self last night, can you?" Sergeant Perv grabbed her arm. Her helmet toppled from her lap and bounced on the sidewalk with a dull *thunk*.

He shoved her against the wall of a closed grocers, already pad-locked for the night against the homeless and the drug-addled. Her jaw dug into the brick.

"What the—"

"Not so funny now, is it?" He cuffed her hands behind her back as another blackcoat rushed down the street to assist him.

As the DNA pen slid into her neck, Tristan slipped out of the alley. He thrust his hands into his pockets, smirking as he slipped back into the Plum Luck Dragon.

Tristan did not look back.

7

Lila sat in a hard wooden chair in front of a cluttered desk. A map of Saxony flickered on the wall beside her, lights blinking here and there, marking crimes. The computer hummed from a little box in the ceiling, running the numbers, collating the data, and projecting the map onto the wall. With one touch, Chief Shaw could bring up the crime statistics for any city or any street in Saxony. With another, he could highlight every militia vehicle on patrol.

Lila had always admired it. She admired it so much that she had slipped into BullNet one night, copied the code, and now had the exact map available in her own office, with no one the wiser.

The door opened. Chief Shaw stood at the entrance, hand twisting the knob back and forth as though it might be her neck, and scowled. He was an older man, a man who carried his pot belly well and hid his hair beneath a sentry cap. Most blackcoats never wore them after making lieutenant, but it was Shaw's habit, a habit carried over from his sentry days, long gone but not forgotten. Unlike the others who wore them constantly, Chief Shaw's didn't cover a balding dome.

"You're lucky I was still here," he growled, finally closing the door behind him.

"It's only seven o'clock. If you go home earlier than this, then you aren't doing your job right. Unless you are," she conceded, "in which case, I'd love a few tips."

"Tip number one. Don't have a side job. That helps."

"Touché."

He slid her palm across the desk. While she checked his office for bugs, Shaw replaced her wooden seat with one of his soft leather chairs, pushed away from his desk by the eager Sergeant Perv when he dropped her off. He had not wanted to offer her any sign of luxury, so sure that he had scored the biggest bust of his career. After receiving the results of Lila's DNA profile, the blackcoat had been shouting about truth serum immediately, something he could only receive from a superior officer.

His nervous lieutenant had recognized Lila immediately, though not from the sketch. He'd boxed the sergeant's ears for his mistake and almost let her go. Even though he thought his sergeant barking mad, he'd called Chief Shaw, clearly hoping he could smooth over the affair before Lila demanded that his sergeant be fired for stupidity.

She hadn't been able to talk her way out of it.

"I stopped the fool boy before he could begin a formal arrest report, and no one saw you brought in except for his lieutenant. Everyone else is too busy canvassing the city. That will keep it out of the press and should keep it from the matrons," Shaw said gruffly, sitting across from Lila after she finished her scan. "That doesn't change the fact that Sergeant Holguín swears you're the woman in this picture."

Chief Shaw slid the familiar sketch across his desk.

Lila dropped her eyes and snorted. "Only senators have ever described me as pretty, what with their highborn manners and all, but I'm offended at the insinuation that I look anything like this woman. My nose is much smaller than hers, my chin much daintier. Why, I even—"

Shaw pushed the sketch closer. "I'll never understand how you made chief when you can't go two seconds without—"

"It's my day off. Be glad that I'm not taking this seriously, for your sergeant's sake. What did this mystery woman do?"

"Drop the act, chief. Mr. Simmons is an amazing sketch artist. If there's one thing about this sketch that's perfect, it's your eyes. You can't disguise them with rubber and latex."

"I don't know what—"

"You were here last night. I should have you in a holding cell right now. I should shoot you up with truth serum and find out exactly what you know."

"Not without a chance to speak first, I hope. That is the law."

"Then speak. Because my suspicion is enough for the serum. Plus there's a sergeant who swears you're a match for our only suspect. I don't care who your daddy is. You're going to talk to me and tell me everything you know or—"

"This is how you repay someone who's helped keep your ass in that chair for the last few years?"

"Were you here last night when the explosion happened?" he asked, leaning forward in his chair.

"You mean, did I witness a bomb go off? Yes, I did. Great job on managing the press, by the way. I could take a few tips from you."

"How did you know it was a bomb?"

"I guessed. You wouldn't be yelling at me like this if it wasn't."

Shaw rubbed at his mustache. "Did you have anything to do with it?"

"What on earth would I have to gain by it?"

His eyes narrowed. "Did you have anything—"

"I had no idea that was going to happen," she said carefully. "I was working on my father's case when the fire alarm went off. I fled, and the bomb exploded as soon as the sergeant pinched me."

Lila didn't mention that Sergeant Holguín had only caught her because he had turned on thermal imaging. None of the black-coats had mentioned it or her disembodied head floating above the street. They would have been thought crazy at the addition, a fact that might have worked in her favor if it didn't also expose her thermal suit. Bullstow and Chief Shaw were both ignorant of her toys, and she wanted to keep it that way.

"So that was you in the compound? You tranqed my men?"

"The idiots deserved it. They were shouting privileged information about your testing protocol. I nearly got away from your men by bluffing with the information. They need retraining. Restraint techniques, emergency crisis—"

"Okay, okay. I get the point. One's a rookie, and the other has never been promoted for a reason."

"What's Sergeant Holguín's excuse, then? The man has violent tendencies. He needs anger management courses."

"What else did you see last night?"

"I saw the flyers, if that's what you're asking. What do you have so far?"

Shaw crossed his arms and considered her. "You had nothing to do with it, then?"

"I had nothing to do with it. I can't believe you'd even ask me that."

"And you do not know who planted it or why?"

"I couldn't imagine what sort of idiot would plant a bomb, especially so near Bullstow."

Shaw's eyes narrowed. "It's never a simple yes or no with you, is it?"

"Oracle's light, chief, my little brother lives here!"

The reminder did the trick. "I'm sorry," he grumbled. "You were my only lead. We've been at it all day, and we have nothing. The prime minister won't approve my request for citywide sweeps with CR detectors. Says it'd be too costly, and they'd ding too often."

"What are you looking for?"

"Nitro."

"Nitroglycerin?" Lila asked, wide-eyed. She hadn't given Tristan as much credit as he deserved. "My father's right. Randolph General would light up like a star, as would most pharmacies, their staffs, and most patients with a heart condition. If you're going to violate everyone's rights, you better be sure it will be worth it."

She thought back to the explosion, remembering the mushroom haze and flames. "Are you sure that's what it was, chief? I saw smoke and fire. Nitroglycerin is used in demolitions. It doesn't give off smoke. Just dust when the building falls."

"They added gasoline and a few other chemicals to the mix. It was a precise explosion, professional, but it was designed to look far worse and far cruder."

"If it was made to look far worse, then they could have made the explosion worse if they'd wanted to. Did you trace the source of the nitroglycerin?"

"That's about all we've been able to do. We tracked it to Weberly Demolitions. The family had a break-in several months ago. They don't have any leads. The thieves were in and out just like with the bombing. We're taking another look."

"What about your security cameras around Bullstow?"

"The footage is all gone. A virus wiped out the recordings. We requested the security footage from the lowborn businesses around the compound, but every single one went down the night before the blast. Someone paid a group of children to knock the cameras out, but the kids couldn't say who had given them the money. The man just walked up to them out of the blue with instructions written on a piece of paper and gave them half the money up front. They hit the cameras and came back for the other half. Then he simply walked away."

"Identifiers?"

"None. He wore a hood over his face, black trousers, plain gray coat, black boots. He never spoke, so they wouldn't even recognize the sound of his voice. There was absolutely nothing interesting or out of place that they could identify. We caught him on a camera a block away, but he ducked inside a building and never came out again. Search turned up nothing. He just disappeared."

Lila didn't believe for a second that the man had simply disappeared. He'd likely escaped by climbing onto the roof.

Dixon enjoyed making such escapes.

"Tech is looking at the virus. Perhaps you'd give it a look too. See what you see?"

"Sure," Lila said. "That's why you thought I had something to do with it, then? Because of the virus?"

"I know that you're not the only hacker in Saxony, chief. I'll admit that I was grasping when I realized you'd been there, but I have nothing. My men are out in the city right now, asking slaves to turn on an organization whose sole purpose is to free them, asking servants to do the same. A third of the workborn have a family member serving a slave's term. I'm not numb to the futility of it, especially when they do not understand why we are asking, but I have to do what I can. These fanatical types never stop at one. They might not have hurt anyone this time, but they'll grow bolder and bolder until they do. It'll be my head when that happens for keeping it from the press."

Lila couldn't help but wonder if Shaw was correct. What if Tristan did strike again somewhere else in the city?

If she turned him into Shaw later, would Tristan flip on her? Would he tell the chief that she'd sat in his office and pretended not to know who had been behind the bomb? Would he smirk at her again, just like he'd smirked at her outside the Plum Luck Dragon?

Perhaps it didn't matter what he wanted to say or what he didn't. As soon as Shaw used the truth serum, Tristan would talk. He wouldn't have a choice. Once the drug hit his system, he'd feel like a drunk wanting to confide in his best friend, only the pull would feel a thousand times stronger. He'd spill everything; everyone did under the serum.

But so far, Shaw had nothing. Zilch. That one fact might be enough to delay her father, perhaps even convince him to overlook Tristan's transgression.

Lila looked Shaw in the eye. "What else can you do? If you talk to the press before you know more, it will only cause a panic."

"All I can do is hope for a lead. Someone, somewhere knows who these AAS people are. There are rats in every organization. We just have to offer up enough cheese."

He slid a packet across his desk. Inside she found the rest of her things, things she had been forced to surrender as soon as she entered the Bullstow holding area.

"At least the bomb covered up your activities, else we would be having a very different conversation. Why are you dressed like that, anyway?"

"Meeting with spies." She grinned innocently. "As unseemly as it is, it's perfectly legal."

"Fake plates aren't. See that it doesn't happen again," he said. "You should probably ditch the bike in East New Bristol, anyway. Half the highborn in the city own one, as well as the richer lowborn. It marks you as one of them the moment you ride up on it."

"No, it marks me as a damn good thief."

An hour later, Shaw cleared her to leave, the virus saved on a fresh star drive in her pocket. She dodged a few men and boys wandering the grounds in impeccably tailored coats and breeches and stepped across the street toward her waiting cab.

Her taxi driver barreled back toward the Plum Luck Dragon and her Firefly. Shaw had apologized that Sergeant Holguín had failed to make arrangements for it. They both knew the neighborhood. Lila didn't have much hope that it would still be there.

When her taxi rounded the corner, she wasn't surprised that her Firefly and her helmet had disappeared.

8

Lila's stomach woke her several hours before her alarm. She stuffed her head under her pillow, doggedly unwilling to venture out from her warm bed to feed it.

Her belly insisted again only a few moments later, growling. She'd barely had breakfast or lunch the day before, and she'd been too angry about Tristan, her near-arrest, and her stolen Firefly to remember dinner.

As four o'clock in the morning was too early for Chef to have anything prepared, she sat at her computer and worked her way through a packet of stale cookies, reviewing the output of several searches she had left running overnight.

She'd made no progress on Zephyr.

Lila clicked on a blinking red tab in her snoop program. Someone had stumbled upon a piece of her Prolix identity during the night, some dusty part of the net she had some measure of control over, but not enough. She had received the alert around two o'clock, and her programs had taken note of the user.

Lila pushed her cookies away. It could have been anyone, but she knew the timing didn't bode well. Zephyr had slipped through the outermost layer of her fake identity while she slept.

It was the first chink in Prolix's armor.

No one had ever gone beyond the first few.

Lila hopped up and paced. There were only eleven more layers of protection between Prolix and Zephyr. Once the snoop burrowed through them, Zephyr would possess enough information to figure out her identity.

Lila pulled out her still-ashy Colt from a drawer and disassembled the gun, spreading the pieces out upon her desk, a task that always calmed her. For the next hour, she cleaned and lubricated each piece until the weapon looked brand new. Sliding fresh darts into the chambers, she carefully aligned the sensors. She didn't trust the old ones. It was the sensor that ejected the proper dose of sedative into each target through the needle, stopping its work based on the target's heartbeat, estimated weight, imbalance, and lurching steps. If the chip was damaged before it struck or gummed up by ash, the dart might inject too much sedative or not enough.

She needed her targets to go down swiftly. She couldn't handle a fair fight. She couldn't even handle an unfair one.

After she'd cleaned and prepped her gun, Lila dressed in black workout pants and a gray tank with the words *Randolph Militia* scrawled across her breasts. She buttoned her blackcoat atop it, then stuffed her Colt and short sword into a gym bag.

Padding out into the hallway and down the grand staircase, she cocked an ear. Only Ms. O'Malley shuffled around the first floor of the great house, making her morning tea and fetching the breakfast linens and china. The half-deaf, half-blind woman was easy to avoid.

Sergeant Galen was as well. The man posted before the great house was far too chatty and cheerful so early in the morning, and Lila usually hopped the fence that enclosed the house just to avoid him. She then darted down Villanueva Lane, which ran from the great house, past the security office, and out through the southern gate of the compound.

The dark sky loomed above Lila while she traveled, shivering in the cold, damp air. The wind shook the trees that lined the streets. Golden leaves rained down, brushing her cheeks and lodging in her hair.

Up ahead, a pair of blackcoats stopped in the dim light of a street lamp, out of curiosity rather than suspicion. There was only one blackcoat who traveled from the great house to the Randolph security office, and she rarely left before seven unless there was a reason.

Lila brushed past the patrols, offering a curt nod, and climbed the stairs to the security office. Rising twelve stories, the building housed the estate's security offices, their training facilities, as well as the barracks and private apartments of the Randolph militia. The coat of arms, two wolves straining and howling in opposite directions, had been sculpted into the front door, welded seamlessly into the steel.

The white tiles in the lobby had been scrubbed and polished during the night. Steel arches hung askew at all angles around the large space like a bird's nest rising in the center of the hollow building. A spiral staircase snaked around the center, climbing up the first ten floors. Four glass elevators traveled up and down the building, positioned to the north, east, west, and south of the lobby. They carried travelers to the top of the structure, upon which a bright dome strained toward the sky, like a child's bubble longing to break free.

The elevators only went to the top two floors if you had the proper key. Lila slid hers into the slot and rode to the eleventh floor, peeking through the glass walls of each office as she climbed higher and higher.

Everything seemed exactly as it should.

With a beep, the elevator's doors opened into the reception area of the plush front office. She didn't bother to turn on the lights; she merely strode through the right hand door, passed through her admin's office, and flipped on the switch in hers. It would be two or three hours before Commander Sutton and the rest of her staff arrived for work.

Her office had been decorated in much the same way as her bedroom, for the same interior designer had worked on both. Inside was an ebony desk and coffee table, a black couch with a few red throw pillows, and a comfortable black leather desk chair. The designer had used the same color scheme on her private quarters on the twelfth floor, a floor she shared with the commander. Or would have shared, had the chairwoman allowed Lila to move into the chief's quarters.

Instead, Lila used it infrequently to nap, to shower, and to change clothes.

She dropped her bag in her office and returned downstairs into the brightly lit gym on the basement level. A running track circled the building. She warmed up with a few laps, then switched to the obstacle course that ran along the outside. The gym master changed the course on a weekly basis to keep her from boredom and keep her skills sharp. She hopped over foam-covered fire hydrants and park benches, jumped atop stair rails, swung across beams, scrambled atop platforms, and leapt to the next, landing in a roll, all the while keeping up her pace. Since she was lousy in a fight, her policy was to run quickly, hide often, and carry a big gun filled with lots of darts.

Before leaving the gym, she hit the weights and stretched, smiling as her limbs loosened all the knots she'd born the day before.

Her stomach growled as she worked, but the cafeteria wouldn't open for another hour.

Lila took a shower in her apartment, changed into a spare uniform, and returned to her office. Several messages from Tristan blinked on her palm. She deleted them all without reading them, then paced around the room sweeping for bugs.

Then she inspected every cabinet looking for cookies.

Sighing heavily when she only found an empty packet, she settled at her desk. Mornings were the best time to catch up on paperwork. She'd only just gotten through half her inbox when a knock sounded upon her door.

"Come in," Lila called out, checking her watch. Two hours had passed.

Commander Sutton strode in and plopped herself in a chair across from Lila. "You were in early."

"Playing catch-up," Lila said, tossing a folder down upon her desk and threading her fingers. "Although I never got to the catch-up

part, so I suppose I lost the game. Any news from the other properties during yesterday morning's holo-conference?"

"Nothing out of the ordinary. It was quiet all day. Had to go
home on time for once."

"Bet your husband liked that."

"The beast hollered at me for not calling ahead. It's always something with him"

Lila chuckled. "Did you have a chance to review the camera
footage from yesterday morning?"

"Yes. Tell the engineers that thermal never sensed you, at least
not enough to trigger an alarm. Captain McKinley might have
noticed it if she had more experience and if she had been looking
right at the camera when you passed. As for the cameras themselves,
I straightened them all yesterday. I even ordered a few more to fill
out coverage. They should be here later this afternoon. I'll boost
their signals, and we'll see if you can slip by them all next month."

"Good." Her commander might not have been technical enough
to work on computer security for the estate, a lack that would
keep her from the chief's office, but she was extremely gifted with
audio and visual security. She could install them, modify them,
and boost their signals as well as manage and alter their output.
Lila trusted her judgment. "If Captain McKinley never noticed
that they'd shifted out of line, she needs more training. See to it."

Sutton frowned. The commander had never really gotten along
with Captain McKinley. Sutton did not enjoy the woman's casual
approach to the chain of command, specifically when McKinley
ignored it and went over her head. "Yes, chief."

"What did Sergeant Tripp and Sergeant Nolan find out at Bullstow?"

"They didn't have much to report, I'm afraid. Bullstow evacu-
ated the area, then charged the family militias with holding the
perimeter. They claimed it was to keep everyone safe while they
cleaned up the site, said they wanted to ensure the gas leak had
been contained. Sergeant Tripp and Sergeant Nolan weren't able to
get close enough to see anything. Both of them tried. Repeatedly.

There were rumors of paperwork on the streets, paperwork that Bullstow was very keen on recovering."

"Paperwork?" Lila hoped the press ran with that scandal rather than digging deeper.

"Yes, files, I suppose. It was a law office."

"They could have been protecting court documents. Legal privacy and all."

"Could have been. They also closed the airspace around the site and kept the press away. I haven't seen a single photograph of the area, apart from the official press release from the governor's office. Half the photo is nothing but smoke."

"Do you think something else was going on?"

"I don't know. The media seems to agree with the official story, but I have a weird feeling about it. Bullstow didn't shy away from letting us get close to the train when it derailed. Why would a gas explosion be any different?"

"Because there were dozens upon dozens of casualties who needed tending? Because we didn't ask, we just threw ourselves in, regardless of whether or not the situation might have been dangerous?"

Sutton grinned. "Well, when you put it like that."

"I suspect it was an abundance of caution on their part. Don't stick your neck out for anything more on this case. I've already put some spies on it. I'll see what I can dig up on my own."

"As you wish, chief. You always manage to figure out these things, anyway. You have a better spy network than your mother."

"Not better and not as well placed. I like to think of it as a close second, though."

"Well, I'm glad that they're on it."

Lila nodded, vaguely annoyed that she had been forced to put any spies on the case, pulling them off their regular assignments. It would have been suspicious not to pretend an interest, though. Besides, she needed to know what the other families were finding out. She needed to know if she had a chance at convincing her father not to hand over Tristan's name to Shaw, not that the idiot deserved it.

Lila holstered her Colt and short sword, then walked Sutton out of her office. She waved at Sergeant Jenkins, her private executive admin, as he rolled his wheelchair behind his desk, the Colt at his waist gleaming and polished to a shine. It wasn't disuse but love that kept it so beautiful. He could outdraw and outshoot nearly anyone in Saxony, even edging out Sutton, who had once been a sniper for the army. Lila had studied hard under his and Commander Sutton's tutelage. She'd even won several state competitions, but only when the pair chose not to compete.

Jenkins settled in front of his computer, his shirt starched and his jacket crisp, and bowed his head toward her. "Morning, chief," he said, pulling off the top to his morning coffee. "It's omelets today, before you ask. French toast, too. I suppose you could pour syrup all over them and pretend that they're waffles."

Sutton snickered.

"I might." Lila escaped her office and headed for the elevator. She rode down to the first floor cafeteria, a large, plain room filled with plants and long rows of tables carved in oak. She filled her plate with an omelet, several slices of French toast, and a pile of fruit salad from the buffet. She then found a seat among her militia, those Randolphs who either had a drive to protect the family or who suffered under dividends that shrank with each generation, due to their birth plunging them further away from the matron's chair.

These highborn needed a contract with the family.

They needed one that paid, and paid well.

It did not take long for a few lieutenants from the overnight shift to settle beside her, wanting a word about militia business and department budgets while they ate.

When Lila finished, she dumped her tray into the slot in the back of the cafeteria and peeked out the window. The sun had risen while she had been catching up on her work.

The sight was too tempting. She'd give herself fifteen minutes before returning to her office.

Walking along the gravel pathway that circled the compound, she pulled out her palm. After deleting several new messages from Tristan, she checked her alerts, those anonymous notices sent by her snoop program.

Zephyr must have been at work this morning, too.

He had chewed through another layer.

Lila sent a hasty message to her father. *I'm killing that damn spider.*

Her mood only worsened when she spied a familiar motorcycle across the street from the south gate. Whereas Lila's Firefly had been built like a greyhound, the black Amazon resembled a pit bull, strong and sturdy with a barreled chest.

The rider dipped his helmet.

Lila thrust her palm into her pocket and stalked past two blackcoats manning the gate house. Both eyed one another nervously, choosing only to salute their chief, rather than offer good mornings.

Her temper thanked their better judgment.

She passed by the Amazon and its rider, continuing two blocks beyond the south gate until she reached Simone's, a restaurant with an outdoor dining area. The windows were dark so early in the morning. Thin chains threaded through the chair legs, tables, and patio umbrellas, each ending in a little padlock. Lila shook a chair loose from the jumble and sat down, waiting.

The rider pulled up beside her and cut off the Amazon's motor. It gave out one last halfhearted sputter and died.

"You're still in the city," Lila said icily. "You should take my advice and leave Saxony with your people. I might not be able to call off my father. I hear Westminster is nice this time of year."

He popped up his visor, not bothering to get off his bike. He set his jaw, either in anger or annoyance.

Or both.

"Yeah, Westminster is nice if you want to freeze your balls off. You didn't even look at my messages, did you?"

"Why would I? I told you that I was done. Don't you understand the meaning of the word?"

"You complained about me not answering my messages?" He dug into a mesh bag on the side of his bike, tossing Lila her helmet.

She barely caught it before it slammed into her chest.

"Your Firefly is parked one block east of the south gate."

"I'm surprised you went to the trouble. Your expression seemed to indicate a certain amusement at my predicament last night."

"Amusement? I winked so you'd know I intended to take care of your bike. How much plainer could I have been?"

Lila considered the gesture. Tristan wasn't the type to go out of his way for no reason. It was either a peace offering or he wanted—

"Go change out of those ridiculous clothes and get your bike. We have real work to do."

Lila's chin jutted out, and she drummed her fingers on her helmet absently, watching his face grow redder and redder when she refused his command.

He had only retrieved her bike because he wanted something.

He always wanted something.

"Thank you for rescuing my Firefly, Tristan, but it doesn't change the situation. I was taken in for questioning once already. I'm done being tethered to you."

"You said that you were done. I never said I was."

Lila propped her boots upon the table, her spirits somewhat lifted when he gritted his teeth. "Done," she sang out, hoping he'd take the hint. She'd seen the stubborn glint to his eyes before. It said he would tie her to the back of his bike if he had to, blackcoat be damned.

Her hand brushed her Colt. Dixon could always pick up Tristan later. A few hours of sleep and a tranq hangover would serve him right. She'd do it. They both knew it, and they both knew how fast she could draw and how accurate her darts were, too. He'd be snoring before he even got off the bike.

"You can't be *done*. I'm here to hire you." He squeezed the grips on his Amazon, just as Shaw had worked at the doorknob the evening before.

"I'm not looking for work. With my dividends, I hardly need whatever paltry cash you could offer me."

"I'm not offering cash. I'm offering you something better."

"What could you possibly offer me that I can't get for myself?"

"Chairwoman Wilson and her estate, a couple of decades early," he said, smirking when her eyes widened. "I thought that might interest you. Go get changed."

Lila considered Tristan, considered the amount of trouble he might get her into with this latest ploy, considered whether or not she could trust him.

The answer was simple. She couldn't.

It couldn't hurt to hear him out, though. Chairwoman Wilson's estate would bring in hundreds of millions of credits for the Randolph family, not to mention what it could do to the New Bristol economy if the businesses had proper management—her family's management.

Even better, her mother would be far too busy with the changeover to talk of senators and babies and the season.

Intrigued, Lila did as he bid.

9

Lila followed Tristan into East New Bristol and turned onto Shippers Lane, passing the Plum Luck Dragon, which now bore a *Closed until Eleven* sign behind the glass.

They stopped next door to the restaurant in front of a run-down gray brick structure. The five-story building seemed slightly out of place in a slum, for the windows on the top floor arched so expansively that they would have fit nicely in a gothic cathedral. The ones on the other floors imitated them like a baby brother emulating his elder. Someone had nailed a piece of weathered plywood over the busted window near the front door. It had been tagged by graffiti dilettantes, rather than artists, with one of them stenciling a red phoenix in the corner. Above the plywood, a neon sign spelled out *Mechanic*. Half the letters had dimmed or cracked. Only the *M* remained whole.

A familiar man with a shaved head sat on a little wooden chair in front of the unfamiliar shop. He balanced on the back two legs, bouncing a green ball the size of his fist, and a purple scarf covered his neck. Before Tristan had even stopped the bike, Dixon hopped to his feet. He tugged on the handle of the steel dock door at the front of the building, allowing it to roll up into the ceiling.

The entire first floor had been hollowed out as a working repair shop. The sign out front had not been mere cover. Tristan rode his Amazon inside, stopping behind several new trucks. All were black Cruz N-47s.

Lila followed him inside, the oil and grease covering the smells next door. She parked her Firefly near a jumble of other cars and motorcycles, many rusted and likely dead. They were so tightly packed that only the most careful driver might untangle one from another. Tool benches and shelves sat along one wall, everything neatly packed in its place.

Lila traded her helmet for a mesh hood and threaded her way through the Cruz trucks toward the front of the shop, pulling her workborn peacoat around herself more tightly.

Two men in their early twenties bent over the frame of a Barracuda, unscrewing rather important-looking parts from the motorcycle, a hushed string of curses flowing freely between them. An old woman dressed in coveralls and a brown coat supervised them from a workbench, underneath a sign that read *Clean Up or Suffer.* She adjusted her bifocals and squinted at a piece of thick tubing in her hands. Several of her fingers and part of an ear were missing.

"Hello, Hood," she said, her voice more crotchety grandmother than criminal mastermind. She didn't look up from her work.

"Hello, Shirley. Hiding the evidence, I see."

"You're one to talk. You ever going to tell me who you stole that bike from?"

Lila shrugged.

"Let me know if it needs a repaint. My boys work fast. I'll even cut you a deal. Course, my prices—"

One of the men dropped the Barracuda's gas tank. Its echo boomed in the metal shop. "Sorry, Shirley," he said instantly, chasing after it.

"I'll let you know about that repaint."

Lila turned and followed Tristan, who had moved toward a door at the back of the shop. "You weren't eating your dinner last night, were you? You were here the entire time."

"I was eating dinner. I just wasn't eating at the Plum Luck Dragon."

"You moved for the food, didn't you?"

"No, it didn't hurt, though," he admitted, pulling open the door. He turned and started up a narrow flight of stairs.

Dixon tapped Lila on the shoulder before she could follow. The tongueless man held up his notepad. A shamrock charm dangled from a silver bracelet at his wrist. Lila skimmed through the notes from earlier in his day, which was something of a guilty pleasure. Dixon never seemed to mind all that much unless he was in a hurry. Today's page had started with a hastily scribbled *eggs and two biscuits please* and led into a boast about a *blonde, mid-20s, nice ass, nice everything* soon after. An all caps *DON'T BE SAD. I'll find another for you tonight* poured into a note about Lila. *Tristan's getting her? Good.*

Dixon tapped his smooth, aristocratic fingers in the middle of the page, and she found her place. *Are you ok? Last night you limped.* He cocked his head to the side, squinting through the mesh, watching her face.

Lila nearly shivered at the intrusion. His blue eyes always seemed to catch more than others, and she sometimes wondered if he knew who she was. "I'm fine, Dixon. It was just a few blisters. Thanks for asking."

You lost me last night. He wrote quickly. *Next time, you won't.*

"Oh yeah, what's the score again?"

Dixon narrowed his eyes, bit the air in front of her hood with a twinkle in his eye, and returned to cover the dock door.

"Words, words, words," she called out.

Dixon flipped her the bird, then rolled down the steel door behind him, returning to his chair outside.

"Are you done yet?" Tristan asked impatiently, leaning on the wall at the top of the stairs.

Lila took one last look around the shop, closed the door behind her, and followed him up to the fifth floor. Someone had strung fairy lights across the entire ceiling in the hallway, which ended in a window at the back of the building. The latch hadn't been locked, or perhaps it was broken, for the window hung slightly out of true. Many things in the building seemed broken, little things like door knobs, the stair railing, the moldings. Lila supposed that

Tristan's people fixed things as they had time, but clearly, Tristan did not give them enough of it.

Perhaps she should speak to Shirley. The woman had proven time and time again that she knew how to handle her business. The whole shop might fall around their ears otherwise.

Lila sprinted forward to catch up.

Tristan ducked into an apartment at the end of the hall. Thick black drapes had been placed over the grand windows to trap in the heat, darkening the interior. He flipped on the lights, though it didn't help much. The front room looked like a cocktail lounge for frugal moonshiners, with most of the kitchen ripped out and styled like a bar. Two wine barrels supported a darkly stained countertop, and four black barstools stretched along one side. Several tables and old black couches lined the sides of the room, couches that had once belonged in the lobby of the old hotel. The room smelled slightly of wine.

Lila pulled off her hood and tossed it on the counter. Pacing from one side of the room to other, she eyed everything like a cat might explore her new surroundings. "Nice apartment," she said at last, falling into the couch.

"It's not an apartment. It's more of a meeting room, though I do sleep here."

Lila peeked through the two doors in the back. A string of bottle caps hung in the window inside one bedroom, while the second was a world of color. Strips of flags hung from the walls as well as posters of bands and sales and festivals, only right side up half the time. They seemed to be collected for color only. Purple, blue, and green took center stage.

"Dixon, the resident magpie, sleeps in that one."

Lila stifled a laugh and crossed her legs on an ottoman. It had been made from a smaller wine barrel, chopped in half and covered with a blue faux-leather cushion. Several like it had been placed around the room. Three coffee tables had been made in much the same way as the counters. The wine barrels had been cut a bit higher than the ottomans, then attached on either end to a stained slab of wood. "What's with the barrels? Did you rob a winery?"

"No, we didn't rob a winery," he muttered.

"Then where did the barrels come from?"

"Here and there." Tristan flipped on a heater abandoned in the middle of the room.

Lila could not find a label or a brand. It was likely that it had been etched into the top of the barrels and cut away by Tristan's people or covered up. "Tell me more about this deal, then."

Tristan opened a free-standing locker in the back of the room and withdrew a bottle of whiskey. "You want a drink?"

"No, I don't want a drink. I don't drink whiskey, and it's far too early for it. I need to get home, Tristan. It's almost nine. I'll be missed."

The whiskey disappeared back into the locker, and Tristan found a bottle of wine. Delicate calligraphy hovered over an orchid on the label.

La Sangre de las Flores.

"You sure?"

"Sangre?" Lila asked, impressed. "I suppose you liberated this as well?"

"I'm always liberating people and things that need it." He poured the wine into two black coffee mugs adorned with the Jolly Roger. "A housewarming gift from Dixon. They suit me, don't you think?"

Lila took a mug and sipped the sweet wine, tasting an under-current of blackberries, breathing out happily at the first sip. It wasn't that she couldn't afford Sangre; it was only that her family boycotted the family who produced it. The chairwoman had a falling out with the Holguíns when Lila was a little girl. Ever since, her mother refused to stock the wine in their cellar, as did every Randolph establishment and every lowborn business who leased land from the family. It had been written into their contracts. The slight had hurt Holguín's label so much that it had nearly gone out of business a year later.

Somehow the label still clung to life. If Chairwoman Holguín and Chairwoman Randolph ever made amends, both stood to make a great deal of money. But for that to happen, a great deal of highborn drama would likely pass first.

"Tell me about this job," Lila prodded.

"Don't you ever just take a break? Is there ever a moment when you aren't all business?"

"I don't have the time."

"Make time."

"If I had the time, I'd rather sleep."

"Fine." Tristan dropped a manila file on the coffee table and sat next to her on the couch. "I told you last night that my people bombed Slack & Roberts. What I didn't tell you is that Toxic downloaded every file on their servers beforehand."

"Why?"

"For information, of course. To prove some suspicions we had. Toxic spent all yesterday morning hacking into their files, and we spent the rest of the day and night going through the data. We didn't find anything in the legal files, of course. Someone important might request them."

"Someone important?"

"You know what I mean. No one puts a smoking gun in a file that Bullstow might request at any time," Tristan said, and sipped his Sangre. "We moved on to the billing data soon after."

He picked up the file on top of the coffee table and dropped it in her lap. "Like I told you yesterday, we've suspected that Slack & Roberts have been colluding with several highborn clients on a number of defense cases, ignoring the people they should be defending in order to pass the prisoners onto the highborn as slaves."

Lila opened the file. "What is this?"

"Billing data on several of their clients. They were all sentenced in a drug raid six months ago on Wilson-Kruger property. Supposedly, some young wastrel son of the chairwoman was dealing black market heroin and trance tabs out of a club on the estate."

"Club 137."

"Yes. The club manager called Bullstow, not realizing that the chairwoman's son was inside. The two blackcoats arrested the kid as well as everyone else they found with drugs, several of whom were Wilson family servants. Chairwoman Wilson, to everyone's great amazement, disowned her son on the spot. Slack & Roberts stepped up to take the cases, since several of their lawyers hadn't met their pro bono quotas for the month. At least, that's what they claimed. These are from the company's private files. Do you see anything strange?"

Lila thumbed through the papers. Given her familiarity with security and legal documents, it took only a few moments to spot an issue. "This source code is the same throughout the stack. 01435. I assume this is a code for pro bono work?"

"Is it? Why would a pro bono case need a billing source code?"

"Because paperwork is anal retentive the world over. Is it a pro bono code or not?"

Tristan took a sip of wine and shook his head. "No, it's not. I'll skip to the good part. The legal fees were paid, and they were paid from the same source. All of them."

"What does the code mean, then?"

"No idea. When we dug a bit more, we found copies of the bank transfers. The sending account is from a bank in Burgundy. The Liberté. I'm sure you've heard of it." He gauged her reaction with a smug little smile.

Lila's head snapped up. The Liberté was notorious in the Allied Lands and the rest of the commonwealth, especially among the highborn. They used it and other such banks in Burgundy as way to disperse bribes, to buy quasi-illegal goods, and to pay off spies. The more inept highborn used them to pay off hackers, thieves, and specialists in corporate espionage.

Of course, those weren't the only reasons why one might use Burgundy banks. They also functioned as intermediaries, a way to shuffle funds in and out of the Holy Roman Empire. It had been traitorous to do business with the kingdoms of Germany and Italy for nearly two hundred years. If a highborn wasn't hanged immediately for conducting business with the empire, then she'd be exiled from her family and her mark would be up for grabs.

She'd not get it back. Ever.

But that only happened if you weren't good enough, weren't sneaky enough to hide your trail from the government and the press. As an independent and neutral country, the Republic of Burgundy could help with that, though it was impossible to obtain a visa to do business in person. Member nations of the commonwealth had long considered Burgundy morally off limits for aiding their enemy in a time of war, at least officially, but the banks in Burgundy were accommodating. Despite their country's status, they had a solid reputation for protecting the anonymity of account holders on both sides. It was what had kept them out of the war for so long, even though they slept between the two great powers. They had found a niche, they proved useful to both parties, and they would do anything in their power to keep it that way.

Liberté meant secrecy. Liberté meant scandal.

Lila flipped to the end of the file and scanned the transfer data. "You think this money is coming from Chairwoman Wilson."

"Yes, but not from any account she could be tied to. That's why I want to hire you. Find the owner of this account. Prove it belongs to Celeste Wilson. She's been selling the workborn into slavery, and I want her in a holding cell where she belongs. In return, you get to bring down the chairwoman a great deal earlier than you thought possible."

Lila stood up, laughing. "You want me to break into Liberté and steal account data? Are you mad?"

"Oh, is it too hard for you? I suppose I'll have to tell Reaper and Toxic that their heroine can't walk on water after all."

"We're not six years old," she said, twirling her sapphire ring. "You can't dare me. It has nothing to do with how difficult it might be. It's about stupidity, and me not having any."

In point of fact, Lila had already broken into the impenetrable bank once, as a test of her strength. It had been young and stupid and childish, and she wasn't proud of it, but she had accomplished it at the age of fifteen. It was an age she had known would protect her from the worst of the fallout. But during the hack, she had been smart enough not to take any data.

Being caught as an adult was far more trouble than it was worth, especially if she had to steal data. The prime minister wouldn't be able to save her even if he wanted to. "We don't need to hack into the bank. There might be an easier way."

"Enlighten me."

"They arrested Simon."

"Yes." Tristan peeked at the file. "Simon Wilson-Craft, age seventeen, Chairwoman Wilson's youngest son. The way I hear it, he was a good kid in his last few months of high school, not a wastrel son at all. Now he'll be a slave for the next twenty years."

Tristan shoved his mug onto the coffee table. "According to the bill of transfer on his mark, Simon will pick grapes in the Masson vineyard until he's thirty-seven. Your mom was the one who bought him. As a present. Wrapped him up in a little bow and sent him to Chairwoman Masson as a gift for the Summer Solstice. Did you tie the ribbon?"

"My mother outbid Chairwoman LeBeau. No one else would."

"Oh, is that what it is? Can't let—"

"Chairwoman Wilson didn't lift a finger to save her son from that woman. You might not be allowed to bid on members of your family, but your allies can. She didn't ask them, though. My mother saved Simon. He would have been sent to a coal mine if she hadn't stepped in, all because Chairwoman LeBeau wanted an easy dig at his mother during parties."

"Yes, because picking grapes in the hot Saxony sun is so much better than—"

"It is better. Safer, too. Simon has always loved the Masson vineyard. That's why he's there. He might not be happy, but he's not miserable and he's safe. My family did the best we could by him, so go vomit your righteous indignation on someone else."

Tristan dropped the folder on the coffee table with a slap. "Since your family still owns him, can you run down to the vineyard for a taste of your slave boy whenever you're hungry?"

Lila's face twisted in disgust. "Oracle's wrath! He's my best friend's little brother."

"Ah yes, of course, I forgot that you like to keep your friends on a leash. How is Ms. Wilson? Does she scrub your dishes after you eat? Wash your boots? Do you make her say 'Yes, madam' or is she—"

"Shut up about things you don't understand. We did the best we could for both of them when they found themselves in very bad situations."

"I think I understand the situation just fine."

"Why? Because you grew up as a slave?" Lila asked, ignoring Tristan's darkening expression. "I know who you really are, Tristan. I research the people I work with. You were well educated— tutored by Amala Devi, no less. I was impressed when I found that out. It explained a great deal, like how a slave can write like a senator."

Tristan looked up.

"Yes, I know about that, too. You could have taken a servant's contract anywhere with your education and abilities. You could have been a proper journalist, but—"

"I am a proper journalist."

"A proper journalist can use his own name, but you can't because you ran away before you aged out. Stupid, really. You had less than a year until your eighteenth birthday. Now you have those months hanging over your head and more time besides for cutting that thing out of your neck."

"I don't regret it."

"No, but I imagine your mother didn't approve of your choice. You hate her a little for choosing to stay with the Holguíns, don't you? Finally free, after all that time. She could take a servant's contract with any other family. She's free now, and well educated, just like you. She could go anywhere with her credentials. She could even open her own lowborn business if she saved up the capital or found an investor. Yet she stays with those people who bought her mark, day after day. She stays with him and the rest of that family. Out of comfort? Out of loyalty? Is she still his mistress? I don't think it's a coincidence that you target the Holguíns so often." Lila held up the mug with its last few drops of Sangre, and his eyes narrowed even more.

"I work in a security office, Tristan. Did you think I wouldn't know? We get tagged all the time by Bullstow for security alerts, thieves stealing this and that. Chairwoman Holguín's sons had a few Cruz trucks go missing last week. A few Cruz trucks happen to be downstairs in your shop right now. What a coincidence." She tapped her boot against one of the ottomans. "If I cut away the cushion, would I find the Holguín label underneath? I knew you and your men hit their warehouse a few weeks ago—technically not their winery, so I suppose you didn't just lie to me ten minutes ago, but I couldn't figure out where you had stored all that wine. I didn't know you and your people had moved into this place, though. That managed to slip past me."

She sat down on the coffee table across from him. "It's always amused me before, this strange habit and vendetta you have against the Holguíns. If your highborn father hadn't retained Devi's services, you would—"

"I would have grown up poor and stupid, indoctrinated and indebted to the highborn so that I'd take any contract offered, rushing into a different brand of slavery the moment I was released."

"Not every family is like the Holguíns."

"No, some are like the Randolphs. You're so used to having everyone below you that you don't even notice the imbalance. Ms. Wilson is not your friend anymore, Lila, not when you own her. Even the most well-treated slaves are still slaves."

"Then they shouldn't have gotten themselves into trouble."

"Like her little brother?"

"Like your mother? Are you still working out your teenage angst? All that jealously toward those rich kids who had everything you couldn't afford as a child? You claim to hate the rich and everything they stand for, but you sure do spend a lot of time stealing their toys and enjoying the spoils of their labor."

"To fund my work," he said, clipping each word sharply at the end. His eyes ordered her from the room, but she knew he would not ask her to do that. He still needed her as a tool.

"Not always. You keep the Amazon and other trinkets when it suits you." She placed her mug on the coffee table. "Not to shoot down your brilliant plan, Tristan, but instead of hacking into Liberté and waving our butts to the militia and the Burgundy government, perhaps we should speak with Simon first. If he knows anything about this, he might be willing to talk."

"To you? Why?"

"Because according to Alex, he has a little crush on me."

"Poor kid." Tristan hopped up, stamped to the door, and flung it open. The knob banged against the wall so hard that it left a hole in the plaster.

He didn't wait for Lila to follow.

10

Tristan's sour mood did not improve on the hour-long drive to the Masson vineyard, located in Massonville, a city named after the highborn family. Unfortunately, Lila had not taken her Firefly. Dixon had already pulled out one of the trucks for their journey, offering a wink, a kiss on the cheek, and a wave to Lila as the pair pulled out of the garage.

Things were fine in the truck; at least, that was what she kept telling herself. Fine also meant awkward, for the truck was much too quiet. The radio did not work, for Shirley never wasted her time fixing unnecessary luxuries, and the silence only highlighted Tristan's lingering annoyance.

Lila didn't bother trying to make conversation.

What would they talk about, anyway? Motorcycles? Wine? Music? The stars? Early on in their working relationship, they used to talk more, joke more. After their first job together, Tristan had even taken her to the top of the Victory Tower and pointed out the constellations. It was something that no one had ever bothered to teach her as a girl and something she'd never seen the point of learning. The stars weren't useful to a young chairwoman-in-training, and even less useful to a future militia chief.

Perhaps the stars and their stories only belonged to the poorer classes.

She still remembered lying on the hard stone, pointing up at the sky, and laughing as they made up their own patterns and stories, half-drunk from stolen bottles of Sangre. There was Whiskers, the manic kitten, who Frigg had put into the sky after biting her ankles one too many times. Rind, who had been put into the sky because Odin was afraid she'd lop something precious off his body should he fall asleep. Amoeba was a hideous monster that kept growing and growing every time one of them suggested a new limb or a new attachment. They decided finally that it was put into the sky to give drunk people something to talk about in the middle of the night.

Lila hid her smile. They had almost been friends.

She'd been stupid to think it, though. He'd shown his true face, for the next morning she'd dug in her pockets and found her palm missing.

Lila had sped to the hotel on her Firefly, pushed past a bleary-eyed sentry, and fired a tranq dart directly into Tristan's neck before he even opened his mouth. Dixon had thought it funny until he learned what had angered her. He'd sheepishly led her into Reaper's room. They'd found the chubby hacker bent over her palm, muttering to himself, still trying to break her encryption.

Reaper had cowered the moment he saw her temper, claiming that he had found it in Tristan's room and just wanted a peek.

Tristan never denied stealing it, though he wouldn't admit to giving it to the hacker.

They'd fought nonstop ever since.

Lila's half-smile turned into a scowl, but she kept her mouth shut. She sent a quick message to Sutton, asking her to handle the morning's holo-meeting with the other Randolph properties, suppressing a snicker when the commander messaged her back.

Anything to keep me away from the Beast tonight.

Lila didn't waste the rest of the drive. As the bluebonnets passed by her window in a blur of violet and white and blue, she jotted down notes on her palm, ideas on how to dig into Zephyr's identity.

Such thoughts left her when an alert flashed on her screen. The snoop had dug through the third layer of Prolix's identity.

Why had she agreed to go to Massonville? She had bigger things to worry about than investigating Tristan's conspiracy theories.

She hadn't agreed for Tristan, though. She cared about Simon, a boy scarcely older than her younger brother Pax, a troubled brother she had not even seen in several days, even though he lived right across the hall.

She was an awful older sister.

Tristan pulled into an empty, crumbling parking lot near the shore of a lake. Several weathered picnic tables and benches had been scattered around the area, lying in pools of mud. "The vineyard is a kilometer up the road. I suggest we walk the rest of the way, unless you want to stroll in to the great house and ask for permission."

"It's best if no one knows I'm here. If you're right and Chairwoman Wilson hears that I visited Simon a day after Slack & Roberts blew up, it might put him in danger."

"My thoughts exactly." Tristan opened the truck door. "It's best if the friend who visits is a nobody like me. I doubt a manager would report that to either family."

Lila buttoned her coat against the chill, and the pair strolled down the muddy road toward the vineyard, one side lined by stubby trees and rocks. Few cars drove by, and Lila turned her head toward the lake each time one passed as though fascinated by the water and the scattered rocks at the bottom, visible through the surface.

It wasn't hard to pretend an interest. Lila had always been so busy, first with the hospital, then with the militia. She'd rarely even seen the lake, much less spent an entire day on it. She squinted at the boats prowling the water, filled with bundled families and fishing poles, the air punctuated with random shouts and random giggles. Lowborns, no doubt, with enough resources to afford a small vessel and a day off work to enjoy it.

The Randolphs probably didn't own a boat. Not unless Jewel had bought one.

For the experience.

Lila rolled her eyes, patting her hip when her palm vibrated in her pocket. *I'm glad,* her father had written. *I'm depending on you, Lila girl.*

"Who was that?" Tristan asked grumpily.

"The prime minister."

"Ah, is he sending you off somewhere to do more of his dirty work?"

"No, it was about my last job." Lila slipped her palm into her pocket. "The work is far from dirty. There are things he can't get Bullstow involved in and problems that they aren't able to solve. Someone has to do it."

"He uses you?"

"No one uses me."

Tristan spun around to walk backward, studying her face. "Some father."

"My father is a good man."

"Fine. Convince me. What was this last job about? Why did he risk his eldest daughter's reputation? Why did he need you to break into Bullstow when he has access to the whole network?"

Lila considered Tristan's attitude, his silence on the way over. She had never told him much about the jobs her father sent her on, even when he was a part of them, and she didn't want to trust him now with the knowledge. She settled on half knowledge, the only knowledge she ever gave him. "Someone has been bribing the highborn."

Tristan cocked an eyebrow. "I figured that happens all the time."

"It does, and usually they're easy to ferret out and take to court. Every family militia has at least one person working bribery cases fulltime. Mine has three, and I might add a fourth."

"It sounds like your family gets up to a great deal of trouble," he said, glancing behind him. "So I'm assuming that sometimes these people aren't so easy to find?"

"Impossible if the target has been up to something they shouldn't have and refuses to come forward. That's what happened in this case. We know people are being bribed, but none of them will cooperate with the investigation, not even to give us a name or a file. We can't even use the serum against the victims. They haven't done anything serious enough to warrant it. My father suspects that the culprit is a hacker who's turned on her highborn clients. What's odd is that the hacker managed to find a highborn who had never hired her, someone who should never have been on her radar. If the victim hadn't gotten greedy and been busted for something else, we never would have known. Chief Shaw was able to use the serum on her, but in the end, it didn't matter. She simply doesn't know who is bribing her."

"What was this highborn doing to get on the hacker's radar?"

"Breaking into Bullstow and doing a horrible job of it. If my father was less of a prime minister, he might not have known what was going on, just like Governor Lecomte has no idea that his own government networks have been compromised."

"So you're saying that someone out there is doing my work for me? I hope you don't catch them."

Lila shoved Tristan into the empty road.

"What?" He chuckled. "You shouldn't put yourself at risk to defend highborn criminals and their lackeys. Whoever is doing this is a patriot."

"She isn't a patriot. She's a vigilante at best. At worst, she's a bigger criminal than her victims. You can't go around bribing people, Tristan, just like you can't go around bombing them. That's what we have a court system for."

"A fallible one. It only works against the workborn and the occasional lowborn."

"And if you had your way, you'd bomb everyone into seeing your viewpoint."

"Talking is masturbation."

"Is writing?" she asked.

"Yes, if you don't back up your words with actions."

"And damn the casualties?"

Tristan shrugged.

"Change comes slowly. You can't do it at the point of a sword, Tristan. That's not a revolution. It's assault, coercion—"

"Maybe some people need to be coerced."

"Is that why you've been prodding the workborn to protest? I counted four last month on the news."

"I wouldn't waste my time."

Lila studied his face, the way his eyes did not run from her. Perhaps he hadn't started the protests after all.

"People like your mother will never end up in a holding cell, no matter what they do," he said. "How is that—"

"Leave my mother out of this. She'd never dream of breaking the law."

"No, she just dreams of ways to bend it."

"Of course. All laws bow before a competent chairwoman."

"Spoken like a highborn. How many times did she make you write out that proverb as a child?"

"Enough times for it to stick. Few highborn break the law, whether you want to believe it or not."

"And you say I'm naïve."

"You are. For a highborn, breaking the law is cheating. It's not sporting, and it's an admission that you are inept. The highborn have more self-respect than that. So if you have a problem with the laws or how the highborn treat the workborn, change the laws so the matrons can't bend them. Complain to your senator, and stop buying that family's products."

"Yes, because that always works," Tristan muttered. "By the way, the hacker is a he."

"A he? How do you know it's a he?"

"I don't, but how do you know it's a she? Must it always be a she?"

"He. She. Who cares?"

"I do. It gets annoying. And I think it's ridiculous that instead of going after the highborn criminals, you're going after the one bribing them. That's part of the—"

"My father is dealing with the highborn and their crimes," she said, trying to cut him off before he launched into another lecture. "I'm just working the other end."

"So you compromised BullNet to draw the hacker's attention?"

"No." Lila had thought she'd be smarter than that, opting to retrace the guilty highborn's steps, to dig around in the system and figure out how Zephyr worked. She had only called in Tristan in case things turned bad.

Bad was an understatement.

It might get worse. If Zephyr found her first and leaked her activities to the press, then Shaw would be forced to arrest her. If the senate voted to execute her or tried to take her mark, then Shaw and her father would come forward and explain their part in it. Not only would they lose their careers for allowing a highborn heir to gain access to BullNet, but they might very well be hanged for the scandal. Her life would be exchanged for two, and her actions would cloud the Randolph family's reputation. She'd not dodge a slave's term, and even if she did, her militia career would be ruined.

At the very least, her mother would exile her from the family.

No one in Saxony would accept that an heir and chief of security had been given access to the entire Bullstow network, which would be exactly how the media would frame it.

Tristan sighed, spinning back around. "You've decided that this is the end of share time. I always think that this time I'll get a meal, but all you ever toss me is more scraps."

The sign for Masson's Vineyard came into view, taller than Tristan, wider than one of his Cruz trucks. A woman's hand had been painted on one side of it, embracing a cluster of red grapes, the green Masson coat of arms taking up half the sign. Tristan turned down the black-paved road, recently swept and scrubbed, just wide enough for two cars to traverse.

Lila might not have wasted much time on the lake, but she had been to the vineyard dozens of times. Senator Dubois had invited her to tag along with Jewel on countless occasions, no doubt trying to make a match between her and his matron's relations. The family held exclusive balls at the vineyard during the season, and everyone lucky enough to get an invitation believed the house was worth the trip.

Even her mother.

Luckily, the Massons had never seen fit to wall off the vineyard. They employed a small complement of militia in a little tower adjacent to the house, supplemented only when an heir was in residence or when the family held an event. Few guards would be around at ten o'clock on a Thursday morning, though, and Lila and Tristan weren't close enough to the house to see it as anything more than a pile of stone and glass in the distance.

It was relaxing to see the vineyard, each row of vines perfectly straight on either side of the road, like lines of soldiers standing at attention before the house. The small-limbed vines wrapped around trellis after trellis as though they had become miniature trees in their pairing. Just two months before, clusters of blue grapes had hung toward the bottom of those limbs like spiders lying in wait, ready to drop from their perches and charge all who came near like eager, poisonous assassins. Though they had been picked in the harvest, she glimpsed a forgotten cluster from time to time, hidden from rushed hands.

"What do you think Simon's doing now?" Lila asked, wrapping her coat around herself more tightly. Grass and mud coated her black boots, and it would only get worse when she left the road. "Preparing the vineyard and winery for tours? Getting things ready for the season?"

Tristan shrugged. "I don't care much about rich people's things."

Lila frowned and squinted into the distance. Up ahead, a crew of slaves dressed in jeans and boots stooped over each side of the road. A parked cart had been filled with small crates of flowers, orange pansies and small yellow blooms she could not identify.

A man in a pair of overalls looked up at his people, focusing alternately on his own work and his crew. He had a stern face, yet it was not cruel. Lila wondered if he was a slave or a servant. Perhaps he was just a restless, highborn Masson who had successfully petitioned for freedom from a desk, like Johnny Beaulieu, the Randolph head gardener. Though younger than Lila, he had assumed control of the entire groundskeeping staff for every Randolph compound and constantly traveled among them.

Behind the crew master, she glimpsed Simon, snatching up a container of yellow blooms from the cart. He still looked young and scrawny to Lila's eyes, but at seventeen, he had begun to acquire the body and height of a man. He would have been scrawnier if he still lived on the Wilson estate. Six months of labor had filled him out somewhat, cut muscles into his arms, given his shoulders a stretch, and tanned his skin.

Alex had visited him over the summer. *Happy* was how she described him, considering everything that had happened.

"There he is," she said, pointing at Simon in his jeans and dark brown t-shirt, marred with dirt and sweat and grass.

Tristan slapped her arm down. "I know his face. I'll bring him to you. Don't stand in the middle of the road like an idiot."

Lila whipped her peacoat and turned away, wandering between two rows of vines, absently pulling off leaves as she passed.

Soon, a laugh erupted behind her, and Simon sprinted forward, picked her up, and twirled her around. His frame had indeed filled out, and he was more muscular than he appeared under his work clothes. "Lila, you've come to visit."

"No, she hasn't come to visit," Tristan grumbled, leaning against one of the metal trellises. "I told you that."

Simon put her down gently. "A visit's a visit." He pressed a kiss to her cheek.

The contact lasted several seconds too long.

"Alex said that you were doing well here," she said, pulling away.

"I'm trying. If it wasn't for you, I'd be at the mines. I know that. Alex does, too. You're a good friend, Lila. I just wish I could pay you back somehow."

Tristan raised an eyebrow. "I bet you do."

Simon's face fell somewhat at Tristan's tone. "Who is he? New money?"

"Far from it. Let's go for a walk. Alone."

"Bullshit. I paid off the crew master for this. Cost me more than it was worth, too."

Simon's gaze passed back and forth between Lila and Tristan. He then thrust his fists into his jean pockets. "You really aren't here for a visit, are you? What's this about?"

"The club raid," Lila replied. "We never really talked about it. You'd already been charged and sentenced by the time I got back from La Porte. It was too late for me to do much but keep you from Chairwoman LeBeau. Tell me what happened."

"It doesn't matter. It's over."

"That's what you told me last time we spoke, and I let it go. But I'm not going away so easily this morning. Something happened in that club. I want to know what it was."

"Why? Nothing's going to change. The courts have ignored my appeal, and I've taken up enough of your time."

"And we just spent another hour on you," Tristan interrupted. "We'll spend another hour traveling back to New Bristol. Don't waste our time, kid."

"Tristan!"

"It's the truth."

Simon shook his head. "I can't talk about it, Lila. You know that. I can't discuss family business with outsiders. Not even with you."

"You're not a Wilson any longer," Lila said. "Do you honestly think your mother will take you back into the family? She'll send someone with your mark the day you finish your slave's term, and that will be the end of it."

"My mother will be long dead before I finish here. I'll be a workborn in the end, anyway. None of it matters."

"Wrong. If you're not guilty, then you could finish high school. You could marry into a new—"

"Highborn do not marry. We liaise. Marriage is reserved for the poorer classes."

"Your brothers married into other highborn families. They can help you do the same."

"I'm not them."

"You'll be one of the poorer classes eventually if you don't. But if you don't want to marry, then fine. Take a servant's contract instead. You could even start a business. You're not yet eighteen, Simon. You have options. You have plenty of time. But you won't have either if you stay here."

Simon frowned and brushed at the dirt on his jeans, fighting a losing battle to keep the muck of the vineyard from his clothes.

Lila grabbed his hands and squeezed, ignoring the grit on his fingers. "Simon, this may feel like some big adventure or a vacation right now, but if you stay here, this might be it for you. If something happened that night, you need to tell me. How far has loyalty gotten you?"

Simon dug his toe into the earth. He did not answer for some time. "I didn't do it, Lila. You know me. You know my friends. I've never even seen heroin before. Still haven't. I wouldn't even know what to do with it."

"What happened in the club that night?"

"I don't know. It wasn't like the militia said. There weren't even that many people in the club. My cousins and I were there to blow off steam and have a few beers after midterms. One minute we were sitting around the table, laughing, the next minute two Bullstow blackcoats entered the club. They didn't even stop to talk to Mr. Sutherland. They just came in and headed right for our table, like they knew us and knew exactly where we'd be."

"Did Mr. Sutherland rat you out?" Tristan asked.

"Why would he do a thing like that? We're kinsman."

Lila ignored Tristan as he rolled his eyes. "Did they search you?"

"Yeah, they didn't find anything, though. It didn't seem to matter to them. They arrested us all anyway, then they took us to the security office on the estate and put us in a holding cell. I'd never even been in there before. There were over a dozen people in the cells already. I heard them talking. Half of them hadn't even been on the estate when the militia took them, and none of us had any drugs."

"No one fought back in court?"

"Of course they did, but they were poor workborn. They didn't have much money for lawyers. I think some of their families were threatened or paid off, because a few just agreed to whatever the blackcoats put in their report."

"Do you have proof of that?" Tristan asked.

Simon shook his head. "No. The prosecution used those who had been turned as witnesses against the rest of us in exchange for reduced sentences. They said whatever the blackcoats wanted, even when it contradicted the militia report. The ones who spoke the truth weren't believed."

"And you?" Lila asked.

"I wasn't about to admit to something I didn't do. Some law firm offered to defend us for free, at least those of us who couldn't afford lawyers, but I guess you get what you pay for. The charges against Dan and Tobias were dropped before my trial, and their parents threatened to take away their dividends if they tried to speak in my defense. I can't blame them for staying quiet."

"Why was Bullstow even on the estate?"

"Our security budget has been strained. The chairwoman has called them in before to straighten out the crowds. Bullstow comes in, makes a few busts, and writes the reports. None of us like them, though. They're both assholes."

"Both?" Tristan asked. "Is it the same two guys every time?"

Simon nodded.

Lila eyed Tristan, who had cocked his head in thought. "How many times have they come out, Simon?"

"Four or five times, at least. That's what Tobias told me, anyway. He was thinking of joining the militia before we realized how bad off the family was. He still patrols with them sometimes, though. Or did. He always knew who'd been arrested on the compound and who brought them in."

"The chances of the chairwoman's call being answered by the same two officers every time is incredibly small," Lila said.

"It's pretty much impossible," Tristan agreed. "Those two men work for your mother, Simon. She's using them to clear out her estate of undesirables. You are an undesirable. I have to ask myself why a chairwoman would set up her own son."

Simon eyed the other slaves as they worked along the roadside. "I have to go now. We've got to get all the flowers planted before the weekend, and then there's painting that must be finished. I've been gone for too—"

Lila put her hand on his chest. "She set you up, and you know it. Why would your mother do that? Why would she throw away her own son?"

"She didn't throw me away. She's going to come back for me. It's just a misunderstanding. After she gets everything in order, she'll bring me home. I've sent her messages, Lila."

"Has she replied to them?"

"She will. She's going to come back for me."

"What is she getting in order?"

"Nothing."

Lila grabbed his wrist. "What is she getting in order, Simon?"

"I trust you, Lila," he said, looking her in the eyes. "Give Alex a message. Tell her she needs to visit Mother. If she waits too long, she'll always regret it."

He squeezed Lila's shoulder and started off toward his crew.

Tristan's hand shot out, gripped his arm, and held him in place. "We're not done."

Simon tried to shake him off, but Tristan held firm. "You idiot child, we're trying to help you. Senator Craft is dead. Your father can no longer help you get out of this mess. Do you really think your mother is going to save you? She tried to dump you in a mine where you would have come out with black lungs if you ever came out at all. She isn't coming back for you, no matter how many messages you send. You're not the only one she threw in the trash, you know. Not everyone was so lucky to end up in a rich man's vineyard."

"You don't know what you're talking about."

"Yes, he does," Lila said. "Why does Alex need to see your mother?"

Simon shrugged off Tristan. "I have to get back to work."

Lila barred his way. "Simon, I promise you that I will not tell my mother anything that you tell me this afternoon, but if you don't tell me what I want to know, then this deal is off. I'll make it my mission to find it out anyway. You know that I will."

Simon glanced back and forth between her face and the work crew, looking like a lost child who must chose a savior from the crowd. "I don't know what to do."

"Then trust me like Alex does."

He frowned and kicked at the grass, his eyes reddening. "I started interning as an assistant to Mr. Heatherstone last year. He brings in new software accounts between our family and the wealthier lowborn. I noticed my mother was acting weird during our meetings. It was just small things at first, like saying no to reasonable deals because the families weren't the right sort of people. The deals wouldn't have brought in all that much money, so I didn't put much thought into it. But then, suddenly, she didn't want us to take on any short-term accounts. It seems odd, doesn't it? I mean, we needed more partnerships, and Mr. Heatherstone brought her several good deals, even one with the Park family. All she needed to do was sign, but she said no to all of them. She said they weren't right for the family, that we had too many other projects going on."

"What other projects?" Lila asked.

"That's what I wanted to know, so I looked into it. We're coding a few software applications. Each deal is worth several million credits, all long-term projects, but we're losing more and more money every year. We have plenty of people to work. Why wouldn't she want us doing anything?"

Simon cracked his knuckles and sighed, his breath steady once more. "I broke into my mother's files and started fishing around the financials. I'm not an idiot child. I know enough to understand when someone is liquidating assets. She's putting her affairs in order, Lila.

My grandmother died when she was my mom's age. I got worried. I wanted to know that she was going to be okay, so I confronted her about it one night after dinner. She got angry that I had peeked where I shouldn't have, said she couldn't trust me anymore. She admitted that something was going on, though. It's the fertility meds she's been taking. I knew they were hurting her. You can't take that many pills and still be okay. She said they've made her sick and that she just needs a bit of time to get things settled. She needed extra money for a doctor up north who might be able to help."

"Then you found yourself with a drug charge?"

"Yes, less than two weeks later."

"Simon, your mother did this to you."

The boy stared at Lila, eyes wide. "She didn't mean it. She's just sick and confused and scared. That's why she's not responding to my messages. She's trying to get treatment, so she can have an heir and save the family, but it's killing her. If the press finds out that she's confused or that she's not well, then the stock price will go down even more. Maybe it's already too late and that doctor up north couldn't do anything. She's just trying to protect the family. I spooked her. That's why she won't respond to my messages." His words came faster and faster, all in a rush. "She just doesn't want to risk anyone finding out before everything is settled. She can't write back, don't you see? She just needs me out of the way for a bit, but she's going to come back for me when she's ready. I've sent her lots of messages, and she'll come."

"What proof do you have that she's sick?" Lila asked.

"She wouldn't lie about it. She's going to get me out of here when she's ready. You'll see. She'll tell them it was all a mistake." Simon's cheeks sank slightly into his mouth, and his jaw clenched.

He had been brave so far, but that bravery was about to fail.

"I've sent her messages. She'll come," he insisted again, his voice cracking.

"I'm sure you're right, Simon. Your mother will come back for you." Lila wrapped him in a hug.

The boy clung to her, sniffling, the years vanishing at her touch.

Lila rubbed his back and pretended not to notice. It was how Pax had come to her months before, after he had lost his best friend, after he had put away his brave face and let her squeeze away some of the shock. It was how he still came to her sometimes, eyes darting around her room, unsure how to start.

She should have checked on Pax before she left the compound. He needed his sister.

She should have brought Alex to visit Simon more often. He needed his sister, too.

Lila offered Simon another silent squeeze, an apology to Pax, to Alex, to all of them, frustrated with herself for allowing her father's case and Tristan's conspiracies to take over her life so completely, frustrated that once again she had forgotten the little things.

When the boy finally pulled away, his eyes were redder, rawer. "You won't break our promise?"

Lila shook her head.

"Simon," Tristan began, "those blackcoats who arrested you? Do you remember their names?"

"Of course. Muller and Davies." Simon spat out the words, all too eager to trade his sadness for rage. "Everybody hates them. They're two of the biggest assholes that you'll ever meet."

11

Lila dodged a picnic bench and a deep puddle near Tristan's truck, stamping her feet to dislodge the mud and grass on her boots. "I'll drive," she said, holding up her hands to catch his keys.

"Not a chance. It's my ride."

"It's not yours. Not really," Lila shot back, climbing into the passenger's seat. She crossed her arms over her chest as he hopped in beside her and slammed the door.

"Well, it certainly isn't yours." Tristan thrust his key into the truck's ignition. "When we get back to New Bristol, we'll go to Rossi's Pub. I want to know more about Muller and Davies."

Tristan started the engine and pulled out onto the road, tires spinning in the muck before catching the asphalt.

"Well, I want many things, but it doesn't mean I'm going to get them." She couldn't imagine Tristan visiting Rossi's, a bar frequented by militia members throughout New Bristol. Not only could she not imagine it, she didn't want to encourage such stupidity.

"Of course, Chairwoman Randolph has everything she could ever want, yet she still wants more. It's a shame you abdicated as prime. You certainly fit the profile of a whitecoat."

"What do you know of it?"

"I saw enough with the Holguíns. More than enough." Tristan's jaw had set like Simon's.

Set and closed.

Bluebonnets and cedar trees flashed by the windows as they pulled onto the interstate.

"I'll look into Muller and Davies," Lila said. "Quietly."

"I hired you to help me, Lila, on behalf of every poor workborn in Saxony. I didn't hire you to protect whatever highborn secrets crawled up your—"

"I'm not protecting highborn secrets, you impulsive nitwit. I'm trying to protect yours. If you go anywhere near Rossi's Pub, someone will spot the scar on your neck. They'll do a DNA stick faster than you can blink, and you'll be off to the mines within the week. Is that what you want?"

"I've been inside Rossi's before."

"Well, it was a dumb move then, and it's an even dumber move now. You don't need to go. I'll dig into Davies and Muller's backgrounds, see what I can find, and contact you later."

"Fine," he muttered.

"You have a lead now, Tristan. A lead that came with zero risk to you and your people. You should be thanking me."

"Thanking you? For more scraps? The boy's militia lead is a poor substitute for hard evidence, evidence that's sitting in Liberté right now. I'm left wondering why we're not hitting that bank. All I have is the word of a scared boy who's too loyal to his mother to save himself from slavery."

"You really can't understand it, can you? Can't understand someone protecting their mother?"

"What I can't understand is that my two biggest leads are those dirty militiamen, and you don't want me to go after them. Are you trying to save Bullstow's reputation?"

Lila turned in her seat. "After all our jobs together, you'd ask me that?"

"I'm asking you that *because* of all our jobs together. So many secrets. It's what I hate most about the highborn."

"Like you don't have secrets of your own. Every day you hate something new about us. It must be so tiring."

Once again, Lila realized that she was fighting with the former slave. She rolled down her window and breathed in the fresh air. "What more do you want from me, Tristan? I've already promised to investigate them. I'm trying to keep you away from trouble. If I come up with anything, I'll share. I promise."

"Thank you very much, chief. Can I do anything else for you, chief? Fluff your pillows, perhaps? Shine your boots?"

Lila smacked the door of the truck and whipped her head around. "What is wrong with you today? You're even worse than usual. I'm sorry I called you out on your bullshit back at the shop, but at the risk of sounding like a child, you started it. Just like you're starting it now. If it'll make the ride back smoother, then fine, I'll go back to pretending that I don't know who your parents are. Is that better?"

"You can't even apologize well. I guess they don't teach the highborn that at Bokington. Why would they? It's not something you'll ever need."

"Why should I apologize? Because your panties are in a twist?"

Tristan pressed down the accelerator, and the truck sped up. "That's rich."

"Slow down and talk to me like a grown man. I don't want to end up in a ditch."

"Yes, because you always talk to me like a grown woman," he said, rubbing the edge of the steering wheel with his thumb. Hard.

For a moment, Lila merely stared at him, not sure how things had spiraled into an argument yet again. Had she started it? Had he?

Was it even a different argument, or was it the same one, a marathon of bruised feelings and frustrations?

Lila couldn't tell anymore.

She wasn't even sure that she cared.

"I have my own spy network, you know," he said, breaking into her thoughts. "Every single highborn family in New Bristol has at least one of my people sneaking information. The Massons, the Holguíns, the Weberlys, even the Randolphs. The highborn talk in front of the help all the time, forgetting that we're there, but we're always listening."

"That's not a secret to the highborn. We use it all the time to our advantage, planting false—"

"Did you know that Senator Dubois is planning a lavish party a few weeks before the season begins? I didn't, not until I read the report this morning. He's hoping that one of his kin will win the hand of a certain unnamed heir this season. Yammered on about it through an entire dinner with his mother on Sunday night. He wouldn't tell her the identity of this eligible mystery woman, but it was obvious to anyone paying attention."

"Slow down," Lila said again, eyeing the speedometer as it crept higher and higher. "I don't understand what you're talking about."

It was a lie, of course. Senator Dubois, her sister's favorite senator, loved playing matchmaker, especially between Lila and his cousins.

She couldn't blame Dubois for the interest. A match with a Randolph heir would make any senator's career, regardless of whether or not Lila wore the whitecoat. She was a highborn, after all, and everyone knew the chairwoman considered her the prime, despite her interest in the militia rather than Wolf Tower.

That was not the only thing that made Lila so valuable. She had no children. A senator always retained custody of an eldest son born to an heir. Turned over to the senator soon after birth, he'd grow up at Bullstow, raised by his father and educated in their schools and university until he was old enough to take a position in the compound. It was how future senators were bred as well as their clerks, their militia, their chefs, their professors, their medics, and their community liaisons and social workers. The men of Bullstow had once been the children of Bullstow, bawling and snotty and laughing, doted on and spoiled by a thousand fathers.

A boy meant a child of one's own and a child shared.

The rewards were even higher with Lila, for Chairwoman Randolph had no granddaughter yet. Such a child would be necessary to secure the hierarchy of one of the richest and most powerful families in Saxony, otherwise Beatrice's sisters might begin to step out of line. The man who could offer that security to the chairwoman would consummate his career between the sheets.

It was really the only way. After their internships, senators began their political careers in the legislatures of the smaller cities scattered throughout Saxony. To advance to a larger, more prestigious city, a senator needed to prove himself behind the podium as well as bind himself to the highborn and elite lowborn in the region. He did that by making matches, or more specifically, by making babies. Seeding an heir for Lila, and by extension Chairwoman Randolph, would catapult most any senator directly to the New Bristol Senate, or elevate him to the Saxony Senate if he had other favorable ties in the region. A Saxon senator might even make it to Unity.

That was why she hated going to events during the season, this endless press of men smiling at her, flirting with her, merely for the chance to become the father of her children.

Children she explicitly did not want to have.

If Dubois's plan hadn't worked for the last four years, it certainly wouldn't work this year.

"You know exactly what I'm talking about. Last night you claimed it was my fault that we wouldn't be working together any longer, but instead you're quitting so that you can bed a rich, pompous senator and pop out a—"

"Tristan, if you'd—"

"When the poorer classes have children, they choose that moment to fight back, Lila, to make the world a better place for their kids. But the rich shrug off their ideals and hide behind the shelter of laws and society. You always said you had no intention of having children, but I suppose that was a lie. You've been beating me up for two years because you think I'm a liar, but—"

"It wasn't a lie. If you'd shut up for one—"

"Fine. You changed your mind. It says a great deal about your character that you'd quit the work so easily. I thought you were—"

"Quitting the work? I never worked for you, Tristan, and I don't belong to you. It's absolutely none of your business what I do or don't do. I'm not going to apologize for not talking about my life choices with someone who has lied to me, someone who has stolen from me, someone I can't trust, someone who has shown a complete disregard for my safety and welfare. Get over it."

"Disregard?" Tristan gripped the steering wheel with white knuckles. "I didn't disregard your safety last winter, you spoiled ass!"

Lila jerked her head away.

Spoiled.

Ass.

Tristan words echoed in the quiet truck.

She settled back into her seat, her fingers trailing out the window. Her hand caught the updrafts as they drove closer and closer toward the city. Tristan was right. He had saved her life, and he hadn't needed to. The job was over when Lila had slipped off the downtown bridge and plunged into the waters below, knocking herself senseless when she struck the surface. She had panicked, not knowing which way was up or down, barely able to hold her breath, barely able to see the lights of the bridge through the murky water.

Tristan had jumped in seconds later.

Though she was too confused to find the surface, she'd seen Tristan. She cut through the water toward him, and he grabbed her waist immediately, pushing her toward the surface with all his strength. He kicked after her, madly mimicking her movements.

It turned out that she hadn't been that far from the surface after all. Her head had broken the surface a short time later.

Tristan's hadn't.

She had been about to dive back down after him when he appeared several meters away, clawing at the water, looking afraid, his mouth barely clearing the surface. "Relax, Tristan," she'd shouted, too scared to get close to him until he calmed. "You're safe. Stretch out like you're sleeping on a bed, and you'll float."

Tristan finally trusted her instructions and calmed. She'd circled him, grabbed him from behind, and started the long trip back to the shore, pulling him along.

They had lain under the bridge for a long time after, panting and shivering. Tristan had dug his forehead into the grass and dirt, clutching at the white wildflowers. He'd reminded her of Pax and of Simon, struggling to get himself under control.

It wasn't until later that night, after they'd returned to the old hotel, after she was bundled in blankets before a heater, that Dixon had told her what she already knew.

Tristan didn't know how to swim, and he was terrified of the water.

Spoiled.

Ass.

Tristan rubbed the leather steering wheel again with his thumb. "So tell me, which highborn prince will invade your tower at the next rich girl's party?"

"Don't be crude, Tristan," she mumbled.

"I'm not. I just want to know. Do you already have one lined up, or will anyone with the right pedigree do? Must he be a senator of Saxony? Are you too good for the New Bristol High House?"

Lila closed her eyes and leaned back into the passenger seat.

"Well?"

Lila ignored him. After a while, he stopped baiting her.

It was a long trip back to New Bristol.

Dixon already had the dock door raised by the time they approached the shop, as though waiting for their arrival. She had already donned her mesh hood, obscuring her face, ready to jump on her Firefly and return home.

Shirley met them at the door and stuffed her hands into her pockets. She looked at Lila over the top of her bifocals and clucked her tongue. "Hood's back."

"Looks like it." Lila shut the truck door. "You seem to have neglected the radio in this one."

"Radios don't get you from point A to B. Radios aren't important."

"Obviously you've never tried to keep up a civil conversation with that one for longer than five minutes," she said, jerking her chin to Tristan. "Trust me, it's important."

Shirley and her assistants smirked. A woman sitting on Shirley's swivel stool cackled as she twirled around and around. "That's what I like about you, Hood," Samantha said, the purple feather in her black derby hat floating while she spun. "You always say the loveliest things."

"Out, all of you," Tristan barked. "It's lunchtime."

Samantha hopped down from the stool and followed Shirley's assistants. The old woman herded a little ginger boy out from behind the tangle of automobiles and quickly joined them.

"Would you mind not insulting me in front of the others?" Tristan grumbled, slamming the truck door after they'd gone.

"Stop leaving yourself open to it, then." Lila snatched up her helmet.

Fighting again? Dixon wrote on his notepad.

When Lila shrugged, he scribbled a second note. *PLD? I'll bring here.*

"Chinese again?"

Dixon rubbed his stomach. His eyebrows twitched roguishly.

"Now that you guys live next door, you're going to get sick of it in a few weeks. I guarantee it."

Dixon shook his head.

"Come on. We have work to do, Dixon." Tristan yanked open the door to the back of the shop and disappeared into the dim interior of the building.

Dixon ignored the order. *He's our chairwoman.*

Lila cocked her head to the side.

He takes care of everyone. It puts him in a bad mood. He means well.

"I'll agree with the bad mood part."

I'm a senator, Dixon wrote with a smirk.

Lila chuckled. "Is that so?"

I negotiate between families. I smooth things over when required. You are a family.

Lila heard heavy boots clomping across wood. Tristan poked his head back through the doorway. "Dixon, come on. We have a new lead."

I know who you are, Elizabeth Randolph.

Lila froze. He'd written her name in large block letters.

Dixon's eyes twinkled. *I could be your senator.* He tugged off Lila's hood and grabbed her around the waist, pressing his forehead to hers.

His eyelashes tickled her cheek.

Lila opened her mouth to say something, anything, not to protest but to ask why. And how? How had he known?

But before she could sort out her thoughts and settle on one question among the press, Dixon tilted his head forward and joined his mouth to hers. He sucked at her lips, nibbling as if she were a particularly sweet strawberry.

Lila didn't feel the lack of what had been cut away from him. She only felt hunger.

Her helmet hit the ground with an echoing *thunk* in the empty garage.

Lila barely heard it. She barely heard anything. All thoughts of Tristan's fight disappeared. All memories of him stealing her palm left her. All memories of their near-drowning vanished. All questions she had for Dixon, about how he'd found out her identity, about why he was kissing her, no longer seemed important.

It all bounced and rolled away like her helmet.

Wrapping her hands around Dixon's neck, she ran her tongue across his lips, testing, tasting, dimly wondering how and when and why their mouths had joined. Her fingers slipped under his collar, and she felt the cut where a slave chip had been yanked out.

She found that she didn't care.

The thump of his heart beat against her wrist, the gentle brush of skin against skin. She had missed this, had wanted it, had needed it, and hadn't had it in a very long time.

Alex had been right. She was starved.

She had a dim realization that she was courting trouble.

Dixon moaned at the brush of her fingers upon his neck and pressed her into him closer, his lips hard against her mouth.

She let her hands fall to his waist, walking him toward one of the truck beds, brain turned off, reduced to only a throbbing, pulsing need.

Lila's eyes strayed toward the door.

Tristan was gone.

12

Lila rode her Firefly directly into the family garage, scarf trailing from her neck in a battered tangle. She barely stopped before swinging her leg over the bike, happy to get off at last. The vibrating engine between her thighs had felt far too pleasant after Dixon's kiss.

Too bad his kiss hadn't led to anything more. He'd pulled away before reaching the truck, writing that it didn't make the most comfortable bed but that he'd wanted to kiss her for a long time. The wait had been worth it, though. For a man with no tongue, Dixon had been good at his job, far better than she could have imagined. She was too hungry not to wonder what else he might be good at. Perhaps the next time she visited the shop, Dixon could show her his room, could kick off those blood-red boots, the purple scarf, his trousers, and whatever else lay beneath. She'd wrap her legs around his waist and let him ease into her—

"No," Lila chided herself, taking off her helmet. "Totally out of bounds." The poorer classes frowned on casual sex. Dixon might make more of it than it was.

He might already have.

"What's out of bounds?" asked Commander Sutton at the open garage door. When Lila didn't answer, she frowned. "I saw you come in at the front gate, and much too quickly, I might add."

"You might add, but I might not listen." Lila snatched up the bugs she had laid on her sister's bike earlier that morning. She slipped them into her pocket before the commander could close the distance between them.

"I don't care if you are my superior officer. It's my job to protect the heirs. All of them. Your life matters more, chief, whether you like the implications or not."

"I don't. I shouldn't matter more than anyone else on this estate."

"That's two different statements. Perhaps it shouldn't matter, but it does." Sutton held up her hand to stop Lila's expected rebuttal. "I also don't want to explain to the prime minister how I allowed his eldest daughter to die in such a trivial manner."

"He wouldn't blame you."

"You obviously have never been a parent." The commander snorted. As the pair walked down a flower-strewn path toward the great house, Sutton filled her in on the morning's meeting.

"So nothing out of the ordinary?" Lila asked after she finished.

"Boringly so."

"Good. That's how I like it. Thanks for filling in." They stopped at the front entrance of Villanueva House. "I'll be working from home for the rest of the afternoon, commander."

"As you wish, chief." Sutton bowed, then stepped onto Villanueva Lane and marched back toward the security office.

Lila messaged the same to Sergeant Jenkins on her palm and stepped inside the great house. She didn't waste much time on her work after she returned to her room. She handled the few things that could not wait, then tossed the rest aside, paging Isabel to bring her lunch.

Using her web of proxies and fake logins, Lila broke into BullNet once more and accessed the militia's employment records. It didn't take long to bring up Muller's file. He was a below-average cop who had never been part of a high-profile bust until the raid on Club 137. Davies was much younger, a rookie, but had already marred his career by wrecking a militia truck after a few beers at lunch the year before. He had been suspended without pay for a week while Bullstow sorted out what to do with him. Though he hadn't lost his job, he had been required to attend counseling for his drinking habit.

She ignored the notes from his time in therapy. It would likely all be lies.

Their biannual evaluations didn't offer much help, either. Both men had been cited for a slew of infractions: poor recordkeeping, tardiness, apathy, and aggression. They'd barely kept their jobs, and had both been tagged for new partners and new assignments in the hopes that they could be retrained.

Their parentage was far more interesting than their biannual reviews. Muller's aunt was Chairwoman Weberly, whose family ran Weberly Memorial, Randolph General's closest rival. Davies's mother was Suji Park, an elite lowborn who had bought her son's way into Bullstow at a very high price.

The act marked the first step into becoming highborn, and from what Lila knew of Ms. Park and her daughters, the family would likely make the transition as soon as the next highborn family fell. They certainly cleared more profit each year than the bottom quarter of highborn families in the state, and several of her sons and nephews had been elected into the Low Houses of New Bristol and Saxony.

If Simon's allegations were true, Officer Davies might have ruined the family's chances.

Lila sent a message to two of her spies, taking them off a few nonessential cases, and transferred them to Rossi's Pub for the evening. Perhaps they'd find out something that wasn't in the files, something useful. Bullstow militia didn't speak freely to highborn heirs, much less to a chief, so there was precious little she had to gain by going to the bar herself.

Not unless she wanted a drink. That was about all she'd get.

That and fawning respect.

A knock sounded on the door.

Lila turned off her monitor. Isabel entered, balancing a plate of turkey and cheddar sandwiches and a kettle of tea. The young woman was twenty, with lush red hair, green eyes, a thick body, and a look of permanent annoyance that could only come from dealing with Jewel on a daily basis. She set the tray on the corner of Lila's desk.

"Thank you, Isabel."

"Will you join the family for dinner?"

"Probably."

"I'll tell Chef, madam." Isabel dropped into a quick bow.

"I'm not to be disturbed for the remainder of the afternoon."

The woman nodded and scampered back to the kitchens. Lila always had the impression that she made Isabel nervous. She'd never met Lila as a child. She'd come into Randolph possession several years ago as a slave, then stayed on after signing a servant's contract. Lila couldn't help but recall Tristan's words, that she'd only stayed on because she was indoctrinated.

Lila knew it wasn't true for Isabel. They'd done a lot for the young woman and her family. Besides, Isabel had fallen in love with the food—at least, that was what Chef claimed.

Lila turned her monitor back on and nibbled on a sandwich. She used her proxies and a fake ID to hack into Bullstow Financial Solutions. It did not take long for her to bring up Muller's and Davies's accounts. As expected, she discovered payments soon after the club raid and Simon's trial, originating from a Liberté bank account. It was the same account listed in Slack & Roberts' files.

"Well, well, well, Chairwoman Wilson. You have been naughty."

It wasn't the only account that she found. A second Liberté account had paid off Muller and Davies around the same date, matching the amount. It could have been a coincidence, but Lila didn't believe in them.

She broke into BullNet once more and dug around in Muller and Davies's case files. From what she could tell, the men had not been on duty the day they received Chairwoman Wilson's payment, and had only been involved in routine matters on Bullstow property the day they showed up at Club 137.

Lila drummed her fingers on her desk and stared at the screen. Two accounts. Two patrons. Perhaps the officers had one price for all their dirty deeds, but Lila hadn't seen the same amount repeated anywhere in their account history.

Her palm beeped with an alert.

Zephyr had broken through a fourth layer.

Lila tossed her palm on her desk and brought up all data from the senate job, looking for a lead on Zephyr. The only thing she had was the fire alarm. Its activation had not been a coincidence. Zephyr must have done it, though she was unsure of the motive. The snoop might have meant it as a distraction, something to help her escape, but any half-competent snoop would have assumed that she could get out of the building on her own. A distraction would have been unnecessary, and calling more guards to the area might have hampered her exit.

Lila doubted the purpose was to assist.

Was it just a case of amusement, then? Had Zephyr raised the stakes so that the game was more fun for both of them? Lila couldn't see how adding a few firemen in the mix would increase the entertainment value.

Had Zephyr meant for her to get caught?

That was much more likely.

Perhaps the snoop had followed her hack, realized her skills were much better than the previous hackers, and decided that hiding from her might be too difficult. It might have been nothing more than a defensive response, and now the snoop wanted to know who had shown up on the playground.

Lila switched her attentions back to the trap itself. It had been crudely buried deep inside the senate's network, clearly without the knowledge of Bullstow. That meant access to BullNet. It also suggested a certain knowledge of security and a team. Even Lila required one.

She tried to dig deeper into the BIRD to figure out when the trap had been set, but she came up empty. She might be able to pinpoint it, but it would take time that she didn't have. There were more pressing questions, and her Monday deadline loomed.

Lila rubbed her eyes, needing a break. She took off her jeans and sweater and crawled into bed, exhausted from staying up Tuesday night and getting so little sleep the night before.

She only meant to lie down, but her eyes soon closed.

She turned her head, unsurprised to see Tristan beside her, the cold stone of the Victory Tower against her back as she stared up at the starry sky.

"Klepto," he slurred, pointing with a wobbly finger, "the oaf who stole Odin's sword. Odin put him in the sky because he believed that no one should suffer the chains of slavery."

"Why not kill him?"

"To isolate him, to make him stare down at everything he couldn't have for all eternity."

"That's depressing. I don't think that's how the story went at all."

"Is that so?" Tristan turned on his side and propped himself up on one arm, watching her face. "Tell me how it goes, then."

"Klepto stole the sword from Odin, you're right about that, but Odin put him in the sky because Klepto couldn't control himself, couldn't stop himself from—"

Tristan rolled on top of her, pressing his lips to hers. His shirt melted away under her fingertips, and she ran her hands up and down his smooth, tanned skin.

The pair no longer suffered on the stone floor of the tower; they kissed on Senator Serrano's large couch instead. Tristan pressed himself between her legs, and Lila fumbled at his belt. She tugged down his trousers with a giggle.

A giggle that stopped in her throat.

For all that she found was another pair of trousers.

Lila pulled away from Tristan's mouth, and he laughed as she unzipped the second pair, revealing a third, and then a fourth.

"How does it feel, Klepto?"

The fire alarm screeched, starting Lila. "We have to go!"

"No. You're going to get caught, Lila. It's your turn to be a slave now." Tristan held her down, gripping her wrists so hard she thought they might break. Lila didn't even struggle. Instead, she tried to reach his mouth, still longing.

Tristan laughed at her and finally shoved her off the couch.

She hit the floor, smacking her head against the rug beside her bed.

Lila gazed around the room, stunned, her mind hazy, half still in the dream.

She'd never fallen out of bed before.

Kneeling on the rug, she reached for her palm on the bedside table. A new alert had popped up on the display while she napped.

Zephyr had broken through another layer.

13

Lila rolled the tip of her cigar in an ashtray perched on her windowsill, then brought it back to her lips and puffed the oaky tobacco. She blew the smoke out the open window, avoiding the thick red drapes tied to the side. Down below, Johnny Beaulieu and a young slave bent over a shaded portion of the grounds, digging despite the chill, calling back and forth to one another in a lesson, rather than a conversation. Little plastic pots of bare twigs sat in a row behind them, looking like claws bursting through the potting soil. The plants were horrid, ugly things, but she knew that after Johnny's care and devotion, the twigs would bloom into red roses.

Highborns, lowborns, and workborn threaded in and out around the pair, dodging each another, finishing last-minute errands before dinner.

A knock sounded upon the door.

"Come in."

Alex's heels clicked against the hardwood floor. "I thought you were working," she chided, snatching up the silver platter of leftover sandwiches.

"I was. Now I'm resting."

"Smoking a cigar is not resting."

"It is when no one's around to nag." Lila balanced her cigar on the ashtray's edge, then dug into her desk for the second. She sniped off the head with a guillotine cutter and handed her friend a matchbook. Lila heard the sharp strike behind her, and Alex puffed and breathed out slowly, savoring the taste.

"Woodsy." She chuckled, joining Lila at the window. "I haven't smoked a cigar in ages."

"You smoked one a few years ago with me."

"That's right. Your promotion. The last chief stepped down to open the florist shop with your cousin. I feel sorry for both of them, having to work under your Aunt Georgina. I don't even understand why she retired."

"She wanted to spend time with her grandchildren. I can't blame her. She missed a lot of her children's lives. I didn't understand how much work it was being chief until I took on the role." Lila puffed again. "I see Mr. Beaulieu in their shop all the time. Helping."

"He should get a cut of their profits. I'm sure he's earned it by now."

"More than. The two fools didn't know anything at all about roses. Still don't, though if you ever want the heartiest strain of tomatoes or the sweetest peaches, Emma can grow them for you. They should have started an orchard."

Her friend put her hand on the windowsill. A smile came to her lips as she watched the back of Johnny Beaulieu. A flood of leaves rained down, flashing in little bursts of yellow.

Alex was not entranced by the leaves.

Lila's eyes narrowed. "Oh, Alex, you didn't!"

"What?" she asked, taking a noncommittal puff on the cigar.

"Georgina ran off too many nannies. I used to babysit Johnny."

"I didn't babysit him. He's not that much younger than we are, anyway. What's five years? Besides, he's fun and eager."

"I hope you're not making him any promises."

Alex grinned. "Of course I'm making promises. I promise him every time he comes over that we'll have amazing, toe-curling—"

"I'm not listening."

"Sex, sex, sex, sex, sex. If you think he can do great things with roses, you should see what he can do with a woman's bud." Alex giggled, a smug, satisfied look plastered on her face.

"It's called a clitoris."

"You need a vacation. Stick a week's worth of condoms in your purse, find a good lay, and don't come up for air until you've run out."

Lila coughed on her cigar smoke, thinking about her dream with Tristan. Whenever she had dreams of impeded sex, it usually meant she was in dire need of it in reality. Perhaps Alex was right. She really did need a vacation.

A sex vacation.

She drooled a little at the thought.

"Is that what you've been doing with Johnny? Taking a vacation?"

"Why shouldn't I? I'm never getting my mark back, not unless the Slave Bill passes, and we both know that's never going to happen. Johnny is just a bit of fun after a very long day."

"A bit of fun?"

"Fine. He's a giant ball of fun. He'd be even more fun if I didn't have to dodge Georgina. I swear, that woman knows."

"Trust me. She doesn't. If Georgina knew or suspected, she would have wanted you off the estate. She wouldn't have asked nicely, either. If you want to sleep with him, fine, but make sure he's worth it and try not to let her find out. I wouldn't let the chairwoman transfer you to La Porte, not if I could help it, but I don't want to think about what I'd have to trade to keep you here."

Alex took a large puff and exhaled. "I'll keep that in mind."

"Are you still seeing Sebastian?"

Alex smiled slyly. "When I'm in the mood. I'll give you his number if you want. You could use someone with his—"

"I was just curious. He was never really my type."

"I'm starting to think your type requires batteries."

"Yeah, well, your mouth requires batteries."

Alex snorted, smoke thickening in the air. The pair watched Johnny and the slave for several long, quiet moments.

"Alex, how long has it been since you've seen your mother?"

"My mother?" Alex asked in surprise, tilting her head. "I haven't seen her since the day of the auction. Afterwards, I mean. In the garden. Why?"

Lila recalled the meeting. Immediately after Alex's purchase, Chairwoman Wilson had cornered the purring Chairwoman Randolph. She had offered half the Wilson-Kruger estate in exchange for the return of Alex's mark. Beatrice had laughed at the woman's proposal, and said that she had no intention of settling for half of the Wilson estate when she'd get the whole thing in a decade or two. She was patient enough to wait.

Lila had tried to reason with her mother but to no avail. Chairwoman Wilson could not hope to match the price that they had paid for Alex's mark, and the land under the estate was worth far more.

Beatrice Randolph had always been fond of land.

"You haven't seen her since?" Lila asked.

"Of course not. When my mother took me into the parlor after the meeting, she told me that I was the stupidest, most selfish brat in all of Wilson history, including my great-great-aunt Sofia. I was worse than an assassin because I'd ruined the prospects of the family. Me, and all alone by her estimation. I was a disappointment to every Wilson and every Wilson ancestor, and she never wanted to see me again. She even went so far as to say that if I hadn't belonged to your mother already, then she would have sold my mark herself. I've respected her decision and stayed away. Happily."

"You don't want to see her?"

"Not even if she was on her deathbed."

Lila nodded and puffed again on her cigar. "It's not your fault, you know. You couldn't have known that Madeline and Lizette would…"

"Die? My mother warned me something like that could happen. She said I needed to stay, that spares were important. She didn't sell me my mark out of the goodness of her heart, Lila. I blackmailed her for my freedom. It was my decision, and my family will pay for it."

"It doesn't mean it's your fault. Maybe it's not hers, either."

Alex laid her cigar on the rest. "What's going on? Why are you asking about my mother all the sudden?"

"Because she might be ill. Don't ask me how I found out, Alex, I can't tell you."

"I don't have to. You went to see Simon, didn't you? I wish I had known. I would have gone with you."

"I didn't know I was going, or I would have brought you along. Keep it to yourself, okay?"

Alex nodded, suddenly looking tired. "Look, about Simon. He told me the same thing when I visited last time. Go see her. Time might run out for the pair of you. He's worried about nothing. He's made up some story about her, just to cope with his situation. It's hard on him, harder because he was always her pet."

"Are you sure it's all made up? Are you sure it's nothing?"

Alex shrugged.

"I wish I'd known before. I might have been able to help."

"It wouldn't have looked good coming from you and your mother. It would only have made things worse. That's why I didn't tell you. You've done enough for us already."

"If you ever did want to say something to her, even if it's just to tell her to go—"

"I already did that."

"Well, if you want to reaffirm that or take it back, it should be soon, just in case. I'll take you. Whenever you want to leave, even if it's in the middle of the night, just say so."

Alex shook her head quickly. "I've said what I wanted to say, and she's said enough for the both of us. I'm done with her."

Before Lila could say another word, Alex grabbed her empty dinner tray and pulled open the bedroom door. "Thanks for the cigar, Lila. Dinner's in ten."

With that, she slipped through the door and hurried away.

Lila turned back to the window. Johnny and the slave had finished planting the roses. The pair piled up the plastic pots, hefted them on their shoulders lazily, and carried them down the sidewalk toward the greenhouse. A laugh rose up between them, carried to her window on the back of the chilly October wind.

They turned a corner and disappeared behind Villanueva House.

Lila rolled out her cigar and dug in her closet, pulling out one of her formal uniforms, not all that much different than her casual one, just shinier and better tailored. She always wore the same thing to dinner with her family. It was a chief's obligation to her matron.

The secret panel in the back of her closet caught her eye. She locked her bedroom door and closed the window, then pulled out a small chest from the hidden compartment. In it sat Captain Beauregard's old bridle; Nubbins, her favorite teddy bear, rescued from the incinerator by Chef when the chairwoman deemed Lila too old for such toys; a ribbon from her first fundraiser for the hospital; a program from its opening; and a tattered notebook, filled with furious scribbling and conversations trapped in time. She sat on her rug and opened it to the back page.

I would have given it to you. Just ask next time.

The words had been written in Dixon's block handwriting. She never understood how he had known that she would take it.

She traced his addendum, a smile coming to her lips. *Keep it. I have loads. Bring me something of yours next time. It's only fair.*

She had brought him a purple scarf.

After he'd kissed her, Dixon admitted to following her back to the Randolph estate the year before. Or at least trying. It had taken him six months and a dozen attempts before he managed it successfully, and another four just to glimpse her face.

He'd put so much effort into the job.

She couldn't help but wonder why.

Lila put the notebook away again and pulled out a palm-sized crimson bag, unfurling the strings carefully so that the contents would not drop onto the hardwood floor.

Alex's mark tumbled into her fingers, nothing more than a small silver coin. Her mother had all the paperwork in a safety deposit box on the property. That and Alex's name on the Bullstow slave registry condemned her to her fate. The coin was commemorative. The coin was meaningless.

It meant something to Lila and Alex, though.

Lila had never admitted to her friend that she owned it, that her mother had given it to her as a present on the same day that she had become the chief of security. It had spoiled Lila's promotion ceremony, the happiest day, the day she felt the most freedom from her mother.

Perhaps the chairwoman had wanted to ruin it. She had been very plain in her words after she handed over the coin. "Even in your duties as chief, remember that friends, family, and slaves are not any less of a threat than your worst enemy."

Family.

A mother could be a threat and an enemy as well.

Lila dropped the coin back into the velvet bag and shoved the chest into the closet, replacing the secret panel.

She was already late for dinner.

14

Lila waited until ten o'clock before she shoved open the secret panel again. She tossed her ash-covered workborn clothes into a satchel and changed into trousers, a black sweater, her cheap work boots, and her leather riding jacket. Adding a star drive to the chain around her neck, a scarf, and her jammer, she slipped through the great house and started out for the garage, shivering as she stepped out in the cold.

Withdrawing her palm, Lila threaded through the dozen luxury cars and antiques and brought up a snoop program. She then passed the device over her silver Firefly, intent on finding any bugs. After several moments of searching, it was clear that the chairwoman's people had not yet replaced the GPS chip or any other equipment. They had been about as productive as her own spies, for she had precious little new information on Muller and Davies that she didn't already know, except that the pair had begun to spend a little more money than others of the same pay grade in the last two years.

Sloppy.

She put on her helmet and gloves, slipped the satchel over her head, and pulled out of the garage.

No one bothered her as she rode toward the guard post. Sergeant Tripp gave her a familiar nod, pushing back his young recruit from the road with a lazy jerk of his arm. After she lifted her visor, he blew out a burst of smoke from his pipe and waved her on.

It didn't take long to reach the mechanic's shop. As she sped past, she noticed a woman she'd never seen before, sitting in chair beside the dock door. She was dressed in a long hunter-green coat, the lapels more ruffle than collar. A dark gray knit cap had been stretched down low over her forehead, and the chill had reddened her nose. The butt of a gun bulged out of her front coat pocket.

Lila turned at the next intersection and cursed Tristan for the tenth time that night. She had called twice since dinner, but he had not returned her call.

That meant he was on a job, perhaps breaking into another office building so that he could plant yet another bomb. Dixon was probably helping him.

Lila parked her Firefly in front a closed Brazilian grocers, the same grocers she had been arrested in front of the night before. She traded out her riding jacket for her workborn coat and typed Tristan's name in her palm one last time.

He did not pick up.

Lila bit her lip. She hadn't the patience to deal with a lookout she didn't know, and she had no desire to stand out in the cold until he came back. She had business with the man. It shouldn't be too hard to break into the building and wait for him to return.

What a surprise it would be if he found her sitting on his couch.

Smirking at the thought, Lila pulled her helmet off and replaced it with her newsboy cap, tugging it down low over her eyes. She grabbed her satchel and leaned against the grocery store's wall, pretending to fiddle with her palm, helmet balanced under the crook of her arm. Over the top of her computer, she watched the door of the apartment building just a few meters away.

It didn't take long for someone to leave. A slim brunette opened the door, dressed in a threadbare coat. She opened the door so wide that it *whacked* against the wall. Shivering, she marched down the street, high heels clicking on the pavement.

Lila lunged as soon as the woman's back was turned, catching the door at the last second, nearly slamming her fingers in the process.

Her boots crunched on shattered glass inside the entryway, the remains of a bulb still rolling on the floor. She crept up the dim stairs, finding yet another bulb on the ground, the only light peeping under the doors of each apartment. Whoever owned the building had not owned it for very long if they still used the delicate lights in a slum, rather than the nearly indestructible light strips across the ceiling. They would learn quickly, or else they'd go broke.

She climbed up to the top floor, the air stuffy and smelling of boiled cabbage. Sounds echoed through the doors and settled in the hallways: the howls of infants, the shouts of roommates and couples locked in arguments, the smashing of glass and fired clay, the sobbing of both women and men, and the moans of late-night sex.

At the end of the hallway, she reached a door and climbed up to the roof. The whirl of temperature-control units covered her footsteps as she approached the ledge.

Across the alley, three meters away, lay the mechanic's shop.

Tristan had been smart with his lease. Likely his people had begun a slow takeover of the apartment building, snatching up vacant units as soon as any tenant moved away. With the apartment building so close behind the shop, Tristan had two exits for his people. There was also plenty of cover on the shop's roof as the row of temperature-control units sliced the roof in two, and a small greenhouse had been built toward the back. Tristan's people could always jump across the gap and defend the shop if needed, or jump back to the apartments and escape.

She could jump over too.

Lila dropped her helmet and satchel in the darkest corner of the roof and squinted across the alley. A man paced around the perimeter on the other building, his hands stuck in the pockets of his thick woolen coat, a coat too small for his frame. The guns he hid inside them peeked out, a secret to no one.

Lila consider his walk, his expression, his limp. A man like him might not load tranq darts into his revolver.

Lila thumbed her Colt, which had been tucked into her waistband at the small of her back. A sleep dart might be effective, but the thought of bring harm against another innocent appalled her.

She ducked as the man turned and stalked toward her position. Counting his steps as he clomped by, she poked her head back up after he passed, then replaced her weapon in the inside pocket of her coat.

Down below, a woman prowled across the alley. Squinting harder in the darkness, Lila recognized the black derby hat, adorned with a purple feather. Samantha would help her get into the shop undetected. She'd probably even wait with Lila in Tristan's garage, either to escape guard duty or to keep watch over her quick fingers.

But where was the fun in that? Lila had an image of Tristan returning to find that she had slipped through his defenses. She wanted to watch the self-important look drop away from his face and change from surprise to irritation.

It would serve him right for how he'd acted.

She took out her palm and checked her messages.

None displayed on the screen.

Sticking the device back into her pocket, she waited for the guard to cross by her position again. When he slipped behind the greenhouse on the opposite side of the building, she hopped up, sprinted across the roof, and launched herself across the alley.

Blisters stinging, Lila's ankle turned as she landed. She tripped. Rolled. Her head barely missed the row of heating units.

The guard's footsteps stopped.

Lila didn't wait. Ankle throbbing, she scrambled back to the ledge and threw her leg over it, letting herself dangle off the side with only the strength in her fingers holding her up.

The fire escape lay a meter to the right.

Lila had gravely misjudged her position.

"Fuck," she mouthed, walking her hands toward the railing.

Lila slid along the roof until the rail was under her feet. She kept sight of Samantha, waiting until she passed under the fire escape and walked toward the end of the alley. Lila's fingers cramped, and she began to sweat under her thick coat.

Waiting in Tristan's room didn't seem quite so funny anymore.

Once Samantha was out of earshot, Lila let herself drop to the handrail, then gently stepped down on to the fire escape, cringing when it squeaked softly under her weight.

Samantha did not turn around.

Lila breathed deeply and limped to the window, which opened into the fifth-floor hallway.

She tugged at the bottom.

The lock was still broken.

Lila ducked into the hallway on the top floor and slid her mesh hood over her face. Removing a set of lock-picking tools from her pocket, she knelt by Tristan's door.

The door opened as soon as she touched the doorknob.

He'd left it unlocked, open to the world.

Sloppy. Tristan trusted his people far too much.

Lila slipped through the door, confused to find Dixon at the window. He peeked through a slit in the drapes, staring out over the front of the mechanic shop. Scars crossed his back as though a thin bicycle wheel had been dipped in silver ink and raked across it, backing over him again and again, scoring his body with thick furrows. She'd seen them before, wondered about them, but she could never bring herself to ask.

They never got any easier to see.

This was the back she'd wanted to explore earlier in the day, connected to a man she barely knew, with a past she'd never uncovered. She had asked Tristan about him, of course, in between sips of wine on the Victory Tower.

"All you need to know about Dixon can be summed up by one sentence," he'd replied, bitterness clouding his mirth. "Dixon Leclair has the most beautiful voice in the world."

She'd looked up, startled and confused.

"He and I grew up together, you know. Whenever Dixon sang, everyone around him stopped. The notes held you like a spell. The notes made you stupid. They made you forget the bad and cling to the good, or they made you forget the good and cling to the bad.

He played all who listened, depending on the song, and people followed him for it. He didn't need the notes, though. He could make you believe you could fly with just a few well-chosen words."

"I didn't know."

"Few do. I'd give my right hand if I could hear him sing again. He doesn't need a tongue for it, but he won't, not since they hurt him. He won't even hum. Assholes knew exactly what they were doing."

Tristan wouldn't say more about it, not that night or any night after.

Lila took off her hood. Dixon turned, cocking his head in confusion, a puzzled little smile on his face.

"Sorry. I didn't know you were here."

Dixon's bare feet slapped across the wood floor as he crossed the room, sandwich perched lazily in his hand. Cheetah-print boxer briefs clung to his swimmer's body.

Lila gulped and tried not to look down.

Dixon took a big bite of his sandwich and stared at her expectantly, sticking his finger in his mouth to move the food under his teeth.

"Avocado and bananas with hot sauce?" she asked, sniffing the air.

Dixon nodded.

"Really? Is it good?"

He grinned and nodded again, pointing at his throat. He had explained once that he could only taste food in his throat and on the little tip of his tongue he had left. He favored strange food combinations, but Tristan had told her once that he'd always been a bit odd about food. That time it had been cream cheese, raisins, pickles, and tuna.

She pointed to his boxer briefs. "They were a gift?"

Dixon shook his head and snapped the waistband. Lila looked down at exactly the wrong moment for a peek.

Or the right one.

Oracle's light, she was hungry.

Dixon winked.

"Sometimes I just don't know about you." She unwound her scarf. It was hot in the room, for the heater had been turned on full blast, rattling between the couches. "May I wait here for Tristan to get back from whatever stupidity he's up to right now? We could talk or something."

Lila could think of several things she'd rather do than talk. She wondered if he'd be up for any of them.

Dixon licked his fingers and picked up a pillow from one of the couches, then launched it at Tristan's closed bedroom door. It landed with a dull thump.

The door opened in a rush. "Damn it, Dixon, what—"

Tristan turned his head, realizing too late that Lila was in the room. He looked down at his black boxer briefs, the only stitch of clothing he wore, revealing a form very much like Dixon's without the scars. "Didn't hear you come in," he grumbled, and slammed the door shut again.

A moment later, he emerged in a pair of black cargo pants and a gray t-shirt. "Turn the damn heater down, Dixon. I'm roasting."

Dixon shook his head.

"Ass," Tristan spat, turning off the heater himself. His gaze tracked to Lila. "What are you doing here?"

Dixon scribbled furiously on his notepad. Seconds later he held it up.

SHE COULDN'T RESIST ME. OUR KISS WAS EPIC.

Lila bit her lip and tried not to laugh. "If you'd bother to check your messages, Tristan, you might know. I've been trying to call you for the last few hours."

Dixon flashed his notepad. *He did.*

"So he's been ignoring my calls?"

Dixon nodded, almost laughing.

"Go put some clothes on," Tristan grumbled. "You're making the chief uncomfortable."

Dixon raised a brow and fell back into the couch. He kicked his feet on an ottoman and took another lazy bite of his sandwich.

Lila tried not to peek again. And failed. "Look, I don't care why you ignored my calls tonight. You asked for my help, and I have new information. If you've changed your—"

"What new information?"

"Stuff."

"Well, that's really specific, Lila. Next time don't bother explaining yourself so thoroughly." When she didn't answer him, he rolled his eyes. "I've already updated Dixon on our progress. You can speak freely. I tell him everything anyway."

Lila pushed her shoulders back and gave a curt nod. "Fine. I need lookouts. I'm hacking Liberté tonight."

Tristan cocked his head to the side. "Wait a minute, you want to break into the same bank that you said you'd be a fool to hack into this morning? What information could possibly have made you change your mind?"

"Does it matter?"

"I suppose not."

Dixon whistled and held up his notebook. *What's the plan?*

"I obviously can't do it from my family's estate. It might be traced back to me or my family. We'll park outside the Wilson compound and use her network. Your people can serve as lookouts in case her militia patrols see us and decide to investigate. Their techs won't even see me in the logs after I'm done. Even if they do, they'll think it was one of their own. Let Mama Wilson sort that one out."

"Have I told you how much I enjoy the way you think?"

"Yes, as a matter of fact, you told me this evening after you returned my messages," she said. "One more thing. I'm not going to make any withdrawals. This isn't a bank robbery."

"I can steal my own money," Tristan said, tugging on his coat.

15

While Tristan and his people prepped for the op, Lila recovered her satchel and helmet from the roof of the apartment building. She limped up the stairs this time, rather than jumping across and risking further injury to her ankle. On the way back, she retrieved her Firefly and parked it in the back of the shop for safe keeping, then changed clothes and stopped by Toxic and Reaper's storage room. She grabbed a sleek Apex for her work. The pair always kept several new, unused laptops on hand at all times, preparing for such situations.

She hopped into one of the Cruz trucks, uploading her snoop programs from her star drive while Tristan darted around the garage, giving last-minute orders. It always amazed her how quickly he could pull together such things, how easily he directed his people, how willing they were to follow his lead. She often wondered if she had no title and no birthright if her subordinates would react the same way.

Probably not.

"You ready?" he asked finally, opening the driver's side door.

"Always," she replied through her mesh hood, shutting Apex's lid. "Were you able to get ahold of Reaper? It would make researching faster if we had an extra hand."

Tristan shook his head. "He won't be back for several days, and I can't begrudge a man for wanting to earn an honest living. I certainly can't afford to pay him what he's worth, either. I called Toxic instead. She just needs the address, and she'll meet us there." He pulled the truck out of the shop carefully while a now-clothed

Dixon signaled his way through the maze of motorcycles and parked cars.

Once Tristan had cleared the dock door, Dixon and four other figures hopped onto a few motorcycles, with two of the men doubling up. The woman in the green coat closed the door after them, and they zipped away from the shop.

"They're going to be too loud on those things. This isn't a parade, Tristan. We should go in fewer vehicles."

"We'll be fine. I have no intention of turning an alley into a parking lot."

Lila thumbed the edge of her laptop as they drove in silence, their earlier fight remembered but ignored by strained agreement.

That was fine by Lila. She had no wish to start another.

As the streetlights rushed past, two of the bikes split off from the group and turned down a side street. Another turned at the next light.

Only Tristan and Lila remained.

"Where are the others going?" she asked.

"Patience. They'll meet us on foot after we find a good place."

"You're counseling me about patience?"

Tristan ignored her and circled the Wilson compound while she gauged the strength of the chairwoman's network on a spare palm. They settled on an abandoned restaurant named Chaucer's Ghost, one of the many businesses around the estate to go bust after the family's dividends had dwindled.

Plywood covered the windows and the windows of its neighbors. All had been painted white, though the blurs of darker colors shone through, far-off echoes of frustration and boredom drawn out in paint. The street had not been swept in months, and only one street lamp still functioned. It slumped over the road as though put upon and exhausted from its efforts.

Tristan pulled into the alley beside the restaurant, killed the engine, and messaged the group. "I didn't see any patrols," he said, tapping his palm computer against his leg when he had finished.

"They don't have the manpower for it. I suspect the chief is too busy taking care of the mess inside. What do they have to steal, anyway?"

"The emperor?"

Lila snorted. The Kruger addition to the Wilson name was not due to birth. It was a bit of pomp that Norma Wilson, Alex's grandmother, had styled for herself. Eighty years ago, a rebellious niece of the king of Germany had slipped into port with the intention of making a new life for herself in America. Up to that point, the women in the Holy Roman Empire were looked at as little more than breeding cows. They lacked the ability to vote, own property, or manage their own finances, if they were lucky enough to have money at all. Ilse Kruger refused to settle for such a life. After her husband's death, she cleared out his bank account in Burgundy, escaped to Saxony, and eventually settled in New Bristol. A master of accents, she even managed to start a business with no one the wiser, and her irritated father had little reason to locate her.

After all, he didn't know she was pregnant at the time.

Unfortunately, the secret didn't last. The king died, and Ms. Kruger's father took the throne, also claiming the abandoned title of emperor. As his only child, Ms. Kruger suddenly became very important. Or, more correctly, her children would become important. Her eldest son would one day become the rightful heir. The emperor dispatched men to find her and return her to Germany. So did his counterpart in Italy, though only to cause mischief, rather than to aid.

Alex's grandmother managed to intercept one of the men. After slipping him truth serum, she sent her people to find Ms. Kruger, nearly bankrupting her family to take over the woman's company. After it lay in ruins, the chairwoman bought the woman's mark at auction, her identity unknown to those attending. Both Ms. Kruger and her young son became Wilson slaves.

The fallout nearly unsettled the ceasefire between the Holy Roman Empire and the Allied Lands. Fortunately, the king's new wife bore a son, and Ms. Kruger and her heir didn't seem worth the trouble any longer—not enough to rescue, anyway. His partner, the Italian king, dissuaded him from going after her because the diplomatic situation was too tense. There were other heirs, and his grandson had never lived in Germany.

What was a daughter but another cow?

What was Ilse Kruger but the most rebellious and troublesome cow of all?

It enraged Lila to think of it. The only thing stranger was the idea that men should handle everyone's affairs. Certainly she had met many competent men in highborn society, but putting them solely in charge of anything, much less an entire country, seemed insane.

But that's how it was in the Holy Roman Empire. Even now, there existed a few aristocratic traditionalists who thought Peter Kruger should be the rightful king and emperor rather than King Lucas, not that the Italians would ever go for it. Lila thought them all barking mad. She had met the man several times growing up, and he was a sad disappointment. He barely knew how to read, and barely spoke when Lila attempted conversation.

It wasn't all that surprising. Lila and Alex had snuck peeks at her grandmother's parties when they were young. The chairwoman liked to drag out the small man from whatever hole he had been set to work in that day, force him to dress up in child's costumes, and serve her guests wine. Occasionally the woman offered no costume and no clothes at all.

That was before the Interclass Abuse Act, which, among its many provisions, forced slave owners to educate their slaves' children and ended much of the humiliation the poor man suffered. Strangely enough, the rightful heir to their enemy's throne had been the inspiration for much of it. Too many highborn had been disgusted by the chairwoman's antics during parties. They had begun taking a longer look at their own actions in response.

It hadn't ended every torment Peter Kruger faced. Like Alex's grandmother, Chairwoman Wilson still assigned him to every unpleasant task she could devise, all in an effort to skate around the act. But at least Mr. Kruger's children could read and did not endure the same humiliations, though they were little better off. They would not be allowed to age out at eighteen, like other children of slaves. As the children of a German citizen, the law still considered them an enemy.

Lila wasn't sure what her own mother had planned for them after she took charge of the Wilson property, but at least she had no interest in humiliation.

Neither did Lila.

They agreed on another thing as well. While Alex's mother and grandmother had always believed Ms. Kruger's capture was their greatest triumph, Lila saw it for what it was. An overextension. A wasteful expenditure of resources on a luxury item that offered absolutely no return on investment. It had sounded the death knell for the Wilson family. They had never recovered from the loss of capital.

Besides, it was just crass. What sort of behavior could one expect from a family who had only attained highborn status with Norma Wilson's rise? If Alex had not shown more decorum, then she and Lila could never have become friends. Her mother would never have allowed it.

"Look alive, will you?" Tristan said, snapping his fingers in her face. "Here they come."

Dixon showed up to the truck first. He opened the truck door and scooted in next to Lila, forcing her to squeeze closer to Tristan. They sat next to one another, not touching, not speaking. While Lila slipped on her hood, Dixon scribbled notes about what he'd seen around the neighborhood.

One patrol on the other side. They're stopped with no lights. Eating. He drew a map beside his words.

"Well, they won't be eating for much longer," Tristan said as he directed the next two men to the roof of Chaucer's Ghost. The other slipped inside the truck cab. The group squeezed closer together, and Tristan awkwardly put his arms around Lila for lack of anywhere else to put them. She smelled his soap, really nice soap, and a hint of whiskey.

Dixon raised an eyebrow.

Out of the corner of her eye, Lila saw Tristan's chin jut out, and he pulled Lila even closer into his body.

Lila had somehow found herself in a tennis match between the two men, and she was the ball.

"Get off," she muttered, pushing Tristan away. She climbed over Dixon and the other man in her haste to escape the truck, nearly kneeing them both in the crotch.

At the mouth of the alley, a petite black woman with thick, natural curls, an electric-blue coat, and knee-high red boots strolled toward them. The young woman reminded her of Pax in movements and Jewel in beauty.

"Toxic, check for a security system," Tristan barked when she stopped before the truck.

The woman scampered over to the side door of the building and pulled out her palm, passing it over the doorframe several times before punching furiously on the keypad. She twisted her ankles back and forth, clicking her heels, while she worked, and Lila heard the smack of bubblegum.

Tristan drifted away from the truck, stalking deeper into the alley toward a bundle of blankets. He squatted in the muck, and his murmurs echoed against the buildings on either side. Something changed hands. Dirty knit caps bobbed in agreement above the blanket, and Tristan drifted back to the truck.

"Spies?" she asked.

"No. Too young for it. Told them to run if more people showed up."

"What'd you give them? Flyers?"

"The number for a shelter, not that they'll go, and a little cash. I've seen them around. They'll buy food with it." He turned back to watch Toxic's progress. "We've never actually given those fliers out—not that it hasn't stopped Bullstow from asking everyone in the neighborhood about them. It's making my people nervous."

"It should make *you* nervous. They're already looking into the nitro heist and the camera vandalism around Bullstow."

Tristan raised an eyebrow. "How did you know about that?"

"It's what I do," Lila said, checking her Colt.

A muffled beep sounded inside the restaurant. Toxic turned, bowed to her little crowd, and added a flourish with her free hand.

"Faster than me," Lila admitted, pitching her voice deeper. "Good job."

Toxic gestured toward Lila with her palm and turned back to Tristan. "Finally, someone appreciates my work. Do you see how easy that is?"

Tristan ignored her. "Let's get in before someone sees us."

"No one will even know we opened the door. I've set the system to keep sending a locked signal."

Lila straightened her mesh hood and crossed into Chaucer's Ghost, crinkling her nose at the smell of mildew and mold and the twinge of something dead. The building still looked like a working restaurant, for the stainless steel sinks and counters and ovens had not been removed. A thin layer of dust coated every surface, including the floor. The group all left boot prints as they trudged through the kitchen. Spider webs stretched across the corners of the room, and Lila heard the sound of flapping wings through a pair of open double doors.

Tristan snapped a tube in his hands and shook it, bathing the room in an eerie green glow.

The group moved into the empty dining room. A dozen pigeons fluttered in place as they entered, offering cooing trills. The birds had left their mark upon the floor. Pockmarked with gray and white droppings as well as a smattering of fuzz and feathers, the large room still managed to drip with the memory of comfortable charm. Though the red brick walls had dulled somewhat, the stained cherry wood still shone in patches, especially on the bar in the back of the dining room. Something had been moved upon it recently, disturbing the dust.

On the wall, a sign had been left up. *Chaucer's Ghost* glinted in twisted metal, still proclaiming its name for invisible guests. Every time Tristan moved, the green light shifted, creating shadows that retreated around the tables. Lila imagined ghostlike patrons pausing mid-bite, suspending birthday wishes, anniversary cakes, and nervous wedding proposals, all in order to watch the little group invade their space. They all existed just out of sight, hiding whenever she turned.

Lila shivered at the thought.

Dixon pointed up.

"Yes," Lila said. "There's an office upstairs. Hopefully it won't be so messy."

Lila followed the light up a familiar staircase. Alex had dragged her to the restaurant many times when they were younger. She'd even met the owner, Mr. Farthing, a man who had left the Wilson family years before by buying his mark from his matron. She remembered not being sure what to make of him, with his wispy sideburns, thin mustache, and ivory cane carved into the shape of a falcon's head. The man was determined to own a business instead of staying with his family or marrying into a new one. He'd even proclaimed that one day he'd own enough restaurants to sit on the Low Council of Judges. When Lila had laughed and told him the council, even the lowborn council, was only for women, he had swiped the bottle of beer she'd been drinking and wandered off with it.

What had become of him after the business failed? Who had bought his mark? She couldn't imagine such a proud man in the mines.

Tristan prodded her in the shoulder when they reached the top of the stairs. She retraced the route from memory and found Mr. Farthing's office. The room was smaller than she remembered, even without the furniture. Several filing cabinets rusted against the wall, and a few open drawers revealed that they had been emptied. Scratches on the cherry wood floor betrayed the location of Mr. Farthing's desk and liquor cabinet.

The rotting stench was absent. At least the birds had not ventured inside yet.

"Watch the truck and the back door, Frank," Tristan ordered the man with the navy coat. "Whistle if you spot something off. We'll do the same."

Frank slipped away, shaking his own green light.

Dixon leaned against the office door, watching him go. He fingered the revolver in his holster, gaze locked on the hallway and staircase.

Lila sat down in the middle of the room, glad that Tristan had posted lookouts, glad that she only needed to focus on the hack. The first and relatively easy step involved shoving open the door to the Wilson-Kruger network. The password was not difficult to guess, not after logging on for so many years as Alex's guest.

Toxic sat behind her as she worked, huddled in a corner, giving Lila her anonymity.

Lila pulled off her hood so that she could work freely, relieved that her identity and her work would not be compromised. As soon as she muttered the password, Toxic connected to the network, eager to assist. "Reaper was too busy for the Bullstow job. I coded the virus and uploaded it myself. I can help."

"I'll keep that in mind."

Lila soon she forgot about Toxic, though, too immersed in her task to care about anything but the Liberté. She prodded her way inside, exploiting the hole in the server's operating system she had used over a decade before.

The entire system now belonged to her.

Lila opened her snoop programs in a small window and created a new employee account. She then logged in as the newest bank account manager for Liberté and looked up two accounts, pulling transaction histories for the past three years. She then saved them to her laptop and star drive. Though she had no intentions of reviewing the data before logging out, her eyes strayed over the second account and lingered on a familiar number.

Natalie Holguín. Lila sometimes bought Sangre de las Flores from her, with both women using cash or untraceable accounts so that their matrons would not catch wind of the trade. Acting quickly, she ventured to Natalie's bank account and saved the transaction history. She then returned to the second account and scanned the list, picking three more Liberté accounts, two of which looked strangely familiar. She saved their transaction history and account information as well.

Time was running short.

She deleted her new employee account and erased all traces of it in the system.

The hack had taken less than fifteen minutes.

Her snoop program still burned with a green light.

"Done," she said, opening the data while her programs deleted the evidence of her work. Tristan looked up from his post at the window, as did Dixon. Even Toxic peered over her shoulder.

"That quick?" Tristan asked.

"Yes, that quick." Lila scrolled through the information on her screen. "Edward Teach. It must be a workborn name. Toxic, see if you can find a record of him in the state registries."

Dixon snorted at the door, and Toxic covered her mouth, a stray giggle escaping.

"Did you say Edward Teach?" Tristan asked, striding forward.

"Yes." Lila shoved her hood back over her face and eyed them all warily. "Is he a friend of yours?"

Tristan peeked at the screen. "You could say that. What did he do?"

"He's the owner of Chairwoman Wilson's account, or at least the account you think belongs to her."

Dixon chuckled again.

"What's so damn amusing?"

No one said a word as Dixon scribbled on his notepad. *Blackbeard.*

"Blackbeard?"

Pirate.

"You can't be serious. You mean pirate, as in the pirates who sailed the seven seas before the Declaration of Peace? The same pirates who almost single-handedly destroyed the alliance among the old countries with all their looting and plundering? The ones who claimed government mandates for the destruction they wrought?"

Tristan nodded. "I suppose they thought it funny. They weren't fans of the alliance."

"That alliance has kept the Romans at bay for several centuries. Doesn't that mean anything to you?"

Tristan shrugged.

"What does Blackbeard have to do with Edward Teach, anyway?"

"It was Blackbeard's real name," Toxic explained, before launching into a vulgar sea shanty.

Lila frowned. The only thing she knew about pirates had come from movies. "So Chairwoman Wilson is funneling money through an account named for some pirate who's been dead for…"

"About three hundred years," Tristan supplied.

"And she's transferring that money into the accounts of two Bullstow militiamen as payment for her dirty work?"

"Looks like it."

"Shiver me timbers." Lila pushed her laptop away. "Lovely. This just gets sillier and sillier the longer it goes on. The woman can't even be a dignified criminal."

"What? It's funny."

"Being cute when you're naming accounts like that can come back to bite you in the ass. It's not funny. It's sloppy."

Toxic sat forward. "How much is in the account?"

"Millions. Nearly fifty million, to be exact." It was stupid of Chairwoman Wilson to put that much in one account. A hacker could just spirit it away with the touch of a few buttons.

Lila could move it.

She could move it anywhere she wanted.

Her fingers twitched at the ready. She could almost see the look on Chairwoman Wilson's face after finding her account empty.

She could almost feel her own arms being forced behind her back and cuffed. The cold seat in the back of a militia cruiser. The look on her father's face. The surprise.

The disappointment.

She'd never actually stolen anything before, not without prior authorization from the owners, and only as a test of their security. Not even Serrano's cigars really counted. He passed them out like candy, especially to heirs.

It wasn't really stealing, was it?

Lila didn't know anymore.

She took her hands away from the keyboard. Moving the chairwoman's money, even if it would belong to her family soon, crossed a line.

"Why does Chairwoman Wilson need millions?" Tristan said, returning to his post at the window. "You don't need that much to pay off a couple of dirty militiamen."

"No, you don't need millions," Lila agreed. "Money not used to make money is money wasted. She's up to something. Could be anything."

"You already know what she's up to."

"I have my suspicions."

"Bullshit. You know as well as I do what she's doing."

Toxic raised her hand. "I don't."

"She's running. She's selling that whole damn empire of hers. Probably been bleeding it dry for years, ever since her daughter lost her mark, squeezing her own family and the workborn around her just to get a few more credits before she flees."

"We don't know that," Lila cautioned.

"Of course we do. She's going to run to Burgundy and retire like all the other disgraced highborns, with or without her family. I suspect without, if you believe Simon is really in the dark about all this."

"Don't start with Simon. He's just a boy."

"Fine, perhaps she'll send for him after he's all used up from the vineyard. But she's running. You know it as well as I do."

"We don't know anything of the sort." It wasn't that Chairwoman Wilson possessed too many scruples for such an act—Lila just wasn't convinced that the woman had enough intelligence for it.

Then again, liquidating assets without an heir and transferring them out of the country was illegal and difficult to manage, unless one wanted a slave's term. If Chairwoman Wilson was smart enough to hide her money without getting caught, then she could have recovered her family's fortune after her mother's idiocy, rather than fallen even lower.

It didn't make sense.

Lila turned back to her laptop. She traced the deposits in Teach's account to a bank inside Saxony, First New Bristol. Not only did Lila bank there, she owned controlling shares, purchased as a way to conceal some of her money from her mother. It definitely wasn't the most honorable of banks, but that had been the point of purchasing it. Her funds would remain undisturbed, and it gave her a good way to spy on the funds of morally ambiguous highborns and lowborns in the city.

Chairwoman Wilson's activity must have slipped through.

Lila did the hack herself, since she did not want Toxic near the bank that held part of her nest egg. She called out a few names, and Toxic searched through several public databases, both of them looking for a match.

After an hour, the pair had an answer. "Some of the money is coming to Teach's account as a consultant's salary from a lowborn business," Lila explained. "That business is partnered with Wilson-Kruger, but you have to go back through a dozen layers to find it."

"What does that mean?" Toxic asked.

"It means that the company is an empty shell within a shell within a shell."

Toxic considered the implications. "Is that proof?"

"Not really. It doesn't prove much at all. It just shows that the chairwoman sent money to a sketchy bank account, and that bank account sent—"

"Bribed," Tristan interjected.

"—*sent*," Lila said over him, "money to a few militiamen after they helped with a particularly difficult case on her property. That is how her lawyer will frame it, and she'll never be charged."

"It bothers me when you talk like them," Tristan said.

"Then get over it, don't listen, or don't ask for my help."

"What about the money in the account, though?" Toxic asked. "Can't we turn her in? It's illegal to hide money like that, isn't it?"

"What reason could Bullstow give for peeking into her financials? The militia can't just stroll up to the High Council of Judges with an anonymous tip and expect to see financial information for a multimillion credit empire. Besides, the money is set up to go somewhere else if that happens, mark my words. Burgundy protects their clients."

Toxic's eyes passed from Tristan to Lila's hood and back to Tristan. "Well, if it helps, I did confirm that there's no Edward Teach in the commonwealth and in Burgundy. There aren't that many Teaches left, actually. I've been in every database I know of. I can't believe that no one would name their kid after a pirate."

"Me neither," said Tristan, nodding toward Dixon when he gave a thumbs-up and a grin.

"I can," Lila added, already digging into the second account.

"You would."

Lila ignored Tristan and scrolled through the transaction history of the other account. She needed more time to dig through the information, and she had a nagging feeling that she was missing something. "Look, I held up my end of the bargain. I found data linking Chairwoman Wilson to Slack & Roberts, even though it doesn't prove much. I need to get home now, though. It's late."

"What do you mean it doesn't prove much?" Tristan said. "It's proof that money—"

"I already told you. It's not illegal to give money to a few black-coats for helping out an estate. Any decent lawyer can argue that away. Besides, if they tried to arrest Chairwoman Wilson for having a fake bank account in Burgundy, even if Liberté chose to assist them at their game, they'd have to arrest half the highborn and lowborn elites in the Allied Lands. It's suspicious, but it's nothing unusual."

"So then we break into her compound. We search her office and find—"

"You mean we jump in feet first and hope for the best?"

Tristan balled his hands into fists.

"How about we do something else first?" she said.

"What?"

"Speak with—"

A whistle cut through the air downstairs.

16

Lila slapped down the lid of her laptop, shoved it into her satchel, and joined Tristan at the window. Downstairs, a cruiser with the Wilson-Kruger coat of arms parked half on the street, half on the sidewalk. The militia lights gleamed on its roof, spinning white and gold, white and gold.

The driver cut the engine, and two blackcoats hopped out. The women put their hands on their hips, fingers grazing their revolvers. The pair stared up at Chaucer's Ghost suspiciously.

"Shit," Tristan said as one of them pointed to the office. "They've seen the glow stick. Toxic, get up. Move!"

Toxic shot up from the floor, not waiting for further instructions. She jammed her laptop into a bag, flung it over her shoulder, and hurtled past Dixon. Lila cringed as the young woman raced down the stairs, her boots clomping against the cherry wood.

"It was the glow stick, right?" Tristan hissed.

"The glow sticks, Toxic's job on the door, the truck in the alley, take your pick," Lila whispered, racing downstairs after Toxic and Dixon, all three much quieter than the hacker. Lila straightened her hood and thrust the star drive into her bag. "Even if their techs saw me on the network, they wouldn't be able to pinpoint my location."

Tristan grabbed Toxic's shoulder at the foot of the stairs. The group paused, peering through the green glow at the front door. One of the blackcoats grunted and kicked the wood. The chains strung through the handle *clinked* and *thumped,* holding the door in place. A thin beam of light shot through the cracks in the frame, shifting through the room like a searchlight.

The pigeons stopped cooing. Wings fluttered and slapped. New pools of white and gray struck the floor.

"Do we have a master key?" said a woman behind the door, her voice hard, yet strangely childish.

"We have a bolt cutter in the back of the truck." Her partner snickered, words already shifting pitch as she stepped away to retrieve it.

Tristan turned Toxic toward the kitchens and gave her a shove, spurring the group toward the side exit. The green light went out behind them mid-flight as Tristan tucked the glow stick into his coat pocket.

Another rolled in the kitchen, back and forth near Frank's body. There wasn't enough light for Lila to see if he was breathing.

Toxic glanced back at Lila, jaw slack, her brown eyes wide and staring. She winced as one of the frustrated women kicked at the restaurant's front doors.

Dixon brushed Toxic back, raised his scarf over his nose and mouth, and stepped over his comrade.

Pushing open the kitchen door, he functioned as the group's canary, freezing in place almost immediately, telegraphing what was in the alley. His gun fell to the ground at his feet, and his hands shot into the air, two fingers raised.

Two fingers. Two people waiting.

Toxic didn't care. It woke something in the young woman, seeing a glimpse of the world, and that something didn't pay attention to Dixon's raised arms.

Lila lunged for her, fiercely clasping one electric-blue sleeve, but it was yanked free of her fingers, the fabric burning her skin as it slipped through.

Toxic ran the last few steps toward freedom and bumped into Dixon on the way out.

There was a puff of air.

Toxic stumbled, and Lila spied the small black dart in her neck.

Dixon grabbed Toxic and helped her slide to the ground unharmed.

Tristan took advantage of the distraction. Scarf masking his face, he burst through the door and charged. Lila drew her Colt and snaked around the door behind him. Two blackcoats, a male and female, swiveled away from Dixon to the new threat.

Tristan barreled toward them with the force of a bullet train.

Lila hid behind the door and fired a dart into the woman's neck while Tristan knocked her partner onto his back. The man struggled to breathe as he hit the ground, and Tristan shot him with a dart.

"Diana to Command, send reinforcements to Chaucer's Ghost," his radio called out as Lila and Tristan dragged the sleeping black-coats away from the truck. While they worked, Dixon tossed Frank over his shoulder and placed him in the truck bed. Tristan slid Toxic in after him.

The bundle of children in the alley had already disappeared.

Lila was glad for it. "We need to leave before the other two realize we're here." She wrenched open the truck's passenger door. "I'm not shooting another blackcoat."

"No way we're leaving. That's some highborn shit right there. We don't run, we take them out, now," Tristan said, spinning around and sprinting toward the mouth of the alley. Dixon offered Lila a small wink before taking off behind him.

Lila shoved her satchel under the passenger seat and followed behind them, Colt drawn, stomach twisting up, every cell in her body sending up an SOS to get away while they still had the chance. She was all too aware of the star drive in her laptop bag and what it contained. The hacked data broke several laws in several different countries. They'd argue over who had the right to hang her first.

"Stupid, sloppy, reckless man," she muttered, running after Tristan, glad that her mesh hood would hide her identity. "Where are the others?"

"Doing their job."

"Which is?"

"Covering our ass," Tristan whispered, sliding to a stop at the mouth of the alley. He peered around the edge of the building, then ducked back again.

Sirens started up near the Wilson compound, only a minute or two away from their location.

A shot rang out at the front of the building, nothing but a puff of air.

One of the blackcoats swung around the corner, her weapon drawn. Tristan fired.

The woman slumped to the ground at his feet.

Above them, an owl hooted, or at least Lila believed it to be an owl. One of the lookouts stood on the roof's edge, revolver in hand, lips curved in satisfaction. He pointed back at the front door and tugged his ear.

Tristan gave him a thumbs-up and spun his finger in a circle above his head.

"Come on, let's go," he said, snatching up her hand as he ran back to the truck. "They got the other one. We're clear."

Dixon shoved the fallen blackcoat out of the street and followed Lila and Tristan down the alley. While Lila hopped into the truck cab, the two men quickly covered Frank and Toxic with a tarp, then piled into the truck with her jammed in the middle.

By the time Tristan backed the truck from the alley, the two lookouts had climbed down from the roof. They didn't leap into the bed of the truck. Instead, they raced down the sidewalk.

"Where are they going?"

"To get the bikes. They parked in a garage a few streets over," Tristan answered, yanking down his scarf and gunning the engine.

The militia spotted the truck before it turned the first corner. Four cruisers, lights whirling and sirens blaring, zoomed behind. The first stopped in front of Chaucer's Ghost, narrowly missing the patrol vehicle. The rest did not deviate from their target. Bystanders on the streets backed away from the curbs and watched the chase as a dog might watch a ball.

Dixon took out his revolver, dumped its darts onto the floorboard, and loaded a magazine full of live ammunition.

Lila grabbed his chin, her eyes wide. "No. You can't shoot people. We're not Roman barbarians."

Dixon batted away her hands. He retrieved his darts and shoved them into his pockets, then spun around in his seat, watching the parade of cruisers following them. He cocked his gun, popped out of the window, and brought the revolver up to fire.

His scarf slipped. He didn't bother to fix it. His gaze had stopped on a teen in an overstuffed indigo coat, standing on the corner. Her blonde hair shook back and forth as she watched the chase.

He mouthed something, a curse with no breath behind it.

"She's right. You can't shoot out their tires without hitting someone on the street. Who's out at one o'clock in the morning, anyway?"

"They are," Lila said, pulling out her computer.

"Yeah, well, they need to stay home next time." He yanked his palm from his pocket and tapped out a number. "I need teams two and three down on Harris now," he ordered, voice much calmer than his driving. "I'll be passing through in two minutes. Be there."

He dropped the palm computer into his lap and jerked the wheel, turning down a street whose lamps still functioned. Mostly. The militia cruisers did not follow as closely any longer, but Lila heard more sirens on the way.

The entire third shift of the Wilson militia must have been sent out to capture them.

Lila opened the laptop and stretched her fingers.

"What are you doing?" Tristan asked.

"I'm going to try and scramble the Wilson's communication system. I just need you to drive back around to—"

"Are you serious?" Tristan slammed the laptop shut and shoved it to the floorboard. "I'm not turning around."

"Right now, they have the advantage. They're going to work together to lead us somewhere and corner us. If they can't talk to one another, then they can't do that, and we'll have the advantage."

"I'm not driving back!"

Lila leaned back into the seat. "Shortsighted little—"

"Same to you," Tristan snapped, sneaking a peek in the rearview mirror. "I can't believe they're doing this for a stupid B&E."

"It's not for a B&E. Someone detonated a bomb two nights ago in front of the capitol, or have you forgotten? They don't know that we weren't planting a bomb in that restaurant. Any security chief with any sense will do whatever it takes to capture us now in case we did. If she's on duty, she'll be at the scene or in one of those cruisers, tailing after us."

"So this is all my fault?"

"Do you know of someone else who detonated a—"

"What will they find if they review the network logs?"

"Nothing. My snoop programs scrubbed them clean as soon as I slipped out of Liberté. They changed the logs to make it look like I had downloaded a flood of tentacle porn."

"Tentacle porn?"

Tristan and Dixon's heads swiveled in unison.

"Keep your eyes on the road, damn it!"

"I am," Tristan yelled. "How long will it take for them to figure out what you were really up to?"

"If they were really good and they guessed what I was up to? A few weeks. However, the Wilson militia has never been that great at computer security."

"What do we do then?"

"If we get out of this, then *we* don't do anything at all. *I* do. *I* go and talk to Chairwoman Wilson. *I* push her to do something stupid."

"Like track us down and put a bullet in our heads?"

"Are you volunteering?"

A black truck swung out behind them as they crossed Harris Street. Lila whipped her head around as another street brought another truck. The second nearly sideswiped them in its haste to join in the chase, and a few people on the sidewalks jumped back, flattening themselves against the buildings. One brave soul didn't flee. Instead he cheered, hooted, and laughed. When Lila looked in the rearview mirror after they passed, he'd begun to gesture lewdly at the Wilson cruisers with his brown paper bag.

The trucks that joined them were the same make, model, and color as theirs. Neither had license plates. Tristan flicked a switch near the radio. Lila heard a tiny motor flip on in the bed of the truck.

"You flipped the plate?" she asked. "Your black truck fetish makes so much more sense now."

"It's about time. Duck."

"What?"

"Duck!"

Dixon grabbed her head and shoved it into his lap, then huddled over her. Their heads disappeared below the seats.

Lila found herself in a very interesting position.

"This only works if they get confused," Tristan explained, retrieving a baseball cap from the dash and shoving it over his head.

The drivers of the trucks, all wearing the same cap, played hopscotch down the street, swerving into each other's lanes and scrambling their positions. After a couple of streets, one of the trucks broke off to the left as Tristan turned right. The last truck continued straight.

The militia struggled. The drivers were too slow to realize what had happened and sort out who should go where. Two cruisers went straight.

Only one turned right after them, tires squealing, back fishtailing before righting itself, catching, and trudging on.

Tristan floored it. "Two down, one to go," he said, jerking the wheel. The truck flew down an alley.

The cruiser followed.

A dull *plink* sounded against the tailgate.

"They're shooting bullets now?"

"They wouldn't dare. It was just a GPS tag." Lila reached inside her front pocket and switched on her jammer, hoping it could scramble the device. "I turned on my jammer, but I—"

Tristan spun the truck into an alley, nearly clipping a fire hydrant. The cruiser following them wasn't so lucky. It raked against the hydrant and clipped the wall of a lowborn shop.

The frame dented as it struck. The engine stalled.

Tristan punched the gas and flew into the next intersection. "Dixon, did you get Toxic's laptop?"

He gave a thumbs-up.

"Good. We're coming up on the garage. When we stop, take the laptops and head to the bikes. I'll take Lila and the others back to the shop."

Tristan slowed down in front of a four-story parking garage. He braked, hopped out, and raced to the back of his truck, squinting at the tailgate while Dixon ran for the bikes.

Lila cursed and jumped out as Tristan knocked the GPS off the truck.

"You don't just leave them. Make them work for you," she said, kicking the tracker into the sewer, hoping it would carry the chip away in a stream of sludge.

Tristan skirted the truck and yanked open the driver's-side door. "Get back in, hurry!"

"It's better if Toxic and I aren't found together. She's a hacker. It wouldn't be a stretch for someone to put two and two together if we're both caught."

Tristan stopped and spun around. "Get in the truck, you stupid woman. What are you going to do? Run away on foot?"

The sirens roared nearby, closing in.

"It's safer for us all. Get back to the shop. I'll meet you there."

"You can't be serious. Get in. I can't keep you safe if—"

"I'm not one of your people, Tristan. I don't need you to keep me safe."

Dixon spun around, already halfway down the street. He sensed the trouble brewing between Lila and Tristan, and motioned for her to come with him instead.

Both men stared at her expectantly, as if they wanted her to choose.

Lila spun and jogged down the street, ripping off her mesh hood as she raced away.

Dixon shouted, emitting an incomprehensible noise, half word, half rebuke.

Lila had never heard him try to speak before.

She wheeled around, eyeing the frowning Dixon, his eyebrows low.

Lila could barely form words. "Go. Both of you. Now!" she shouted, before scrambling into an alley next to the garage. It would be just another getaway for her in a world of getaways. Just another night, hiding after a job.

"Fuck!" Tristan kicked the truck's tires. He took several steps toward her, then glanced at the sleeping figures in the truck bed. Giving one last kick, he yelled for Dixon to get to his bike. He jumped back into the front seat, pulled out into traffic, and drove away.

A cruiser bounded along, narrowly missing Tristan's escape. They turned the wrong way, barreling forward as though they had his location.

Lila hoped they didn't.

Before she moved out, a motorcycle pulled out of the garage. Dixon circled the block several times before he too gave up. He finally rushed off in the opposite direction, bound for the shop.

Lila breathed easier, listening to the sirens, none of them nearby. She turned down a side street, thrust her newsboy cap on her head, and slid from shadow to shadow, just like any other workborn out for a solitary stroll.

17

Lila spent the next hour walking from street to street, hiding among a thinning crowd of Thursday night revelers. Wrapped in scarves and warm coats, each stumbled back home from bars or their lovers' embraces. Half the horde preyed on the other half, and she saw at least a dozen pickpockets working the streets. The whores tipped their collars as they passed her, desperate for a last transaction or an hour away from the cold. They didn't even notice the soft planes of her face. That inattention was likely why they were still on the street so late.

Others noticed her too, or at least her limp, thinking she was an easy mark until they saw the gun in her front coat pocket. Once the adrenaline had left her, her ankle had begun to throb, still sore after her misguided leap across the alleyway and all the running after. In addition, her heels had rubbed against the leather in her cheap boots and scraped against her blisters.

It beat a holding cell, though. If she had been caught, her mother would not spare a moment's thought at distancing her from the family. Chairwoman Wilson had exiled Alex out of anger, but Beatrice would do it out of preservation, out of necessity. It would be the most efficient solution to a new liability. One must think of the family before the individual.

Lila checked the time on her palm. A quarter to two. Her fingers twitched once again, keen to summon a taxi. Several had passed already that night, but she hadn't bothered to flag one down. She didn't have enough cash. She couldn't call for one of her people to pick her up, either. Too many questions.

She slipped her palm back into her pocket and continued on, stretching her sore ankle, wrapping her coat more tightly to fight the cold. She'd just have to make it to the shop on her own. It was only another one or two kilometers away.

The familiar purr of a Firefly turned the corner. A silver Firefly. Her silver Firefly. A helmet obscured the rider's face. Was it Tristan? Dixon? Someone else?

Did she care?

The bike sidled up next to her on the abandoned street. Its rider cut the engine, and Lila gratefully stopped beside it.

The rider took off his helmet.

"Why are you limping again?" Tristan frowned.

"It's nothing," she answered, grabbing on to a streetlight for support. "I just walked on it funny."

"You should have holed up somewhere and called me."

"How was I supposed to know you'd answer? I tried to call you after the Bullstow job, and you ignored me. I tried to call you tonight, and you ignored me. How would I know you'd actually pick up this time?"

Tristan closed his mouth and stared at the kill switch. "I shouldn't have ignored you before, but I would have come and picked you up if you needed me."

"That almost sounded like an apology. Why are you here, and on my bike, no less?"

"Shirley's team is already taking everything we used tonight and prepping for new paint jobs. She's pretty pissed she's having to redo it so soon."

"You could have ridden your Amazon."

"I could have, but I knew you'd recognize your Firefly. I got worried something had happened to you. I thought maybe you'd been pinched. I've been driving around for the last half-hour looking."

"Where are the others?" Lila asked, stretching her ankle.

"One of the trucks is still out, but they shook off the militia. They're just lying low until they can work their way around back to the shop. Fry and Dice made it back on the bikes before I did. Doc says Toxic and Frank will be fine, by the way. They're in a spare room back at the shop, sleeping."

"And Dixon?"

"He's fine too." Tristan shifted on her bike and squeezed the grips, head ducked low. "Look, Lila. I wanted to talk to you about Dixon. This thing you're starting up with him—tread carefully. He doesn't get mixed up with women often. Certainly not highborn women. He didn't even know who you were at first, or it wouldn't have gotten started up in the first place."

"Because highborn women are horrible monsters?"

"Occasionally, some are. Look, just don't… If you aren't into him, don't lead him on."

Lila stopped mid-stretch. "Okay, Mother."

"Don't mock me."

"Don't leave yourself open to it. Dixon's a big boy. I think he can manage his sex life on his own. I know I can."

"Don't you think he's got enough shit to deal with?"

"Yeah, I pity him."

"Pity? He doesn't need your damn pity."

"Sure he does. He has to live with you, doesn't he? I couldn't imagine the horror. Now slide back. You're on my bike. A bike I actually paid money for."

Tristan reluctantly scooted back, and Lila swung her leg over. She put on her helmet, which he'd stuffed into netting behind him. She barely felt it when Tristan put his hands on her waist.

"If you don't hold on tighter than that, you're going to fall off. I really don't want to see your temper when I start laughing my ass off about it."

He gripped her a bit tighter. She smelled his soap, the hint of whiskey, and the shop. His scent and touch were so inviting that she had to stop herself from leaning back into him. It was so inviting that she had trouble thinking about anything else while she rode. His warmth upon her back, his arms on her hips.

The vibrating motor between her legs.

She definitely needed a vacation. After she wrapped up the Wilson case, she'd take a week off and head to some highborn resort a million kilometers away from New Bristol, the security office, her mother, the High Council, the next season, Tristan. She wouldn't even have to worry about condoms. Alex would slip them in her luggage for her.

She'd done it before.

When they rounded the corner onto Shippers Lane, Dixon pushed off the wall and flung open the dock door. The pair rode into the shop, narrowly avoiding Shirley and her team, who'd already removed several panels off the first truck.

Two small, mismatched socks poked out an open tailgate of another, and a flash of ginger peeked out of a blanket at the other end.

"Couldn't get him to his bedroll. Had to move it down here. He says he wants to help," Shirley grunted. "Told him I'd wake him up later so that he could learn how to sand down the paint. It put him back to sleep, at least for a while."

"He won't sleep easy until everyone's back," Tristan said. "Not for a long time yet. He'll either grow out of it, or he won't."

Dixon pointed up.

"Yeah, let's go," Tristan called out to Lila, who parked her Firefly away from the dock door and Shirley's work.

Lila took off her helmet, slipped on her hood, and trudged after the two men.

Tristan poured himself a whiskey as soon as they reached his apartment. "I want a copy of that data," he demanded, filling a mug with Sangre for Lila. "Dixon?"

He pointed to Lila's mug, and Tristan handed him the rest of the bottle.

Dixon tipped it back and breathed out slowly at the taste.

Lila had to agree with Dixon's sentiment. She almost felt spoiled by a second round of Sangre in the same day. "I'll give you the data I found on Teach, but it's not going to help you any," she said, removing her hood.

"You let me be the judge of that. We might find something that you didn't, especially if we cross-reference it with the data we took from Slack & Roberts."

"I wouldn't mind seeing that data myself." Lila slid her star drive into the waiting computer on his coffee table. She uploaded Teach's account history and sipped her wine while the files from the law office saved to her drive. "You should move everyone out of the city, especially after tonight."

"Screw that. We live here. This is our home. We're not going to run. No one saw our faces today."

"What about the bombing?"

"They didn't see them then, either."

"Yeah, but my father—"

"I'll think of something before Monday. I always do."

What next? Dixon wrote on his notepad.

"I'm going to speak with Chairwoman Wilson tomorrow."

"And if you don't find out anything?" Tristan's *if* sounded more like a *when*.

"It's my business to find out things. Let me worry about that."

"I'm not a man who's fond of being handled. This is my job, remember? I brought it to you."

"Yes, I'm assisting."

"Assisting me or taking over? Do you even know the difference?"

Lila drained the rest of her mug and grabbed her satchel, ignoring his taunt. "May I change somewhere?"

Tristan waved his arm absently toward his bedroom.

His new room was very much like his old one back at the hotel. He owned very little, just a bed and a dresser. A dented filing cabinet tilted in the corner, rusted at the top. Papers poked out from several of the drawers. Weapons were strewn about: knives, bows, guns of various calibers, even a mace nailed to the wall, perhaps for decoration. The string of bottle caps hung on a peg near the window, all containing letters and numbers scribbled inside with permanent black marker. Lila had studied them once, trying to figure out Tristan's code, but it was impossible to tell what they meant. She had her suspicions. Something so innocuous could contain valuable information, a way of passing information to Dixon or the rest of his people should something happen to him.

Lila didn't like to think about it.

She changed clothes quickly and instantly felt more like herself. She wished she had grabbed her militia boots before she left that evening, but that small comfort would have to wait.

She emerged moments later with her bundled workborn clothes and stuffed them back into the satchel. She handed it to Tristan before sitting on the couch beside Dixon, who had poured her another glass of wine. "Last one, okay?"

Dixon offered her a small, mischievous smile.

"I mean it."

"What is this?" Tristan said, holding her satchel awkwardly by the strap.

"I need someone to wash them"

"You want us to do your laundry now? We aren't your slaves, chief."

"I'm not asking you to be, but I can't exactly have the house staff wash them. My mother left instructions for them to throw away any unmarked clothing, just to make my extracurricular activities more difficult. I'd use the cleaners I normally do, except that they reek of smoke and gasoline."

"That's not my problem."

"Isn't it? I thought you wanted my help. You have machines for this, don't you? Just get one of your people to toss them in."

"These people aren't my slaves either." Tristan tossed the satchel back to her. The flap came loose in midair, and her clothes scattered across the floor. The smell of gasoline rose up from the sooty mess. "I'm not yours, either."

"Why must everything be a fight with you? Why do you take everything so personally?"

"How am I supposed to take it?"

"It's just business."

"Business? I forgot. You're a highborn heir. Everything is always business for you," he said. "While we're on the subject again, stop shooting down my orders in front of the others. It subverts my leadership and makes everyone confused. It's also annoying."

"I'm not going to apologize for having better plans. Here's some advice: if you want to be a better leader, think before you blurt out your thoughts and stop being so sensitive."

"Would you say that to another chief? To one of your commanders? Do you undercut them all the time?"

"My commanders think before they act."

"Of course, because everyone is so perfect on your highborn—"

Dixon held up his notepad. *Relax. She hacked Liberté for us.*

"You're taking her side?"

Dixon shook his head.

"Good. She didn't do it for us, and you know it. She doesn't do anything if there's not something in it for her. Don't ever forget that."

Dixon stood and returned Lila's clothes to the satchel. He pointed to himself, winked at Lila, and hung her satchel on his doorknob.

Tristan shook his head. "Tread carefully, Dixon." He retreated to the window and took a long pull on his whiskey.

Dixon pulled Lila up from the couch with a laugh and put his hand around her waist. He twirled her around the room until she giggled alongside him, dancing to imaginary music, still hobbling on her ankle but not caring one bit. They seemed to hear the same tune, and she leaned back perfectly when he dipped her. She might have been at the Closing Ball, dancing with a highborn senator.

"Stop fooling around, Dixon. We need to talk about tomorrow."

Dixon ignored Tristan. Instead, he scooped up Lila, a still giggling Lila, and pushed her against him, holding her close. All at once, he tilted her chin and pressed his mouth to hers.

Lila closed her eyes this time, sliding her fingers around Dixon's neck, letting out a little moan when he sucked on her lip and bit down, just enough to make her gasp.

She smelled…nothing. Nothing but La Sangre de Las Flores.

When she opened her eyes, Dixon pulled away, twirling her once more around the room.

Their dancing didn't seem as lively as before. The steps weren't as fluid. She hadn't even been thinking of Dixon as they kissed.

She was mostly thinking about getting laid.

"What did you mean about—" Lila said, turning, but Tristan had already gone into his bedroom and closed the door.

Dixon chuckled at his absence and plucked Lila's riding jacket off the back of the couch, helping her put it on. He then grabbed her hand and led her out the window in the corridor and onto the fire escape, checking first that no one was around to glimpse her face.

He motioned for her to sit beside him and put his arm around her shoulders, warming them both up. His breath heated her cheek and came out in smoky wisps from the chill. His stubble brushed against her skin.

"Dixon, we need to talk," she said, trying to ignore how nicely his body felt against hers. She pulled away, but he stiffened and held her in place.

He gave her a little squeeze and pulled out his notepad, writing with one hand in the dim light that streamed through the window in the hall. *I know. It's cold, though.*

"What do you know?"

That we would never work.

Lila sighed. "That's not what I was going to say, Dixon."

We're friends. I know. I feel the same way.

She turned in his grasp and stared at his face. "What on earth are you doing, then?"

He grinned and scrawled on his notepad. This time, Lila watched him as he wrote every word. *I said I wanted to kiss you. I didn't mean I wanted more.*

"Why?"

Jealousy is a powerful motivator.

A hammer hit Lila's chest as she read his simple words. Dixon and Tristan always roomed together, always seemed to finish each other's thoughts, and always moved with the precision of one person. Other things came to her, like Tristan's annoyance after Dixon had kissed her and his constant overprotectiveness toward his friend.

"Wait a minute. You and Tristan are together?"

Dixon's jaw opened so wide that she could make out the small nub of his tongue in the back of his mouth. "No!" he mouthed, then wrote it out, adding many gratuitous exclamation marks. *Gross. He's my brother.*

"There's nothing gross about—"

Dixon pointed at *brother* again, then *gross.*

"Wait? He's really your brother? As in you both share a parent, you're not just friends?"

Dixon nodded.

"Same mom?"

Dixon shook his head.

Lila leaned back into the building. Tristan's father had been a highborn. She could only guess at the man's morality now that she knew he had slept with two slaves on his family's estate. It wasn't wrong for the highborn to bed the poorer classes; it wasn't even wrong to intermarry, though it made life more difficult for the couple. It was only immoral for a highborn male to have unprotected sex with a female slave, creating children forced to grow up in servitude. No wonder Tristan and Dixon felt bitterness toward the highborn. Their father had used his slaves for more than just work.

That was no highborn man. Not a proper one, anyway.

"Who are you, Dixon? I could never figure it out. It shouldn't be hard to find the identity of a man like you, but no slave children aged out of the Holguín estate who met your description. Only Tristan's."

Dixon shrugged. *Mystery.* He winked.

Lila didn't like that answer. Her mind flashed back to the dance around the apartment and how he had twirled her so perfectly. It was as though he had been born to do it, as though he practiced, as though he'd been tutored by a dance master. "Just now, when you danced. That was a waltz. A perfect waltz. You've had training." Her mouth opened wide and she stood up, still shocked. "You're not from the poorer classes at all. You're a highborn. Your father was highborn, and so was your mother."

Sit down.

Lila sat.

Long story.

"You had a slave chip."

He tapped *long story* again with his finger. It was clear he would not tell the story that night, but it didn't matter all that much.

Lila could do her own search.

I know you, he wrote, seeing her expression. *Don't dig into my past. I'll tell you some other time.*

"When?"

Dixon shrugged. *One day.*

Lila shook her head. "I don't know if I can promise that, Dixon. I've seen the marks on your back and your tongue. How does a highborn man end up like that, much less a slave?"

Try? For me?

"I still don't understand why you kissed me like that. Twice now. That wasn't a kiss between friends, Dixon."

No, it was a kiss between highborns. He pointed back to the top. *Jealousy is a powerful motivator.*

"For what? Whose jealously?"

Tristan's.

"So Tristan would be jealous of whom?"

Me. I can't talk, but I'm not blind. He walks into a room, you look. You walk into a room, he looks. I'm tired of the looking and the fighting. Fuck already.

Lila coughed. "What the—"

Dixon pointed to *fuck already.*

Lila's face grew warm. "Why would you even think—"

He pointed once more. *I can't talk, but I'm not blind. Jealously is a powerful motivator.*

"Jealousy? If this was just about making Tristan jealous, why did you spend a year trying to figure out who I was?"

To see if you were worthy. Don't worry. You passed that test. He paused for a moment, considering his words carefully before beginning again. *You've been so busy that you've walled yourself off from men, and I bet you never even noticed. Someone had to wake you up.*

Lila ignored the last bit. "It's not like that with us. We can barely stand each other."

He only fights because he doesn't know how to ask for what he wants.

It was hard for Lila to understand that. She walked into rooms every moment of every day, not just asking, but demanding. She didn't ask for obedience; she expected it from everyone around her. She placed those who did not offer it into two groups: those who should be demoted because they couldn't handle authority, and those who were to be promoted, for they were intelligent enough to have better solutions than hers and fight for them. She tried to surround herself with the latter sort. She valued them. She needed them in her position. "That doesn't make any sense."

Slaves can't ask. Dixon scratched out his words before beginning again. *Slaves can ask, but they'll never get. Not from the highborn. He's okay with others, but with the highborn, he's stuck in the past.*

"I don't—"

He told me you're quitting. You'll be gone soon. He's running out of time. He's still not asking for what he wants, and he's being an idiot. So are you.

"Fuck you."

He laughed. *Yes, fuck. If you can't stand him, then why are you blushing? Why do you look?*

Lila ignored his question.

Dixon doodled on the side of the page for a few minutes before scrawling. *He always lets me have what I want even when he wants it more.*

"Why?"

Slave's habit? Because he loves me? Sometimes he should love himself more, don't you think?

Lila rested her cheek on Dixon's shoulder, not knowing what to say. He squeezed her closer, and they looked up at the stars for a time. She nearly drifted away to dreams despite the cold. It was then that Lila understood why she enjoyed being around Dixon so very much.

He calmed her. He quieted the whirring and clinking in her mind. His silence and the silence it created within soothed her like a warm fire on a cold night. He had always been difficult to turn away from.

Tristan flicked the switch, made it spin in double time. He tired her out.

"You're impossible, Dixon."

No, just improbable. Don't think well of me. I wanted bragging rights. I won't ever let him forget that I kissed you first. Not ever.

Lila poked his ribs, and Dixon squirmed and laughed. In the alley below, Samantha looked up from her patrol.

"I have to go, Dixon," she said, hiding her face. "Thanks for taking care of my clothes."

No problem. Tristan and the others are proud. It meant more than laundry to him. Try to remember that.

Lila nodded and ducked back through the window.

18

Lila slipped on her fluffy white robe and flopped down on the edge of the wet tub, applying ointment and a few bandages to her heels. Her stomach churned at the smell. She had stayed up all night digging into the second Liberté account, an account owned by Sun Leasing Company, a company in name only. It possessed no ties to any highborn or lowborn companies in the commonwealth, not even in the empire as far as she could tell, and there was no trace of an owner or receptionist. Even the company's address had been a lie, for it belonged to a small museum up north, a museum devoted to a long-dead composer.

While the account holder had been careful, the people sending money or receiving it might have been sloppy. Lila soon turned her attention to them, hoping for a break. Natalie Holguín, along with scores of others, had been making regular payments to the company on the first of every month. Lila might have dismissed the payments as rent, but the amounts were too high. Why had a leasing company paid off two blackcoats, anyway? Why had it paid off Slack & Roberts? They were lawyers who specialized in criminal law, not real estate.

Why did several of the accounts seem so damn familiar?

It hadn't been until she received the sixth alert on her palm that she realized where she'd seen them before.

The BIRD job.

She'd pulled up the folder on her desktop computer immediately, nearly kicking herself for not realizing the connection at Chaucer's Ghost. The folder contained all the information her father had sent her for the BIRD job. Lila had done extensive research on every highborn that had been bribed. She'd then made a list of their bank account numbers, looking for patterns.

It didn't take her long to track down the two familiar accounts. One belonged to Bo Park, a distant cousin of Suji Park. Chairwoman Weberly's niece owned the other.

Natalie Holguín also graced the list.

The three names and accounts could not be a coincidence.

Sun Leasing belonged to Zephyr.

That meant that Muller and Davies also worked for the snoop, just like Slack & Roberts.

When the seventh alert hit her palm, she hadn't let it fluster her. She just needed a bit more time. Zephyr might be racing through the layers of her fake identity, but the snoop still had to put together those small inconsistencies, the bits she did not have the access to change, like a photograph torn into pieces must be reassembled to glimpse the whole.

This photograph would not reveal a person, though; it would only reveal an amalgam of personalities. Pieces that could never quite fit together, slightly jagged and mismatched, shreds of different portraits of different people.

The finished photograph would give Prolix away in the end.

But that wouldn't happen until Zephyr tried to put it together and recognized something was wrong with the data. It wouldn't be possible, shouldn't be possible, until all the layers had been stripped away.

Only five remained.

But Lila had found Zephyr's trail at last.

Unfortunately, she still had a day job. A day job that required more attention than she could give it at the moment, and required several cups of coffee to attempt. She dressed and returned to her office on a nearly healed ankle, handling the most urgent reports first, letting the rest of her paperwork pile higher and higher.

Luckily, Commander Sutton picked up the slack, becoming concerned when Lila did not rush down to the cafeteria at breakfast.

Lila only skipped waffles or pancakes when she was sick or stressed or busy.

To her credit, Sutton didn't ask for an explanation. She slipped a plate of food on Lila's desk and took a stack of reports, asking if she might have the pleasure of handling the ten o'clock commanders' meeting.

Then she'd kicked Lila out of her office before noon, shooing her back to the great house for lunch.

Lila didn't complain; she'd intended to return all along.

She strolled back into the great house five minutes before noon and wiped her boots on the front mat, declining to surrender her blackcoat to Isabel. The workborn had been cleaning a vase when she entered. Isabel bowed nervously as Lila padded deeper into the house and closer to the worst sort of racket. The noise emanating from the kitchen rivaled the most petulant teenager's room. A pop-punk tune blared through the speakers, each verse sung in French while the chorus blurred by in rapid-fire Spanish. Chef bobbed at the counter, tilting a large metal bowl, and whisked its contents in time to the beat. A bag of chocolate chips perched precariously on the edge of the counter.

Lila frowned, a bit annoyed that she had pressing business on the Wilson compound. One never missed Chef's cookies.

Not ever.

Alex paused mid-chuckle from her perch on a barstool and turned down the music to a dull throb. "Chef's making cookies."

"I can see that."

"Her cookies are so much better than Chef Louisa's." Alex's fingers darted toward the bag for a chocolate chip.

"You can compliment me all you want. You're still a vulture." Chef smacked Alex's knuckles with her whisk. Chunks of dough sprayed the counter.

"I stopped trying things like that when I was seven," Lila said, and kissed Chef's cheek. "Apparently you're a slow learner, Alex. Chef's sweet as sugar, but one does not steal nibbles from her."

Alex slumped on her barstool and rubbed the back of her hand. "I take it back. Your cooking is horrible."

"I wouldn't say things you don't mean. Chef has an annoyingly long memory."

Chef measured out a space between her hands, then kept extending it and extending it.

"Yes, yes, I get it! Smartasses. Both of you."

"I like our side better." Lila grinned at Chef, peeking at the dough.

"I think Chef should open her own restaurant, don't you, Lila? Then I could just buy her cookies no matter what I've said or done. She'd make twice the credits she makes now, maybe more."

"I don't have the money to go into business for myself."

"I've told you a million times that I'd invest," Lila reminded her, hopping up on the counter. "I'd even let you buy me out later as long as I get to eat free for the rest of my life."

Chef fixed her with a glare, and Lila quickly abandoned the counter for a barstool. "Just say the word, and we'll go look at properties."

"Why on earth would I do that? If I went bankrupt, I'd lose my mark."

"So? Mother would buy you back in a heartbeat. She increased your salary by fifty percent after Chairwoman Holguín offered you a contract. There's no way she'd let you go to someone else no matter how much anyone bid. You'd just have to stay with us for the rest of your life as a slave. How is that any different than now?"

"All I'd have would be pocket money from my slave's stipend and no mark. I couldn't even leave the compound or use a palm without permission. Owning a business is overrated. It's a fool's game, and I'm too old to play it." Chef tossed a few handfuls of chocolate chips into the bowl and began to stir them into the dough.

"What if the Slave Bill passes?"

"What if it does? I'm happy where I am. My servant's contract is exceedingly generous."

"Yeah, but you'd be the boss," Alex said. "No one would be able to tell you what to do or where to—"

"Except for every customer who comes through the door, complaining that their soup is too hot or too cold, that their entrée is too salty or not salty enough, that the cookies don't have enough chocolate chips or that they have too many."

"Blasphemy," Lila interjected.

"Right now, I cook for the most influential family in all of Saxony, and not a one of them complains unless I cook liver."

"Jewel complains all the time," Alex pointed out.

"That's President Randolph to you, young lady," Chef corrected her sternly. "And she doesn't count. When someone complains all the time, no one listens. What's in a business for me, anyway? What's the point if I'll only chase my tail every hour of every day? My kids are grown. If they want to want to be lowborn, they'll have to earn it on their own."

Lila knew Chef's children, had played with them as a kid, even though both of them were slightly older. One had become a nurse, the other a phlebotomist, both acquiring jobs at Randolph General. It had only taken a whisper into the right ear to ensure they were hired. Chef suspected. Her children did not.

Both had been affected by their elder sister's illness and death, prompting them to enter the medical field. Lila would do anything to keep that sort of talent and motivation at Randolph General.

Besides, they'd earned their place.

"Just say the word, Chef. If you ever change your mind, I'll help make it happen."

"You're a good kid when you aren't being a bossy, sarcastic little grouch," Chef said, patting her cheek.

Lila's lips crooked in a smile. "You forgot sneaky." She held up a handful of chocolate chips and backed out of reach of Chef's whisk. She popped them in her mouth and sighed theatrically. "Come on, Alex. I'll take you to Violet's. We'll get some proper chocolate."

"Really?"

"You won't get any cookies today after such slights, and neither will I."

"I'd give you a cookie, but only one. I'm sure there's a clause in my contract about it. You're vultures, both of you."

Alex had stopped listening. She was too intent on Lila's face. She hopped off her barstool and followed Lila, stopping only to collect her coat.

After the pair reached the garage, Alex leaned against Lila's silver Adessi roadster and refused to go any farther. "You didn't ask me to come with you for chocolate. You want something. I can see it in your eyes."

"I didn't try to hide it."

"I know. Out with it."

Lila slid her fingers over the glossy paint of the antique car, stalling. "Yesterday we talked about you visiting your mother."

"I remember. I was there." Alex stiffened. "My answer is the same as yesterday. I have nothing to say to that woman."

"I remember. Unfortunately, I have to ask you again."

"Why?"

"Because I need a ticket into your mother's office."

Alex's eyes narrowed. "Is that why you asked me yesterday?"

"No. I did that because Simon wanted me to, but late last night some information came into my possession. That information has led me to your mother. I need to see her, and I need a way to do it without stirring up tensions between the Wilsons and the Randolphs. You're the only way I can think of, not unless I want to wait until the season starts. That's more than a month away, though. It might be too late then."

"Why do you need to see her?"

"I have a few questions."

"You're talking like she's some suspect you've found trespassing on Randolph property. What is this about, Lila?"

"You already know what it's about."

Alex studied Lila's face. It took several moments for her face to lighten. "Simon? This is about my brother?"

"Of course. What else would it be about?"

"You won't convince my mother to budge on Simon. She's too hardheaded."

"I'm not going there to convince her. If I'm right, then the end result of this meeting could result in Simon's freedom."

"Oh," Alex said, mulling over the implications. "It's bad, isn't it? What she's done?"

Lila nodded. "I'm not going to bullshit you. If I'm right, your mother is involved in something serious. She'll go to trial, and she'll likely be hanged. You'll be part of what tied the noose around her neck. You don't have to be a part of this. It's a heavy burden."

"It's also a heavy prize. Maybe she deserves it. Maybe I want to be involved."

"You don't mean that."

"What if I do? Do you think you were the only one who played games with her matron? Some of us weren't so lucky. Some of us would still be playing if…" Alex brushed a bit of flour from her skirt. "What makes you think that she'll even see me?"

"She'll do it to save face. The season is coming. There's no telling what I might say if I'm annoyed with her, no telling what rumors I might spread and who I might spread them to. She'll want our business long concluded before the season starts. She needs willing senators if she's going to have an heir."

Alex rubbed the little scar on her neck, the healed over imprint of her slave's chip. Healed, but marked and not forgotten. "I'll do it. I'll help you."

"Are you sure?"

"I'm highborn," she said, drawing herself up to her full height. "Daughter of Senator Elias Hardwicke-Craft and prime to the Wilson Empire. Becoming a slave hasn't dulled or rusted my mettle. I might not walk among you any longer, but my nature hasn't changed."

Lila took down a set of keys from a peg near the door, unlocking the Adessi. While Alex buckled up, Lila connected her palm to the vehicle's port. One of her programs came up immediately, allowing her to disengage the GPS system. She then used the palm to locate and toss out all bugs she found hidden inside the roadster.

Lila patted her pocket, which contained the bug stolen from her motorcycle. She had played with it after dinner while waiting for Tristan's call the night before. It only responded to her and her receiver now. She had learned well from her mother and her commander.

Lila pulled out of the garage and passed by the gatehouse, waving to Sergeant Hill and his rookie. The radio in the Adessi had been tuned to opera, and neither woman reached out to change it. Not even Alex, who loathed such music. She remained quiet as they drove through the city, head cocked to one side, eyes roaming the streets, the buildings, the cars, the signs. She studied life outside the compound hungrily, as it was something she rarely saw unless Lila had time to take her out. Her hands sat in her lap, thumb tapping, betraying her thoughts.

Too soon, they reached the crumbling Wilson estate. A battering ram or a semi might have bent the front gate, given the large dent in the center. Engineers had replaced a bolt in one of the bottom hinges with a thick beam of steel the size of an infant's arm. Dark smudges marred the Wilson coat of arms on the gate, two intertwined serpents ready to strike. Someone had welded it back together after a bad break. *Make Your Own Good Fortune* peeked beneath the weld. Wires flowed out of the instrument panel in the guard post beside them, some taped together with worn duct tape.

The gate's electronic lock sparked suddenly, arcing into the sky in a sizzling blue light.

Alex's brows rose. "You've been sparing my feelings, haven't you?"

"What good would it have done you?"

"I'm an adult, Lila, not a child."

A guard knocked on the car window—a sergeant, by the stars on his collar.

"Name?" he asked when Lila rolled down the window. His voice was bored and hoarse, as though he had been yelling all night. He clicked the tip of a pen and started writing the time on his clipboard.

Lila rested her elbow on the window. "Elizabeth Victoria Lemaire-Randolph and Alexandra Craft-Wilson, here to see the chairwoman."

The guard dropped his clipboard to his thigh and stared back and forth between the two women. "Do you have an appointment?" he asked, face paling, voice rising.

"No."

"Please state your business."

"My business is none of yours. Tell Chairwoman Wilson that I am here to escort her daughter into the compound. See that she accepts a meeting, or I'll remember you when my family takes over, sergeant."

The blackcoat wheeled around and sprinted back into the guard post. He yanked an earpiece from the wall and shouted into it, gesturing into the air.

Soon after, the gate opened.

The sergeant did not return.

Lila drove into the compound. A Wilson militia cruiser sat on the other side, waiting to follow them in.

Her initial amusement faded quickly, for the inside of the estate was much worse than she could have imagined. Chairwoman Wilson had shuttered half the buildings, chained the entrances, boarded up the windows, then left them for the elements and scurrying beasts to claim. The broken roofs had been ignored, as had the crumbling bricks and splintered doors. Wilson's disgruntled family had done the rest, tagging them with more graffiti than a workborn slum. The word *waiting* crept up frequently, written in block letters, as did *existing* with a giant question mark. Here and there, a red phoenix had been stenciled, no larger than Lila's palm.

Even the buildings still in use had not escaped the barrage. Only plywood and an open door told the difference between them.

The destruction had started before Alex left the compound, but her leaving had greatly exaggerated it. She cringed at every corner, at every building, at every familiar face locked in unfamiliar circumstance.

Once upon a time, the Wilsons had been the epitome of fashion. But today, groups of teens, young adults, and the elderly plodded along, bound for nowhere in particular, dressed in fraying suits and dresses several seasons out of date. The poorer classes walked among them, donning soiled clothes several sizes too small or too large, holes at the knees and elbows.

Lila wasn't sure why the servants didn't take up contracts with other families. Perhaps there were no servants left, and these were slaves. Or perhaps these servants were the most desperate, unfit for much more than the poorest lowborn family. Everyone had to work somewhere. Everyone had to eat. Perhaps this was the best some of them could do. Perhaps they were just as trapped as the highborn.

If there had been a waiting prime, Celeste Wilson would have been assassinated by her own family for such incompetence.

Lila parked in front of Wilson Tower, surrounded on all sides by rows of empty spaces. A decade before, the lot would have been full. On a day like today, the tower should have caught the sun, glittering like a precious gem on the crown of a queen. Now a thin layer of grime covered every mirrored surface, stealing its beauty. It might have been made of plastic and paste, nothing more than a child's tiara.

A man emerged from the tower, clad in a well-worn golden blazer marked with a serpent coat of arms, hands clasped behind his back. His face lightened when he saw the women exit the vehicle, the dimple in his chin more prominent as he smiled.

"They said you were at the gate, but I didn't believe them." He picked up Alex in a large hug.

"Patrick." His sister beamed after she was returned to the pavement. "Have you seen Simon?"

"No. Mother has forbidden it, just like she forbade us from seeing you." The dark circles under Patrick's eyes didn't seem that far removed from the state of the compound. When the Randolphs took over the estate, every building would need extensive repairs and renovation. Of course, that assumed Chairwoman Randolph didn't raze the structures and rebuild it all from scratch.

It would probably be cheaper.

Patrick took his sister's arm and escorted the pair inside. They crossed over threadbare carpet, passed by peeling wallpaper, moved around the mismatched chairs in the waiting room, sliding by the spaces where priceless art had once hung on the walls. Alex stopped in front of a bright square nestled among the faded paint. "The Rembrandt. *The Mill.* It was here."

"It sold at auction last year in the Netherlands. It was one of the first to go." Patrick picked at the hole where the nail had once been. "I tried to stop her from selling it. I always thought you'd find your way back somehow, and that it should be here when you walked through the doors. Mother was adamant, though. We needed the money. I'm sorry, Alex."

"What exactly was the money used for?" Lila asked.

"Making more money, I suppose. You have to spend money to make money."

Lila and Alex locked eyes. Though Jewel's age, Patrick had always been a little dim. It was lucky he was so handsome. He'd make someone a fine husband, as long as that someone wanted a sweet, beautiful puppy.

Patrick led them to the elevator, doors marred by a long dent and a curious round indentation that looked suspiciously like a bullet hole. Patrick would not meet her eyes after she touched it. As the doors rattled shut, Lila feared that the elevator might not be strong enough to reach the top of the tower.

"A serviceman was out here last week for the annual inspection. It'll hold," Patrick assured her.

"Did it pass?"

Patrick nodded.

"With or without a bribe?"

Patrick ignored Lila's swipe.

The still-rattling doors opened directly into the chairwoman's waiting room. They were the last indication of the infection raging throughout the Wilson compound, for the twentieth floor of Wilson Tower was a genie's bottle of opulence and elegance. Cream-colored chairs lined the walls in the waiting room and matched the hand-painted wallpaper. Peace lilies sat atop mahogany tables, potted in gilded vases. Everything had been replaced recently, the entire office redecorated and renewed in keeping with current trends.

Everything but the art. The same pieces still hung proudly upon the walls.

Patrick bowed and opened a door. "I will inform the chair-woman that you are here."

Once he retired into the other room, Lila glanced at her friend. "He's become her secretary. I don't want to sound rude, Alex, but—"

"He's not bright enough?"

"Well, I wouldn't have phrased it so bluntly, but it's suspicious that she's using someone like Patrick to help her now, someone who doesn't know enough to understand when things are a bit sketchy. She's hiding something."

"I agree, and I don't like it." Alex studied the art on the walls. "These aren't the originals, you know. That Rembrandt over there? It's a forgery. A very good one, but it's still false. I used to sketch the original when I was little, whenever I was waiting for my mother to finish her work. It was worth millions. Every painting in here is gone, as are the ones downstairs. What has she done, Lila? I never thought it could get this bad."

"That's what I'm trying to figure out." Lila retired to one of the arched windows, realizing that Chairwoman Wilson must have more than one secret account if so much of her estate had been sold off. "She'll probably have us waiting at least twenty minutes. That's time to make an inventory of the property."

While they waited, Alex pointed out building after building that had been shuttered and what might have been moved or sold.

A teenage boy interrupted them mid-conversation, wheeling a mop and bucket behind him. He couldn't have been more than fifteen, but his body was small for his age.

"Hello, Oskar," Lila called out.

The boy inclined his head. "Hello, madam." He shuffled into the restroom before she could say more, face blank, eyes fixed on the sloshing water, careful not to make a mess.

"He's growing up fast, isn't he?" she asked Alex, remembering Peter Kruger well enough to recognize his son after so many years.

It was in the eyes. Exhausted. Hopeless. Dead.

"I bet my mother still makes Peter scrub the sewers. Oscar's twin sister is probably in the scullery as we speak, washing the dishes or the oven or even the walls. When I first found out I was going up for auction, I worried that I would end up like them. I still do. Sometimes it's hard for me to remember that I have it so well. Sometimes I feel like I have to do something to ensure that I'm not scrubbing sewers for the rest of my—"

A door burst open in the back of the waiting room, and Patrick returned. "The chairwoman will see you now," he said, bowing. "I'll wait for you out here."

He smiled kindly and sat on one of the cream-colored chairs, pulling out his palm. Lila wondered if it was for work or play. Probably some sort of game, knowing Patrick. What sort of work could he possibly have to do in such a place?

Alex followed Lila into the chairwoman's office, awash in gold. The woman sat upon a golden couch in a little nook to the left of her desk, a painting of a golden serpent with bared fangs on the wall behind her desk chair. The matron's silvercoat had been impeccably tailored, and the embroidered coat of arms matched the golden dress underneath. A framed Van Gogh loomed over them, with Japanese characters painted along the edges of the piece.

The chairwoman motioned to two plush chairs across from her couch, both upholstered in the same golden hue. "Speak quickly, girls. My lunch is waiting."

Alex gaped at her mother. Time had worked quickly, or perhaps it was all the medication. She had lost weight and height in the last year, and her arms and legs had dwindled in size. Her eyes bulged in their sockets, and her gray hair flowed freely past her shoulders, frizzing in the damp, foggy afternoon. It gave her a squirrel-like, neurotic appearance.

For the first time, Lila understood how Simon might have mistaken his mother for being ill. Lila had seen the chairwoman during the last season, but only in the soft light of the ballroom and only under several layers of makeup. It had been enough to hide her stress and wrinkles, but the harsh light of the office only made them worse.

The chairwoman's eyes hardened at Alex's presence. "You fought so hard to be free of me even after I warned you to be careful of what you wish for. What do you think of your new life now?"

Alex stared at the floor. "Hello, Mother."

"Don't call me that, slave. How dare you come into my home now after you've been cast out of it. Just look at what you've done to us."

The words slapped at Alex, clearly hitting their mark with more force than a fist.

"I don't believe Alex had much to do with this," Lila said. "Besides, we didn't come to visit. Simon's worried. He said you've been ill. He made me promise to bring Alex to visit you. I would have brought him along if I thought the Massons could spare him."

"You saw him?" The chairwoman crossed her legs and sat up straighter on the couch.

"Yes, I did."

"What could you possibly have to talk about with a boy ten years your junior?"

"This and that." Lila loosely held the audio bug she had palmed while in the waiting room. "Are you going to ask us to sit?"

The chairwoman waved at the padded chairs across from her, fixing her eyes on Alex with a disgruntled sneer. "Not you, slave. These chairs are new."

Lila sat down while the chairwoman's attention was on her daughter. Under the pretense of adjusting her short sword, she brushed the bug under her seat. Her finger lingered and pushed, sticking it into place firmly.

"So? How is he?" the chairwoman prompted. "I suspect he's gotten taller."

"You haven't visited him?"

"Of course I haven't. The boy turned into a delinquent. Selling black market drugs on my own property, after all my care and attention? It's reprehensible," she said. "Besides, it takes two hours to get out to Massonville and back again. I refuse to give the boy that much of my time."

"Simon didn't sell any drugs," Alex protested. "You know that he wouldn't do that."

"Oh, I don't know about that," Lila said. "People will do a lot of things for money, won't they, chairwoman?"

Alex shook her head. "Not Simon."

"What exactly are you implying, Chief Randolph?" The chairwoman intertwined her fingers in her lap. Her thumbs tapped back and forth.

"I'm not implying anything. I'm just saying that I can understand why the kid might have done it. He's always been a well-behaved, studious boy, but even well-behaved, studious boys have desires. Anyone can see that your family is struggling, so I can understand why he might have been tempted to sell a few trance tabs here and there, just to make some extra—"

"We're not struggling. And it wasn't just trance tabs."

"Is that so?"

"We're doing fine. I've shuttered a few non-productive businesses recently. I've restructured a bit of debt. We just won several new contracts. We'll be back to our former glory in no time. With a new heir. Very soon." The chairwoman's eyes narrowed into slits.

"Of course you and I understand business, but young boys rarely do. If Simon didn't understand the state of the compound, the reason why your purse had closed, he might have taken matters into his own hands. Highborn schools can be just as rough on declining families as they are on new money. You'd know about that, wouldn't you, chairwoman?"

"Your backhanded slaps are tedious, Chief Randolph."

"My apologies," Lila said, braving her friend's irritated glances. "I only meant to say that perhaps the boy wanted money for new clothes, new shoes, perhaps a new designer belt to prove his worth to his friends."

"I gave that boy everything that he wanted. How dare you come in here implying otherwise. We were and are doing fine. He had no reason to betray his family like that."

"Betray? That's a strong word, isn't it, chairwoman?"

"No. I don't think it is."

"Mother, even if he did sell drugs in that club, it was just—"

"Be quiet, slave. No one asked you to speak."

Alex sucked in her breath. To her credit, she refused to stare at the floor again.

Lila studied the chairwoman's unblinking face and her still-tapping thumb. "Bringing Alex to visit wasn't the only reason why I stopped by. My Aunt Georgina has been thinking of procuring a new software contract, something to streamline her growing bridal empire. The poorer classes do so love their weddings. If you had time for a meeting next month, I'd like to set something up. I can't guarantee that you'd win the contract, but I'll put in a good word for you during the—"

"We don't do brides."

"Really? I suspect that if I were in your shoes and it would save my family, then I'd do the rightful king of Germany."

"Lila!" Alex shouted, eyes wide.

Her name echoed in the small room, spurring the chairwoman's burning gaze. The thumb kept tapping.

"I'm sorry. That came out wrong." Lila smirked. "I just meant that no matter what state the Randolphs might be in, we'd never turn down an opportunity to make money if there was enough money to be had in a deal."

"We don't need any new deals."

"Is that true? Judging by the state of this compound, I'm under the impression that you do. In fact, you seem desperate for them."

"Mother, take the meeting," Alex pleaded. "You obviously need the—"

The chairwoman's head swiveled. "I told you to be quiet, slave. If you need an occupation, then you can join Oskar in the restrooms. We can always find toilets for our slaves to clean."

"Yes, I'm certain it takes all their effort to wade through your family's shit." Lila smiled. "I'll ask you one more time. Would you like a meeting with Aunt Georgina or not?"

"No."

"I must confess I'm surprised by your answer. It was Simon who asked about possible deals between our families. He mentioned that he couldn't please you with the deals he helped bring in. They were never the right terms or with the right sort of families. He wanted to discharge his duty to the family by bringing you a deal worthy of the highborn. He said you needed the money for something important."

Chairwoman Randolph's thumb stopped twitching. "Simon is a child. Children make mistakes."

"They certainly do. With that understanding, I have to wonder why you aren't forgiving your son for his evening of stupidity. He is a child, after all, and a mistake is just a mistake. A mistake is forgiven."

Chairwoman Wilson stood up and pointed at the door. "That will be all, Chief Randolph. My lunch is waiting."

Lila did not move from her chair. "Simon still loves you. He cried while talking about you."

"I said that will be all." Strands of hair fell into the chairwoman's eyes. She looked the part of an ancient oracle, those long-dead queens, shouting curses at the raiders circling their town, boasting that their gods would protect them from harm even when they knew they had no hope. "Get out, or I shall have Patrick carry you all the way to the gate."

Lila stood and straightened her blackcoat. "I'll spare your son the exertion. After all, he's still a highborn. For now."

Alex followed Lila out. As soon as they entered the waiting room, Patrick shoved his palm into his pocket. He was too late to hide the telltale signs of colored pixels on its screen. A few bars of tinny eight-bit music still hung in the air.

Patrick led them to the elevator and happily punched the buttons, seemingly oblivious to their mood. He spent the entire walk through the building trying to convince the two women to stay for lunch.

Lila opened her mouth to accept, but Alex shook her head. "I have work that I must get back to, Patrick."

"Perhaps another time, then? You'll come back to visit, won't you?"

"I have a better idea, Patrick," Lila said. "Perhaps one day you could go to lunch outside the estate. If Alex and I just happened to be there, you wouldn't be breaking your mother's rule if we asked to join you. After all, it would be impolite of you to refuse another highborn."

Patrick laughed at the idea, and a dimple peeked from his chin. "I'd like that. Give me a suggestion of a place I should check out. Just"—he paused, considering his scruffy boots—"maybe not anywhere expensive. Mother will probably have her spies there, and it's tacky to spend so much these days, isn't it?"

"Very tacky," Lila agreed, "and boring."

Patrick grinned and tried to engage his sister in conversation, but Alex only spoke in hard pleasantries. Her brother didn't seem to notice. When they arrived at the Adessi, he hugged both of them off the ground and twirled them in a little circle.

Lila watched him jog back into the building. "I've missed your brothers. I should have convinced them both to meet us away from the family compounds ages ago."

"Patrick and Simon have always done whatever Mother told them. Times haven't changed that much. I doubt they would have agreed."

"Patrick might meet us somewhere," Lila said, climbing into the Adessi.

"Maybe."

As the militia cruiser braked behind her roadster, Lila dug into her blackcoat and pulled out an earpiece. She fiddled with one of the controls and popped it into ear. She heard a muffled voice and took her hand off the wheel to increase the volume.

"You didn't have any questions at all, did you?" Alex said as Lila backed out the parking spot. "You just wanted to plant a bug in my mother's office."

"Of course I had questions. I just knew I wouldn't get anywhere with them. What do you think about her answers? About her?"

"She looks worse than I had imagined. I wasn't prepared for it. Perhaps she is sick and half mad, Lila, just as Simon said. I thought he made up his story, but now I'm not so sure. The woman who raised me would have taken the meeting with your Aunt Georgina even if it was only staged to mock her, just on the off chance that it might be real. Mother always said that pride doesn't nurture business. What's changed?"

"I don't know."

"She didn't like it when you offered her the deal. You insulted her with it."

"No, I insulted her when I implied that she should sleep with Mr. Kruger. I hit a nerve when I offered that deal. Am I mistaken?"

"No. She got nervous when you mentioned Simon." Alex turned her head, and her bun crushed into the headrest. "My mother framed Simon, didn't she? She's the reason why he lost his mark."

"Probably." Lila drove through the serpent's gate. The militia cruiser followed them for several blocks before turning back to the compound. "Your brother is why I planted the bug, Alex. I'm sorry if you feel betrayed. I'm sorry if Simon will feel betrayed, too, but my loyalty is to you and Simon. I couldn't care less about your mother."

"I'm not mad. I figured there was something more to it. Even your angles have angles. You're like your mother in that."

Lila stopped at a red light and turned to her friend, not knowing if she wanted to be compared to the chairwoman. "No. You know what, it's not all right. I should have been up front about my intentions beforehand. You're my best friend, and you agreed to—"

"Don't apologize, Lila. I've always admired that about you. I've always wished that I could play the game at your level. I didn't lie when I said I wanted to help. I just didn't realize…" Alex pinched the bridge of her nose. "I always knew my mother was capable of doing something like that to me. I've always been more of a rival than a daughter, but to do something like that to Simon? She loved that boy. What is she doing, Lila? Where is all that money going?"

"Do you really want to know?" Lila asked carefully, digging into the glove compartment before the light had a chance to turn green. She plugged a spare cord into her earpiece and slid the other end into the car's sound system.

It only took a few seconds before the audio rushed through the car's speakers.

"Something's come up. I'll need them by tomorrow morning," said a mechanical, sexless voice, filling the car. It was robotic and crackled over the line, a jumble of waves and pitches. Chairwoman Wilson had installed an external filter, a device that scrambled and strained all sounds in her office, bending the waves until a bug could no longer pluck them from the air. The only transmitter that could slice through the tangle would be a computer with the right key. All others would hear nothing but static.

Lila didn't have the key, but Randolph engineers had devised a counter. Or at least a prototype of one. Unfortunately, the program jammed the speaker's voice through too many transformations and alterations. The voices were hardly recognizable as anything more than human on the other side.

The High Council would never accept a single word as evidence. Lila could still gain information, though.

"Yes, I know, and I don't care," the voice said after a pause. "Plans change. I don't want to hear that it's short notice. I'll pick them up tomorrow morning. Nine o'clock."

"That's not a lunch order," whispered Alex as they came to another red light.

"Clearly, mine is the most important," the voice continued, "but I need the boy's too. Finish them, and forget about the others. The girl is of little use, as is… Yes, I expect your work to be completed when I arrive in the morning. No excuses, Ms. Schreiber."

A crash nearly blew out the speakers, Wilson's palm computer smacking against the desk, if Lila had to guess.

Alex swallowed. "Do you think she was talking to—"

"Valandra Schreiber? It's likely."

"What does my mother need a forger for?"

Lila shrugged. "Valandra Schreiber is as good at creating fake documents as…"

"As your mother is at making money. I'm not sorry that I helped now. This is about more than revenge. More than Simon, too, by the sound of it."

The pair drove down several streets before Alex spoke again. "Do you think she's leaving? Mother said that the girl was of little use. You don't think… Lila, the boy could be Patrick."

"Could be."

"But then why would she need to forge anything for Patrick? He's not a slave. He could go anywhere at any time. You don't think she's talking about Simon, do you? That she's moving him somewhere he could be free again, like Brazil or Burgundy?"

"It's hard to know what she meant from such a short conversation."

Alex's thumb twitched. "You're appeasing me again."

"I've only had a moment to think about it."

"You wouldn't rat her out for that, would you? You'd let her take him away?"

Lila turned down another street, getting closer and closer to home and her security office. "I'd keep my mouth shut if she took him, or you, for that matter, so long as she took you somewhere nice. Some place tropical, with a nice beach, and lots of men who look like Johnny Beaulieu."

"Wouldn't that be nice?" Alex gave a half-smile. "I don't think that's going to happen, though. Ms. Schreiber is from Burgundy. She specializes in Burgundy—"

"Zephyr?" interrupted the voice through the static. "You were right. She came by. Take care of it. I don't care what you do, just do it right."

19

"Damn it, Lila, I said no." Alex turned on her heel and scooted into the kitchen.

Chef eyed the slave as she snatched an apron from a peg near the door and slipped into the scullery. The music, an instrumental punk waltz from Burgundy, paused instantly. "Ms. Wilson is willingly doing the dishes?" Chef asked, gesturing with a knife laden with chunks of zucchini. "Have the gods gone completely bonkers?"

"Something like that." Lila frowned, searching the countertops for cookies. "She's just upset. Will you see that she eats lunch?"

Chef nodded. "I saved a plate for both of you. Cookies, too, so stop eyeballing my kitchen."

"Yes, madam." Lila bowed, far more deeply than an heir should bow to anyone, much less a workborn.

Chef chuckled and smacked her in the arm with her dishtowel. "Would you like to eat in the dining room? I'll send Isabel to get it ready."

"No, my bedroom. I have work to do."

"Bedrooms and desks aren't the place for eating. You work in there too much lately. You eat without focusing on your food."

"When was the last time you sat and focused on your own lunch?"

"Don't use my own words against me."

"Of course," Lila said, brushing her finger across the countertop. "Look, Chef, in a few minutes a blackcoat named Sergeant Tripp will attend to his new post here in the kitchens. He'll be looking after Ms. Wilson for the next couple of days. I'm sorry for the inconvenience."

"Looking after her? Is she in danger?"

"It's just a precaution. I'll feel better if someone is watching out for her and those around her. She's agreed to that much, at least, but I'd rather not have Sergeant Tripp tromping all around the great house. It'll be harder for him to do his job."

"I'll inform Ms. O'Malley about Ms. Wilson's amended duties," Chef said, unpausing her music. "Isabel will be along shortly with your lunch, madam."

Lila nodded her thanks, then climbed upstairs to her room and woke her computer. As she typed in her ID, her mind strayed to the question of Dixon's identity once again. It had stuck with her all night, all morning, and all afternoon, like an intense craving she couldn't get rid of no matter how much she ate. It would be easy to spend a few minutes recalibrating her search parameters. It could run in the background and wouldn't even take up that much of her computing power.

But she had promised.

Besides, she had other work to do.

Isabel roused her from her trance with a knock on the door, bringing her lunch.

Nibbling on Chef's curried chicken salad, Lila checked her palm. Sutton had sent a message, informing her that the militia patrols had been doubled, just as Lila had asked. Sutton had sent another confirming that the Masson militia would pull Simon from the vineyard immediately, excusing him by illness, and place him under guard. Since Commander Sutton's sister-in-law was the commander at the vineyard, Lila had faith that the job would be taken care of discreetly, with no word leaking to either the Massons or the Wilsons.

Lila's luck had run out by the third message. Sutton insisted that unless Lila gave her an explanation for the orders, she'd request a protective guard for her, too. Lila typed out a reply, assuring the commander that she had no intentions of leaving the compound that afternoon.

But Lila knew Sutton. The woman was no fool, and Lila had exhausted her patience. Her commander knew something was going on, something that had spooked her chief. She'd start demanding answers the moment Lila returned to the security office.

So would her mother.

Lila wasn't even sure if she was overreacting or not. Every scrap of information she found on Zephyr said that he was just a hacker. Bribery was recent, something he had branched into during the last couple of years. He'd never featured in any reports of physical violence, at least none that she had heard about. His attack, if one came, would come from online.

But she wasn't about to take any chances with her friends.

She added a thank you to Commander Sutton and skimmed the auto-transcription file from Wilson's bug. Nothing more had been captured by it.

With security in place and no new information, Lila turned her attentions to Valandra Schreiber. Finding the forger meant trapping Chairwoman Wilson, which meant capturing Zephyr. Then, and only then, would the threat looming over her father's head, Shaw's head, and her own be lifted. Only then would Tristan be ejected from her life. Dixon might have been right: perhaps she did like looking at Tristan. She liked looking at a lot of men, but that didn't mean anything. Highborn casualness wouldn't suit a former slave.

After she wrapped up the Wilson situation, they could both go on with their lives. She was just hungry. She'd take a short vacation. Perhaps she'd even let Dubois pair her up with one of his cousins this season, if he was so keen to play matchmaker.

Lila slipped a few grapes into her mouth, thinking of the Closing Ball, and set her programs to search for Ms. Schreiber. She even tried a few manual searches, all longshots but valid nonetheless.

But after an hour, she'd still found nothing.

She didn't have time to continue searching on her own. The forger had always been good at erasing all traces of herself on the net. Or, at least, paying the right sort to do it for her.

She bit into a chocolate chip cookie and typed a familiar name into her palm.

Max Earlwell.

Named John Poole by birth, Max had a modest start to life. His mother had been a slave, caught stealing corporate data from the Salazars, an old highborn family based in La Verde. Trudy Poole might have dodged the loss of her mark if she had been highborn, but with no family to pay her lawyer's fees, she had been sold at auction. More correctly, she had been given away. Even a steep discount had not been enough to tempt any of the highborn families into allowing a corporate thief onto their property. Wolf Industries had been the only family to acquiesce, for Beatrice Randolph had understood Ms. Poole's unique worth.

She also knew she wouldn't have to pay for it.

Lila had not understood as a child that every rule, every barrier preventing her from visiting Ms. Poole had been carefully constructed by her mother to entice her. Ms. Poole had been Lila's cookie jar, set up on the highest shelf in the kitchen. Always there, always ready to teach Lila something new. A new way to infiltrate a family's network, a new way to sneak into locked buildings, a new way to disengage security systems, a new way to divert an alarm. Visiting her father and Shiloh at Bullstow had been test runs for Lila's future mischief. How far could she take Ms. Poole's lessons? Could she go one step further?

Could she go one step after that?

Lila wondered if her mother had ever intended for her education to go so far. Instead of her daughter learning corporate defense, Lila had reveled in its offense.

Max had also learned at his mother's knee, had competed against Lila in silly, childish games, even as he aged out and left the estate. It was Max who had bragged that he would break into Liberté one day, though to Lila's knowledge, he had never attempted it. Perhaps he had been successful and not revealed it, just as Lila had kept her own victory to herself, for she had been well tutored by her mother against such trust. She didn't require a high five from Max or a hug from Ms. Poole after a job well done.

No, Liberté had always been a quiet, hidden pride. Every time she polished her sapphire ring, the ring she had commissioned from Jewel as secret congratulations for herself, she felt the glow wash over her anew, felt a smile come to her lips. She flaunted her mischief in front of everyone, and no one else could decode it.

Now she'd done it twice.

Max might not have matched her feat with Liberté, but he had definitely succeeded in ferreting out useful information for Beatrice Randolph over the years. It was what he was good at; his skills were superior to both Lila's and the chairwoman's. After he had found an information leak that led to the arrest of five Randolph workborn and two family members, as well as the recovery of three million credits, Max had earned a condo for himself and his mother in one of the nicest buildings on the Randolph estate. The chairwoman also promised him a lucrative contract after he aged out.

Max took the condo and declined the job offer, leaving the estate one week after his mother's death. Eight years later, he lived on the lake in a house fit for a highborn heir.

Lila chewed her cookie, waiting for her old friend to pick up.

"Lila, you little minx," he said at last. "What box of trouble will you throw me in today?"

"The best kind. The finding kind."

"You know me too well. Who am I finding?"

Lila poked at her cookie, smooshing it in half. "Valandra Schreiber."

"Valandra Schreiber? You want me to find Valandra Schreiber? Just like that?"

"Yes. Just like that. I need to find her before nine o'clock."

"Nine o'clock when?"

Lila slipped a chocolate chip into her mouth. "Tomorrow morning."

"You're not even joking, are you? No one ever finds Valandra, Lila. She finds you. If you need some forgery work done, send a proxy.

Oracle's wrath, I'll go for you at half my usual rate. Valandra's an ugly little creature, but she's a bigger flirt than I am. We always have a fun afternoon."

"And a fun night?"

"I have a fondness for hotels and ugly little creatures. I'm fairly ugly and little myself, except where it counts."

"Chairwoman Wilson knows where Ms. Schreiber is, Max. She's meeting her at nine o'clock tomorrow morning."

"Wilson is lying. She knows a drop address at best."

"Even so."

Max sucked in a breath. "I'm not going to rat out Valandra. She's a business acquaintance, Lila, a profitable one. She's also a friend. Besides, I know several highborn families who would share an interest in finding the snitch who ratted her out. You couldn't pay me enough to be that guy."

"Point taken. My beef's not with Ms. Schreiber, anyway. I just need to know where Wilson is picking up whatever she's getting from her."

"Forged visas, most likely. That's Valandra's bread and butter."

"Probably. I already have an idea where the chairwoman will go after that. She'll be headed to an airport, a private airstrip, most likely, somewhere she doesn't have to file a flight plan. I just don't know which one."

"You either don't have a bug on her, or you do and don't think she'll be dumb enough to talk about her plans. Or you think she'll find the bug before she says something useful."

"She's either gotten smarter, or she was never as dumb as I imagined. Either way, I can't rely on my bug. Just find her."

"Double my usual rate. This is a speed job."

"Twenty percent above the usual."

"Lila—"

"Twenty. Otherwise I'll send out my entire militia to tail every car that comes out the Wilson-Kruger compound, as well as cover the local airstrips, and you'll get nothing. It's risky and involves a great deal of paperwork and overtime, but it'd be cheaper than hiring you."

"And you'd alert every spy in the city to your intentions before you even left the Randolph estate, and you'd get nothing in the process. Fifty."

"Done."

"I'll stick a GPS tracker on her car. It'll be more discreet than tailing."

"Good." Lila drummed her fingers atop her desk. "One more thing, Max. Have you ever heard of a hacker named Zephyr?"

Max breathed out. "Heard of him, yes. Seen him, no. He's like Valandra. Word is he rarely meets his clients. He used to be just a small-time hacker, but he's moved up in the world in the last couple of years. A little too quickly, if you ask me. Why? Are you looking for him too?"

"Maybe."

Max laughed. "Well, good luck with that one. I wouldn't even know where to begin. I'm not even sure if he's real."

"Good to know. Always a pleasure, Max. Tell Ms. Schreiber to go on vacation for a while. There will be questions after this. Questions she won't want to be around for. I'm doing her a favor this time, and only because it's you."

Lila ended the call in the middle of Max's grumbling complaint.

She ate the rest of her cookie and then turned her attention to more pressing problems. For the next hour, she searched for more information on Sun Leasing, Muller and Davies, and anything that might help locate Zephyr. Unfortunately, she found nothing.

Time was growing short. Trapping Chairwoman Wilson might give them more information, but it also might spook Zephyr into running. It was a risk, but one that she'd have to take. After all, a running Zephyr was a busy Zephyr. She'd have more time to search.

After putting her computer to sleep, Lila padded downstairs, bound for the security office once again. She eased behind Isabel, who dusted the bookshelves in the study, *Alice's Adventures in Wonderland* propped open with a heavy silver statue. Isabel wiped absently with the feathers, too engrossed in the text to hear the footfalls behind her.

Isabel never stole the silver. She dealt with Jewel's craziness, as well as the chairwoman's cold perfection, on a daily basis with little complaint. If the worst thing the woman did was read while dusting, the family should count themselves lucky.

Lila left Isabel to her dreaming.

A flood of leaves fell over Lila as she ventured from the great house, little bursts of yellow carried on puffs of wind. The sky threatened, heavy and gray, as she walked to the security office, dodging a few scrambling slaves laden with bags, bundles, and crates, intent on their Friday afternoon errands.

If Lila hadn't been searching the horizon for rain, she might not have noticed the flash of brown on a roof across the street from the estate and the flutter of short, dark hair.

Waving to Sergeant Hill and his rookie in the guard post, Lila strolled across the street. She used her master key to gain access to the building and sprinted up the stairwell, each floor painted in perfect yellow lines and smelling of metal.

Moments later, she emerged on the roof.

Tristan leaned against a temperature-control unit, face turned away. "Your family owns this building, don't they?"

"Of course. We own, lease, or have some sort of stake in every-thing around the property for two or three blocks, but you already knew that."

"It wouldn't do for the poorer classes to get too close."

"It wouldn't do for anyone to get too close. There are security issues, Tristan. Not everything is a class issue."

Lila dug her palm from her pocket and brought up her messages. Another alert.

"Did I miss your call?"

"No. I didn't bother. I didn't want you to dismiss me with a few words."

"You want an update already?"

Tristan shoved his back off the temperature unit. A dark red bruise had formed over his right eye, which was slightly swollen. "I already know—"

"What happened to your eye?"

Tristan looked away, turning toward the empty streets around the Randolph estate. "It's nothing. Don't change the subject. You already went to see Chairwoman Wilson. I want to know what you learned."

"Are you following me again, Tristan?"

"One of my people saw you drive in with the chairwoman's daughter. You didn't even bother to call me."

"Of course I didn't." Lila said, taking another long peek at his eye. "It was only a couple of hours ago, and I have a lot of other business on my plate right now."

"What did she say?"

"She confessed to everything, Tristan. Cried for an hour, begged me not to take her to Chief Shaw. We hugged, sang songs, drank Sangre, and braided each other's hair. What do you think she said?"

"Okay, so then we break into her—"

"The bug I planted in her office offered much more intel than our conversation. Nothing I learn through the bug is admissible as evidence against her, and I'll be surprised if it isn't discovered by the end of the day, but I did find out she's meeting with Valandra Schreiber tomorrow morning."

"Valandra?"

"Thought that might interest you. Something I said spooked her, and she's decided to run."

"I knew it. She's going to Burgundy. We have to get to her before—"

Lila shook her head. "We aren't going to do anything. I already have someone tailing her. She and her guest will be in a holding cell by noon tomorrow, compliments of Chief Shaw."

"Her guest?"

"Chairwoman Wilson asked Ms. Schreiber for some sort of forged documents for herself and a boy. I suspect they'll be entry visas to Burgundy. Alex believes that either Simon or her brother Patrick will be accompanying her. Maybe both."

"You don't believe that. I don't either. Who do you think it really is?"

Lila shrugged. "Simon's a long shot. If he went missing from the Masson vineyard, it would raise an alert, and it would make it more difficult for the chairwoman to escape. She wouldn't risk taking anyone with her who might get her caught, not unless the person was precious in some way. Simon is nothing to her now. He's of no use, just like Alex."

Tristan studied her face. "I didn't ask who it wouldn't be. I asked who it would. You already have an idea, don't you?"

"Perhaps."

Lila kept the idea to herself. It seemed too ludicrous to speak aloud. Overhead, a few birds called out, as if agreeing with her, the only noise over the closed shops around the estate.

"So how will we get to her before she runs?"

"We don't. Like I said, we let Bullstow scoop her up."

"You can't be serious. All she'd be charged with is carrying fraudulent papers to Burgundy. That's a few years at best. She made sure her son got twenty."

"Fraudulent papers would still give her a sentence. She's a chairwoman. Her auction price will be so high that she'll never be able to pay it off. Any sentence is a life sentence."

"She has fifty million credits hidden outside the commonwealth. She'll pay off her mark after she completes her sentence. Even if the Holguíns become her master, it's still not enough."

"What would be enough? How long would a highborn have to spend as a slave before you'd be appeased?"

Tristan rubbed his cheek, flush with stubble. "I don't hate every highborn."

"Just most of us?"

"Why aren't you pushing for more? Because she'll lose her position as chairwoman the moment she's convicted? Because Bullstow will turn over the estate and accounts to Wolf Industries after her trial? I know you. That's not your end game."

Lila considered Tristan, considered the chance he would do something stupid if she did not share, at least some part of her suspicions. "You're right. That's not my end game. I suspect that Chief Shaw will find something else in the car that's far more damning than fraudulent papers."

"Which would be?"

"Just trust me, Tristan. Come tomorrow morning, she'll be taken care of. Legally. Then you and my mother can both get off my back for a while," she said grumpily, stepping back through the door.

Tristan, thankfully, did not follow. She jogged downstairs and shoved open the side door of the apartments, emerging in the alley.

She was so irritated that she didn't notice the gun. Not at first, and not quickly enough.

Peter Kruger took a step toward her, a revolver in each hand. His tan skin bore few wrinkles and no scars despite his age and experience, and his mud-brown hair fell to his shoulders. He wore black trousers, a sweater, and a cheap workborn peacoat, which fell to his hips. He seemed like a cross between a senator and militiaman and a slave. Perhaps he would have fit in all three worlds. Perhaps he fit into none.

Lila reached for her Colt.

"No." Mr. Kruger aimed at her chest. "Hands up, or I will shoot the one on the roof after I'm done with you. I won't use tranqs."

Lila's hands faltered. Even she couldn't beat a loaded gun already pointed at her heart. She had messed up. She'd put a guard on Alex, she had increased security around the estate, but she hadn't taken along a guard for herself. "I suppose Zephyr ordered this?"

"Zephyr?"

"Your boss."

"I don't know this Zephyr," he said, his voice soft with disuse, never rising above her own.

Lila couldn't tell if he was lying.

"Chairwoman Wilson commands you, then? Did she tell you to tranq me?"

"Only one of these guns holds tranqs, madam, but I'd do it that way if I could. I hear that a tranq overdose is more pleasant than a bullet in the brain, but I don't know how to override the sensors. I'm sorry for that."

"Working in the sewers prepared you for this?"

"I don't just work in the sewers. I'm quite good with a knife. I can butcher a pig in less than forty-five minutes. They say there's not much difference between a human and a pig. I guess I'll find out. I'm sorry for that, too."

Lila shifted her weight, ready to spring past the man, but he'd already fired.

A dart hit Lila's neck.

She flinched at the bite and yanked it out as soon as it landed. She might have been pulling out a bee's stinger.

"It already dosed you, madam, and you know it. Maybe not the full dose, but enough."

Lila's chest and back warmed suddenly, and the world spun around her. She lurched in place and grabbed the wall for support, then rested her cheek upon the cool, painted brick.

"I am sorry, for what it's worth. You always smiled. You always gave me the courtesy of a title. You always told me 'Good day, Mr. Kruger' whenever you saw me, even when I stank of piss and shit. Not many people bothered. I wish it had been someone else."

Lila slumped, crumpled onto the pavement, and landed on her shoulder. She struggled to flip onto her back so that she could see her death approach, so that she could know when it would happen.

Overhead, the sky rippled like the surface of a pond in a fresh rain.

Kruger bent over her, gun cocked in his hand.

Tranq darts did not fill the chamber.

"After you go missing and no one finds your body, you'll live on as some sort of ghost story. The missing heir. People will claim to see you everywhere. They'll tinker with your story, trying to prove what happened to you and why. Books will be written about you. You'll live on far longer than you ever would have behind the walls of the Randolph compound. I promise you that."

Kruger's words made little sense to Lila. She didn't want to be the ghost of an heir. She wanted to live. She wanted to eat Chef's cookies, to spend another morning in the gym or at the gun range, to have her argument with Commander Sutton, to smoke another cigar with Alex, to hug her brothers and her father, to scowl once more at her mother and her sister. She wanted to see Shirley and the little ginger-headed boy. She had never even found out his name or why he wanted to help so much, and now it seemed so important for her to know.

She wanted to brag to Max that she had slipped into Liberté. Twice.

She wanted to see Dixon again, to read his notebooks, to best him in a race over the city's rooftops, to share another waltz and another bottle of Sangre.

She wanted to see Tristan, not just see him, but wrap her arms around him, inviting him in for a kiss. She wanted to wrap her legs around him, inviting him in for more.

She wanted to know if Dixon had been right about them.

She wanted to finish her dream.

She wanted Tristan to say that he wanted her. Just once.

The sight of the gun brought her out of her stupor, out of her futile wanting and wishing. It was too late for all of that now. She'd spent all her time like bags of coins wasted and tossed away in a wishing well, all for the purchase of leather blackcoat and an empty bed.

She'd become an empty shell soon.

Switched off and gone forever.

Soon after, she'd become chunks of meat served up for Chairwoman Wilson's pleasure.

The gun hovered in front of her face, but her arms were too heavy to bat it away. Her tongue was too thick to call for mercy.

She couldn't even cry.

As the sedative coursed through her, warming her blood, numbing the force of her impending death, Lila found that she didn't even care anymore. Not about any of it. Her family would get along without her. Tristan and Dixon would get along without her. The season would start without her.

She remembered caring only seconds before, but it seemed so hard to remember why.

Lila took the easy path and let the drugs take her.

20

"Wake, Lila of New Bristol. We do not have much time."

Lila's eyes fluttered. She opened them with effort, finding herself on the morning room floor. Dishes peeked over the table, witnessing her yawn: a half-filled glass pitcher of orange juice, pulp glued to the side; a plate covered by a half-eaten pancake, drowning in maple syrup; eggs and bacon, piled near an abandoned fork; and two glasses of wine, standing watch over an empty bottle of Gregorie. Breakfast with her mother. She'd walked out for some reason, but she couldn't remember what they'd argued about.

Apparently her mother had walked out, too.

"Wake, Lila of New Bristol," came the voice again. Lila chased it, turning her head at the dispassionate tone. A blue-eyed blonde stood over her and nudged her shoulder with a boot.

A boot lined in fur.

Lila sat up and scooted away from the odd figure. The woman might have come from a movie, with her worn and dented leather armor. The well-used hilt of a sword peered over her shoulder, the grip fashioned to its owner hand, not by crafting, but by years of battle. A handmade bow had received the same treatment, a companion in war and travel. Taller than Lila, the woman had muscles that might have been sculpted by artist, if his muse had carved them by hard and bloody practice. She wore two large pearls around her neck, speared by leather.

Lila knew the woman at once: an oracle of old, a battle queen, both blessed and cursed by visions from the gods.

"Rise," the oracle commanded.

It was the voice of a woman used to being followed, not in life but in battle.

Lila licked her lips and obeyed, nearly tripping over the hem of her blackcoat. She rested her fingertips on her Colt, brushing the grip. The woman's eyes tracked the movement.

Lila did not remove her fingertips, but she didn't draw her gun, either.

The pair stared at one another for several moments.

"I was…" Lila paused, unsure of where she had just been and what she had been doing.

"You were about to die. Poison runs through your blood."

"Poison?"

"The kind your people carry in their weapons. The man who came for you weakened you before striking. He is a coward, too afraid to test his might against you in a fair fight. He will not go to the Halls."

Lila nearly laughed. She could not remember any poison nor any man who might have come for her, but she knew that such a man hardly cared about some imaginary afterlife spent feasting and drinking and recounting sagas from—

With a start, Lila realized that she couldn't remember what else people did in the Halls. She'd tuned Chef out whenever the workborn had begun to speak about them.

Her mind backtracked, pondering the oracle's words. "Then I am dead?"

The oracle turned away. She prowled along the windows, her disdainful eyes piercing the glass to judge the garden beyond. "This room is a coffin. You feast daily inside it, all the while locking yourself away from the beauty that grows on the other side of these walls, and yet you worry now about being dead?"

"It's only the one room."

"I am brought to battlefields. You bring me to the table."

"I'm rather fond of tables." Lila kept her distance while the oracle paced and glared at the world outside.

"We don't have much time," the woman said at last, pausing before the center pane of glass. She studied Lila, her eyes dropping from her

face to her boots like a scanner. But rather than search for weapons, she seemed to search for some small modicum of usefulness.

Lila wondered if she found any.

"You have whittled away years in this place, wasting time on things that do not matter."

"My family does not matter?"

"No."

"Well, I'll be sure to send them your regards."

"What will you tell them? You do not even know me." The oracle crossed her arms over her chest, seeming all the more imposing as her biceps hardened. "I would succeed where my sisters and brothers have failed. Perhaps that means I must defer to the daughters of Sileas this time. When you wake, you will go see the one in your village. You will listen to what she has to say."

"You want me to go see the oracle?"

"Yes. You have seen her before."

Lila cringed. Alex had dragged her to the New Bristol oracle as a teen, but only as a lark. The pair had waited for five hours in the temple, both hiding their palms as they watched movies, both trying not to snicker whenever a lilac-robed women flitted by, telling everyone to pray until the oracle called them.

Lila hadn't obeyed. She'd had better things to do than pray to storybook figures from other people's imaginations. She'd never had time to watch movies, and she'd finished two before the pair had been called.

"I saw her mother before she died. I'm guessing her daughter has learned the same parlor tricks. I bet she even gives the same prophecy to every heir who steps into the temple."

"Go again."

"I'd rather not."

The woman drew her sword in one deft movement, the blade hissing against the leather.

Lila drew faster.

"The nerve. You would point a weapon at me?"

"You drew first."

Lila's grin faded as her Colt shivered in her palm. A searing heat burned her hand. Lila dropped the gun, her hand weak, her skin burning.

The weapon landed at the oracle's feet with a dull thunk.

It was the oracle's turn to grin, but she didn't. The woman merely raised her nicked blade to Lila's throat. "When you wake, you will go see the oracle. You are running out of time, Lila of New Bristol. You are all running out of time."

"All?"

"Some more than others."

The woman pulled her arm back. The flat of her blade crashed toward Lila's face, smacking against her skull.

Beeping woke her. Its steady cadence, its pitch, its closeness to her head, its likeness to an alarm clock—it all worked together to eject Lila from her deep slumber.

Rudely.

Lila covered her ears. "Kill it to death."

The noise quieted, though not enough to soothe the headache looming behind Lila's eyes. Dr. Helen Hardwicke-Randolph peered over her, an OB/GYN by practice, but the only doctor that Lila had trusted since she turned eighteen. Her beautiful silver hair, wrapped in a bun at the nape of her neck, contrasted prettily with her dusty orange scrubs. Scrubs that were out of place against the light blue décor behind her.

Blue. Calming. The sea.

"Emergency room," Lila muttered, nose crinkling at the smell of rubbing alcohol and cinnamon-scented cleansers.

"Yes. Do you remember being brought in?" Helen twisted a ring on her thumb, turning on its bright light, then brought it up to Lila's face.

"Do it, and I will eat your brain."

Helen turned off the light and sat on a rolling stool beside her bed. Snatching up her stethoscope, the doctor listened to Lila's breathing. Several machines leaned over the pair, filled with numbers and blinking lights that Lila did not understand. She only knew that she was connected to a few of them. An IV had been taped to her arm, and something was clamped to one of her fingers. She tried to shake it off, but Helen smacked her fingers and reseated the clip.

Lila had been given a private room on the highborn side of the hospital, rather than a nook with a curtain. She even had a real bed encased in plastic, instead of the cheap foam tables that the poorer patients were given. It crunched and squeaked underneath her as she rolled her body.

"Do you remember being brought in?" Helen asked again as she flipped her stethoscope back over her head.

"No." Lila yawned. "I picked the color scheme for the hospital. Blue is calming. I thought it worked best in here."

"So you are responsible for making me wear these ugly orange scrubs every day?"

"I could change the color. Do you want to risk it?"

"I might. My coworkers might want to as well."

"Put it to a vote, then," Lila said, thumbing the clamp. "What happened? Why am I here?"

"How are you feeling?"

"Like I got shot by a tranq. Why do I feel like I got shot by a tranq?"

"Because you got shot by a tranq. You'd think it was a bullet by the way your mother and Commander Sutton are carrying on. They nearly came to blows in the middle of the emergency room."

"Is that so?"

"Yes," came a familiar voice from the doorway. As Sutton brushed a gray strand out of her eyes, Lila glimpsed a few drops of dried blood on the sleeve of her red jacket. Her blackcoat was missing.

Lila's eyes opened wider.

Commander Sutton was on guard duty.

In a hospital.

"Don't sit up, fool. Not yet," Sutton warned. "Get a bucket, doctor."

"But you're in Randolph General."

"So are you. I'd much rather be guarding the door than in your position. Lie back—"

Lila lunged toward the side of the bed, barely grabbing the basin Helen offered before she gagged. Her brain spun in circles and slammed against her skull as she hunched over it. The chicken salad she'd eaten for lunch clawed at her throat, but Lila stubbornly held it down.

Memories of academy training at Bullstow flooded her thoughts. A quick announcement after physical training. Mats dragged out and spread on the gym floor. The humid air. The smell of sweat from exercise and nerves. The new recruits pacing in drenched workout clothes, hoping their physicals had found them fit enough for the full dose. Their mentors, those they'd be partnered with in their family militias after graduation, loading the tranq dart in front of them. The sting when the tiny dart hit their neck. Falling. The aftermath.

Oh, for oracle's sake, the aftermath.

Sutton. Sutton shot her.

She had looked just as sympathetic back then, too. Sutton knew what it was like. They all did. Everyone had to go through it at least once. You had to know its effects so that you didn't start shooting everyone just because they annoyed you. You also had to be healthy enough to take the full dose, or you couldn't join the militia.

Perhaps it was karma for tranqing so many people lately.

Helen patted her back. "Get it out, you'll feel better."

"No, damn it. I'm fine." Lila pushed away the basin.

"Stubborn child."

Sutton brought her a glass filled with ice-cold water. Lila accepted it gratefully and gulped down half the glass in one long swallow.

"Your mother nearly had Commander Sutton in a holding cell after they found you." Helen settled the basin in Lila's lap.

It was only then that Lila remembered what had happened. Peter Kruger, his guns, and the thoughts that had gone through her head as she lay in the alley. The ancient oracle, invading her dreams while she slept.

She patted her chest, her head, her belly, her neck, but felt no wounds.

"Bullstow would never accept the charges." Lila gagged again over the basin, knowing she'd be sore from it later. "It didn't happen on the compound."

"So you do remember?"

"It's coming back to me."

"Well, the chairwoman doesn't care where it happened," Sutton said. "She said I should have known something was up when you increased security. I think I'm only alive because she's trying to decide between handling it privately or orchestrating a very public accident."

"How long was I out?"

"Only four hours. You were hit with a standard militia tranq dart, but you must have pulled it out before the injector triggered completely. Could be that you won't get as sick."

"I should be that lucky."

"You already are." Helen rolled her stool next to a computer at her bedside with a loud squeak. She typed a few notes into Lila's medical records. "Your blood work came back an hour ago. We barely got a blood sample in time to test for tranqs. From what we can tell, you received the standard sedative. There's no poison in your system."

Lila breathed out in relief. She hadn't even considered the possibility.

"How much do you remember?"

"I don't remember blood." Lila pointed at Sutton's sleeve. She hadn't bothered to hide it.

"Lila, what happened?"

"I don't know. I went to go look in on one of the apartment buildings and then...nothing. I don't remember anything after that."

"Nothing?" Sutton asked.

Lila shook her head, stalling, lying.

Helen swiveled back to the bed. "It's not unusual for tranq darts to make the last few moments of consciousness fuzzy, especially after a stressful situation. The memories might come back, but they might not. We'll just have to wait and see."

"I was hoping you could tell me more," the commander said. "It all happened out of range of our cameras, except one of the new ones I installed yesterday afternoon. Unfortunately, I hadn't finished setting them up, so it's a miracle that it was even pointed in that direction. All we have is an out-of-focus clip of a man in a peacoat herding you back into the alley. Twenty seconds later, he falls, bleeding."

"So you have him in custody?"

Sutton shook her head. "Two men picked him up and tossed him in the back of a dark-colored truck. We didn't get a good look at any of them. The camera was pointed much too low for that."

"A dark-colored truck?"

Sutton nodded, withdrew her palm, and cued up a blurry picture. Lila's body lay half out of frame, completely vulnerable to anyone who might happen by. The bottom half of a green truck sat in the right foreground. A figure jogged toward it, caught mid-stride by the camera. Only his black pants and dark crimson boots had been captured.

Dixon. Dixon had been there.

The other figure must have been Tristan. Both had walked by and left her like she was nothing.

But they had saved her life, hadn't they?

Why had they taken Peter Kruger with them? Why had they left her behind?

"We've had no luck tracking the truck. The suspects took your gun, too. We only found your tranq. I didn't even know you carried a live backup. On any other day, I would have thought it a bit much."

Lila licked her lips. Sutton now thought of her as some Roman barbarian, ready to kill at the slightest provocation.

"I have to give you credit for shooting him after you were tranqed. All those lessons with me and Sergeant Jenkins paid off, even if your hand-to-hand training never did."

"How did you find me?"

"Someone who lived in the apartment building heard the shots, saw the blood, and fetched Sergeant Hill at the gatehouse. It went out over the radio as a shooting. Took about ten minutes to get the information straight, but by then your mother was in hysterics."

"Don't worry," Helen assured her. "I saw photos of the scene. Unless that truck delivered your assailant directly to a trauma center, there's no chance he could recover with that amount of blood loss. Even if he made it to an ER, he might not pull through. We've sent messages to every hospital within a hundred and fifty kilometers. No one has been admitted anywhere near New Bristol with a gunshot wound. He's crawled into a hole, and he'll die there."

Helen's palm computer beeped, and she retreated from the room to check it.

"Chief, I promise you, I will find the man who did this," Sutton said. "I shouldn't have let you go without an escort, not after you increased security. I should have found you and asked why. I should have been taking your security much more seriously. Just because you're not the prime anymore, doesn't mean that others accept it. Assassinations are rare, but they still happen. I should have—"

"You shouldn't have done anything. I'm the chief of security. I should be able to handle myself."

"Not against an assassin. All it takes is one slip. I won't make another mistake. I promise you that I will keep you safe from now on."

"Stop it. You're wigging me out with all the—"

Helen walked back into the room and sat upon the swivel stool, her mouth slack, eyes wide. "The results just came back on the blood. They wouldn't release them before, kept saying they needed to re-check. I thought…"

"What?"

"The blood belonged to Peter Kruger."

Sutton laughed, a nervous little skitter that died in her throat when Helen and Lila did not join in. "You're serious. Peter Kruger tried to murder the chief?"

"Peter?" Lila asked, feigning ignorance.

Sutton raised a brow.

"The asshole tried to kill me. I refuse to call him Mr. Kruger ever again."

"It's his blood at the scene," Helen confirmed. "Tell her about the other thing, commander."

Sutton dug into her coat pocket and handed Lila a baggie filled with a single piece of cardstock. Lila instantly recognized the flyer for the American Abolitionist Society. The red text swam as though she had been hit by another dart.

"This was found, pinned to your blackcoat under one of your stars. We couldn't pull any prints or DNA off it, but it looks like Peter has friends. I'm trying to run the name of this organization, but so far…"

Lila gripped the sheets as Sutton droned on, suddenly feeling very exposed in the hospital, just as exposed as her body had been in the photograph. Her breathing quickened, and she heard the beeping of her heart-rate monitor slowly increase.

Tristan had left her.

He'd left her after he'd done something to her body, and then just walked away.

All that she'd felt after Peter's dart struck her, all her feelings for Tristan, all her wants, all her desires, all of it crumbled.

It didn't leave a shell behind; she became the shell, and all at once, that shell filled with stupidity.

She'd trusted Tristan before and found it misplaced. When would she learn?

It had been a stolen palm and a jammer almost every time they met, but she knew the score. Stealing led to bolder and bolder crimes. Tristan had been angrier and angrier with her lately, more impatient and more demanding, especially after she'd told him it was their last job together. Chairwoman Wilson was all but in a holding cell. She'd told him as much on the roof.

He'd left her there, pinning the evidence to her coat to be done with her. She was the only outsider who knew about the AAS, and she'd already admitted to Shaw that she had been at the scene.

Tristan had always said he'd protect his people no matter what.

He'd only saved her so that he could frame her.

If Shaw didn't suspect her before, he certainly would suspect her now.

Lila's heart-rate monitor increased its pace, and she ripped the clamp off her finger. "When can I get out of here?"

"Now, if you wish." Helen pulled out her IV. "I just need to finish the paperwork."

"Commander, how many people know what happened to me?"

"Not many. We've tried to keep it under wraps as much as possible. You know how the press gets."

Lila nodded. The press was so very predictable.

And predictable could be useful.

"I'll fetch Sergeant Norwood from the lobby," Commander Sutton said. "We'll bring around the car after we check it for… After we make sure it's safe for you. Give me half an hour." She patted Lila's hand and turned to leave.

"Wait. Who's going to be on the door after you're gone?"

"Lieutenant Nathaniel Randolph. He's a good—"

"I know of him. Leave him guarding the door after we depart. This door. No matter who occupies the bed. No matter what my mother says against it. And relieve Sergeant Tripp from his current assignment."

"Chief?"

"You have your orders."

Sutton nodded and left the room, bound for the lobby.

Helen followed her out.

Lila, alone in the room, shoved away the flyer.

21

Lila did not remain alone for very long.

She had just taken a sip of water when the door opened. A man entered, dressed in a pair of pale blue scrubs. A surgical mask had been tied around his face, obscuring his mouth. One eye bulged slightly.

Tristan locked the door behind him and pulled down his mask. It caught on one ear and dangled to his shoulder.

"Please tell me that you haven't been operating on anyone in that getup." Lila slid her hand toward her gun holster. She cursed silently when she found her Colt missing. Some well-meaning nurse had set it on the room's back counter.

Tristan yanked the mask free and shoved it in the back pocket of his scrubs. "You're awake early. That's good, right?"

"Neither good nor bad." Lila shrugged, squinting at his face. "Are you wearing makeup?"

"Maybe. Do you honestly think that Sergeant Stick Up His Ass wouldn't notice the black eye? Do you honestly think that he would have let me in?"

"That's Lieutenant Stick Up His Ass."

"Whatever." Tristan's gaze fell to the baggie containing the AAS flyer. "Good. They found it."

"It was kind of hard to miss."

"It was a spur-of-the-moment decision. My people are worried that this heat over the bombing won't go away until they have suspects in custody. When I saw that guy bleeding on the street, I thought he might be our ticket out of the heat. The AAS doesn't just do bombings now. They've gone in for assassinations. At least it'll muddy the waters."

Lila thumbed the edge of her holster, eyes fixed on the AAS flyer. "It certainly has."

Tristan cocked his head, noticing the placement of her hand under the blanket. "Damn it, Lila. You think that guy worked for me, don't you?"

"I don't know what to think. All I know is that Chief Shaw will be looking at me much more carefully for the bombing. I've been his only suspect for days, and now I turn up with one of those damn flyers he can't seem to find anywhere else, and I'm not shot but tranqed? That's convenient, don't you think? It's almost as if someone planned it that way."

"You're not a suspect. You're a target now."

"Yes, I'm sure that's what he'll believe. I'm sure that's what you were going for."

Tristan sat on the side of the bed. "You still don't trust me. Even after all this time. I don't even know what to say to that."

A wave of nausea rolled over Lila. She gripped the basin, but refused to throw up in front of Tristan and give him the pleasure. "You shot Peter?" she asked through gritted teeth, changing the subject.

"Peter? Peter who?"

"Peter Kruger."

"That was Peter Kruger?" Tristan whipped out his palm and swiped at the screen. "I didn't shoot him. I just thought he'd make a good scapegoat. I didn't care who he was. The asshole tried to kill you. We thought he'd likely die anyway. I had no idea…"

"If you didn't shoot him, who did?"

Tristan slipped his palm back into his pocket. "Dixon. I didn't know that he followed me. He was on the next roof, waiting for us to finish our…discussion. He's the one who saw Peter. I tried to get down there in time—"

"Seems like you did."

"No. Dixon stayed on the roof to cover me. He was too far away for a dart, though. I pinned the flyer on you, and we took Peter with us. Doc's trying to save him. I hope he fails."

"I owe Dixon my life. Tell him I said thanks, will you? It might be days before I see him again." Lila pushed the basin away, dizziness fading, and finished the rest of her water. Things made more sense now. Perhaps she'd jumped to the wrong conclusion, but it wasn't her fault. Tristan brought it on himself, over and over.

He took the empty cup from her lap. "So who do you think sent Peter?" he asked as he refilled it from a pitcher beside her Colt.

"Chairwoman Wilson. She called a hacker named Zephyr to deal with me."

"Are you sure it's Zephyr?"

"Yes. What do you know of him?"

"Enough to know that he doesn't kill people—at least, not in any of the stories I've heard. Why would Peter Kruger take orders from a hacker?"

"Not from him. From the chairwoman. Zephyr just told her how to fix the problem."

"Okay, so why would Peter Kruger commit murder for her? He could win his freedom for blowing the whistle on a highborn, German citizen or not."

"If he wins. If he trusted Bullstow to protect him during the process, to protect him once it was over. Tristan, he didn't do this for Chairwoman Wilson, and she's not running to Burgundy. She's heading to Germany. Tomorrow morning, the chairwoman will board a flight with Oskar Kruger and use the boy to gain safe haven, either from King Lucas or from his enemies. No one in the commonwealth will be able to touch her there, and Oskar will no longer be a slave. Peter was doing it for his children."

Tristan's eyes widened as he gave her back the cup. "Are you sure? What of the daughter? What of Maria Kruger?"

"I suspect the chairwoman promised she'd take the whole family. She might have kept her vow, too, but I spooked her. She wasn't ready. She told Valandra Schreiber not to even bother with the other two visas. She'll take the only person who really matters."

"That's what you meant before when you said the chairwoman would have something more damning with her. You knew what she was planning all along, even when you spoke to me on that roof, and you didn't even tell me."

"I had my suspicions after we broke into Liberté," Lila said, and sipped her water. "I didn't know for sure, though. All I knew was that she was liquidating assets. Oskar Kruger is an asset, one she could sell or use to her advantage. If I had told you, would you have believed me?"

"Of course I would have."

Lila raised an eyebrow, and he looked away. "If the chairwoman is caught with the boy and fake visas, it'll be clear what she's doing. Come tomorrow, she'll be arrested for treason. They'll look into her records, and they'll see how she paid off Slack & Roberts as well as Muller and Davies. They'll all be punished enough, even for you. Let Bullstow do its job. Sometimes the system does work."

"Sometimes. Other times it fails miserably. How many people from the poorer classes have to pay for the occasional win? How much injustice is acceptable?"

"How much injustice pays for another bomb? What happens when you hit innocents in the crossfire? Will you justify a few casualties the same way I justify the current system? Do you even care about justifying it at all?" she asked. "You know, I think most of the time, you're so angry about your past that you want to destroy the world, rather than build it slowly into something new. You want people to pay, people who had nothing to do with whatever happened to you and Dixon, and fuck improving anything for anyone."

"That's not true. I just want everyone to be free. What's wrong with that?"

"Abracadabra," she said, waving her hand dismissively. "All slaves are free. Now what do they eat? How do they put a roof over their heads? How do they school their children? Broader still, how will we grow our food when we have no slaves to harvest the crops? How do we run our manufacturing plants, our oil platforms? What do we do with our criminals? Half the world runs on slave labor, Tristan. Disrupt that, and you're left with anarchy. You can't destroy the world, shake it up, and expect it to change all at once. It takes time, time that's better spent building than cleaning up after an implosion."

"You don't give people enough credit."

"So that's your way of saying you have absolutely no idea what to do after everyone is free? That we'll just figure it all out later?" she asked. "You should change your focus to piecemeal victories, Tristan. Changing the world is a marathon, not a sprint, and it's a lot less dangerous than bombing a city. I don't want someone's death on your conscience, Tristan. You couldn't bear it if you hurt someone."

"How do you know what I can and can't bear? You don't know me."

"Don't I?"

"Apparently not. You thought I might have hired Peter."

"I was shaken up." Lila said, knowing that wasn't the only problem. Her shell had not softened while Tristan spoke to her. Indeed, it had just grown harder and harder. The sting of it, her feelings of stupidity, of anger. It didn't seem to matter that he had explained his intentions.

She just didn't care anymore. His intentions were sloppy. His intentions had absolutely nothing to do with her, and everything to do with himself.

"What will you do with Peter?"

"If he dies, I'll leave his body in the old hotel with a few spare bombs. Bullstow will find him eventually. If Doc heals him, I'll think of something else. It's hard to have sympathy for someone who tried to murder one of my—"

"I'm not—"

"One of my people?"

There it was. That was what had bothered her the most. That was what hurt her the most. She had been a tool to him at her most vulnerable.

Just like Peter.

He had intended to use her just like he would soon use her would-be murderer.

Dying or unconscious, leaving them both as evidence for Bullstow and Chief Shaw, all to take the heat away from himself and his friends.

His real friends. His family.

What would he have done with her body if she had died?

She shivered, not wanting to know.

"I was worried," he said at last.

"So you didn't just come to yell at me again?"

"I was worried," he repeated, sitting next to her. "Lila, I have to tell you something."

"What?"

But Tristan didn't say anything at all. He cupped her cheek and leaned toward her.

His lips slid in between hers.

She tasted whiskey. Her stomach rolled, but she calmed it by force of will.

Tristan scooted closer and wrapped his arms around her. The smell of his soap filled her mind. Skin met skin as his hands slipped under her blouse and jacket, calmly stroking her spine, lips pulling on hers, swallowing them up, tugging gently, tongue tracing.

His heart thumped in his chest.

Hers thumped too, but for a different reason. It was the *thump thump thump* of outrage and anger. This was her chance. This was her chance to get the idiot out of her mind, to finish it once and for all, so that she'd never have to regret him the next time someone like Peter tried to put an extra hole in her head.

Screw Tristan. If he could use her as a tool, she could use him like one too. She didn't have time for a vacation, anyway.

She wound her fingers around the back his neck, threading through his hair, grazing the scar where his slave's chip had been cut out. Pulling him to her harshly.

Tristan moaned at the contact, and she flicked her tongue.

His eyes closed, lashes dark against his cheek. His lips crooked into a small smile before meeting her lips for another kiss.

The smile rubbed at her, hit her the wrong way.

She ignored it.

The thin blue scrubs offered little cover, but it was too much for Lila to bear. She recalled the glimpse of him the night before, his chest bared to her, and her arousal deepened.

She closed her eyes tight, only wanting to feel. She wanted him pressed against her, hard, wanting to be lost in his warmth, those hands stroking all over her body. Any hands, any at all would have done the job.

At least his voice was finally silent, their anger spent in other ways.

She yanked the top of his scrubs over his head, and Tristan complied, pushing her back onto the bed, still kissing, moving atop her. His hands, such soft, quick hands, snaked over her blouse as he undid each button one by one by one, his lips never leaving hers.

He undid the clasp of her bra, and she shoved it and her blouse over her shoulders.

When her breasts met the cool air, she wrapped her legs around him, felt his erection against her trousers, watched his face pull back as her thighs squeezed. He chuckled at the pressure and kissed her nose.

She took his lips, hard, hating him for his easy mood. She rocked her hips to meet him, tugging at the drawstring around his waist.

He dug his face into her neck. "Lila," he murmured, his voice soft, accent heavy on his lips.

He left a trail of kisses across her skin while his hand slid over her hard nipples, warming them.

His mouth moved to her chest. He sucked on her breasts while his hands dipped lower and lower, unbuttoning her trousers.

Every part of her wanted him to touch deeper. To feed her.

His fingers slipped inside her trousers, grazed her, found her clit. "I've wanted you for so long." He kissed her neck as he rubbed her, warmth spreading, gasping.

She nearly came at the first stroke.

Her back arched, knocking his hand free.

Her eyes snapped open as she processed his words.

He wanted her.

She pushed his hands away, pushed at his chest to roll him off her.

Tristan would not roll easily. "Don't. What's wrong? You feel for me. You're wet for me."

"I'd be wet for anyone right now." She shoved him away again, but Tristan wouldn't be shoved. He would not let go. He held her tightly, stroking her back with his fingers as though calming some wild thing, his cheek resting against hers.

He smelled too nice. He arms were too warm, too inviting. He was the warm bed in the morning that kept you trapped when work was waiting.

And this bed was far too confusing.

"Stop it," she said, stiff in his arms. "Let go of me now, or so help me, I will shove my Colt straight up your ass."

The mattress dipped. Tristan stalked around the room, sneaking peeks of her body while she clasped her bra and buttoned her blouse and trousers. "I don't understand. I know you feel for me. Even Dixon noticed," he said as she fastened the last button. "For a long time, I thought there was something going on between—"

"There's nothing going on between Dixon and me. There never was."

"I know. We had a discussion last night. It cleared up a lot of things."

"A discussion gave you that black eye?"

"There were words involved, too." He stopped and backed toward the counter. "Am I not good enough for you? Just because I'm not one of those highborn assholes—"

"Tristan, look at me. I am one of those highborn assholes. I'm those people you hate so much, who you can't shut up about hating every single day. You hate my mother, my sister, my brothers. You even hate Alex, regardless of whether or not she's a slave now, and I think sometimes you hate me even though—"

"I don't hate you. I just want..."

Lila frowned as soon as Tristan trailed off. One minute the man was wrapping her up with a bow, ready for the militia to carry away in his place, the next he was making claims on her. She squeezed her hands into fists until her voice calmed. "What? What do you want, Tristan? Because right now, I don't understand you."

"You do understand me, or you wouldn't have kissed me back like that. You wouldn't have gotten so..." Tristan snatched up the top to his scrubs and slipped it over his head.

"Wouldn't have gotten so what, Tristan? I'm highborn. Sex doesn't mean the same thing to us that it does to you. I'm trying to be responsible."

A sliver of guilt overcame her earlier anger.

She'd taken it too far. He was a slave—an escaped slave, but still a slave.

She was a highborn. No matter how annoyed she'd been, she was the one who was supposed to fence in her temper, to remain moral and calm and temperate.

Besides, sleeping with him was what he'd wanted for a long time. She had no intention of giving that to him now, not after what he'd pulled.

"Don't try and be responsible on my account."

"Do you even remember that I kissed Dixon too? Judging from the bruise on your eye, you didn't take it well. That's why I can't go any further with you. None of this is personal for me. It's just sex."

"If that kiss wasn't personal then you need to look up the word personal."

"Did it look personal with Dixon?"

Tristan wouldn't meet her eyes.

"I haven't gotten any in a while. That's all. It's something that I will rectify soon, before it gets me into any more trouble."

"I'm trouble? I'm standing right here, Lila. How much sooner can you get? We both want it. I don't understand why you're holding back."

"Yes, I want sex, Tristan. I'm starved. But you're definitely not asking for sex. You're asking for more than that."

"Is that so wrong?" Hunched near the sink, he seemed so much smaller than she had ever seen him before. "I'm not asking for marriage, Lila. I just want to be with you. I want it so much that it hurts. I don't understand what's wrong. You highborns have relationships all the time. Why not with me?"

"I don't have relationships with people I don't trust. You want to know why I thought you might have been involved with Peter? How about the fact that you try and steal from me every chance you get? How about the fact that you tried to break into my palm—"

"Not this again. I told you, I never asked Reaper to break into it."

"Then why did you have it?"

Tristan opened his mouth, then shut it again. "Forget it." He reached out to turn the lock on the door.

"Don't contact me—"

Tristan whipped around. "Screw you, Lila. You want to know why I took your stupid palm? I wanted something of yours. That's all it ever was. It was an idiotic, pathetic snap decision that I wish I could take back, but I never even turned the damn thing on. If I could do it all over again, I'd take your scarf. It was just a palm. You're rich. I figured you'd just buy a new one. How could I have known you'd be so attached to the damn thing?"

"You expect me to believe that? When you can't stop taking my jammer every time—"

"I'm a better thief than that, chief. If I wanted your jammer, I could have had it."

"Then why do you do it?"

He shrugged. "It's funny."

Lila stood up and slipped on her red jacket. "Funny? I'm so glad that I entertain you." She whipped her blackcoat around her shoulders. "I find you funny too, you know. Funny that you'd use my unconscious body as bait for Bullstow, and just a few hours later, you want to use it for something else entirely. Who does that? Who looks down at someone they claim to care about and does something like that?"

She hadn't meant to say it out loud, hadn't wanted to admit to it.

Her Colt and short sword lay on the counter in the back of the room, but before she could get to them, two arms circled her, pinning hers to her sides. "It wasn't like that," Tristan said, laying his head on her shoulder. "Don't go. Talk to me."

Lila shook him off and slipped her Colt and short sword into her holsters. "We're not talking. We're fighting. We're always fighting, and I'm exhausted by it."

Lila marched out into the hallway and let the door swing closed.

22

It was the knock that finally woke her, dimly echoing in her bedroom like a splitting maul against a stump, hacking away at log after log after log. The room was warm, too warm for blankets and sheets. They had twisted around her legs in a sweaty mess as she slept, evidence of her second conversation with the ancient battle queen. The woman had stolen into Lila's dreams again, demanding she cast her worldly concerns aside and visit the New Bristol oracle.

Chef would enjoy that. She'd had labored her whole life to bring Lila and her siblings to the gods. If Lila but mentioned her dream, Chef would switch off her music and oven, then drag her to the temple, likely taking along a thousand cookies along as an offering.

Lila's stomach rolled at the thought of food, and the pounding came again. She turned her head, squeezing a pillow atop it, hoping the incessant beating would go away. Soon.

Finally the blows stopped.

Her stomach lurched. She curled her body, worried that she'd be sick in her own bed.

"Lila, wake up. It's almost six in the morning," Alex whispered. A dull *thunk* sounded against her bedside table. Her friend pressed something soft and cold against her hand.

"You wanted me to wake you at five, but you barely opened your eyes when I shook you. This is my third try." She lifted the pillow off Lila's face, grabbed the cold thing, and put it on her forehead. Then she disappeared from view. "Drink the water."

Lila closed her eyes. She pressed her face against the cold pack as though it might heal her or, at least cool her down.

Then she hid under the pillow once more as Alex switched on the light in the bathroom.

Water flowed, striking the sides of the tub like a waterfall.

Too loud. It was all too loud.

The bed dipped suddenly as Alex sat next to her. Lila grabbed her stomach at the movement and gagged under the pillow. Luckily, nothing came out. "How do you feel?"

"I could take out my tranq gun and show you."

"Don't be fussy." Alex pushed a water glass into Lila's hand. "Chef is making pancakes. They'll be ready downstairs in thirty minutes. She said if you can't make it downstairs, then she'll send up plain oatmeal. I just thought you should know."

Lila sat up, moaned as her head protested, but drank the proffered water in three long gulps. She slid the empty glass back on her bedside table. "I hate oatmeal."

"I know. Chef knows too, but she said that if you can't manage to get downstairs and eat, then you're probably too sick to eat anything but oatmeal. I agree with her."

"I'm not sick."

"Close enough. I started a bath for you. Commander Sutton said it would—"

Lila jumped out of the bed suddenly and rushed to the bathroom. She gagged over the toilet, barely opening the lid before she began to throw up wave after wave of the water she'd just swallowed.

"Well, at least you're out of bed," Alex said at the doorway, glass in hand. She refilled it from a pitcher of ice water and set them both on the bathroom counter. Two tiny pills jingled, bouncing as she placed them nearby. "I'm putting these here for your headache. Take them after you're done puking out the rest of your intestines."

Lila nodded and reclined against the bathtub, wiping her mouth with the back of her hand. Her stomach had settled, at least for a few moments.

Alex knelt down, sliding Lila's palm into her hand. "You should go back to bed."

"I have work."

"You're exhausted, Lila. You slept four hours at the hospital and another eight or nine after you got back home. It wasn't enough. Whatever work you have to do, give it to Commander Sutton."

"She's already handling too much. I'm fine. I just haven't slept much the last few nights. Add a tranq on top of that…"

"And this is the result?"

"Yes."

"I still think you should be in bed. The news is going crazy, just like you said it would. People think you're in the hospital, dying. Even Patrick called. He was freaked out and worried."

"You didn't tell him it was just a tranq, did you?"

"Of course not. He would have gone straight to my mother."

"Good. That's good, Alex." Lila rested her forehead against the cold tub.

"Can I get you anything else?"

Lila shook her head.

"Okay. Take the pills on the counter after you stop throwing up. Commander Sutton said they would help. I'll come back up in fifteen minutes to check on you."

When Lila opened her eyes, Alex was gone.

Lila crawled onto her bathmat and curled up, checking her palm. Overnight, she'd gotten two more alerts for Zephyr. She deleted them and moved on to her messages. The first was from her father. She'd been nauseated and exhausted on the ride home from Randolph General, but she'd managed to send him a message before they arrived at the compound. *Reports of my demise are an overstated fiction, but it's convenient. Act concerned. I'm getting close to that damn spider.*

Her father had replied soon after. *Even though I know it's false, the news is breaking my heart.*

Lila moved on to her next message, this time from Shaw. After arriving back at the great house, she'd spent twenty minutes in her bathroom, finally letting herself puke up her lunch. Once she was done, she had lain on the bathmat and called the Bullstow chief, telling him an abbreviated version of her suspicions about Chairwoman Wilson. She had not explained how she'd found the information. They'd put together a quick plan for the chairwoman's capture anyway. Lila hoped he'd fleshed it out since then.

Everything is ready for tomorrow, his message read. *I'm trusting your friend to be a better tail than my men. I could get her now. I have cause.*

Lila stood up and shuffled toward the counter. It was bravado on Shaw's part and nothing more. The chief knew he wouldn't get the chairwoman for anything serious that way, for her security would spot them before he got close. Lila had sent Max in place of her own militia for the same reason.

Lila swallowed the two pills with a few swigs of water, hoping her stomach would behave long enough for them to kick in.

She scrolled through a whole list of other messages while the tub finished filling up. It seemed like everyone she had ever known was trying to contact her, all wanting to wish her well, to fight on. It was touching in a morbid sort of way. Useful, too.

Her plan was working. As soon as she had disconnected with Shaw the night before, she'd tipped off a few reporters to the shooting, reporters with a history of not checking their facts before breaking their stories to the world, so adamant that they be the first. Lila had claimed to be a resident of the apartment building where the incident had occurred. In her version, Elizabeth Victoria Lemaire-Randolph had been shot, perhaps killed, and the Randolphs were trying to cover it up, even going so far as to intimidate her into silence, threatening to evict her from her apartment if she spoke the truth. She even claimed that she'd seen the bullet land.

Initial reports at the scene backed up her story.

The ruse had worked.

Half the reporters had gone on camera almost immediately. Viewers would flock to their station, not merely because someone had tried to assassinate an heir, but because they'd used a gun to do it. The other reporters had shown more patience, only going to air after when they learned a Randolph blackcoat guarded the door of a highborn room in the ER.

He wouldn't be there unless the eldest daughter of Chairwoman Randolph languished inside.

No matter how much her mother denied the story, reports grew and grew about "the heir who favors black." Everyone in New Bristol knew who the phrase referred to.

The story grew even larger after sources close to the chief could not reach her. Especially when Commander Sutton refused the chairwoman's order to remove Lieutenant Randolph from the ER. It was a standing order from the commander's superior officer. Lila's authority trumped the chairwoman's.

Her mother was probably livid.

Lila couldn't help but giggle at that. She deleted the messages from well-wishers, not returning any of them. If only she could get away with such things every day.

She sipped at her water and composed a new message to Dixon, thanking him for saving her life. It wasn't enough, but she didn't have time to say it in person.

Besides, it would be a little awkward with—

She closed her eyes. She didn't want to think about Tristan.

Lila put down her palm and slid into the hot water.

Soon after, her fingertips turned to prunes.

She was glad that Sutton had demanded that she take the day off. It would make her absence far less noticeable, for she had no intention of remaining on the compound and staying in bed after she finished her bath.

Alex knocked at the door.

"I'm not dead yet," Lila called out, eyeing the soap bottle on the edge of the tub.

It was so very far away.

"Glad to hear it," her friend called through the door. "I'll check on you again in fifteen minutes and see if you're dead then."

"Okay."

The next time Alex checked on her, Lila was just slipping into plainclothes for the day, nothing marked with a Randolph coat of arms. Every bit of energy had been sucked out of her muscles. "Tell Chef I'll be down in twenty minutes for my damn pancakes. I've earned them."

Alex nodded, the sides of her mouth twisting as she click-clacked from the room.

Lila switched on her desk computer and placed a call to a private office inside Bullstow. Turning on her external filter, she made sure that the call had been bounced from at least a dozen locations. No one would be able to trace it. No one would know who had placed it. No one would know who was speaking.

"I trust you're ready?" she asked after Chief Shaw picked up.

"I have a few teams in the field, but their locations are based mostly on guesswork," he said, sensible enough to mirror Lila's vagueness. "I have another team waiting in reserve. I just need to tell them where to go. You better be right about this."

"I am, and you know it."

"Meet me at Bullstow in an hour if you're planning on coming along. We're taking Tiny." He offered up a rare chuckle.

Lila grinned. Tiny was Bullstow's roving communications center, built like a wolf hidden behind the face of a kindly grandma. Constructed inside an old mail truck, it offered a whole host of features for Bullstow to use while conducting surveillance and covert operations. Wolf Industries had developed it, winning the contract not through price, but through sheer optimism of its features. Even Lila had a hand in writing the proposal, for she had to ensure that their own wagon could outstrip and counter Bullstow's capabilities. After all, Bullstow might use it against her and her people.

"So you're coming too?"

"Yes, just to make sure that all procedures are followed to the letter. I can't let her get away on a technicality."

"Understood. I'll be there soon." She hung up, noting Shaw had said nothing of how she'd been found the day before, or the AAS flyer.

Lila started a call to her father, bouncing the signal around once more, but didn't initiate it. Her father might be worried about her, but he might not even be awake yet. Best to let him sleep.

Besides, she'd know more about Zephyr after Chairwoman Wilson's interrogation. She didn't want to contact him until Zephyr was in a holding cell.

Lila closed the program and gathered her things, scrambling downstairs to eat breakfast in the morning room. On the way, she hid her coat and scarf in a cupboard so that she could retrieve them later. She just hoped the rest of her family had not woken up early. She didn't have time for a long conversation.

Lila breathed a sigh of relief when the room was empty. A plate had been set at the table, already loaded with pancakes and eggs and bacon. Chef must have done it, hoping that Lila would eat more than if she served herself.

It didn't work. Though she'd begun to get her appetite back after her shower, the last thing she wanted was to lose her breakfast in front of the Bullstow militia and Chief Shaw.

Alex stuck her head through the doorway as Lila finished up. "Feeling better?"

"A bit," Lila said, following her out into the foyer. She climbed the main staircase and paused halfway up. "You know, I think you were right about going back to bed, Alex. I'm exhausted. Tell the others not to disturb me today. I'll be resting. I'll come down if I want anything"

"Okay. Feel better." Alex disappeared around the corner, entering the morning room to clear away the breakfast dishes.

Lila turned immediately and retrieved the coat and scarf she'd hidden on her way to breakfast. Then she slipped from the house and into the dark morning.

It was still an hour before sunrise.

Checking her watch, Lila darted behind a tree until the expected patrol passed by Villanueva House. She wound her scarf around her head to obscure the bottom half of her face and avoided the security cameras. Even if someone saw her, they wouldn't be able to tell who had been caught on screen.

With some difficulty, she climbed over the wall around the great house, a wall she usually hopped over easily, and nearly lost her breakfast as she flopped onto the ground on the other side. She then slipped into the shadows, dodging the occasional patrol that crossed her path, always managing to find a hiding spot well before anyone spotted her.

It was an easy feat, since she had designed their routes.

Scrambling up the stone wall of the compound proved more difficult. Her muscles felt like rubber and barely responded. She might as well have gained a hundred kilograms for how difficult it was to pull herself up.

It took four attempts before she successfully scaled the wall.

Luckily, her taxi was already waiting on the corner of Aunt Georgina's bridal block. She ducked into the back seat, pulling up her scarf until it obscured her jaw and nose. Her unbound curls spilled over the rest of her face.

"Take me to Eclipse," she said, pressing cash into the taxi driver's hand. Eclipse was Suji Park's cash cow, a coffee shop chain that had spread around the entire state, open by six o'clock in most locations.

"Which one?"

"The one by Bullstow."

"You gotta be more specific than that, madam. The one by the east gate, the west gate, or the north gate? Come to think of it, I think they just built one by the south—"

"The east gate."

After a quick drive, the taxi dropped her off on Leclerc Street, a block away from Bullstow. Women and men dressed in business clothes bustled up and down the street, ready for another Saturday at work. Half of them formed a line in front of the brightly lit coffee shop, a line so long that it snaked out of the building and twisted in on itself. The front of the building had been made of glass, and a large sign covered the entire top third of the store, its name spelled out in blue.

Eclipse was not exactly subtle.

She threaded through the crowd unnoticed and popped out beside the Bullstow gate, right in front of what remained of Slack & Roberts. Sergeant Holguín had taken her into the compound from a different direction on Wednesday night, which meant that she hadn't seen the destruction. Now it was cast before her in gloomy relief, a blur of twisting shadows highlighted by street lamps and Bullstow floodlights.

They had all been luckier than she had realized that night. Chunks had been chipped away from the stone wall around Bullstow as if it had been hit by gunfire and a mist of acid. It was even worse near the gate. If the sergeant had taken her there instead of merely dragging her across the street, not everyone in the group would have walked away so easily.

Only one had remained at the gate, though, closed in the guard post, protected by bulletproof glass.

Slack & Roberts slumped across from it, bricks charred and blackened, roof collapsed, building pancaked from three floors to one in some places. The whole back wall of the building still stood upright as if it were an unfortunate witness, back bent and cracked by the assault. Filing cabinets stood in a row along one section of the wall, blackened, dented, but unmoved.

A whistle split the air.

Chief Shaw waved her over.

"Almost didn't recognize you under so many meters of scarf." He ushered her toward Tiny, which had been disguised as a bread truck. *Bite me* had been written above a cartoonish rendering of bread loaves, with a green, childish monster swallowing each one whole.

"Bite me?" Lila asked. "This is why men shouldn't go into marketing."

"It was Captain McGraw's turn to paint the truck his month. It was either this or paint Tiny up with a couple of women in bikinis drinking beer. We voted for the less stupid of the two ideas."

"Good choice."

He paused at the door. "You okay after yesterday?"

"Why wouldn't I be?"

"I read the report, chief. That would have shaken anybody up."

"It helps when you don't remember much."

"All the same. Given the circumstance, I'm going to have to ask you to stay in the truck away from the suspect, away from the other officers. I can't give the High Council any reason to toss her case." He scratched his forehead under his sentry cap. "You understand, don't you?"

Lila nodded. It was already starting to happen. Shaw wasn't quite sure of her anymore, wasn't sure that Tiny shouldn't race after her next, wasn't sure about her and the bombing and the AAS, wasn't sure that he shouldn't fill her with truth serum and get answers.

"Of course I understand, chief."

Shaw nodded and opened the back door of the truck. The two chiefs slipped inside. A rack of computers hummed along one side of the truck, and two blackcoats sat before them, chairs bolted into the floor, ears covered by headphones.

"Hello, cousin," both men, the eldest sons of Randolph highborn, said at once. They turned to their screens before Lila could respond.

"Let's head out," Shaw called to the driver. He and Lila strapped themselves into the chairs behind her cousins, and Tiny lurched away from the curb. For such a large truck, the shocks absorbed a good portion of the bumps in the road.

"I have three teams out in the field near the airports," Chief Shaw explained as they passed through downtown. "One's only a kilometer from NBI, and two more are near Martins and Stevens. We don't want Wilson's spies to tip her off, so we're just waiting for now. When we go in, we'll claim an anonymous tip has alerted us to black market drug smuggling through the airports."

Lila's palm vibrated, and she scrolled through Max's message. *As I thought, it was just a drop-off location. Wilson didn't even get out of the car. I managed a tracker, but it's not seated well. It might come off.*

She called out the tracker's ID, and a little blip appeared on the cousins' map of the city. They pumped the verbal directions through to the front of the truck, and Lila heard the muffled, disembodied voice of Jewel Randolph calmly relaying the next street.

"I can't believe you kept the voice," she told the chief.

"Your cousins like it. Reminds them of home."

Lila held her tongue. The Randolph compound had never been their home. They belonged to Bullstow.

It only took her cousins five minutes to figure out that Chairwoman Wilson had not chosen New Bristol International or Stevens for her flight. Instead she had chosen Martins, a small private airstrip outside the city. While their reserve team brought up the rear, a kilometer behind the chairwoman's car, Tiny passed Wilson's limo and sped to the airport. The group radioed back and forth to the team already in position, planning the last-minute details of their trap.

"We already have a team in plainclothes at Martins. It's our own good luck she picked that one. The strip is small and manageable, and Captain O'Bryan is leading the team. It's his aunt's airstrip. She's leaving him and his boys to their playacting, all too happy to assist. She's told none of her people what's going on."

"Of course she'll help. The bust will be good for his career. What helps him helps the family."

"Doesn't anyone do anything just because it's the right thing to do?" Shaw asked, rubbing his salt-and-pepper mustache.

"Chief, I didn't know you were such an optimist."

The driver pulled into the airport and hid behind a fuel truck. The two chiefs peered over the shoulders of Lila's cousins. As the men brought up the lapel cameras and microphones on the plainclothes blackcoats who roamed the airstrip, Chairwoman Wilson's limo slid through the gates and pulled inside the hangar.

Captain O'Bryan approached the back window of the limo seconds later. The rest of the blackcoats surrounded the car on every side while Martins staff closed all but one hangar door, blocking the exits. Shaw's reserve team pulled in front of the last door and parked outside it, waiting.

The chief winked.

"Good plan. Nice execution," she whispered while the cousins turned up O'Bryan's mic.

The captain knocked on the limo window. His reflection disappeared as the glass rolled down, farther and farther, until all that was left was a dark hole.

Lila leaned closer to the monitor, the interior of the car too dark to penetrate.

"Oracle's light," Shaw mumbled beside her.

She cocked her head as someone peeked out of the window, sunglasses obscuring half his face. It had to be a male, for the jaw was too square and broad to belong to the shrunken chairwoman.

There was a familiar dimple in his chin.

Patrick Wilson removed his sunglasses. "What seems to be the trouble?"

23

Lila squinted at the monitor, mouth gaping at Patrick's face. "I don't understand. The chairwoman..."

Shaw rubbed his mustache. "I thought you said—"

"Is the chairwoman inside? Is the kid?"

Captain O'Bryan leaned down in front of the window, giving the two chiefs a better view of the interior. Someone sat next to Patrick, hidden in shadow, but it was impossible to see the person's face. "My name is Captain O'Bryan, sir, and I'm a member of the Bullstow militia. We need to search your car, then we'll get you on your way. We're sorry for any inconvenience."

"Search the limo? Why would you do that?" Patrick chuckled and turned his head, noting for the first time that every hangar exit was blocked. He shifted in his seat. "I don't understand what's going on."

"It's just a routine search."

"Is this a joke? Is someone playing a prank?"

"No, sir. There have been reports of drug smuggling through the airports lately. We take those reports seriously. Everyone's being searched today. Please step out of the car."

Patrick tilted his head to the side. Licking his lips, he slipped out of his good humor. It shattered like a thin shell under the pressure of a thousand leagues. "Do you know who I am?"

"No, but I know who you can be. You can either be a cooperative gentleman or a pain in my ass. Which will you choose today?"

Patrick glared at the blackcoat and started tapping away on his palm. "You have absolutely no reason to stop me, officer. I'm calling my mother's lawyers. Pray to the oracles that you are not still here when they show up."

Lila tilted her head to the other side, her mouth hanging open wider than it had before. She'd never heard Patrick speak with such distaste in his voice. It was as if a puppy had suddenly turned rabid and ripped into his owner's leg.

Oskar Kruger was the leg. He sat forward, clutching a satchel to his chest, peering up at Captain O'Bryan and his lapel camera. His eyes were wild and scared, and he stared back and forth between both men.

"So I see you've decided to be a pain in my ass," the captain said. "Please step out of the vehicle, sir. This will be last time I ask nicely."

Lila finally closed her mouth. "It can't be Patrick."

"Looks like you're only half right about this one. I'm sorry, chief."

"You don't understand. I've known him all his life. He didn't send Peter Kruger to kill me. He's my best friend's brother, for oracle's sake! I grew up with him."

She remembered the day Patrick came home from the hospital, hands wiggling, mouth stretching open in a yawn. She remembered every birthday after that, his tedious violin recitals, his demands for ice cream dinners, the first time she caught him in the music room with a girl and a pillow over his lap, the half-hour before leaving for his first event of his first season when she and Alex stood around taking pictures and straightening his cravat.

She remembered all the smiles, all the winks, all the silly jokes.

Every time he'd teased Simon about his crushes on older women. Every time he'd teased Alex about her conquests. Every time he'd teased Lila about the criminals she would tranq.

He was charming and pretty and dumb.

He was not a master criminal. He was not a murderer.

She would have known. She would have seen it.

She was Chief Elizabeth Victoria Lemaire-Randolph, for fuck's sake, in charge of security for the entire Randolph family.

She would have known.

Her mind slipped back to her near-death in the alley, realizing that Peter had never answered her question. He'd never said that Chairwoman Wilson had ordered him to kill her. He'd dodged the question, and she'd assumed.

That was sloppy of her. Very sloppy.

"I know you're close with his sister," Shaw said, squeezing her arm. "Don't let that blind you now."

Captain O'Bryan yanked open the door to Patrick's limo and hauled him out. He ducked as Patrick punched, and two militia-men tossed the flailing highborn onto the ground. They pinned him while Captain O'Bryan cuffed his hands behind his back. "Don't touch me! I'll ruin all of you for this." He kicked and groaned at every push and pull that came his way.

Oskar cowered in the car, still squeezing the satchel to his chest.

Once the team had secured Patrick and the driver in the back of a militia cruiser, the captain knelt on the cement beside the car. "Oskar, could you please hand over that bag?" The captain spoke calmly, as though approaching a frightened kitten that might bolt at any moment.

Oskar merely shook. Not his head but his whole body.

Captain O'Bryan did not reach in and drag him out. He merely talked. Patient and gentle.

It was Bullstow's way with children.

In the end, it took an hour and a pair of Bullstow social workers before Oskar surrendered the bag and left the limo. Like Captain O'Bryan, they spoke in soothing tones, offering Oskar something to eat if he came out, assuring him that he was not in trouble. The boy cried anyway. Tears streamed down his face as they held his hand and led him away, a boy of fifteen hugging a stuffed blue teddy bear as though it might spirit him from the hangar if he just held on tightly enough.

He cried for a lost dream, for a new life in Germany, promised and stolen away again.

Lila wondered if Patrick had told him about his father.

While the social workers managed Oskar, Captain O'Bryan took the satchel to Tiny. The two chiefs rummaged inside it, digging through the paperwork. As Lila had deduced, the forged visas made it clear what Patrick had planned.

There was no doubt he'd been behind it. The visas belonged to him and Oskar. Lila had given him too much credit, though. Not only had he possessed forged Burgundy visas, but he also had German ones.

Shaw wouldn't even need a confession.

After a search of the limo turned up nothing more damning than a couple of overnight bags, the group turned toward home.

It was a long trip back to Bullstow. Shaw tried to engage her in conversation, but Lila only half attended it, too focused on Patrick, their history together, and her memory of his always-smiling face.

A smiling face that had ordered her death.

When had the switch been flipped?

She was so engaged with their history that she didn't even notice or care that Zephyr had broken through another layer of Prolix's fake identity.

Only one barrier stood between them.

It was almost a blessing when Tiny pulled into a parking spot outside the Bullstow security office. She paced outside of Shaw's office, drinking cup after cup of hot chocolate, waiting for the officers to process Patrick and wrangle him into an interrogation room.

"We're not generating a formal report yet. We wouldn't want to tip off your snoop and give him a chance to run." Shaw ushered her into a room beside Patrick's interrogation chamber. From inside, she could peek through the one-sided glass and watch the entire process, participating through a headset. Given the delicate nature of the investigation, Shaw had been reluctant to allow Lila into the room.

At least that was what he claimed. She knew the real reason she was being pushed to the side of the investigation. She couldn't even blame him for it.

"I have a team discreetly searching Mr. Wilson's office and personal quarters right now. We'll hold off searching further for now, but we won't be able to keep this from the press for long. It's not like the bombing. We can't evacuate the whole compound. We don't have cause."

"What's done is done." Lila slipped on the headset. "We'll just have to find Zephyr in Patrick's files. He has to be in there somewhere. There's no way Patrick has done all this himself. I don't care what you say. He's not smart enough for all this."

She thrust her fists inside her coat pockets.

Shaw left the room.

The door to the interrogation chamber opened. Two blackcoats escorted the irritated figure of Patrick Wilson inside. They ran a chain through his cuffs and into a metal loop on the ground. He still wore his golden jacket, ripped at the shoulder and armpit from all his futile flopping around during his arrest. They had him sit on a wooden stool not unlike the one in her father's office. He laid his elbows on the table, the only piece of furniture in the bare room while they shortened his chains with a padlock.

Then the blackcoats left.

Chief Shaw and his colleague, Dr. Adams, entered shortly after, both pushing heavy office chairs before them. Dr. Adams was thin, middle-aged, and wore a tailored burgundy coat and breeches.

As an attorney and psychologist, Dr. Adams's role was to circle, dodge, and strike, getting closer and closer to any information the target held while keeping their questions within the realm of the law. It was important for the High Council of Judges to note what data a suspect had given up freely to the authorities before any truth serum was introduced. It helped them ascertain the most fitting sentence after trial.

Lila hated the circus of it all. This dancing about with a witness was hardly worth the trouble in Patrick's case. The law did nothing to protect traitors to the commonwealth, and as someone who planned to travel to Germany with a German citizen, Patrick could not be considered anything but a traitor. Legally, Bullstow could do anything they liked to him, just shy of torture.

But the niceties must be observed.

Dr. Adams sat in his chair and steepled his fingers. "Tell us your side of the story."

She watched the pair work on Patrick, with Dr. Adams offering platitudes and gentle nudging, and Chief Shaw offering nothing at all but question after question. Shaw had not even removed his blackcoat or sentry cap before diving in.

But after two hours, they had gotten very little.

Chief Shaw leaned back in his chair and cut his eyes toward Lila. He scratched his forehead, lifting his cap ever so slightly.

It was a sign.

It was finally Lila's turn.

Shaw cranked up his earpiece.

Lila pulled her headset's microphone closer to her mouth. "Ask him about Zephyr."

Shaw echoed her question, and Patrick's head snapped up, his eyes instantly latching on to the glass in the back of the room. He knew at once that someone else had been behind it, perhaps even knowing who.

"I don't know anyone named Zephyr."

"As I mentioned before," Dr. Adams said, "the more information you give us freely, the less likely you are to see a noose."

"I'm not stupid. The visas will see me hanged. It's only a matter of when."

Shaw snorted. "How many family members do you want hanged beside you?"

"Don't answer that," Dr. Adams advised. "Chief, you cannot intimidate a suspect in that manner. It could be perceived as a threat."

"It's not a threat. We have every right to bring in each and every member of his family for interrogation. Should they say anything suspicious, we also have the right to search all their personal data for links to his case. That's bound to net quite a bit of trouble for them, judging by the state of his family's compound. I'm just warning him what will happen if we have to dig deeper to find our answers. Is that what you want, Mr. Wilson? Do you want company in your holding cell?"

Patrick stared at the floor, picking at the hem of his jacket. "Zephyr is no one. He just gives me information or advice sometimes when he thinks I need it."

"He? You've seen Zephyr?"

"No, but I've heard his voice plenty of times."

"What sort of information does he give you?"

"All kinds."

"Did he tell you where to find Ms. Schreiber?" Lila prompted.

Patrick's head shot up when Shaw repeated the name, and his eyes darted around the room. "Yes."

"Who is Zephyr?"

"I don't know. I know very little about him."

Lila leaned on the glass. "Did he tell you how to send money to Burgundy?"

Shaw's eyes shot to the mirror, but he repeated the question.

Patrick followed his gaze. "Who do you have back there, Chief Shaw, feeding you all these lines?"

"Quite a few people. You're very popular at the moment. There's almost an entire shift of patrolmen conducting a sweep of your living quarters and offices. Your mother has even been brought in for questioning. I wonder what we'll find out when we speak to her."

Even after knowing Chief Shaw for her entire life, it was still difficult for Lila to tell when he was bluffing. But it was there, his eyes just a little more intense than usual.

"My men are making short work of your logs and files. Your attempts at subterfuge were not nearly as good as you seem to believe. We've already found quite a few links between you and Burgundy. You aren't going to tell us anything we don't already know. So I will ask you again, Mr. Wilson, did this Zephyr tell you how to send money to Burgundy?"

"Yes."

"Did he set up the auctions for his mother's artwork?" Lila asked, considering Patrick's face as Shaw related the question.

"Yes. We couldn't have slipped the money out of the country if we hadn't."

"And did your mother know that you were sending the money to Burgundy?"

Patrick nodded.

"Who is Zephyr?"

"I told you. I don't know. What does it even matter? He's nothing more than a hacker. He has good business sense. He gives me tips that I can pass along to my mother, but that's all I know of him."

"Who approached whom?"

"He approached me," Patrick admitted, eyes glassy as he thought back. "I'd already been using him for years to help me on certain projects. One day, he said that he could help me save my mother's estate."

"How?" Shaw asked before Lila could prompt him.

"After Alex lost her mark, I mentioned to Zephyr that my mother was having difficulty managing another heir and that the family's business interests were suffering for it. Zephyr said he'd think about options."

Dr. Adams sat forward in his chair. "Did he?"

"Yes. He said there was a company in Burgundy that would like to do business in Saxony. They just needed someone to represent their interests and get around the sanctions. They'd pay a premium for the privilege. We just needed to liquidate enough capital so that we could buy our way in."

"Which company?"

"Sun Leasing."

Lila fiddled absently with her headset. Zephyr had a company called Sun Leasing, but it was just a front. He never intended to do any business with them at all, just take a large chunk of their money and leave them bankrupt and destitute.

Patrick still didn't understand that.

"When did he hand over the money?" Lila asked.

Patrick shifted in his chair at the question. "Sun wanted half up front. We'd pay the rest in installments. I was supposed to send the first after the plane took off."

"How much did Patrick skim from his mother's activities?"

Chief Shaw relayed her question with a disapproving grunt.

"I took enough to set me up in Germany, only a few percentage points, a commission. I earned it. I set up everything to ensure that my mother could save the family. What else am I supposed to do? Twiddle my thumbs in Saxony? Wait until my mother dies before I lose my birthright and get tossed to the poorer classes? Just because I was born a man? What a bunch of crap. I could have been as good as a chairperson as Alex."

"Who is Zephyr?"

"I have no idea!" Patrick shouted, his cuffs rattling against the wood. "Did you know that Alex is bound to the Randolphs, Chief Shaw? Smug little highborns that they are. Simon, my youngest brother, is busy cleaning up the Masson vineyard, right at this very moment. My mother's seen to it that my other siblings and cousins are either in the senate or married."

"What's your point?"

"My point is that I couldn't care less about the rest of them. You and your little boys in the tech department can dig through every computer on the Wilson estate for all I care. Whatever the rest have done, they've done. Just like I have."

"Are you refusing to cooperate?"

"It wouldn't matter either way. I know what you're up to. You're trying to find out about Zephyr so that you can put him in the cell next to me. Mark my words, Zephyr knew the minute your men snatched me at the airport. If he didn't know then, I'm sure he knew when the money wasn't transferred into his account. He's gone, and you'll never find him."

Lila couldn't argue with his logic.

Something tugged at her memory, something Patrick had said earlier in the interrogation. She cocked her head to the side, parsing the man's words once again. "Ask him when Zephyr broke into BullNet for the first time and what files Patrick asked him to retrieve."

Shaw's head shot up, and he frowned at the window as he repeated the question.

"I have no idea what you're talking about."

But Chief Shaw wouldn't let it go. He and Dr. Adams circled the question for the next half-hour.

Soon their patience was spent. Shaw finally called for a guard to fetch the truth serum as well as Dr. Booth, a doctor at the Bullstow health clinic who was qualified to administer the drug.

"No, wait," Patrick shouted, chains rattling. It was common knowledge that the serum had a host of terrible side effects, triggering migraines, nausea, stomach cramps, diarrhea, incontinence, and a whole other host of painful and embarrassing side effects that lasted for a week after the injection, and sometimes longer. The shot itself might be pure bliss, but the aftermath made some beg for death. It was far worse than the sedative used in militia darts, yet it had been ruled as legal. It could only be used in the case of serious crimes, though, and only if Bullstow suspected the prisoner withheld information that could lead to great bodily or financial harm.

No one would argue against the serum's use on Patrick Wilson, and he knew it. The life of an heir hung in the balance. The wealth of a family teetered on the brink.

"It was one of the first tasks I gave Zephyr," he started, words flowing like a waterfall. "I asked him to break in and find dirt on the Randolphs. I'd heard a rumor about Jewel Randolph's time at university. I thought I might be able to blackmail her and ask for Alex back. The elder Randolph daughter has always been good with computers. I figured she might have helped hush it up, whatever it was. It was the only way to save the family. My mother certainly couldn't do it, and no one would give me a chance to try."

"What happened?" Shaw asked.

"Nothing happened. Zephyr didn't find a thing."

"Did you send Peter Kruger to murder Chief Randolph?"

Patrick opened his mouth. Closed it again. Staring first at Dr. Adams, then Chief Shaw. "I had to, don't you understand? I heard her speaking with my mother. The bitch knew too much. I told Zephyr to take care of it. He called me back later with a plan."

"Then you knew what was going to happen to Chief Randolph? You asked Peter Kruger to murder your sister's best friend?"

Patrick tried to stand, but the cuffs tugged him back down to the stool. "She's no friend. Haven't you been listening to me? The bitch had it coming. The Randolphs did this to us. They ruined my sister's business. They became her jailor. They even bought Simon and sent him away." The chains clinked and pulled at his wrists as he gestured, cutting red swatches into his skin. "I bet you they even killed Madeline and Lisette. It all ruined my mother. We had to do what we could to survive. It's their fault, don't you see? They should be in here, not me. The only one who deserved it more than that stupid bitch is her mother."

His words echoed in the tiny room.

Lila could say nothing against Patrick's words. It might have been everything she had ever said to her mother, and everything Tristan had yelled in a moment of anger. It was all mixed together and lobbed at her, lit on fire like a bomb.

She couldn't even dodge and avoid it.

"What about Simon?" Shaw asked. "Why did you frame him in the Club 137 raid?"

"He got too curious. I didn't trust him to keep quiet. Do you see what those women made me do? He's my little brother."

"That must have been very difficult for you, Patrick," Dr. Adams agreed. "Tell us more about Peter Kruger and his connection to the AAS terrorist group."

When Patrick claimed to know nothing about the AAS, Shaw nearly called for the serum, but Lila gently prodded the men to question Chairwoman Wilson first. She had just arrived, for as soon as Patrick had implicated his mother, a team at the Wilson compound had brought the matron in for questioning.

Unlike her son, the chairwoman refused to confess to anything at all, ignoring question after question from her interrogators. After an hour of watching the chairwoman fume, Shaw summoned Dr. Booth. They needed information to find Peter before he came after Lila again, not to mention locating Zephyr. Shaw suspected the chairwoman was a part of the case, a conspirator to treason, and she refused to defend herself against such charges.

Dr. Adams ruled that it was an allowable use of the serum.

Dr. Booth arrived ten minutes later in a pair of burgundy scrubs, the Bullstow rose stitched upon his breast, a black case in his hands. The chairwoman bucked and screamed while Shaw and Dr. Adams held her, all so Dr. Booth could slide a needle underneath her skin and inject the dark red liquid into her veins. As she flopped in the chair, her arms shot back and nearly ripped the seatback away.

"I think something might be interacting with the serum," Dr. Booth said, gripping the chairwoman's shoulders. "I checked her medical files, but there might be something missing."

"Lots is. Had to take stuff for the baby," the chairwoman slurred. "Shouldn't be here. Did nothing hardly at all." Her head flopped forward at last, and several locks of hair slipped loose from her bun.

Dr. Booth gently pulled out the pins in her hair so that she wouldn't injure herself. This time, she didn't look like a squirrel. She looked like a ghost tied to the world by gravity and iron chains, tied so she would not drift away.

The doctor slipped a blood-pressure cuff over her frail arm and recorded a few numbers on his palm. "She's stable for now. I suggest you get his over with quickly, though."

Dr. Adams nodded. "Tell us your story, madam."

"Hired a doctor, is all. Patrick's little friend found him for me."

"What doctor?"

"Doctor Asshole." The chairwoman frowned, laying her head upon the table. She sighed heavily and closed her eyes against the light. "Docs in Saxony promised me a girl for ages, but the eggs never took. Found another in La Verde said he could do better. Said I'd be pregnant with a new prime inside of three months. A girl if he gave me the right drugs beforehand. You don't know what it's like. He promised me. He gave me his word."

"What did you give him?"

The matron rubbed at her eyes, kohl smearing. "A third of the family's capital. Millions. All that money for a miracle, but he just took the money. Closed his office and ran away to Burgundy."

Lila added it to her list, just something else her family had caused.

The chairwoman rolled her forehead on the table, hiding her face from the blackcoats. "I messed up. I messed up so bad."

"What did you do?" Dr. Adams patted her hand, then slipped her several tissues from a small packet.

"Had to make up the loss somehow, didn't I? His little friend found another doctor. German. Too expensive, though. Didn't have enough left to hire him, so Patrick's friend found a business opportunity with a Burgundy company. Promised we'd make it all back and more."

The chairwoman rocked back and forth. "I knew I'd get caught, but I had to try. Family's counting on me. Five hundred and twenty-eight souls. You don't know what it's like. They look at you like the dairy cow that's come to feed them, always ready for slaughter if you can't produce. They pick and they pick and they pick. Never grateful, either. Never grateful for anything that you do."

She smacked herself in the chest. "I won't be carved up for dinner. I'm the butcher. I make the rules. Me. You better do what I say, and let me out of here, or I'm going to have you both at my next party. In costumes next to Peter. You'll serve us drinks. The family will think I'm the cow again, a golden cow to be adored."

She looked around, lost suddenly, and grabbed Dr. Adams's jacket sleeve. "Can you get me a baby? Please, I need another daughter. I had three once, but now they're all gone. My poor Madeline and Lisette trapped under the ground and my little Alexandra, always falling behind."

Lila wrinkled her nose as tears spilled over the chairwoman's cheeks. She pulled off her headset and turned away from the window.

Patrick and his mother had both been led by Zephyr. If they'd used the hacker for business advice, other highborn might have used him, too. How many had listened to his whispers? How many had spread his false information to their matrons? How many did whatever he suggested? How many had been caught in his traps, bribed, or coerced?

Would she be next?

Her palm vibrated in her pocket.

Zephyr had just broken through Prolix's last layer. If the hacker had any sense, then he'd just figured out that her identity was a fake. If he didn't, then he'd figure it out very soon.

The clock had wound down.

Zephyr would be looking for her now.

24

Lila handed her last bit of cash to the taxi driver and disembarked from the cab, several blocks away from Tristan's shop. Since she was supposed to be fighting for her life in Randolph General, she wrapped her scarf around her mouth and nose and threaded through the crowded streets, hands in her pockets, holding her nose against the stench of rotting trash in the dumpsters. Her stomach couldn't handle the smell with gagging, and her head did not fare much better. It throbbed against her skull in time to her footsteps.

Luckily, no one looked her in the face, not that they could see much of it.

She should have asked the taxi driver to take her home after the interrogation. She should have turned her attention to finding Zephyr. The hacker would be searching for her now, and she had nothing on the snoop except that he was male.

But the last place she wanted to be was at the great house. Alex loved Patrick just as much as she adored Simon.

What was Lila supposed to tell her? That Patrick would be hanged soon? That there would be no appeals, given the evidence and his taped confession?

Lila rounded the corner onto Shippers Lane and slipped on her mesh hood, trying to put her friend out of her mind. Samantha sat outside the shop, purple feather waving as she followed the movements of those walking up and down the street. A loud racket came from the garage, and dust flew from the open shop door. Most pedestrians crossed Shippers Lane to avoid it.

Lila's head throbbed harder at the noise. Her pain medication was wearing off.

"Hey, Hood," Samantha said, lifting her chin. "You here to see the boss?"

"I suppose."

Samantha led her inside. Several figures wearing breathing tanks and thick hoods with plastic cutouts across their faces stood around a truck, sandblasters passing over the metal. This was the source of the dust, the fine layer of sand that clogged the air and choked Lila's throat. They were so intent on their work that none of them even looked up as she passed through the shop.

They met Dixon on the third-floor staircase. He cocked his head, pointed to Lila and himself, and then waved goodbye to Samantha.

"See you around, Hood," Samantha said as she trundled downstairs.

Lila watched her go. "You saved my life yesterday."

Dixon shrugged.

"I don't even know what I'm supposed to do with that. Saying thanks seems worse somehow than saying nothing. It seems dismissive. Inadequate."

Dixon put his arms around her, giving her a big squeeze.

Lila hugged him back. "This is all you want?"

He snuck a kiss on her cheek and took up her hand, attempting to tug her downstairs.

Lila didn't budge. "Dixon, did you know Tristan pinned that flyer on me?"

Dixon nodded sheepishly.

"You shouldn't have let him do that. It was wrong."

"I'm sorry," Dixon mouthed. "Really sorry."

It was a rare occurrence for him, using his mouth to communicate. He shifted his weight back and forth on the step. When she didn't say anything more, he tugged at her hand again.

"Where are we going?"

Dixon did not explain. He just pulled at her hand until she trudged after him.

The second-floor landing opened out to a short hallway. A man stood in front of a door in a black t-shirt and cargo pants, Colt holstered at his hip. He nodded to Dixon and stood aside as the pair entered. "Doc and our other guest are having a late lunch in his quarters. They'll be back soon," he said, closing the door behind them.

Lila found herself in an apartment, much like Tristan and Dixon's, except the little kitchen had not been redone with wine barrels. Looking at the cracked countertops and holes in the cabinets, Lila could see why the pair had altered theirs.

She had to wonder how shabby the building had been before Tristan had moved in.

"Who stays here?"

Dixon led her through the living room, opening the door to one of the two bedrooms. It held nothing inside but a bed and table, with a wine barrel stool pulled up next to the bed. A little bedroll lay on the floor beside it. In the middle of the room, a heater chugged, struggling to keep the space warm. The air smelled stuffy somehow, warm and thick and tinged with blood.

An unconscious lump dozed in the bed, curled on its side, head hidden in the blankets. Lila didn't need to pull them back to know who it was. His breaths came deep, as though he'd been drugged.

Dixon crouched, withdrew a knife from a hidden sheath in his boot, and extended it to Lila. There was a hard cast to his eyes, a harder look than she'd ever seen from him before.

"Does Tristan know you're offering this to me?"

Dixon shook his head and pushed the handle of the knife into her hand.

Lila pulled up her hood. "I don't need it, Dixon. I carry a knife in my boot, too. Did you know that?"

Another no.

"I've never wanted to use it before today, but I'm not going to. He's not even awake. I'd be no better than him."

Dixon took out his notepad from his pocket. *He started it.*

"True."

I'm sorry about yesterday. We shouldn't have done that. We weren't thinking. Tristan's sorry too. He's been sad since you both spoke at the hospital. His shoulders slumped, and he feathered the corner of his notepad with his thumb.

In that moment, Dixon reminded her of Pax as a child, the look on his face when he'd clumsily tumbled into a briar patch on a hiking trip and taken Lila with him. It hadn't been the cuts on his face and neck that had made him cry, but Lila's sprained wrist. He'd never hurt anyone before that, and he'd been miserable and apologetic and scared for her the whole way to Randolph General, watching her wrist swell to twice its normal size.

"I know you're sorry."

The pair left Peter before the doctor returned, and climbed the stairs to the top floor. Tristan emerged from his room as Dixon opened the door, shirtless and dressed in black pants. He wiped at his hair with a damp towel. "Dixon, I swear, if you don't turn down that damn heater, I'm throwing it—"

He broke off, seeing Lila come through the door.

She pulled off her hood.

"You look awful," he said, his eyes not meeting hers.

"Thanks."

"I didn't mean it like that. You just look exhausted and pale. You should rest."

"I'll rest later."

Tristan excused himself and returned to his room. He came back a moment later, towel gone, black t-shirt pulled over his head.

He turned down the heater and dropped onto the couch.

"I just came by to tell you what happened this morning," Lila said, sitting down on the opposite end. She squeezed a pillow in her lap and recounted the arrest of Patrick Wilson and his mother, embarrassed once again that her prediction had been so wrong.

"So let me get this straight. Patrick Wilson has been behind the false arrests this entire time? It's been Patrick paying off Slack &

Roberts? You can't expect me to believe that Chairwoman Wilson didn't know."

"Of course she knew, or at least condoned what was going on. Chief Shaw and I suspect that she was too busy trying to get pregnant to pay close attention to what Patrick was doing. He did a great many things in her name."

"He ordered Peter to kill you?"

"Zephyr told him how to do it, but yes. Killing me kept both their secrets. I misjudged Zephyr. He's not afraid of spilling blood."

"Do you think he knows that Patrick and his mother have been arrested?"

"Yes."

Do you think he'll run?

"No. He's not sure how exposed he is yet. He's got too many highborns in his pocket to give it up that easy, especially since he lives right here in New Bristol."

"You found him?"

Lila shook her head. "Think about it, though. Everyone he bribed has lived in New Bristol or near it. Plus he had to have access to Bullstow in order to plant his trap in the code. I think he's local, and I don't think he'll want to move yet."

Will he try to hurt you again?

"I don't think so, at least not until he realizes who Prolix is. Patrick pushed him into coming after me. It wasn't Zephyr's idea."

"That doesn't mean he won't try again now that the idea is in his head," Tristan pointed out. "He's dug himself into a hole, and people do stupid things when they're panicked."

What next?

"I find Zephyr before he finds me."

Tristan perched on the coffee table across from her. "Chief," he said, rescuing the pillow in her lap and placing it beside her.

It was just one simple word. One word said in the place of another.

She'd grown to enjoy the way he said her name, his rolling accent, the way he stretched the vowels.

That was gone now.

"What?"

"Ask for help."

She almost chuckled. "Chief Shaw can't—"

"Not from Shaw."

Lila leaned back against the couch, finally understanding. "You want me to ask you for help? You're enjoying this, aren't you?"

"Not even a little. Is it so hard to ask your friends for help?"

"Friends?"

"Yes. Friends."

"That's an interesting word coming from you. I don't need anyone's help. I can do this on my—"

"Maybe you can, but you don't have to."

Lila snatched the pillow back and curled her legs underneath her. "Fine. Help me find Zephyr, then."

Tristan nodded and pulled out his palm. It was his usual stance when starting a new job.

"I suppose you want money?" she asked.

"No."

"What do you want, then?"

"Nothing."

"You always want something."

"You might not believe this, but most of the jobs you've asked us to participate in, we would have done for free. They nearly always align with our interests. You always want to give us something, though, as if you wouldn't trust us otherwise. It's why I always make deals with you. That's all you understand." He tapped on his computer for several seconds before looking up at her expectantly. "Tell us everything you know about Zephyr."

Dixon moved to the couch, his notepad in his lap, ready to chime in.

"You must want something." Lila's eyes straying over Tristan's face.

She saw no trace of deception in him, though, only a bit of frustration in his heavy sigh.

Forgiveness.

"No," Tristan muttered. "You're making it worse."

Dixon looked down at his notepad and scratched out the word with his pencil, drawing line after line after line. Eventually, he pulled the page out of his notebook, crumpled it into a ball, and tossed it onto the floor.

Lila watched it bounce away. "I don't understand how you're going to help me. Toxic and Reaper are fine at what they do, breaking into buildings and finding a few records here and there, but they'd be lost—"

"Humor us. Perhaps you just need a fresh set of eyes."

Lila sat up. The couch had begun to get a little too comfortable. She couldn't afford to fall asleep now, not until she found her quarry. She was too tired to think of the implications and too exhausted to worry if it was the right thing to do. Perhaps Zephyr wasn't the only one who had begun to panic. Two men's lives and reputations hung in the balance, for Shaw and her father would be hanged, or at least ruined and exiled from Bullstow, if her part in the investigations came to light.

Not to mention her own career, her own place in the Randolph family, and her own neck.

In a faltering voice, Lila talked about things she shouldn't. She told Dixon and Tristan everything she'd learned about the Sun Leasing Company, about Zephyr, about the Liberté bank accounts, about her father's file.

Tristan listened, flipping a silver medallion forward and back around his knuckles as she spoke, occasionally snatching it up to type into his palm. "I don't think you need new eyes on it," he said after she was done. "I think you just need a new approach. You need to stop all this sneaky highborn shit and do what we would do."

"What's that?"

"Confront him."

Lila snorted. "If I could find him, then I wouldn't be in—"

"You don't need to find him. You just need to find someone who knows him, then get that person to draw him out. You said Natalie Holguín is on that list, right?"

"Yes."

"Has she been arrested?"

"Not yet. Bullstow hasn't completed their investigation."

"Good. I know Natalie, or, at least I did." His eyes darted to Dixon. "I think we should hire a new hacker, Dixon, don't you? Since ours are only fine at what they do."

"I didn't mean it like that."

"I didn't either. Where is Natalie living these days? I know she's not staying at the family vineyard."

"Why do you want her address?"

"Because I'll need it if I'm going to turn up on her doorstep, with cash, asking her to set up a meeting with her most capable hacker."

"What if she tells you to get lost?"

"Then we'll threaten to turn her in."

Dixon shook his head so quickly that Lila thought it might swing off. He started scribbling on his notepad faster than Lila had ever seen before.

No. Natalie is trouble. She'll do something. We'll get caught.

Tristan clapped Dixon's shoulder. "It's going to be okay. We're not going to get caught."

Dixon pushed him away. He snatched up his notepad and moved to the corner of the room, his gaze fixed on a point outside the window.

Lila watched him go. "What are you going to threaten her with?"

Tristan smirked. "I've had a few of my people following her the last few months. Natalie loves selling Sangre to people she shouldn't."

"She's selling to the empire?" Lila shook her head. Natalie was a lot of things, the least of which was opportunistic, but Lila never thought she would stoop that low.

"No, that's not what I meant. The Holguíns are proud. Chances are if your mother ended her boycott today, Chairwoman Holguín still wouldn't sell to her. Long memory and all. It doesn't matter much, since the vineyards aren't a key part of their business. She doesn't need the money, but Natalie does. Her matron would be very interested to hear that Natalie is selling Sangre to the same families who are boycotting her."

"That's your plan? She'll help you, or you'll tattle to her matron?"

"Why not? The woman loves her blood squad."

Lila shivered. Every highborn matron had access to a special force, altogether separate from her militia, whose jurisdiction remained valid only on her property. The group handled serious crimes against the family, usually violent and usually perpetrated by a family member. Matrons had begun the practice to deal with internal assassination attempts, preserving their family's safety when the courts might not get involved due to flimsy evidence. Since High House valued the safety of their matrons, mothers, siblings, children, and the mothers of their children, they had never struck down the practice. The death of an occasional innocent, so long as it kept their families safe, was an acceptable sacrifice.

Low House rarely got involved either, for blood squads rarely touched non-highborn. It was beneath them. It was a job for the militia. Besides, any Low House senator who tried to bring legislation against the practice could kiss his career goodbye.

"I'm surprised you'd threaten a person with that," Lila said. "Even someone like Natalie. I figured you'd be against blood squads on principle."

Tristan cut his eyes to Dixon, who'd retreated even further into the corner. "I am. I didn't say I'd actually turn the information over to her matron. In any case, I have a list of who she's been selling to, and amounts, sometimes even photos. Even you once, you little sneak. I might not have proof of her other crimes, and she is guilty of much more, but we at least have this much to use as leverage. It will all be useless anyway once Shaw arrests her."

"When that happens, what's to say she won't turn on you and tell Chief Shaw about you for a lighter sentence?"

"Oh, that's exactly what she'll do, but what's there to tell? That two slaves escaped from her family's compound in Beaulac seven years ago and now live somewhere in New Bristol? I'm sure the head of the Bullstow militia will get right on that."

Lila sat back in the couch. "Why would Natalie introduce Zephyr to anyone? It exposes her."

"Because she, like most of the women in that family, love taking slaves down a peg. The idea of me wanting something that she has, even if that something is broken, will be too much for her. She won't be able to let it go."

Lila narrowed her eyes. "Why would Zephyr take the job?"

"Because we'll offer him something money can't buy."

"What's that?"

"An emperor and a princess."

Lila's mouth opened. "Maria? Tristan, you didn't—"

"Of course we did. We weren't about to leave the girl there. I refuse to let your mother offer her up to the highest bidder. She's just a child, a fifteen-year-old girl who doesn't deserve what's happened to her. She's done nothing to warrant such a life. Neither did her father, for that matter, at least until yesterday."

"What will you do with her?"

Tristan thumbed his palm. "What do you think?"

"You want to send her to Germany, don't you?"

"If she wants to go."

"That's treason."

"If that's treason, then I curse every patriot. You should, too."

Lila's brain pounded against her skull. She needed more of Sutton's pain pills. "How did you even get her off the compound?"

"There was a lot of chaos when Bullstow knocked on the door this morning. My people nabbed the girl from the scullery in the confusion. Everyone was so concerned about Chairwoman Wilson and her son that no one noticed Maria Kruger. I'm told she came quietly, didn't even put up a fight. It was sad, really, hearing them tell me how easy it was. She's so very used to doing what she's told."

"So you're not going to hand Maria and her father over to Zephyr?"

"Of course not. I just need the man to believe it, at least enough for him to meet me." He caught Dixon's eye and winked. "You see, we need a hacker who can break into Liberté. He'll recognize his own bank account number, and I just know he'll want to take the job. He'll want the carrots I'm dangling. He'll meet."

25

Something brushed Lila's arm, ticking her skin.

She shot up in bed, panting.

Tristan crouched over her, grasping the ends of a gray woolen blanket, illuminated by the light from the adjoining room. Behind his head, a string of bottle caps dangled from the dark window, and a heater hummed near the bed. It hadn't been there when she had fallen asleep.

"I didn't mean to wake you. You were curled up in a knot like you were cold." He gently pushed her back to the mattress and settled the blanket around her shoulders.

"What time is it?"

"Eight o'clock. Go back to sleep. I'll—"

"Eight?" Lila flipped over and thrust her hand into the pillowcase. She withdrew her palm, thumbing on the display.

Tristan frowned. "You hid it in the pillowcase?"

"Yes. Where else would I have put it? It's not like this has a pocket." She tugged at the chest of her cotton shirt, washed to softness.

Not hers.

Tristan's.

It smelled like him. Not soap and whiskey but the scent that pooled in the crook of his neck, the scent that begged her to lean over, to breathe him in deep.

The bed smelled like him too.

She pressed her thighs together, her blood rushing throughout her body, recalling a sea of light blue paint and a creaking plastic mattress.

His hands upon her body.

His hands attaching a piece of cardstock under her officer's stars while she'd been tranqed.

"It's late," she said, knowing she'd not be able to go back to sleep after such thoughts. "Why didn't you wake me before?"

"Because I've been hit with a tranq dart. I know what it's like. Exhaustion, nausea, sore muscles." He ticked off each symptom on his fingers. "You needed a nap."

"Five hours isn't a nap." She scrolled through the messages on her palm, focusing on one from Alex, written two hours earlier. *You snuck out, I see. I'll cover for you as long as I can. Are you okay?*

Lila sighed. She had not escaped the problem she'd faced that afternoon, only deferred it. At some point, she'd have to return home and tell Alex what had happened to her mother and brother.

She'd have to tell her friend what *she* had done to them.

It needed to happen soon. She couldn't let Alex hear it from someone else.

Lila lay back into the pillow and tapped on her display. *Yes. I'll be back in a few hours. Thanks, Alex.*

"You look better. You even have a bit of color in your cheeks."

Lila rolled onto her back and stretched like a cat, flexing each muscle as far as she could reach, relieved they responded at almost their full strength, sharpness, and quickness.

Tristan was right. The extra sleep really had done her some good.

It didn't mean she had to admit it, though.

"Did you set up the meet?"

"Yes. I had to blackmail her for it. Zephyr will meet us tonight in one of the abandoned factories on the Wilson-Kruger estate."

"Where?" she blurted.

"It's a good spot. The Wilson estate is neutral territory for both of us, and it's in limbo right now. At least half of the Wilson militia has walked off the job since the chairwoman and her son were taken into custody this morning, and Bullstow can't touch the place until they formally charge her."

"And Chief Shaw isn't going to do that because he doesn't want to spook Zephyr any further. An arrest means they'll go after him next."

"Exactly."

"It's not the worst plan you've ever had."

Tristan bowed dramatically. "If you're not going back to sleep, then come and eat. It will help."

Lila nodded. After he closed the door, she changed back into her own clothes and padded into the makeshift kitchen. Several Styrofoam containers filled with takeout had been lined up in a neat little row on the counter, along with a bag from Plum Luck Dragon. Her stomach growled at the smell of grilled meat.

"Where's Dixon?"

"He's making a few last-minute preparations. There's a lot to do."

"Bullshit. If there were any last-minute preparations to make, you'd be handling them."

Tristan took out the last container from the bag and added it the row, lining it up perfectly with the rest of the food. "Pick whatever you—"

"Tristan..."

"He's not hungry. I'm not even sure he could eat anything right now, so I haven't pressed it."

"I've never seen him like this before. It's because you're dealing with Natalie, isn't it?" She eyed Tristan carefully. "What exactly happened to him on the Holguín estate all those years ago? His tongue? The scars? His voice? You've hinted, but you—"

"That's his story, not mine. I won't tell you what he won't."

Lila sat down in one of the barstools at the counter. "Fine. Tell me who else isn't eating," she said, pointing to all the food.

"I didn't know what you'd want. I'll take whatever's left down to Doc and the others. Someone will eat it."

Lila popped open the containers from the Plum Luck Dragon one by one. The first held pork lo mein, her favorite. She usually requested it whenever they ate at the restaurant, but sometimes she'd ordered the other dishes instead.

Lila tugged the pork lo mein nearer. "I guess you've been paying attention."

Tristan didn't answer. He opened the Plum Luck Dragon bag, dug out a plastic fork, and slid it across the counter. Then he began closing up the other meals and packing them back into the bag. "I'll be back later. I should—"

"Tristan, wait. About yesterday—"

He turned toward her all at once, abandoning the food. "I'm sorry. I didn't think. I didn't think about any of it, and I know I can't take it back. You don't trust me anymore. I see it every time you look at me. It cuts me up."

She hadn't been expecting an apology, and she wasn't sure that she wanted one yet. "Tristan—"

"Let's just forget it, okay?" He gathered the food, working much faster. "I fucked up. I'm sorry. Let's just pretend I didn't say anything at all. That I didn't do anything. We'll just go back to—"

"No. We're not going to just ignore it, Tristan. I can't do that."

He closed the bag and lifted it off the counter, unwilling to meet her eyes.

"This is the part where you tell me not to order you around."

"I don't feel like fighting anymore, and I don't know how to fix this."

"Maybe I don't want to fight anymore either. Have you eaten yet?"

He shook his head.

"Have dinner with me."

Tristan didn't react right away. He considered her face, the closed apartment door, and then turned back to Lila. Slowly, he placed the food back on the counter.

"Do you have any plates, Tristan? Real plates?"

He opened a cabinet behind him, messy with plates, steel utensils, and glasses.

Lila joined him, her mind on Dixon's words. It wasn't just washed clothes. It wasn't just a plate. "Go sit down," she said, grabbing what they needed.

Tristan did as he was told, watching her transfer everything to plates. She handed him a real fork and took down a couple of wine glasses, for a bottle of Sangre had appeared on the end of the counter when she turned her back. She opened the bottle and poured for them both.

It was strange to be around him for so long without yelling. It reminded her of how they used to be, so very long ago. Much of her distrust toward Tristan had started because of the stolen palm, had continued because he kept taking her jammer. What if he really had been taking the device as a joke? What if he had taken the palm because he just wanted something of hers to hold on to?

They'd both hurt her when they pinned that flyer on her coat, but Dixon had saved her life. Tristan had saved it as well. He'd jumped into the water to rescue her even when he couldn't swim.

They'd never failed to help her when she needed it. She'd always thought it was for money, but maybe it wasn't.

Could she say the same? She'd agreed to help them with the Wilson case, but she had done that to help Simon and Alex.

There'd always been something in it for her.

"Do you remember that night on the Victory Tower when we made up all those constellations?" she asked, handing him his glass of Sangre.

Tristan's face fell. "I told you when I stole your—"

"I didn't bring it up because of that. Did we ever come up with a constellation named Klepto?"

Tristan sipped his wine while she sat down at the barstool next to him. "I don't remember one named Klepto. I remember one called Buster, though," he recalled, grinning.

"Buster?"

"Yeah, you said he was Rind's guard dog. He bit Odin in a delicate place after leaving her house. We kind of got into a discussion about divine anatomy after that, and whether or not the gods actually had—"

Lila couldn't hide her smile. "I forgot about that one."

Tristan chuckled and swallowed a bite of chicken stir fry. "I didn't think you remembered them at all, just what I did after."

"I remembered. It was a fun night. We used to have fun."

"We could still have fun. Is this really our last job together, Lila? We could start over. I'd like to start over."

Lila dug around in her lo mein. "I was supposed to turn you in the moment you admitted to the bombing."

"You didn't."

"I should have. You didn't just destroy a building, Tristan. You destroyed the contracts of dozens of people at that law firm: clerks, paralegals, admins, janitors, people who had nothing to do with—"

"The payout for their contracts is higher than what they would have received if their bosses had gone into a holding cell. The workborn will have a larger cushion while they look for a new contract, and Bullstow will still get to investigate the information we're sending them. That was why I did it that way. I figured it would take a long time to bring their bosses to court."

"You also damaged the buildings around Slack & Roberts."

"Yes, we did," he admitted, and sipped his Sangre. "The blast was a little more powerful than we meant it to be. It's been a few years since Shirley did that sort of work, and the army never cared much about precision."

"My family owns most of that block. Insurance will reimburse us for the repairs, since it was ruled a gas explosion. If I thought you really meant to hurt people, I'd—"

"I didn't," he said. "Perhaps I should have done it in the first place, and I don't mean that because of the heat from Bullstow. I didn't even realize how far I'd gone until we met the next day, until I saw how upset and angry you were. You call me a criminal all the time, but that was the first time you meant it."

"I'm sorry—"

"No, you're not, and I'm not sure that you should be," he said, stabbing a stray piece of chicken. "I really screwed things up, didn't I? I screwed them up all over."

Lila didn't know how to answer without sounding like an ass. "Now who's not arguing?"

"It's a good plan. The one tonight, I mean."

After a few awkward moments, the pair turned back to their earlier conversation. They spent the rest of their meal trying to recall more constellations from their night on the Victory Tower. When their memories failed, they started making up new stories, both pretending they saw stars among the little flecks on the stucco ceiling.

Her palm vibrated in her pocket. An alert had gone off, but not an alert for the Prolix identity. She had set this alert to capture something else entirely.

"What is it?"

A news story opened on her palm. *Corruption and Highborn Betrayal: The Heir Who Favors Black Hacks into State Database.*

Lila skimmed the article, fearing the worst.

She was not disappointed.

26

At nine o'clock, Lila and Tristan trudged downstairs and joined the assembling group, threading through the jumble of cars, the truck frames on blocks, and discarded machinery. At least a half-dozen of Tristan's people had gathered in the garage, all talking at once as though they attended a cocktail party with guns.

For the first time, Lila was glad that a mesh hood covered her face, leaving her eyes invisible to the world. She'd let Tristan read the article, but hadn't been able to talk about it. There wasn't anything she could say. Zephyr had posted his suppositions on some anonymous server. It was out there, perhaps being read by any number of people, and she didn't have time to hack into it and delete the story.

The only bit of luck was the page stood alone, not part of any larger website, seemingly disconnected from the online world. How would anyone find it? Few people had the sort of programs she'd used to capture it.

It was out there, though, waiting to be discovered, and it would remain so until they trapped Zephyr and brought him back to Bullstow. Only then could she hack into his server and delete the file.

She couldn't even get Toxic to work on it while they dealt with Zephyr. She didn't trust anyone with such a secret.

Except for Tristan, apparently.

She joined Dixon by the front window. He stared out into the night through a small gap in the plywood. His eyes had unfocused, and he didn't move when she called his name.

"Are you okay?" she asked, placing her hand on his shoulder.

Dixon startled at her touch. He nodded quickly and poked at the plywood hole.

"No, you're not. What's got you so jumpy?"

He shook his head and refused to take out his notepad to chat. Lila didn't press him. Since she had no idea what to say, she put her arms around his waist and hugged him as hard as she could. It was what she would have done for Alex or Pax, had either of them been upset. It was what Lila would do when she finally returned to the Randolph estate and faced her friend.

Perhaps Lila needed a hug, too.

Dixon wrapped his arms around her, holding on to her so fiercely that she thought her ribs might break. His hands trembled on her back.

"It's going to be okay," she whispered into his ear. "I won't let anyone take you. Even if they do, I'll buy your mark at auction, no matter the cost. I'll send you some place pretty, and Tristan and I will break you out the same afternoon. You'll be back by dinner."

She felt him nod, and the shaking lessened.

Lila only hoped she'd be able to keep such a promise. Zephyr might not be the only one in a holding cell by the end of the night.

There was a rustle behind them, and Toxic giggled. "Hood, are you sweet on Dixon?"

"Who isn't?"

"I'm not," Samantha hollered across the garage, trudging through the dust with a shotgun. "He's like a foreign film. Looks nice, but you have to do too much reading."

Dixon reluctantly let go of Lila. He dug his notepad out of his pocket and scribbled on a new page. *I don't need my notepad in the dark.*

"Yeah, only because your hands are too busy holding your—"

"We're leaving in five," shouted Tristan on the other side of the garage, his head under the hood of a beat-up green truck.

Lila squeezed Dixon's hand and kissed his cheek, then joined Tristan, who had been listening to Shirley drone on about the engine. "How old is this thing?" Lila asked, running her fingers over the rust and peeling paint.

Shirley slapped her hand away. "She's not old, Hood. She's experienced and reliable. Besides, she's all we have right now that doesn't need to be repainted or repaired. She'll get all of you there and back again."

"So, no quick getaways for us tonight?"

Shirley gently closed the hood, and her mouth twisted into a smile. "Oh, she'll fly. I've made sure of it."

Once Tristan pulled out onto Shippers Lane, his foot became too heavy for the truck's smooth ride, proving Shirley's point. Lila watched the speedometer climb higher and higher, warning Tristan to slow down several times as he barreled through the late evening traffic. Lila's regard for Shirley rose. She suspected that the only parts that the old woman hadn't tweaked or replaced were the frame and the interior.

Lila's eyes strayed to her side mirror. Dixon and Frank rode on Tristan's Amazon, with Fry and Dice trailing behind on a second bike, the lapels of their coats fluttering in the wind.

It took twenty minutes to reach the Wilson-Kruger estate. The group parked a few blocks from the front gate, near one of the only businesses left in the area, Brewer's Pub. While Tristan's men paced on the sidewalk, peering at the silhouettes that crowded around the entrance of the bar, Lila hacked into the chairwoman's security system.

"That's not a good sign," Frank said over her shoulder. Few cameras still operated on the estate. Many of the lenses had been broken or covered with spray paint, or were no longer sending images. She picked a dozen such cameras at random and reversed the footage. All but one had been vandalized in the last eight hours. "What do you think's going on in there?"

"Rage," Tristan answered. "A lot of it."

Lila couldn't disagree. "It happens occasionally when families fall. Instead of facing their change in status gracefully, they..."

"Fight back?" Frank asked.

"Harsh words for it, but I suppose it's appropriate."

"It's not harsh," Tristan said. "Just because it's not proper for highborns to turn to blood and violence, doesn't mean that they don't. You did tranq me once, remember."

"Darts aren't the same thing," Lila mumbled, stashing the laptop under the passenger seat. "Besides, the Wilson family was never that proper."

Tristan led the group away from Brewer's Pub. Shuttered businesses loomed over them on all sides, windows boarded, front doors chained. Lila's hand stayed on her Colt as they walked, for too many people marched up and down the dirty sidewalks for such a wasteland, trampling the litter and trash that had been piled into the streets under worn boots. They came in singles, rather than pairs and groups. Many held paper bags filled with booze, and lumps poked out from their pockets. The air crackled as though it might be the hour before a party.

Or a riot.

"The two gates are guarded by whatever militia the chief of security has been able to scrape together, but she doesn't have enough bodies to secure any other part of the compound. That's why we're going over the wall instead," Tristan explained, turning down a dark street that bordered the west wall of the estate. The bulbs had been shot out from every street lamp on the block.

Fewer people traveled here. The ones who did lowered their eyes and kept to themselves.

"Several of my people are inside the compound in case we need them. They say that this is the best place to cross."

"I'd say they made sure of it," Frank grunted.

"They weren't the ones who did this. The word is, Bullstow whacked a hornet's nest when they took the chairwoman and her son this morning. We should be careful while we're inside. Don't provoke anyone." Tristan led them behind a group of oak trees planted too near the wall. "This is the place."

Lila considered the conveniently placed cover. Someone had planted the trees to hide this part of the wall, but more importantly, someone had let them to grow and had never cut them down.

She pulled Tristan aside as the men began to scale the wall. "Are you sure this is the best place? I have a similar spot on our estate. I installed turret guns loaded with sedative in the trees, ready to eject anyone stupid enough to jump over, as well as a bank of cameras to catch their idiotic, surprised faces. It makes prosecution incredibly simple. We call it the Hangman's Noose. Eighty percent of the intruders that try to sneak into our estate pick that spot."

"I'm sure. My people took care of the cameras along this part of the wall, and your jammer will take care of any we missed. As for the rest of it, the chief doesn't have your resources. The chairwoman revoked most of her funding a long time ago."

"I know, but—"

"My people have been slipping in and out for months without trouble, right here, even taking Maria this morning. Peter could have broken out himself and his children at any time. It's only habit that kept them in."

Lila nodded as Tristan's men tried to scale the wall, a wall that was too high and smooth for them to climb. They fell off again in a flurry of grunts. "So many cameras have been destroyed that it won't be hard to avoid the ones left," she said.

"Good. You'll keep us from them?"

"Of course." Lila backed up and ran at the wall, grabbing the top easily, as though it were another morning at the obstacle course. While the men changed tactics and boosted one another up, she held herself at the top, peering into the compound and the people who dwelled inside.

Tristan had clearly chosen this spot for another reason, for the warehouses and old factories sat before them, row upon row of abandoned and shuttered buildings.

Darkness would not be a problem. A few of the abandoned structures had been set on fire. Mobs milled around the burning structures, some swinging cut lumber at their sides like bats. Others passed around metal flasks. From time to time, a member of the crowd tried to get his or her neighbors to start up a chant, but it never seemed to gain any power.

It would, though. Soon. They only needed a few more fires, a few more sips to fuel their thirst.

Reluctantly, Lila swung herself over the wall.

"Shit," Frank said when he hit the ground beside her, staring at the mob. "How badly do you want this guy, Tristan?"

"Very. Walk quietly."

The group crept in the shadows toward an old factory, only a few buildings away from the mob and their fires. The crowd wore torn and dirty clothes, and wandered the area like starved zombies. Some of them had tied red strips of cloth around their right arms.

Lila didn't have a chance to wonder about the meaning, for Tristan unlocked the back door of the factory and held open the door. She heard cracking inside, like popping knuckles on bubble wrap, as Fry and Dice broke a few tubes. The men shook them and dropped them inside the back entrance.

A green glow lit up the interior.

Most of the machinery had been ripped out of the factory, but several conveyer belts remained, pushing the ghosts of Wilson industry through the abandoned space. The belts seemed so small without the machines beside them, cutting, stamping, and snarling.

Frank sneezed. The noise echoed off the metal walls.

Tristan checked his watch. "I told Zephyr to use the back entrance. We'll keep the front locked, so there's less chance of surprise from the mobs outside."

"That's also one less exit if things go bad," Lila said, her boots making prints in the dust. "The back might get blocked."

"There's nothing we can do about it. We do have a last resort, though." Tristan pointed to a row of broken windows along the side of the factory, all placed just a bit too high to reach. His people started off immediately for a lounge in the corner. They dragged dusty, half-broken chairs across the factory floor and placed them under the windows, sweeping away the shards of broken glass from under the chair legs.

Lila wasn't sure if the rickety furniture would hold her weight, much less Fry's. The man was a giant. He might have cleared out the entire factory by himself, one machine at a time.

"If things get bad, we go through the windows," Tristan said.

Frank, Dice, and Fry disappeared behind the maze of conveyers, each taking up positions in the dusty gloom.

"Let's hope things don't get bad," Lila said after they hid. "Let's hope we're all still well enough to climb if they do."

"Yes, let's do that," came a voice at the door. A short, chubby, balding man, with two black-clad bodyguards in tow, entered the room. Dressed in a shabby pair of trousers and a brown leather coat, he had a Weberly revolver holstered at his side, a weapon he'd likely never shot in his life.

At least, she would have thought that an hour ago.

"Reaper?" Tristan asked, head tilting to the side.

Lila swallowed hard. Here was the man who had written the article. Here was the man who could ruin her father's career.

And hers.

Reaper looked back and forth from Tristan to Lila's hood, his face twisted in startled confusion.

Dixon closed the back door with a *whack*.

Reaper and his bodyguards spun.

Fingers twitched.

Reaper's twitched.

Lila noticed.

When Reaper wheeled around and aimed his Weberly at her head, she didn't budge. She'd already drawn her Colt, just as she'd practiced so often with Sergeant Jenkins, trigger ready for one short pull.

She could have taken them all down, perhaps should have, but she needed to be sure that she had the right person, that Zephyr hadn't sent a lackey in his place.

Dixon and Tristan's weapons followed a half-second behind, covering the bodyguards.

No one said anything at first. Lila passed her gaze them all, hoping no one fired. Best-case scenario: everyone took a dart to the neck and Fry, Dice, and Frank carried them all back to the truck. On the other hand, perhaps not everyone's gun was filled with darts.

That was the worst-case scenario.

Even if it didn't come to that, she had to make sure she got Zephyr to Shaw before he had the chance to speak to anyone else, before he had a chance to send his article to the press.

She couldn't do either of those things if she had a dart in her neck.

"You're Zephyr?" Tristan asked.

Reaper shrugged, his eyes remaining on Lila. "I have many names. Many jobs. Natalie didn't tell me that I'd be meeting you. Perhaps I should have figured it out from your message, but who would have thought that you'd meet with your former masters? Who would have thought you'd need another hacker?"

Well, that answered one question. Reaper really was Zephyr.

"Put down the gun, Reaper," Tristan said. "I'm here because I need someone to do a job that Hood can't."

"Won't," Lila corrected, playing along.

Reaper bit his lip. "You're right. There are far too many guns in this room." He holstered his, motioning for his men to do the same. He then strode forward and clapped Dixon on the shoulder. "You almost gave me a heart attack, you tongueless—"

Dixon shoved him away angrily, rubbing his shoulder.

"Too hard?"

"Quit screwing around. Can you break into Liberté or not?"

"Perhaps." Reaper grinned. The smile did not go to his eyes.

Outside, the shouts of the mob increased. Whistles pierced the air. Catcalls. Dares. Something had changed in the tenor of their voices.

The hairs rose on the back of Lila's neck.

"They've stopped laughing." She eyed the windows.

Tristan's hand moved to his holstered gun. He'd felt it too. "How soon can you start the job?"

"Not so fast, boy. Let me explain how this works, since you're new. You tell me what information you want, and I'll tell you what information you need. In my experience, clients often don't know. They think they need one thing, and often they just need another."

"I know exactly what I need. I need you to break into Liberté. Natalie should have already given you the bank account number from—"

"Take my advice and things will go smoother for you. I give great advice. I'm sure Natalie explained that."

"You assume I trust Natalie. I don't."

"Of course you don't. You're not an idiot. I'm curious, though. Why do you need information about that particular bank account?"

"It's bound up in a job. I need to know who the account belongs to. That's all you need to know."

"Did you bring the payment you mentioned in your message?"

"I have the girl waiting in a safe spot. The emperor comes later. Much later. After I have the information that I need. After you make this partnership worth my while."

"You have other jobs for me, then?"

"Had. That was before I knew who you were. You've either been holding back on me all these years, or you're not nearly as good as Natalie claimed. I don't know if I'm wasting my time here."

"You get what you pay for, Tristan. If you recall, I've been giving you money, rather than the other way around. Do you really think that if I had a rich uncle, I'd be passing the money on to you?"

"Stranger things have happened."

"Yes, like Tristan DeLauncey offering up a slave girl as payment."

"She's not a slave. She's a prisoner of war."

Reaper rubbed his stubby chin. "The girl is worthless, but I'll take her as a down payment. The emperor is the real prize. I'm sure I'll find something useful to do with his brat in the meantime, though."

A sneeze broke the silence in the factory.

Two puffs of air followed, less than a second later.

Both bodyguards fell.

Tristan sprinted toward Reaper before he could draw his weapon, barreling into him with his full weight, knocking him onto the concrete floor, getting in the way of Lila's shot.

Dixon followed, a few seconds too late.

The men wrestled on the floor, a collection of curses and grunts. A Weberly revolver spun out of the fray toward Lila.

By the time she reached them, Tristan and Dixon had Reaper's arms spread and pinned.

"What are you doing?" he growled as another sneeze cut through the air.

Frank and Fry emerged from behind the conveyer belts. They picked the hacker up from the ground and dragged him to the side of the factory, securing him to the wall.

"I'm sorry, Tristan," Frank said after sneezing again.

"It's okay. The conversation was boring me, anyway."

"Natalie set me up?" Reaper shouted, fidgeting in Frank and Fry's grasp. "Does that bitch know who she's dealing with? Do you?"

"Apparently not. You've been selling out the workborn."

"I've been making money."

"Is that why you've been digging into the BIRD?"

Reaper laughed. "I could cut you in, Tristan. Bribing the highborn is a lucrative business, more lucrative than playing the wronged avenger. You couldn't even guess who I have on the end of my hook."

"Tell it to Bullstow, maybe they'll care."

"Bullstow? Since when do you work—"

Dixon wobbled suddenly beside his brother. At first Lila thought he meant to punch Reaper, but his hands didn't fly high enough, didn't move quickly enough or with enough purpose.

Tristan reached out, catching his brother as he stumbled drunkenly. "Careful, careful, careful," he chanted, as though he only needed a bit of coaching.

Dixon looked up, opened his mouth as if to say something, but all that came out was a groan.

Lila helped Tristan guide his brother to the floor, taking care of his head, which had begun to loll from side to side.

Tristan unbuttoned the neck of Dixon's shirt.

"A little earlier than I'd planned," Reaper said, flinching when Frank pulled back his arm for a punch.

Tristan looked up. "What did you do?"

"Oh, that's cute. You really are surprised by this. Did you people honestly think I'd come unprepared? I deal with people much nastier than you on a regular basis."

"What the fuck did you do?"

"I call it Reaper's Back Door, though I'm sure it has a much more scientific name somewhere. I stick it in someone whenever a situation makes me nervous. Like seeing you and Hood somewhere that you shouldn't be."

"It's okay, Tristan. He's breathing," Lila whispered.

"Not for very long," the hacker said. "The poison is harmless, more or less, as long as he gets the antidote within the hour. If he doesn't, he'll be dead. So my question is, how badly do you want Bullstow to have me?"

27

"Do you expect us to believe that bullshit?" Tristan hopped up from his brother's side and strode toward Reaper, grabbing his collar. "What the fuck did you do to him?"

"Exactly what I told you. You can either believe me now, or you can believe me in an hour after he's dead." Reaper smirked. "Don't worry. One of my men outside has hidden the antidote. When I leave the factory safely, he'll—"

Tristan let go of Reaper's coat, then slammed the hacker's head against the wall, stunning him. After Tristan's arm pumped back, Reaper screamed so loudly that he drowned out the shouts of the mob outside, including the crackling of a fire in a nearby warehouse.

A knife protruded from Reaper's shoulder.

Blood trickled from the wound as Tristan yanked it out.

Reaper screamed again, panting as though he'd run for blocks.

Lila dug her forehead into Dixon's chest, rubbing his cheek as he moaned on the factory floor, his face pale and sweaty. She'd never seen Tristan turn to naked violence before, never seen him do anything worse than throw a punch. He'd acted with all the speed and force of a bullet train, and with all the apathy.

Only the poorer classes showed such violence.

But if that was true, why did Lila want to draw her own knife and join in?

"You stabbed me!"

"No, that was just me asking politely. Tell me where the antidote is."

"It doesn't work like that. One of my men hid it. Even I don't know where. The only way to get the antidote is to—"

Tristan dug into Reaper's coat, found his palm, and pressed the device into his chest. "If your man doesn't bring me the antidote in the next five minutes, I'm going to put my blade through your heart. How do you like *my* back door?"

Reaper's clutched at his palm. His fingers shook on the touch screen. "Okay, I'll—"

A shot cut through the air outside.

Everyone looked up and turned toward the windows, listening.

Everyone except Reaper. He tapped the screen, ignoring the world. "I have to get out of here. Shouldn't have agreed to this. Shouldn't have come."

"Watch him," Tristan told Frank and Fry. "If he does something you don't like, stab him between his legs."

Reaper whimpered and typed even faster.

Tristan returned to Lila and Dixon, kneeling down at his brother's side. He dug into Dixon's pockets, opened the notepad to a random blank page, and placed the pen in Dixon's fingers. "I know you feel like shit, but you have to tell us what's going on. If we can't get the antidote from Reaper, I need to tell Doc what—"

The pen slipped from Dixon's hand. He pitched forward suddenly, gagging, and a river of coffee spewed over the floor.

Tristan and Lila dragged him back from the mess and rolled him onto his side.

"It's okay," Tristan told him, patting him on the head. "We'll figure it out. Just hang tight. We'll get you to Doc soon."

Chants started up outside the factory.

A burning piece of lumber flew through one of the open windows and struck the floor. It flamed in the center of the factory.

"I think things just got bad," Lila said over the catcalls and whistles of the crowd.

"We have to get out of here before the building goes up in flames. If we lose Reaper, can you tap into the security system? Can you find his guy with the antidote in the security footage if we fetch your laptop?"

"If the cameras still worked, sure."

Another burning piece of wood sailed into the building, bounced off one of the conveyer belts, and rolled into the center of the room.

"Sooner or later, they're going to get bored with that and torch the sides," Frank called out. "We have to get out of here."

"Dice," Tristan shouted into the dark.

Tristan's last man slipped out from behind one of the conveyer belts like a shadow. "We packing it in yet?"

"Damn straight. Frank, Dice, drag the tranqed men outside. Hood and Fry, take the weasel. Make sure he doesn't get away. I'll get Dixon. They—"

Lila ignored his directions. She sprinted to the window, ran up the side, and grabbed on to the frame, crying out when shards of glass stabbed her palms.

But she refused to let go.

Members of the Wilson family and contracted workborn, both old and young, sprinted around the building, makeshift clubs lifted, guns firing into chaos. Some of them fired real bullets.

She couldn't tell what the crowd was firing at, though, not at first. There were too many heads in the way, too many clubs raised in anger, too many shadows cast by the burning buildings.

Then all at once, the crowd parted. Blackcoats had taken up positions around several of the structures, golden roses stitched onto their coats, guns aimed, pumping darts into the crowd.

People fell around the buildings, grabbing their necks.

Blackcoats fell, grabbing bloody shoulders and legs.

"Oracle's light. It's a war. Bullstow's here. There are dozens and dozens…" Lila caught sight of a blackcoat nearby. He darted a man in the shadows, a man who wore the same clothes as Reaper's bodyguards, a man who fell forward into a fire.

The flames caught quickly.

He didn't scream. He didn't get up and move away. He had been sedated. He couldn't even run or roll out the flames.

No one noticed him burn.

No one moved to help, at least not at first. A Bullstow officer finally noticed him. He tugged at the man's boots and dragged him out of the fire, but it was too late to do much but pat the fire out.

Lila dropped back down to the factory floor, yanking a shard from her palm as soon as she hit the ground. There was too much glass lost among the blood to find them all by sight. She'd have to rely on pain.

"Was your man outside wearing the same thing as your bodyguards?" she asked Reaper, wincing as she tugged another shard free.

"Yes, of course."

"He's dead, then. I just saw one of Bullstow's finest dart him before he fell into a fire. I don't think they pulled him out in time."

Tristan lunged toward the door.

"Stop! If I thought we could get to him in time, I would have gone through the window myself. It's chaos out there, Tristan, and he's tranqed anyway."

Another burning log stuck the floor. This time it was too close to the wall. Dice sprinted forward and kicked it back.

But he wasn't fast enough.

A corner of the wooden structure caught fire.

"We have to get out of here," Dice shouted, backing away, as the flames spread. He sprinted back to one of the black-clad bodyguards, tossed him over his shoulder, and carried him toward the back door, ripping it open before he even peeked outside.

There was no time for precautions. Whatever lurked outside couldn't be worse than what would happen to them inside.

Frank holstered his gun and grabbed the other bodyguard.

Tristan stole Lila's scarf off her neck and approached Reaper. "If you utter one peep, I'll put my knife through your heart."

"You can't do that. You don't know what your friend has pumping through his veins. If you shoot me, you won't have me around to help you anymore. If I don't get out of here safely, he dies."

Tristan shoved Reaper against the wall and grabbed his hands, tying them tightly behind his back with the scarf. "If my brother dies tonight, I'm going to find out what it feels like to torture a man. You better pray I don't enjoy it. If I were you, I'd get to work on remembering the name of that poison, and don't you dare open your mouth until I say you can."

Lila pulled out another shard of glass from her hands, heart thudding when she saw how much blood poured from the wound.

She needed stitches.

Fry threw Reaper over his back. "I'll get him," he said, eyeing Lila's hands. "Stop pulling out the glass. Let Doc do it back at the shop."

Tristan picked up Reaper's gun and rolled Dixon onto his shoulder. The group dashed through the back of the factory just in time, for the flames had spread to the ceiling with a furious *whoosh*, licking the timber beams.

It wasn't much better outside. The smell of gasoline had gotten much stronger. Smoke hovered in the air like a thick fog, rising toward the sky in thin wisps, choking her throat.

She coughed and struggled to breathe, her lungs crying out for fresh air.

It was like Slack & Roberts all over again, but worse, for she was inside it in this time.

Fires raged around them with small lanes between the buildings, filled with the mob, slumped bodies, and the occasional blackcoat.

Another shot. An abbreviated scream.

Frank and Dice abandoned their charges in a clearing behind the factories, near some tranqed members of the Wilson family, stumbling over limbs.

There were a few sharp cracks as Dice stepped on a man's fingers.

"You got the weasel?" Tristan called out.

"Yeah, boss," Fry replied. "Weasels aren't heavy, didn't you know?"

"Let's get back over the wall."

The Wilson family must have also known the easiest place to cross, for the thickest part of the crowd had gathered there. Half of them had given up on the idea of burning down the estate.

Instead, they fought in a grand arena against Bullstow, swinging their makeshift weapons at the blackcoats, heedless of the darts that flew through the air. Guns had been abandoned all over the field of battle, tossed away when they had run out of darts.

Many still clung to their revolvers.

Some still had bullets.

Tristan and his men faced the crowd, bracing themselves, ready to charge through.

Another shot rang out.

Someone screamed as though they'd been hit and not silenced. A woman back-pedaled into the wall, grabbing her shoulder. Blood pumped out, and she cried out once more, red lips opened in fear.

A blackcoat, the likely target, had been standing nearby.

He turned and slipped deeper into the crowd.

"Not that way," Lila said. "If Bullstow is here, they'll have called in the family militias for support. The entire compound will be surrounded, and they'll be rounding up everyone who climbs over the walls."

Tristan hefted Dixon higher on his shoulder. "Where, then?"

"The tunnels under the estate. I know an entrance." Lila led the group away from the chaos of the main battle, back through the lanes between the buildings, with Frank beside her and Dice bringing up the rear.

Half the mob still fought in between the factories. Fires raged around them. Rocks and wood sailed through the air. Alarms and sirens cut through the night sky.

Frank pulled her back from an angry man's fist as they skirted too near a fight, and he kicked the man back into the crowd.

Seconds later, Frank stumbled, struck by a dart.

Dice scooped him up almost before he hit the ground, grunting under his weight.

The group pressed on, dodging the purview of the cameras. They advanced though the smoke, finally reaching fresh air and quiet a block away from the fires.

The men clumped closer together, wary of the empty buildings.

Lila led them to the center of the compound, to a rectangular brick building designed with little imagination and even a smaller amount of money. A golden sign had been posted above the door, marking it as the Wilson-Kruger mail facility.

"Frank's going to be so pissed when he wakes up," Dice said as the group stopped at the door. "He said if he ever got hit by another dart, he'd track down the asshole who did it and beat the shit out of them."

"Good luck with that." Lila kicked the touchpad, then cracked it open, pulling down her sleeves to cover her bloody fingers. She only hoped she wouldn't leave any DNA behind. Sore fingers typed in a code.

There was a *click* as the door unlocked.

Fry yanked open the door, and they followed Lila inside the darkened building. She led them past a long counter with a half-dozen computer stations, screensavers twisting the Wilson family coat of arms around the screen. They dodged several islands, laden with packing boxes, weigh tables, and labels.

Lila brushed past it all, kicking over a stanchion and velvet rope that blocked access to a hallway. Mailboxes lined each side, boxes only large enough to hold a pair of slippers.

The group hurried to the end of the hall. Lila led them down a set of stairs and into the basement filled with boxes and signs and clutter.

"How do you know where to go?"

Lila ignored Tristan's question and turned the last corner. They'd reached an iron door, which led into the tunnel system underneath the Wilson compound.

She wrapped her hands in her sleeves again and began working on the keypad.

Tristan heaved Dixon farther up his shoulder. Reaper's gun peeked out from his front pocket within easy reach. "How long will it take you to—"

The door popped open.

"I thought you said Toxic was faster than you."

"She would be if I had to brute-force it. Luckily, I know the back doors to most systems. Come on."

Lila led them into tunnels, tunnels that Alex's grandmother had dug eighty years before. It was shoddy work all around. The cement spanned only a meter in width, and the lights had been placed too far apart to be of much use. Cracks had been patched over many times. The whole system always made her nervous. It was like something out of a disaster flick. It wouldn't take much for the tunnels to collapse.

"Rest a second," she said once they were all inside. "I need to get my bearings."

"Your bearings?" Tristan let Dixon slide to the damp stone floor of the tunnels. At some point during their exodus, he had passed out. A thin string of vomit ran down Tristan's pants.

While Dice settled his charge on the ground next to Dixon, Fry merely leaned over and deposited Reaper onto his feet.

"Stay there," Fry grumbled, hand on the hacker's shoulder.

"Please tell me you've been in here before," Tristan said, mopping up his brother's pale face with his shirt.

"Of course I've been here before. I wouldn't have led you here if I hadn't. It's just been a long time. I need to—"

Reaper jerked his arm back suddenly, popping Fry in the nose.

While Fry stumbled back, nose gushing, Reaper lunged toward Lila, yanking her wrist and spinning her before him.

Her Colt clattered to the ground.

Reaper's arm crossed her shoulders, pinning her, the useless scarf trailing from his wrist. A blade scrapped against her throat under the mesh hood.

Tristan and Dice drew their guns.

"I wouldn't do that if I were you. I'll slit her throat before your sedative does its work. This is where Prolix and I get off this bloody merry-go-round."

Reaper squeezed Lila closer and laughed. "You know, I didn't realize who you really were until I watched you break into these tunnels. I didn't realize that Prolix and Hood were one and the same. You went along with Tristan to the bombing, didn't you? You snuck right into Bullstow and put your sticky little fingers to work in the BIRD. My, my, my, isn't Daddy going to be angry when he finds out? Not only are you hacking into confidential databases, but you're a terrorist as well."

Lila sucked in her breath. Reaper knew, and he didn't just have her body trapped, he also held her future, her reputation, her father's esteem, and now her life, for she'd never beat a terrorism charge. He had everything important, everything she'd built over the years, everything she treasured, and he thought it funny.

Reaper pulled her farther down the tunnel, causing her to stumble, nearly causing her to fall. "Thanks for carrying me all that way, Fry. I know you must be tired, so I'm going to make this easy for all of you. I'm taking Hood with me, nice and slow, through the tunnels. As long as I get out of here without—"

"Shhh!" Lila turned her head away from the knife and stared down the opposite end of the tunnel. Even Tristan and Dice divided their attention, eyes straying for a few quick peeks.

"Don't you—"

"Shhh," Lila hissed again. Reaper shifted his body, slowly walking her back so that he could face the end of the tunnel.

But Lila didn't cooperate.

And she damn sure didn't wait for him to settle.

"Chief Shaw!" Lila shouted, imbuing the name with all the truth she could muster, the peace of sliding onto her Firefly after a tough day, the happiness of seeing her younger brothers' faces, the relief when she spied Tristan in the water under the bridge.

Reaper loosened his grip slightly, turning his body so that Lila shielded him.

In that moment, half a dozen scenarios should have come to her mind from hand-to-hand training. Complicated releases, ways she could shift her weight, ways she could squeeze her arms into Reaper's body and put him in some sort of hold. But nothing came to her, and Lila had never been good at any of them anyway.

Instead, in that moment of imbalance, Lila did the first thing that popped into her head. She yanked Reaper's arm, turned her chin slightly, and bit the fuck out of his forearm.

Reaper screamed and nearly dropped the knife. His wrist twisted and turned by her cheek as he tried to stab her, but he could not work the blade into position.

Warm blood filled her mouth, but she held on like a pit bull, too scared to let go until she came up with another move. Seconds later, she drove her elbow into his wounded shoulder and collapsed onto the floor like a limp doll.

"You crazy bitch!" Reaper towered over her and raised his knife.

A shot rang out, echoing against the concrete walls.

Reaper jumped as though a hiccup had startled his body.

Blood spurted from a wound on his neck, gushing as his heart pumped more and more of the crimson fluid down his shirt. His eyes unfocused, and his mouth moved.

No air carried his words.

The gun in Tristan's hands smoked.

Reaper's gun.

Tristan turned toward Lila, his eyes wide with shock. He'd hit the man in the neck, the perfect placement for a dart, but Reaper hadn't filled his gun with darts.

Tristan dropped the gun and backed away before his eyes lit on his brother. He sank to his knees and bent over Dixon's still form.

Fry held his bloody nose, guilt spreading into his eyes.

Dice merely watched as Reaper's mouth muttered the breathless words of the dying.

Lila ignored them all. She dug through Reaper's pockets, the shards of glass stabbing deeper into her hand as she searched. "Dixon's going to be fine. Reaper got the poison into Dixon somehow. Whatever he used, it's here. We just have to find it."

Tristan did not look up from Dixon's body. He refused to sit up, refused to move, refused to speak.

Fry and Dice exchanged glances, but they said nothing while she ripped at Reaper's clothes and pockets, tearing the cloth. But no matter where Lila looked, she couldn't find any needles. "He's got it. I know he's got it somewhere."

"His rings. Check his rings," Fry suggested, his voice stuffy from his broken nose.

Lila grabbed Reaper's wrist and twirled off his rings. Both were flat on the top as though a thick coin had been welded onto a band. The reservoirs were deep enough to hold a small amount of liquid.

Lila thumbed a latch on the side of one ring.

Something bit into her skin. She yelped and dropped the ring. A small spike had shot out the top like a tack.

"Are you okay?" Fry said.

Lila nodded. A million thoughts flitted through her mind as she snuck a peek at Dixon, but when she retrieved the ring and squinted into the reservoir, she saw nothing inside.

The second ring looked full.

"I think this one was empty, or nearly so. The other…"

Tristan finally looked up, his eyes red and raw. "Do you think it's the antidote?"

Lila shook her head. "The man's a coward. If he had carried the antidote, he would have traded it to you. I suspect this is his backup. We have to get to Randolph General. Now."

"If we take Dixon to the hospital they'll DNA-test him."

"Not him. Me. Drop me off, and I'll get the lab to analyze the poison in the ring."

"How are you going to do that?" Fry asked.

Lila ignored him.

So did Tristan.

"I'll bring the antidote to the shop as soon as I can," she said.

"That could take hours—"

"It's his only chance."

Tristan studied her, then squeezed his red eyes shut, keeping them from spilling over. "I told him he'd be okay."

"So did I."

Tristan breathed out heavily and opened his eyes once more. "Okay, let's move."

Fry knelt down and retrieved his knife. "What about the weasel?"

"Leave him. He's dead weight." Tristan wound Lila's scarf around her hands, trying to stop the blood.

After he tied off the ends, Lila retrieved her Colt and slid it back into her holster, eyes unable to avoid Reaper's twisted face and the pool of blood around his body.

Tristan picked up Dixon. "Please, Lila. Get us out of here. Fast."

If her fingers hadn't hurt so much, Lila would have crossed them for luck. She started down the tunnel, hoping she would remember the way.

The path began to look more and more familiar the deeper she walked into the tunnels. She turned off a path and led them up a flight of stairs, holding on to dim memories of late nights out with Alex a dozen years before.

Covering her fingers with a clean piece of scarf, she punched in the code beside an iron door. The lock snicked with a booming echo off the concrete walls. Fry swung it open.

The group emerged in the basement of an abandoned restaurant, clutter and dust spilling into the tunnels.

"We should be near the truck," she said.

Fry cracked a glow stick and lead them through the boxes and linens. They crept up the stairs. The restaurant was not unlike Chaucer's Ghost, except that the tables still waited for patrons.

No pigeons had found their way inside, either.

Fry burst through a sheet of plywood nailed over a window. It clattered as it hit the sidewalk outside.

Lila stuck her head through the space, squinting back toward the estate. They were only a block away from the Wilsons' front gate. Militia reinforcements paced around the stone wall, staring at the top, tranq guns drawn and ready. None of them seemed to care about what might be going on behind them.

She even couldn't tell which family the blackcoats belonged to from so far away.

"The militia is busy guarding the wall," she told the others. "It's clear, but we should tread carefully."

Fry lifted Frank from Dice's arms and ducked through the window, helping Tristan pass Dixon through immediately after.

Lila winced as Dixon's face passed under the light.

His skin had paled, and his lips had turned blue.

28

Lila paced in the lab's staff lounge, hood in the front pocket of her coat, her boots clomping on the white tile, passing back and forth in front of the red curtains and chairs. One of the phlebotomists sat at a table, wide eyes following her movements, vainly trying to focus on her hamburger and fries despite Lila's presence. The smell of fast food clawed at Lila's nose. Rather than making her hungry, it made her nauseated.

She'd also begun to yawn every time the woman took a bite. The pacing was as much for her nerves as it was to stay awake.

The ring that had injected her hadn't been empty, after all.

Chef's daughter, Rosemary Tirel, leaned through the doorway. Her red scrubs matched the curtains, and her dark hair contrasted against her pale skin. She crooked a finger, and Lila followed her into the lab, walls white with pops of red cabinetry throughout. Several machines hummed on the tables as they passed.

"That was fast," Lila said, checking the display on her palm. She'd been in the lab less than fifteen minutes.

"Well, you told me to rush, and your information let me narrow down the search considerably."

Rosemary pulled out two stools from under her workstation, but Lila refused to sit. She didn't want to fall asleep.

"It's not poison," Rosemary assured her. "It's Midazolam, a general anesthetic. If someone injected this into your friend, then they should be brought to the emergency room immediately. The drug can cause respiratory arrest if you're given too much."

"Could the amount in that ring been too much?"

"Not if he's healthy. It would be just enough to give him a hard time. He'll need a doctor watching over him for the next few days, but I suspect he'll be fine."

Lila breathed out in relief.

"You should be fine too. I'm guessing you'll sleep very well tonight. Go to bed as soon as you get home so that you don't fall. My mother would kill me if anything happened to you."

Lila nodded. With her sore fingers, she tapped out a message to Tristan, hoping he had already made it back to East New Bristol and the shop.

Doc's here, he wrote back immediately. *I'll let him know.*

Rosemary took the palm away and stuck it in Lila's coat pocket. "We had an agreement. I'd do a rush analysis on the ring, and you'd go to the emergency room. My payment's past due, chief."

Lila glanced at her hands. The bleeding had slowed considerably, but her fingers and palms had begun to hurt more and more. Dozens of glass shards still peeked out of her skin, a few of them larger than the reservoir on Reaper's ring. But now that she knew Dixon would be okay and that she didn't have poison creeping throughout her body, Lila's mind had filled with Reaper's article. It still lingered online, waiting to expose her.

She didn't have time to fuss about with a doctor.

She had to get home and find the article, and she had to do it drugged.

"I don't think it's serious. I'll fish out the glass when I get home."

"If you yank those out the wrong way, you could lose the use of your fingers." Rosemary popped up the sides of Lila's collar and snatched up a scarf on her lab table. She wound it around the bottom half of Lila's face, hiding her identity and the shallow cut in her neck from Reaper's blade.

Lila followed Rosemary down three flights of stairs and through a locked staff door. It was as though they were sneaking around the Randolph estate as children again, hiding from Rosemary's brother and Jewel in a game of hide-n-seek.

At last, the pair emerged in the back of the emergency room. They slipped into a dark, empty patient room, barely avoiding the watchful eyes of Lieutenant Nathanial Randolph.

"I'm going to get chewed out for this." Rosemary sighed.

"I'll make it up to you."

"How are you going to do that?"

"Want to go to a party at the Masson vineyard? If you can get me out of here and back home without being seen, I'll even buy you a fancy dress and shoes."

Rosemary's face brightened. "You're serious? A highborn party? New clothes?" She clapped her hands like a child.

"I thought the vineyard would be the exciting part of that invitation. You do realize that highborn parties aren't like the fun ones you've dragged me to before?"

"No, I don't, but I will," she said, rocking back on her heels. "Okay, I'll get Dr. Daniels if I can. She's discreet."

Moments later, Dr. Daniels slipped into the room with Rosemary trailing behind. A few strands of gray dotted the doctor's red bob. Lila was surprised a woman in her profession had not succumbed and dyed it early, but supposed that working at one of the top hospitals in the country made her hair color a moot point.

"Rosemary, this is highly irreg—" The doctor's gaze stopped on Lila, who sat in a plastic chair in the back of the room.

Lila smiled innocently. "I cut my hands."

Dr. Daniels toed a stool toward her and slipped on a pair of latex gloves before sitting down. "The magnifying lamp," she said to Rosemary.

The young woman tugged it over.

Dr. Daniels fussed with lamp for several moments, then gingerly turned Lila's hands this way and that for a better look. "How did this happen?"

"Dropped a glass figurine. Tried to sweep it up with my fingers."

"Really?" Dr. Daniels raised an eyebrow. "Next time, use a broom."

"What's a broom?"

Rosemary's lips twisted, and she turned her head away.

The doctor peered into Lila's face. "You'd be surprised by how many highborns come in saying similar nonsense, chief. The only difference is that I believe them. I don't believe you."

"Too much?"

"These cuts tell a different story. They're all in a line, and the way they're imbedded… Were you doing handstands in the shards?"

"Yes, that's exactly it. It was a dare. Rosemary is an evil and demanding wench."

Dr. Daniels snorted. "I've been on for the last twelve hours, and I'm tired, so I'm just going to pretend that I believe you. And because I like my job and I want a raise at my next review, I'm not even going to ask why you smell like smoke and gasoline or why half the staff believes you're in exam room four."

"I like you already. I'll see what I can do about that review."

The doctor washed out Lila's cuts before injecting her palm with a small amount of local anesthetic. With a tweezer-like tool, she pulled shard after shard from her fingers, dropping them in a metal container in Lila's lap with a little plink.

Lila bit the sides of her cheek with each tug.

"I think that's the last one." Dr. Daniels twisted Lila's hands under the arm of the magnifying lamp one last time. "You're lucky. You don't need surgery, just an awful lot of stitches."

The doctor quickly sewed up Lila's palms. After wrapping her hands with bandages and administering a tetanus shot, she cleaned the shallow cut on her neck. Then Rosemary and the doctor fetched a tube of ointment and extra bandages and scooted Lila out through the staff door, down the staircase, and into the parking lot.

Rosemary drove Lila back to the Randolph estate in her green sedan. Despite the music blaring from the radio, her eyes drooped.

"You're not going to tell your mother you saw me in the hospital, are you?" Lila yawned as Rosemary stopped in front of Simone's. Though Rosemary could easily get inside the estate, Lila had no wish for the blackcoats to start asking questions.

"I like telling my mother secrets, but I like highborn parties and new clothes more. Don't let my mother find out, and I'll take care of Jackie back at the lab."

"Deal."

Lila stuffed her ointment and bandages into her pockets and closed the car door gently.

As Rosemary's car pulled away, she turned on her jammer and dodged the restaurant's chained-up tables and chairs. Punching a code into a panel by the door, she slipped inside, racing through the darkened space, lit only by the glow from the display cases.

She found the iron door in the basement, typed in her code once more, and ventured into the tunnels. After a ten-minute walk, she found the exit for the great house's basement. She wasn't sure yet how she'd explain away the bandages on her hands, so she crossed her wrists behind her back, keeping them out of sight.

Slipping through the scullery, she found Alex, sitting on a stool in the dark. She flipped on the lights as soon as Lila's boots met the tile.

Lila bit her lip. She'd hoped that she could hack Reaper's server before she spoke to her friend, but perhaps that was part of the problem. She should have spoken to Alex hours before, immediately after her mother and brother's arrest.

She'd make time, and then she'd deal with the article.

Then she'd go to bed and sleep for days.

"Where have you been?" Alex hissed. "I had to eat your dinner as well as my own. My stomach is killing me."

Lila saw nothing but confusion and frustration in her friend's eyes. It was obvious that no one had told her yet about her family. Perhaps the staff hadn't turned on the news. Perhaps the story had not even hit yet. The militias had only been called an hour before. The reporters might have only just descended, kept too far away from the compound to ferret out the story.

It was a small stroke of good fortune. One last chance to talk to her friend.

"I'll tell you upstairs. Is the way clear?"

"Probably. Everyone else is getting ready for bed."

Alex led Lila up to her room, stopping only when Ms. O'Malley ventured from her workborn quarters for a last cup of tea.

When the elderly woman turned toward the kitchen, Alex and Lila padded up the stairs as quickly as they dared. Though Ms. O'Malley might not hear them, other staff might be lurking in the great house.

"What happened to your hands?" Alex asked as they reached Lila's bedroom.

"It's a long story."

"Fine. I'll start you another bath," she said, wrinkling her nose. "You reek of smoke."

"Alex, no, we need to talk." Lila gestured for Alex to sit on the couch while she perched on the edge of the coffee table. "I have to talk to you about your mother."

"That's where you were?"

Lila nodded.

"She's been arrested, hasn't she?"

"It's more serious than just that."

Alex stared at Lila while she recounted Patrick's arrest and the chairwoman's interrogation. She finished with Bullstow's forced invasion of the Wilson-Kruger estate, leaving out how and why she'd come to be there. "Your mother's chief must have called them in a panic when they started burning down buildings. People were hurt. I messaged Chief Shaw on the way over. He promised to send me a copy of his—"

Alex shook her head. "You're joking, aren't you?"

"No."

"Patrick couldn't have done any of that. You have to tell Chief Shaw. He's just a boy."

"He's Johnny's age."

"Don't throw that back in my face. You're wrong about him. The whole thing was my mother's doing, not Patrick's. Patrick's not very… You know him. How can you even think for one moment that he had anything to do with my mother's scheming, that he could come up with anything like that?"

"Because I was there when he confessed. Patrick's not innocent in all this. He was the one supplying her with—"

Alex slapped Lila's cheek.

Both stared at one another in shock.

Alex looked away first. She walked into the bathroom, stood before the mirror, and smoothed her blonde hair back into her bun.

Lila hopped up on the counter beside her, her cheek still burning.

"I lost my temper," Alex said, watching Lila's face from the corner of her eye.

"I know. I also know this is difficult for you to hear, but Patrick tried to murder me, Alex. He tried to—"

"Maybe you deserve it," Alex said quietly. "Did you ever think about that? You've stolen me from my family. You've stolen Simon and given him away. You've killed my mother now as well as Patrick. Right now my family's estate is burning to the ground, all because of you. What do I have left?"

Lila stared at the floor, not sure how to answer. Wasn't this why she couldn't face Alex earlier in the day? Because she knew what her friend would say? Because she had destroyed Alex's family, her home? Because she was the reason that Alex would lose her mother and her brother in a few months?

There wasn't a way to fix it. There wasn't any magical phrase that could turn her friend's anger away. At least she couldn't think of any, not with her friend's large eyes searching her face, waiting for her to reveal a punch line, to claim it was all nothing more than a prank.

Lila wished it was.

"Say something," Alex snapped.

"What can I say? I thought your mother was behind everything. You did, too, or you wouldn't have helped me. I was wrong, though. We were wrong. Alex, I—"

"Don't you dare call me that anymore," she hissed. "Was it even real when you took me to my family's estate? All that stuff we overheard in the car?"

"Of course it was real."

"No, it wasn't. You wanted to keep me as your pet while you tore my family apart, just like after your mother bought my mark, and I was stupid enough to play along because I can't remember my place."

Lila hopped off the sink. "You're upset. I understand that. I'll take care of Simon. I'll make sure that Chief Shaw revisits his case. He'll be turned over to us as a minor slave, and I'll get my mother to put him back in school until he graduates. I'll do the best I can for him and for you. But Patrick did this. He's guilty whether you want to hear the truth or not."

"No, he's not. And don't you dare go near Simon. I don't want him anywhere near you or your family. You turn everything to ash."

Lila tried to grab at her friend's shoulder, but Alex brushed her off, nearly knocking her off balance.

"Let me go. I have to go clean something before I'm the next one sent to Bullstow."

"Alex—"

Alex turned, red-faced, and poked Lila in the chest. "I said not to call me that again. Not ever. I don't understand why you couldn't have just waited until my mother died. Do you and your mother really need the money right now? Did you have to frame Patrick to get it?"

"I didn't frame—"

"Oh gods." Alex breathed in. "Your family really did kill them, didn't you? Lizette and Madeline. I was in that car too, Lila! I heard them cry out. I watched them bleed and die waiting for an ambulance. I almost died, too. Were you there when it happened? Did you watch?"

"Gods, no! I had nothing to do with it, and you know it. They were like sisters to me. If I thought for one moment that anyone in my family was involved, I'd bring them to Bullstow myself. Alex, I—"

"I said don't call me that!"

"You saw your mother's compound. You know that what I'm telling you is the truth!"

Alex's fists bunched at her side.

Lila knew her friend was far too close to the edge. "You should probably go now before you say or do something you'll regret."

Alex bowed low to the ground. "Of course, madam chief. Whatever you wish. I'll consider myself dismissed."

Alex turned on her heel, marched from the room, and slammed Lila's bedroom door.

29

Lila sat in Chief Shaw's office three days later, out of uniform, sipping a mug of chocolate at six o'clock in the morning. He'd zoomed the map on his wall to East New Bristol, centering on the Wilson-Kruger estate. Lila followed the lights as they zoomed down the streets. Shaw did the same. He seemed unwilling to look away, as if it might erupt into fireworks if he took both eyes away for more than a fraction of a second.

"How are your hands?"

Lila slid the sleeves of her sweater over the bandages. Only her fingertips poked from the gauze. "They're fine. It was just a spill on my Firefly. I was going too fast."

Shaw leaned back in his desk chair with a squeak. "I'm sorry that I haven't had a chance to meet with you before today. We've been busy resettling the highborn into public housing until they can find servant's contracts. Our tech department has been digging through the security footage, or at least what's left of it, and processing those who were arrested. Governor Lecomte is demanding trials for anyone responsible of violence. Seven dead, four of those highborn. A dozen more in critical care. Scores injured. It's a nasty bit of business."

"I knew three of the dead through Alex."

"I'm sorry for your loss. Hers too. I hope she wasn't close with the child."

Lila shook her head. A boy of fourteen had caught a bullet in the shoulder, bleeding out on the way to Randolph General. A son of a third cousin with few dividends, he likely would have spent the first few years of his adult life as a slave, for his parents had frittered away what little money they had on clothes and cars.

His anger had led him to the riot.

His anger had gotten him killed.

"He was in the wrong place at the wrong time," Shaw said, shaking his head. "Just like the rest. What a waste."

"He was part of a riot. They all were."

Shaw shifted in his chair. "Highborns do not riot. Neither do lowborn. The workborn mob dragged them from their apartments. We have witnesses."

"You have stories from highborns who were injured during their own foolishness. What they claim and what really happened are two different things. With the exception of the militia, I didn't see anyone who didn't want to be there. They were angry at Bullstow, angry at everything and everyone in their compound. Your own men can confirm that. I'm only surprised more weren't killed."

"Well, we'll let Dr. Booth and his team finish their medical reports."

"You and the press both. I'm just glad your men were wearing vests. How many got shot?"

"Over a dozen. They should all pull through, all except for Captain O'Bryan. His funeral is this afternoon." Chief Shaw scratched his mustache. "I don't want to sound uncaring, but New Bristol isn't coming out well in the media. We're the leading topic on every newscast in the Allied Lands, every front page, every conversation. We look like violent heathens after the bombing and the riot. Several of the matrons have already contacted me, fuming about the expected dip in tourism."

"The press is easily distracted. They'll move on to something new in a few days."

"How's Ms. Wilson taking all of this?"

"Not well. She's not talking to me. She won't believe Patrick's guilt until it comes from his own mouth. Chef's agreed to bring her down once he's cleared for visitors, but I suspect that Alex will still blame me."

"Give her time. It's a lot to take in. She lost family, and she'll lose more in the end." He took a sip of his coffee. "I'm not happy that you were there, chief."

"I'm not happy I was there either. I almost died in a fire and nearly got my head cut off." She stalled, trying to remember the story she'd told him. Zephyr had called her to the tunnels alone in an attempt to bribe her. When Lila had refused to pay him off, he'd tried to kill her. She'd shot him in self-defense with his own gun, a gun he'd loaded with bullets without her knowledge.

She hoped Dr. Booth was too busy to do a proper autopsy.

"Did you find Zephyr?" she asked.

"Yes, Dr. Booth and I found him inside the tunnel right by the door, exactly as you said. We've recorded his death as a heart attack, and we haven't included it in our official account."

"Who was he really?"

"Nicodemus Poulin, according to the DNA results. He lived in an apartment in East New Bristol."

Lila pulled out her palm. "Give me the address. I'll head over and start digging into his computer—"

"We already raided his apartment two days ago, chief. We found nothing. Zilch. He wiped the memory of every computer and gadget he had before he went to see you. Even his palm."

"That's not possible."

But Lila knew Shaw told the truth. It made her failure sting a little less, for she'd fallen asleep shortly after returning from the hospital, far too tired to locate the article that night.

She'd paid deeply for that rest. The quick nap she'd promised herself had turned into fourteen hours, for Isabel had been too timid to wake her. During the night, she'd had another dream of the ancient battle queen, prodding her to visit the New Bristol oracle. This time, the woman hadn't asked nearly so pleasantly, and Lila's skull had ached for the next twelve hours. She'd lived on coffee ever since, too wary of falling asleep lest the dream come again, too scared of the article's release to abandon her search.

Unfortunately, she'd failed to locate it. The server and the story had disappeared while she slept. Now that she knew Reaper's electronics had been wiped, it made more sense.

It also explained why she hadn't seen the story in the press.

"I don't understand. Why would he wipe everything?"

"Who knows?" Shaw replied. "I know how you're feeling, chief. We both wanted a clearer picture of what Zephyr was up to, but it looks like there's nothing to find. You're free to rifle through his computers. Maybe you can figure out a way to recover his files. I'll have my men deliver them to your office if you wish."

"I wish."

"Good."

"No. Not good. I needed him alive. I needed him—"

"We've been through this, Chief Randolph. It's not going to help."

"The man had a partner, and we both know it. He didn't go from a two-bit hacker to a man who influences a chairwoman overnight. His tech didn't just wipe itself, either."

"I'm not disagreeing, but Zephyr is dead. We don't have a complete list of his contacts yet. We have nothing except the gaping hole in our security plugged."

"This case isn't over."

"What do you want me to tell you, chief? Our programmers are reviewing the patch you delivered for the BIRD. Since it breaks Zephyr's trap but doesn't delete it, his partner might assume he hasn't been caught. We might still have a chance to catch him. In the meantime, we'll just have to work backward from Wilson's bank accounts and figure out what he was up to that way. If he had a partner, we'll find him."

"I could help."

"We don't need that sort of help from you right now. My men can handle it," he said. "We could use another kind of help, though. Chairwoman Wilson and her son will be ready for trial soon. We're just waiting for the New Bristol High Council to convene. Since you sit on that council—"

Lila shuddered. "They're my best friend's family. I'm recusing myself, chief. The rest of the families will have to deal with it. I've hurt Alex enough."

"I apologize. I shouldn't have asked." He cleared his throat. "You can tell Chairwoman Randolph that we've already contacted Burgundy and ensured that every Wilson account will be turned over to your family by court order. They stopped their bellyaching when they realized your mother gave birth to several of the prime minister's children. I'll send the chairwoman a message when I find out more information."

"She'll appreciate that." Lila drained her mug of chocolate. "Call if you need any extra blackcoats, chief."

Lila stood, but she had not made it two steps from her chair before Shaw called her back. "Wait," he said, rubbing at his mustache again. "Have you turned on the news this morning?"

She raised her brow and sat back down. Her stomach pretzeled as her mind rushed back to Reaper's news story.

Perhaps it hadn't only been on his server.

"Something happened last night. I figured that I should be the one to tell you, to… Oracle's light, I don't know." He scrolled through his palm and slid it across his desk.

A video had frozen. Lila touched the screen to let it play.

Peter Kruger stood before the capitol in Vienna, dwarfed by the Emperor's Palace. In rusty German, he claimed that he had shot the American prime minister's eldest daughter and bombed Bullstow for the glory of the mighty Holy Roman Empire. He'd then stowed away on a barge headed for the homeland. He spoke so quickly that she could barely read each English caption before it disappeared.

When he finished his speech, a large crowd cheered around the newest member of the aristocracy, the king's elder half-brother returned home.

The rightful king. The rightful emperor.

Lila wondered how long Peter would last. King Lukas had not yet released a statement, and the men surrounding Peter were known critics of the crown. At best, he'd be a slave again, a pawn to bored and bloody aristocrats.

Perhaps he knew and didn't care. He'd been a pawn to the same sort in America all his life. At least now he wouldn't have to clean the bathrooms.

"I'm sorry, Chief Randolph. I'm sorry he got away." Chief Shaw looked at her as though he held a glued-together vase.

But Lila had known the vase would be broken.

Tristan had called, asking for her permission. The plan was good. Peter had wanted to leave the Allied Lands, and had been overjoyed that Lila had forgiven him and given him her blessing. He even agreed to claim responsibility for the bombing, knowing it wouldn't hurt his reputation in Germany. Tristan had told him plenty of details about it. He'd even given Peter a few AAS flyers before burning the rest at the shop. Then he'd left the rest of the nitro so that the militia could find it after Peter's confession.

Tristan had not been sorry to see the explosives go. He'd told her that he didn't have a use for the stuff any longer. The violence of the Wilson mob had tempered his excitement for armed rebellion. A child had died in the fighting, a consequence he had never before considered.

He finally understood the tragedy of causalities.

Peter had shaken hands on their agreement, vowing to drop the nitro's location into his speech. He claimed it was the least he could do, for no one had ever done anything to help him before, not in his entire life. His only request was that Tristan keep Maria safe while he tested the ice in Germany.

Tristan had done him one better. He'd promised to try and recover Oskar as well.

Deep down, Lila knew they weren't helping him. Not really. She'd offered halfhearted counsel, asking him to stay, but Peter wouldn't hear of it. Like Oskar, he'd spent his entire life dreaming of going home to Germany. He was merely being cautious. He was merely setting up a place for his children to live.

He was walking into a devil's trap.

Perhaps if Peter had not tried to murder her, Lila might have spent more time persuading him. And she couldn't silence the thought, deep down inside, that Peter's return would shake up the empire and would waste a great deal of King Lukas's energy and focus.

There was still a war, even if there was a lull in the hostilities.

"It's not your fault, Chief Shaw. My own militia couldn't find the man. I should have put more blackcoats on it. I thought discretion would be a better way of handling it. I was wrong."

"Well, for what it's worth, I doubt he stayed in New Bristol for very long. I still find it hard to believe that a slave bombed that law office, though. From what I've heard, the man can barely read."

"He doesn't need to know how to read to set off a bomb. Besides, look how wrong I was about Patrick Wilson."

"True. He also has information that we did not put in our official reports. He couldn't have gotten it any other way. I don't know why it's bugging me so much."

"Because you're ignoring the help he had carrying it out. He didn't act alone. I doubt he did anything but watch."

Chief Shaw slumped in his chair. "Yes, according to Peter, we've had German spies in New Bristol this whole time, and we didn't even know it."

"I doubt his conspirators were German spies. I suspect Zephyr hired them to hide something for the chairwoman and her son. That's why you can't find the others. He probably bused them back to wherever they came from the moment they were finished."

"I'm not sure if that makes me feel better or worse."

"It is what it is," she said. "You can waste time shooting up the chairwoman and her son with truth serum, but I doubt they knew what Zephyr had planned."

"You think Zephyr bombed that law office?"

"I think he planned my attempted murder and called Peter in for the hit. Find out how that law office connects to the Wilsons, and you'll have the evidence you'll need to close that bombing case."

Shaw studied her face. "What do you know?"

"Perhaps I was looking into Slack & Roberts as well, chief. Get a warrant for their records. Pay special attention to the files from the raid on Club 137 six months ago. You'll want to look into the bank records of the two blackcoats involved while you're at it. Do it quickly, please. Simon Wilson-Craft and the others who were caught in that disgrace of a raid shouldn't be forced to spend another day in slavery. Besides, I owe Ms. Wilson the return of at least one member of her family, don't you think?"

"You're serious about this, aren't you? You think the Wilsons had something to do with the bombing?"

"Something they said or did caused it. Of that, I'm absolutely certain," she said, lying with the truth. "There won't be any more bombings, chief. It was only a distraction."

An hour later, Lila walked out of Shaw's office after having made an official statement about Reaper for Shaw's confidential files, files that only he and the prime minister had permission to access, files she couldn't even hack into because Shaw didn't keep them on the Bullstow network. She caught a taxi and gave the directions for the Randolph estate.

Halfway home, she had a change of heart. "Take me to Starfield Dry Cleaners."

The grizzled old man in the front seat sucked his teeth, gave a heavy sigh, and did a sharp U-turn.

Lila settled into her seat as the taxi carried her toward East New Bristol, a block away from the mechanic shop.

She knew that she'd end up on Shippers Lane when she left that morning. She wasn't actually due in the security office until the afternoon, and she'd brought along her hood and extra cab fare. She'd worn nothing with identifiable Randolph markings or colors as well.

She'd done it all for a reason.

She'd had a lot of time to think since the riot.

Lila disembarked from the taxi and walked to the mechanic's shop, sliding the hood over her face as she rounded the corner.

Samantha spied Lila the minute she came into view. She poked the brim of her derby hat, lifting it slightly in greeting, and hopped out of her chair next to the dock door. "Hey, Hood."

"Hey, Samantha."

"I'll take you up."

Samantha must have had several cups of coffee during the night, for she bounced rather than walked. Dust coated the floors, and Lila wondered if Shirley and her team had made much progress on the trucks. All three frames still sat on cinder blocks in the middle of the garage. It looked as though they had not yet finished the sand blasting.

Tristan answered the door on the first knock, his t-shirt marred with a small splotch of green paint. "Is something wrong with—"

He stopped at the sight of Lila, the dark circles under his eyes almost like bruises on his pale face, his eye still ugly and black from Dixon's fist. "Thanks, Samantha."

"You're welcome," she said, not budging.

"Goodbye, Samantha. Go check on Maria."

"Great. You're pawning me off on babysitting duty. Hood, keep him from sandpaper, hammers, and paintbrushes for five minutes, will you? He's driving us all crazy."

"Shut up, Samantha," Tristan called out as she clomped downstairs. He bit his thumbnail and jerked his head toward his apartment. "Come in."

Lila tugged off her hood and stepped inside the room. It looked as though a hurricane had hit the apartment, a hurricane of slaves who suffered from massive OCD. Everything in the room had been scrubbed and polished and repaired, and every wall had been prepped to paint. Even the knob-shaped hole behind the door had been fixed. She peeked back into the hall and noticed that the window had been fixed. The baseboards had also been repaired and scrubbed and painted green, one of Dixon's favorite colors.

"It looks nice," she said, tossing her hood and coat on the counter.

"Things have been a mess. I let them go too long." He paced around the room and gestured to one of the couches.

Lila ignored him. She peered into Dixon's room, but the bed hadn't been slept in. All his posters and flags had been removed, leaving sad, barren walls. They'd also been prepped for paint.

"Doc wanted to keep an eye on him downstairs. He seems okay, just tired and sleeping a lot. Can't keep anything down, either. He writes that he feels okay, but I suspect he's just trying to—"

"Get you to relax?"

"I don't need to relax."

"Yes, you do. You're worried about your brother."

He dropped his hands to sides. "Dixon's fine."

"Are you?"

"Of course."

She quirked an eyebrow. "Yeah, sounds like it."

"Sometimes I clean."

"And bite your nails?" She gathered up his hands and looked at his fingertips, wincing at how close they'd been cut. "And paint?"

"Dixon's been complaining that there's no color in here for ages. He says that it's too boring." Tristan pulled away. He marched over to a few canisters on the ground and started lining them up. "I'm doing the main room in purple, then I'm going to do his room. I bought a ton of tacky colors. Which do you think? I thought it could be a surprise for when he gets back. I could do each wall in a different color, or maybe even stripes. I'm kind of curious if a room can be too colorful for him."

"Is the hall window a surprise as well?"

"No, it just needed… That's how you came in the other day," he said, spinning around. "You jumped across." His eyes went from amused to worried in a split second. "What on earth were you—"

"Don't worry. You've fixed it. I'll have to find another way in the next time I want to be a brat."

"How are your hands?" he asked, biting his thumbnail again. "I thought you said they were fine. They're all wrapped up."

"It's just a few stitches, Tristan. I can't ride my Firefly for a few weeks, but I'll be fine."

"That looks like more than a few stitches. What about your neck?"

"It's fine."

"I was worried." He stepped in close and put his arms around her. He held on a little too long, and he knew it. "I'm like the silly boy at the vineyard now."

Lila didn't let him pull away. She smelled whiskey, his soap, the smell that covered his sheets and clothes. She closed her eyes and held him around the waist, leaning her head upon his shoulder, breathing him in. "Everything's okay, Tristan. You're fine. Dixon is fine. I'm fine. All of your people are fine."

"How is any of this fine? I told you that you'd be okay, and you almost died. Reaper had a knife at your throat." Tristan's heart beat faster and faster against her chest. "Dixon…"

"Dixon is okay."

Tristan pulled away from her arms and backed against the wall. He thrust his fists in his pockets as though he didn't know where to put his hands. "No, he's not. I chose, Lila. Reaper raised that knife, and I chose."

"Chose?"

His gaze strayed to the heater. "If that had been poison, I would have lost my brother."

"You didn't choose. You didn't have time to think. Reaper was going to hurt someone, and you acted."

"No, he wasn't going to hurt someone. He was going to hurt *you*."

"Tristan—"

"I didn't just act. I thought. I decided. I chose, knowing what could happen. I chose you, and I don't know if Dixon is ever going to forget that."

Lila frowned. "Did he say something?"

"He hasn't said anything, but he knows. He's got to understand what I did, what I—"

"Tristan." She touched his arm, but he batted it away.

"I have to get the place fixed up for him. It's a shithole."

"Do you regret it? Would you take it back if you could? Would you have let Reaper stab me?"

"Oracle's light, no."

She grabbed his waist, insistently this time, and slid her arms back around him. "Then stop."

After several seconds, he sighed, loud and long, and dropped his head to her shoulder. "I killed him, Lila."

"You saved my life."

"I see him. I close my eyes, and I see him. That look."

"He loaded that gun. He did it to himself." Lila cupped his cheek. "Tristan, when's the last time you got any sleep?"

"I'm not tired."

"If you can't remember, then it's been too long." She grabbed his hand, leading him to his room. He stood at the door awkwardly while she turned down his bed. "You need to sleep."

"I'm not tired," he said again.

"Fine. Stand there and watch me, then." Lila kicked off her work boots and lifted her sweater over her head, tossing it on the dresser. The strap of her undershirt slid off her shoulder, and she slipped in between his sheets.

"What are you doing?"

"I've been up for days, catching up on reports, dealing with the Wilson estate, and coding a patch for Bullstow. I'm not due back in the security office until this afternoon, and I could use a nap," she said, placing her palm on the dresser. "Are you in or not?"

Tristan looked back at the paint cans in the living room.

"It will all still be there when you wake up, Tristan. All of it."

He stepped into the room at last, his t-shirt joining her sweater on the dresser.

Other Titles by the Author

About the Author

Wren Weston grew up writing fantasy and science fiction stories, but one chance book club encounter with a romance novel changed her favorite genre forever.

She became addicted.

Not only can she not stop reading them, she can't stop injecting shades of the genre into everything she writes.

You have been warned, darlings.

To contact Wren, visit www.wrenweston.com or drop her a line on Twitter or Facebook.